Seventeen-year-old Nessa Clarkson is full of questions and confusion. How does she fit into the new household Dad is forging with his partner, Cindy, and Cindy's son? What will being a lesbian mean in practice? And why is their neighbour so reluctant to talk about her past?

Moira Cavendish had been famous for a while, in the 1980s. Then she fled the bright lights of London, leaving only a mystery behind her.

Moira and Nessa shouldn't have anything in common. But when their paths cross, and they bond over their shared love of knitting and the ginger tomcat that can't decide whose home is best, they find themselves on intertwining journeys of discovery.

HOW TO SHARE A CAT AND OTHER LIFE LESSONS

Evelyn Fenn

A NineStar Press Publication
www.ninestarpress.com

How to Share a Cat and Other Life Lessons

First Edition, January 2024

ISBN: 978-1-64890-725-8

Also available in eBook, ISBN: 978-1-64890-724-1

CONTENT WARNING:
Mention of past violence, drug addiction, and overdose.

To CAHC who believed I'd do it one day (although I doubt this is what she had in mind).

Prologue

D rizzle glistened in the amber streetlights and the Underground sign reflected red and round in the pavement puddles as Moira Cavendish emerged into the London night. She pulled her neck into the collar of her denim jacket and hunched her shoulders, bracing herself for the walk to Nikki's house.

She heard the party from two streets away. She wished... But there was no point in wishing. This was the way things were, and her only choices were to put up or...what?

At the end of Nikki's road, Moira paused in the lee of a phone box. Nikki's house pulsated with people and noise. Flashing lights and music spewed out of open windows, and the party spilled through the front door and into the garden. Everything about it was too loud, too busy, and too full of hangers-on hoping to be touched by fame.

That week, "Will You (Ask Me Out)?" had reached number one in the singles chart, their third number one, and the first from their upcoming album. Today was a day for celebration.

Nikki hadn't asked how Moira wanted to celebrate. Instead, she had thrown her arms out and invited everyone within earshot to a party. As they were in a television studio recording that week's episode of *Top of the Pops*, the invitation list immediately ballooned beyond the comfortable capacity of her house.

Moira had been reeling from the enormity of Nikki's invitation when Nikki had pulled her aside and dropped another, larger, bombshell: she'd sold the label on the idea of turning the Diptych into the Triptych, with Robin breathing fresh ideas and sex appeal into the band.

It was a terrible plan, but Moira failed to find the words to explain why, her reasoning clouded by her visceral dislike of Nikki's boyfriend. Moira hated how much Nikki liked him and how Nikki chose to spend her free time with him instead of her. Moira also hated the way his presence made her feel: petty, jealous, and confused. She should be happy when her best friend fell in love, shouldn't she? Would she have been happy if Robin had been someone else? Moira didn't know. All she knew for sure was she didn't like the person Nikki became when she was with Robin. He made the drinking and the drugs much worse.

Moira longed for the way it had been in the beginning, when it had been uncomplicated and fun, and just the two of them. She was working hard to keep things together and their friendship alive. Working hard meant coming along to evenings like this, full of hedonistic people looking for hook-ups or highs. She would dutifully put in an appearance and pretend everything was fine. She might even lie and say she was having fun, but hard work on its own wasn't going to salvage their partnership.

The rain soaked her backcombed hair and trickled down her face and neck. How long had she been standing there? She stepped out of the shadows.

Moira excused her way through the throng on the steps and under the portico, using her elbows when words alone were not enough.

Desperate to see a familiar face, she moved through the hallway and into the living room, keeping her eyes open for Nikki's distinctive turquoise mullet. Moira drew a blank. The pounding bass vibrated in her chest, making her queasy. Anywhere else, the neighbours would have called the police, but no doubt Nikki had avoided the problem by inviting the neighbours too.

Nikki wasn't in the dining room, where the sound system made the floor shake, and screaming, writhing bodies danced to "Ant Music".

The kitchen heaved with guests and smelled of weed, but there was no sign of Nikki there either. Moira yelled into the ear of a man holding a spliff. "You know where Nikki is?"

He puffed smoke into her face. "Who?" He must be a gatecrasher if he didn't know the name of his host.

Moira flinched away from the smoke and didn't inhale again until she regained the cleaner air of the hallway.

She tapped someone else on the shoulder, but they didn't know where Nikki was. At least they knew who she was.

On a fourth attempt, someone suggested Moira try upstairs. "That's where the good stuff is."

The good stuff? Oh, no. Surely, they didn't mean...

With new vigour, Moira shouldered her way up the stairs.

In the first bedroom, Moira found a couple having sex on a pile of coats that had been thrown on top of a bed. She shut the door and beat a hasty retreat. She stumbled across more cuddling couples in a second bedroom and some suspicious-looking powder on top of the toilet cistern in the bathroom.

The door to the master bedroom opened, and a man stepped out.

He smirked at a woman who was leaning insouciantly against a wall. He opened a fist to show her...what? Moira didn't know, but she hazarded a guess.

Moira wasn't Nikki's keeper, but this was worse than anything she'd witnessed before, and she was worried. She had to find Nikki. Had to!

Please, God, don't let Nikki be dealing now!

Full of trepidation, Moira went into the room. It took a few moments for her eyes to adjust to the low light.

Nikki lay between the two forty-watt lamps that flanked the bed. She was flat on her back, eyes half shut, mouth hanging open, and drooling. The disarray of the bedding and her clothing left no doubt as to what had happened not long before.

Robin was sitting at the foot of the bed, clad in tight jeans, a tighter T-shirt, and his usual, heavy rings. He was surrounded by money and drugs, and even if Nikki wasn't dealing, her boyfriend definitely was.

Moira didn't try to hide her horror and disdain.

Robin sneered.

Moira tore her eyes away from him and looked at Nikki.

Who wasn't moving.

Eyes half open.

Was it Moira's imagination or a trick of the light, or had Nikki's skin taken on a bluish hue?

Moira rushed to Nikki's side. Hands trembling, she reached out. "Nikki? Nikki!"

Nikki didn't respond. Her skin was cold.

Moira shook Nikki's shoulder, gently at first and then harder.

No reaction.

"Nikki!" she screamed.

A memory from a long ago, mostly forgotten first aid course

surfaced, and Moira called out, "Nikki! Can you hear me?"

No reaction.

Pulse?

Slow and thready.

Breathing?

Barely.

Moira's head spun.

Moira turned to Robin. "You've got to help me!"

He stared at her.

"She's not responding! Help me get her onto her side!" Recovery position. That was what it was called, wasn't it?

Robin didn't move.

"What did she take?"

He didn't answer.

Did he not know? Or did he not care enough to say?

Moira pointed at a telephone extension sitting atop the dresser. "Phone for an ambulance!"

"No."

Moira, still struggling to move Nikki, paused long enough to say, "What do you mean, no?"

"No ambulance. She'll be fine."

Moira didn't believe him.

She managed to roll Nikki over. Had she done it right? She didn't know, but hopefully what she'd done was good enough and was better than leaving Nikki on her back.

"If you won't do it, I will." Moira moved towards the phone, but Robin moved faster.

He clawed her shoulder and pulled her backwards. "I said, no ambulance. No ambulance! No police! No fire brigade either!"

His ringed fist collided with her nose.

For a second that stretched towards eternity, Moira couldn't fathom what had happened. She touched her face. Warm, sticky blood poured from her nose. Her hands shook.

He was on her again, swinging and punching, and she screamed for help and screamed without words.

Nobody came.

She resisted him as she scrabbled towards the dresser. She grabbed hold of its edge and tugged at the telephone cable, trying to pull the phone towards her. Her fingers grazed the plastic as Robin yanked the phone away, tore the cord out, and threw the phone across the room. It crashed into a mirror. Both shattered in a spray of sharp shards.

He turned on her again, pounding into her sides, her back, wherever he could reach. He knocked her into the sharp corner of the dresser. The skin at her temple tore.

Out.

She had to get out.

She had to save herself.

Get help.

Out.

She kicked blindly, and her foot connected with something. He screamed in pain, and she'd bought herself some precious seconds.

She scrambled to her feet and stumbled to the door, driven by instinct more than sight. She barrelled along the landing and down the stairs, pushing people out of her way.

Was he following her? She didn't know and didn't dare pause to check, but she felt him bearing down on her anyway.

There was another phone in the house. Where? Somewhere in the hall?

The crowds.

The noise.

She plunged through the front door and onto the road, staggering towards the phone box.

She yanked its door open.

Lifted the receiver.

Oh, sweet, blessed dialling tone!

She pressed 9-9-9.

Interlude

I started at the girls' grammar school as the last of the wartime generation of schoolmarms were retiring. They were strict and staid, redoubtable women given to wearing tweed suits, cameo brooches, thick tights, and sensible shoes. They stood no nonsense, called us "gels" (with a hard G), and lived in denial we would have anything to do with boys.

Pupils came from across the county. At the start of the day, buses converged on the school gates, where they disgorged their passengers. The convoy of school buses returned at the end of the day to take us away again. Lots of us had to switch buses at the local bus station, and the station, where pupils from the boys' and girls' grammar schools mixed, was snogging central.

Every time I saw kids from upper years sticking their tongues down each other's throats, I would be...repulsed. For the longest time, I assumed it was because I was so much younger, and I would grow into snogging. However, as I grew older, the age gap between me and the snoggers grew smaller until it was my contemporaries who were doing the snogging.

I still didn't see the appeal.

What was wrong with me?

Chapter One

Nessa waited to be allowed inside St Drogo's great hall. On the plus side, milling around like this meant she got to ditch her books and spend a few precious minutes with her friends. On the downside, she was a bundle of stress, nervous energy, and panic, and hanging around outside the exam room had to be the least fun anyone could have with their mates.

Next to her, Meg dropped her lucky ballpoint, swore, bent over to pick it up, and got flustered for an entirely different reason: Tim wolf-whistled.

Meg straightened. Her cheeks flamed but she brazened out her discomfort. She struck an exaggerated pose, hips out and spine twisted in a way that would have pained anyone less limber, formed her lips into a pout, and cooed, "Like what you see, do you?"

Nessa and the rest of the crowd, including Tim, laughed. For a fraction of a second, the pre-exam tension eased.

Meg was Nessa's best friend. She had red hair, which almost touched her shoulders. It was unfashionably curly and had volume and body, and Nessa envied the way it looked great, no matter how little effort Meg put into styling it. Meg didn't bother much with make-up either. All throughout puberty, her skin had remained enviably acne free and smooth, and she wore her freckles with pride.

Like Nessa, Meg was also stressing. Nessa could tell by the way Meg was bouncing on the balls of her feet.

If Tim—tall, devil-may-care, and an extrovert—was nervous, he hid it well, and better than his best friend, Tarone, who looked as though he might pass out at any moment. Not surprising, given he was about to sit an art history paper. When it came to the practical side of his favourite subject, Tarone was a force to be reckoned with, but his creativity was offset by his performance at anything more academic. Writing essays was not his strong suit.

Tarone was tall, had brown skin, and almost-black hair. He had caused a minor stir a couple of years before, when in a relationships-and-sex-education class, he had mentioned his dad was transitioning, and he now had two mums. Possibly the stir would have been greater had the lesson not been online in the middle of an English lockdown.

Tarone was fiercely proud of and loyal to both his mums, and they to each other. When the school restarted face-to-face teaching, he'd returned to lessons with a trans ally pin on his lapel, which the teachers told him to remove. Begrudgingly, he had done so, but he made up for his loss by putting an ally sticker on the lid of his laptop where everyone could see it and the teachers couldn't argue he was violating the dress code.

Nessa not only admired him. She liked him. A lot.

As a friend.

*

Moira parked on her favourite side street and walked the few hundred yards to the craft shop, on the way dodging around roadworks and nipping into a bakery for a bacon roll and a takeout coffee.

In a desperate attempt to lure people into the town centre, money had been, and was still being, poured into efforts to improve the public realm, even though it was too late to save a lot of things. Some stores had closed entirely. Others had downsized. Moira had read that, in big cities, offices now encroached on areas where retail had once reigned supreme. There wasn't the same demand for offices in Oban, so some retail spaces were being converted to holiday apartments instead.

The onslaught of change was ongoing, and several high-profile buildings remained empty, caught in the limbo between a glorious past and a yet to be determined future.

No doubt, in ten, twenty, thirty years, commentators would say the pandemic had been a watershed, but, in reality, change had set in years earlier. All Covid had done was accelerate the demise of the nation's high streets.

Juggling her second breakfast, Moira got the key out of its key safe, opened the front door, and disabled the alarm. She was hit by a strong smell of banana, telling her the bin hadn't been emptied the night before.

When had the shop switched from being a joy to a chore?

The last Friday in every month, Moira went into the shop she managed on behalf of a craft co-operative. Following a day spent behind the counter, she would hold a meeting with the other crafters. In theory, the meetings improved team dynamics by giving everyone quality face time together. In practice, judging by the number of people who found excuses not to attend, Moira wasn't alone in thinking they were a pain in the backside.

During the pandemic, amidst its lockdowns and restrictions, Moira had seen the shop through a haze of rose-tinted nostalgia. She'd forgotten the everyday battles involved in covering shifts and getting other co-op members to pull their weight. She'd looked forwards to returning to the shop; she'd been excited at the idea of seeing people again and of business returning to normal.

But getting back to normal brought its own challenges.

Normal meant people shirking their shifts, not cleaning at the end of the day, missing meetings, and taking everything she did for granted. All the things that had niggled before, but which she'd forgotten during the Covid crisis, had resurfaced to torment her.

*

Friday morning's exam over, Nessa sought Meg out. Together they ate their lunches picnic-style, sitting on top of the wall that flanked the steps leading to the school chapel. A quartet of Year 10s sat on the wall opposite them, content to be ignored, and ignoring the two Year 12s in return. On fine days, like today, the wall was a good place to hang out, legs dangling, and watch the world go by.

"They moved into the new house a few days ago." Nessa pulled a prawn cocktail crisp out of its packet. She eyed it dubiously. What gave it its lurid colour and strong flavour? She read the list of ingredients on the packet and frowned: what was prawn cocktail seasoning made of? Shellfish wasn't listed under the allergy advice warnings, so not prawns.

Maybe she'd look it up later as a break from revising.

Meg swallowed a mouthful of sandwich. "You still wish you'd gone with them?"

Nessa didn't answer directly. Instead, she said, "I know it makes sense for me to finish school here, but it's going to be weird at the end of term, going to a house I've never seen. And I never got to see all our stuff being packed." She hadn't got to say a proper goodbye to the house she'd grown up in.

St Drogo's, named for the patron saint of shepherds, coffee, and unattractive people, was a public school. About two-thirds of St Drogo's pupils attended the school on a daily basis; the remainder boarded.

Like most public schools, St Drogo's worked on a system wherein each student was allocated to a house, which they usually stayed in throughout their time there.

The houses had once been named after alumni, but a recent review of the alumni's accomplishments had suggested they should not be celebrated in a woke world. Had some of them been statues, the more idealistic students would have taken great pride in defacing them or upending them in one of the school's ponds.

The idea to rename the day houses after mammals and the boarding houses after birds of prey had been intended to rob them of uncomfortable political baggage. Unfortunately, the new names came with baggage of their own.

Nessa had started out as a day pupil, but two months ago, because of the impending house move, she had switched to boarding. Although Nessa had known the adjustment would not be easy, it had proved harder than expected.

Nessa had had to change houses. She had moved from Beaver, a name which was supposed to evoke ideas of studious students eagerly toiling away but which, unfortunately, led to any number of crude jokes that had nothing to do with academic accomplishment, to Hobby, which rhymed with jobbie. The move meant she no longer had close contact with the peer group she'd come through the school with. Boarding also made it harder to hang out with Meg. Getting together at the weekends now required permission forms signed in triplicate for sleepovers.

"But you've settled in okay, right?"

"Yeah, I guess." Nessa had been lucky; she'd been given a small room to herself. She'd feared her new housemates might have been jealous or resentful, but they didn't seem bothered. Those students who shared had long since learned to accept their domestic arrangements and had no wish to disturb the status quo, and some of them, like Dinah and Dhriti, were happily inseparable.

Nessa, who had always had a room of her own at home, hoped she would be lucky again, come September, but she'd been warned the odds weren't in her favour. If she had to share, she hoped she and whoever she found herself with would get along.

Moving into the boarding house had been stressful, and she'd barely had time to get used to it before she'd been faced with the added stress of exams. Her mind drifted to the morning's paper. She felt sick. She was sure she'd got question three wrong and she'd managed her time so badly she'd left the last two questions undone.

Appetite lost, she put the crisps aside and left her sandwich in its wrapping. Even if the results of these exams didn't count towards her A levels, they were still important. Her predicted A level grades would be based on her performance, and the predictions would influence whether she got accepted into her preferred university. She couldn't afford to make a mess of another paper.

"Only a few more weeks of term," said Meg, oblivious to Nessa's inner turmoil. "Then you'll see what the house is like."

"I guess. But I'm not going to know anyone there." The family had relocated to the west coast of Scotland, to a place with a name Nessa could barely pronounce.

"That's what the internet's for, right?" Meg nudged her. "I'm only ever a connection away. And you'll get to drive!"

Nessa smiled. "At last!" She planned to take her theory test as soon as possible, maybe even on her birthday, and she was looking forwards to getting behind the wheel. "Hopefully I'll be fully licensed by the autumn."

"And I'll be getting my own car soon."

Meg, one of the oldest in the year, would turn eighteen in September, and her parents had promised her a car. Even if she didn't get the shiny red vehicle she'd been dropping hints about ever since her seventeenth birthday, Meg would have wheels. It was cool to know how to drive. Cooler to have access to a car. Coolest to have a car of your own. Meg had been using her mum's car to drive herself to and from school ever since she'd passed her test, saving her parents twenty-mile round trips twice a day from their farm, which was in the local hills. The novelty of driving herself had yet to wear off.

"Hello, Nessa." Ms Breckenridge waved perfunctorily as she trotted past.

"What'm I? Chopped liver?" muttered Meg, who hated being overlooked by anyone, even a teacher.

"Don't take it personally. She's my Head of House. She has to say hello to me."

Ms Breckenridge passed through the school entrance and came to a halt on the pavement beyond, where she glanced at her watch.

She was too far away for Nessa to be sure, but Nessa suspected Ms Breckenridge might be tutting impatiently. "What's she doing?"

Nessa didn't have to wait long to find out. An estate car pulled up on the zigzag keep-clear markings, and a lanky boy unfolded himself from the front passenger seat.

"Is that—?"

"—Thomas Mitchum," finished Meg. "St Drogo's very own bad boy."

"Didn't he get expelled?"

Thomas had been done for possession during a police raid on a club two towns over, and the school had a zero-tolerance policy when it came to drugs.

"According to Dad, the school couldn't expel him, no matter how much the Head wanted to. It's not like he was caught on school premises, and he's a day pupil, so he wasn't under the school's care when he got caught. Dad says the Head and his parents came to an agreement. Thomas was told not to come to lessons, but as most of them had finished by the time he was caught, that's not much of a loss. And he's allowed on the grounds so he can sit his exams; however, he has to be accompanied at all times."

Ms Breckenridge retraced her path, this time with Thomas trailing after her, slouching and with his hands in the pockets of his jeans. She acknowledged the girls but didn't say anything this time. Thomas ignored them entirely.

"Do you think he's making a point, wearing those clothes?"

"The marijuana leaf motif on the T-shirt? I'd say so."

"Pillock!"

A group of townies shambling along South Road paused long enough to point at the "posh kids". Nessa and Meg caught their eyes and stared until the townies looked away and walked on.

"Was that Jez?" asked Nessa incredulously.

Nessa, Meg, and Jez had all gone to Tovington Primary School, although they hadn't been in the same class.

"Yep!"

"Wow. He's changed."

"I know! He's fit! Never saw that coming when we were ten!"

Nessa reflected for a moment. "We've changed too." It had happened gradually, and they saw each other so often, it had barely registered. But, yes, they were taller and had gone through the rights of passage of braces and training bras. Their bodies had shifted from childhood androgyny to obviously female.

"Don't you think he's gorgeous though?"

Nessa glanced at Meg, whose countenance had taken on a dreamy, besotted appearance. She quirked an eyebrow. "He's okay, I suppose."

"You suppose! You need to get your eyes tested if you think he's only okay."

"There's nothing wrong with my eyes, thank you very much." But she couldn't see what Meg was making so much fuss about. The boy was tall and built and good looking, but so what? That was true of lots of boys, and she had never found one who affected her the way this one, or Kai, the crush of Meg's life, affected Meg.

For a long time, Nessa had feared she was a late developer. Now she knew her interests lay in a different direction, although she had yet to admit it to anyone other than herself.

One day soon, after their exams were over, she would confide in Meg.

Meg clicked her sandwich box shut, shoved it into her backpack, stood, and dusted off her skirt. "French exam on Monday. I guess I'd better get cramming."

"Me too. I've got my next chemistry paper on Wednesday, and I can't afford to mess up again."

As Meg hoisted her backpack over her shoulder, her sandwich box popped out and landed on the ground. Nessa picked it up and handed it to her. "What is it with you and dropping things?"

Meg returned the sandwich box to her backpack, which she didn't bother to fasten. "To the library?"

"The library," Nessa agreed.

*

Emily dropped by the shop before closing time. She was one of Moira's favourite crafters: young, enthusiastic, creative, and didn't take her crafting too seriously. Unlike most of the others, Emily had a day job; for her, crafting was a side hustle, something she did for pleasure and pin money in equal measure. She was always willing to lend a hand, and she helped Moira prepare for closing by bringing in the sandwich boards and vacuuming the floor while Moira balanced the till.

Emily had a thing for rainbows. They'd always been good sellers, but during Covid, rainbows had surged in popularity as they became a symbol of support for the NHS. Moira had bought one and put it in her front window, not that anyone other than the postman saw it so far up the glen.

It had taken Moira an embarrassingly long time to figure out Emily didn't draw rainbows because they were pretty but because they were a political statement, a symbol of pride. Once she'd figured it out, she joined in Emily's quiet amusement that people were buying the message unawares.

Moira had just finished cashing up when her mobile rang. She glanced at the screen, expecting the call to be one of the crafters explaining they were running late, had got caught up in something else, or were not coming to the evening meeting at all.

To her surprise, it was someone else entirely.

She answered the call. "Gareth? What's up?"

"What makes you think anything is up?"

"It's not year end, so you can't be phoning about royalties, and you never phone for a casual chat, so..."

"Okay. You got me." He hesitated, and Moira drew no comfort from the length of the pause. "I've got a proposition."

"What kind of proposition?"

"It's a TV show. *The Cats' Meow.*"

"Sounds ghastly. The answer is no." She always said no.

"At least hear me out."

"It won't matter what you say, and this way saves us both time."

"Humour me."

Moira huffed, a sound somewhere between a laugh and a sigh. "Go on. Give me your pitch."

"Hour-long, Saturday night, prime time. It's a feel-good 1920s flapper-themed competition in which pop singers, cool cats, perform jazz versions of their songs, and a panel of judges made up of professional musicians and comedians give their opinions on the performances. And, of course, there will be a public vote to see who carries on to the following week's programme."

"Of course," murmured Moira. The format was tried and true, and it was one she hated with every fibre of her being.

"There will be dedicated hashtags for social media, an official Yapper account, and a ViewHoo channel. Plus, there'll be payment for all participants. So what do you think?"

"Like I said, it sounds ghastly, and now you've explained it to me, my answer is even more of a no than before."

"One day I'll have something that will change your stubborn mind."

"Don't hold your breath."

"I won't. And I admit this one plumbs new depths of horrible, but I had to ask."

"Good grief! It must be awful if you're saying that!" She paused for a moment before she asked, sombre again. "Does Nikki know about this one?"

"Yeah. The producers want her for a judge."

"And?"

"Her manager thinks she can be persuaded."

"Why?"

"She's going through a slump. And she's desperate."

"You know she's more likely to agree if I'm not involved."

"Maybe, maybe not. The thing is, the producers want you both. They think it could be a ratings winner if you two are pitched against each other. Hence my having to ask."

"So, if I say no, I'm the bad guy."

"Moira..."

"Tell me I'm wrong."

"You're not wrong."

"The answer's still no."

Chapter Two

Most of the time, Moira dealt with bad days by keeping so busy she didn't have time for the bad to crowd in. Sometimes, when bad visited on a non-shop day, the only thing she could do to keep negative emotions at bay was attack her garden.

Moira assaulted the earth ferociously, digging around a particularly well-entrenched dandelion.

Moira had new neighbours: a man, a woman, and a young boy. She'd seen their car and the removal van pull up two days before.

Moira hadn't spoken to them yet, but she'd heard them. They'd thrown the windows open, presumably to air the place out, and they'd shouted good-naturedly at each other as they arranged things, made one another cups of tea, and asked one another how they were getting on.

One of the first things the man had done was erect a swing set for the boy, who was currently squealing with glee as he pumped his legs hard enough to raise him parallel to the ground. At that height, the boy could peer over the fence and into Moira's vegetable patch. Moira guessed he was about seven or eight, but she had limited experience of children, so she was probably wrong.

His eyes bored into her every time the swing reached the top of its arc, and her skin prickled. She hated the feeling of being watched.

She was being unreasonable. This was no worse than the family seeing into her garden from the upstairs rooms in the same way she could see into theirs.

Music drifted out of the neighbours' open windows and back door. Moira could hear unintelligible segues from a DJ, which meant they were listening to the radio. Thanks to the patchy reception, there was a limited choice of stations, which was why Moira had recently developed a fondness for streaming services.

Interspersed with the DJ's links, she heard occasional jingles and the recognisable sounds of Spandau Ballet, Duran Duran, and David Bowie: a radio station playing golden oldies. She could even pinpoint the year, which meant it was only a matter of time until...

Yep.

Here it came.

The distinctive opening chords of the Diptych's most enduring hit, "Will You (Ask Me Out)?"

Moira had mixed feelings about the song itself and hated the memories it carried with it. She dug aggressively, trying to get lost in the mindless motions as she scooped more soil away from the dandelion's tap root. To her horror, she found herself singing along.

> *Will you ask me out, a fancy restaurant, a slap-up meal?*
> *Will you be my mentor, show me what life's meant to be?*
> *Will you make me feel how I'm meant to feel?*

Will you awaken the love that waits inside of me?

Dammit. The new neighbours were unsettling!

Oh, how she missed old Dougie! He'd been stooped, slow of body, quick of mind, excellent company, fond of jazz, and comfortably familiar.

After he'd died, change had been inevitable, although it had been a long time coming. Moira told herself it was a good thing a family had moved in next door, bringing new life to the middle of nowhere.

She didn't want to poke and pry into their lives.

She didn't want to be rude by not introducing herself.

She didn't know what to do for the best, so she had done nothing more than wave tentatively at the boy and take out her frustrations on the weeds infiltrating her brassica beds.

"Hello." The voice was high-pitched and young.

Moira startled. She leapt up and spun around.

The boy grinned at her. Moira had been so absorbed in her weeding and her melancholy she hadn't seen him get off the swing. Now he clung to the top of the fence with his fingertips so he could peer over.

"I'm Finlay. Who are you?"

"I'm Moira."

"You've got grey hair. Are you old?"

"Hmph!" Amusement won out over affront. Barely. Amusement was good, and a sign today's bad might be wearing off. "I'm older than you."

At least he hadn't asked about her slightly crooked nose or the ragged white scar which ran across her right temple, almost into her eye. Possibly he was polite enough not to comment. More likely he hadn't noticed. The scar had faded over the years, and sometimes even Moira struggled to spot it in the mirror.

By way of conversation, Moira said, "I see Mr Gillespie has found his way into your garden. Again."

"Mr Gillespie?"

"The cat." Moira tilted her head in the direction of a big ginger tom. "Also known as Dizzy."

"He's yours?"

"I prefer to think of him as a free spirit who deigned to let me take over feeding him when his human died."

"Eh?"

"Dizzy belonged to the man who used to live in your house. I took him in. Poor Dizzy still misses his owner, and he's confused. Before you moved in, he'd spend hours sitting on your kitchen windowsill, and now there are people in the house... He's trying to go home again."

"That must be why he keeps coming inside. Mum keeps shooing him out. He sits on your shed roof too. I've seen him from my bedroom window."

"The roof gets warm when the sun comes out. He likes the heat."

"Finlay! Leave our neighbour alone!"

Finlay dropped to the ground. He trotted towards the cat who decided he wasn't in the mood to have his head scratched. Finlay pouted as Mr Gillespie streaked away and vanished into an overgrown herbaceous border.

"I hope he hasn't been bothering you." The woman stood in the spot so recently vacated by her son.

"No." Moira could hardly say yes, could she?

Cindy smiled. "Good. I'm Cindy, by the way. That was Finlay."

"He told me."

"And my partner is Joe."

So, they were not married, but there was no stigma attached these days to the lack of a wedding ring, and they might as well be married if they were committed enough to move from England together.

*

Before boarding, especially when Dad worked extended hours, Nessa had spent a lot of time on her own. She'd chafed at the social restrictions imposed by Covid, and she had missed spending time with friends. But boarding life was too far towards the other extreme. Hobby House was full of noise, and there were people everywhere. The common room was usually crowded, the dining hall, used for morning and evening meals, echoed with clattering cutlery and crockery and raised voices, and even when she was in her room, Nessa felt people pressing in on her. Sometimes, more often than she liked to admit, Nessa longed to escape to somewhere quiet.

Breakfast was one of the times Nessa found hardest to tolerate. The clamour bounced off the walls, making her head pound. As a result, she wasn't in a great frame of mind when, two days after her first exam, Elspeth, a Year 10, made a grandiose pronouncement: "I'm going to do ten hours of revision today."

Elspeth was determined and driven, which should have been admirable. Instead, it was annoying. She was inclined to say things like, "I did three hours of prep this evening!" and leave everyone around her feeling inadequate.

Everyone in earshot forced themselves not to groan. Across the table from Nessa, Dinah mimed vomiting motions, which made her nearest neighbours, Dhriti, Su Mei, and Yi Wei howl with laughter. Nessa almost choked with the effort not to join in.

Having got the reaction she wanted, Dinah hurriedly turned her attention to her food. By the time Elspeth looked around, sensing she was the butt of a joke, she could see nothing untoward. Forking scrambled egg towards her mouth, Dinah was a picture of innocence.

Dinah was Malay Chinese. She'd been a student at St Drogo's since she was eight. She spent most of her holidays with relatives in London, only returning to Malaysia during the summer.

For some reason, unlike her cousin, Yi Wei, she used an anglicised name. Nessa had asked about it once, and Dinah had tried to explain, but Nessa didn't get her logic. Dinah's Chinese name, Jing Yi, wasn't hard to pronounce. Still, Dinah wanted to be called Dinah, so Dinah she was.

Nessa was a great believer in respecting a person's preferred names and pronouns.

*

Five hours and one lunch later, Nessa sat at her desk, headphones on, trying to study. She plaited a thin strand of her hair as her mind wandered.

Even though it was fine, and she had to work hard to keep it smooth and tangle free, Nessa's long, dark hair was possibly her best feature. Except when she was on the playing fields, in the swimming pool, or worked in the labs, she liked to wear it as loose as the school dress code allowed, and she was given to playing with its ends when she was nervous or bored. Like now.

Nessa rubbed her temples.

If Nessa had been at home, she'd have closed her books, put them aside, and gone into the living room to watch the telly. Everyone needed a break from the books from time to time, right?

Everyone except Elspeth, anyway.

She considered going to the common room, but she couldn't face it. Because she'd moved in so late in the year, she still felt new. She had yet to find her niche and, right now, the idea of trying to be sociable was too much.

Nessa continued to sit at her desk, staring at her notes, unproductive and frustrated. A blanket of homesickness and longing for the house that was no longer hers smothered her.

She gave in to the temptation to switch playlists. Dad's compilation of 1980s songs was comfort music. It was also the height of uncool, a guilty secret that reminded her of happier times. Before the pandemic. Before Cindy. Before *this*.

Her phone dinged. She scrabbled to retrieve it from under a pile of paper and checked the screen.

A text from Dad! Her heart leapt. Had she summoned him by playing his music?

All fine here. We're still unpacking. U OK? Lots of love, Dad.

The message was typically him: concise and factual. But she wanted the kind of details she only got when he phoned and she got him talking. The text was a sign of the rift growing between them.

Ever since he got together with Cindy...

Nessa now had a not-quite-stepmum and an almost-stepbrother. Was Dad going to drift away the same way her mother had done?

Nessa couldn't rid herself of the nagging suspicion she was being squeezed out. Rationally, she knew it made sense for her to board. Emotionally, she felt resentful. She wanted to be with Dad, but Cindy, Finlay, and their new life were stealing him from her.

Nessa wanted Dad to be happy. He deserved happiness after everything he'd been through in the last few years. But did he have to be the walking cliché of a doctor who fell for his nurse?

Was it proximity or temperament that brought doctors and nurses together?

Mum hadn't been a doctor or a nurse. She'd been an accountant, and she'd left them when Nessa was three.

Mum was a remote figure, happily remarried and living in Australia. A few years ago, they had talked about Nessa going to visit when she was old enough to travel alone, but that had been before Covid and travel restrictions, and nothing had been mentioned since.

Through her mother, Nessa had two half-siblings and three step-siblings, but they were even more remote than Mum. Mum sent photographs every Christmas, so Nessa had some idea what they looked like. But she didn't know them. They weren't even friends on social media.

Unlike Meg, who had an unfortunate habit of measuring her personal worth in likes, shares, and followers, Nessa didn't have much time for social media, and she only friended people she had met.

Once, in primary school, Nessa had drawn a family tree; she'd been amazed at how many people she was related to, and there had been additions since, including Cindy and Finlay.

On paper, family surrounded Nessa. But they weren't close, and sometimes Nessa asked herself what the point of family was.

She didn't need all these people.

The people she needed were Dad and Meg.

The music was suddenly far more bitter than sweet.

She turned it off and let silence play through her headphones.

Chapter Three

Dad drove from Scotland at the end of term, a journey that took him ten hours, plus coffee and lunch breaks. The night before he picked Nessa up, he stayed in a bed and breakfast next to the motorway, but the night's sleep didn't do him much good. When he pulled onto the forecourt of Hobby House at 9:30 am, he still looked tired.

With the help of Dinah, who wasn't due to leave for another few hours, they bundled Nessa's things into the car. Nessa hugged Dinah, made her farewells, and at a few minutes after ten, she and Dad were on the road out of Tovington.

Nessa had thought she had a lot to tell him, but she ran out of news somewhere around Bristol. He didn't seem to have too much to say either, which might have had something to do with the way he concentrated on the road, looking out for lane changes, and the number of contraflows he had to navigate.

They stopped for lunch at a service station near Birmingham, where they ate cold, greasy bacon rolls, which left them unsatisfied and, in Nessa's case, queasy. At least the tea was hot and the water refreshing.

Somewhere around Wolverhampton, Dad put on some music, and she found herself singing along with him to the soundtrack of her childhood.

Will you ask me out, a fancy restaurant, a slap-up meal?
Will you be my mentor, show me what life's meant to be?
Will you make me feel how I'm meant to feel?
Will you awaken the love that waits inside of me?

Dad took his eyes off the road long enough to glance at her, possibly surprised she hadn't protested at his choice. She smiled, a closed-lipped, secretive smile. The moment and the songs were precious and, for once, uncomplicated. Today, she appreciated the music for what it was. They were listening to it as they were meant to: together. There was no bitterness, only sweetness.

They stopped for a second time on the edge of the Lake District, where the food and drinks were much better, and they had a second attempt at lunch.

Revived, they set off on the next stage of their journey, which took them through the Scottish borders. The traffic ran freely, and the countryside was expansive, with rolling hills on either side of the motorway, their tops peppered with wind turbines.

As they edged around Glasgow, the road grew busier, and the scenery increasingly urban. They headed away from the city again. The motorway turned into a dual carriageway, and soon downgraded further to a single lane in each direction.

They travelled past Loch Lomond, went inland at Tarbet, rounded the head of another loch, and headed uphill and over the Rest and Be Thankful, and what kind of name was that? Nessa recognised U-shaped valleys from her half-forgotten geography classes and marvelled that something she'd learned about in books existed in the real world.

They headed downhill again and followed the shores of yet another loch, this time for what seemed like miles.

Nessa got out her phone and consulted a map. She was astonished at how few and how sinuous the roads were, and how long tongues of water fragmented the coastline. They'd gone north, and now they were heading south again. Apparently, nobody travelled in straight lines around here.

Dad paused in Inveraray from where they gave Cindy an ETA. They also took the opportunity for a toilet stop and stretched their legs. They parked in a small carpark next to the water, which they had to share with upwards of forty motorbikes. The riders, clad in leathers, milled around, eating fish and chips and quaffing soft drinks out of cans.

Inveraray was a pretty, white village with a castle, a street of shops mostly catering to tourists, a petrol station, a scattering of restaurants, a chip shop, and a couple of hotels. The breeze coming off Loch Fyne was fresh and cool. It tugged at Nessa's hair and clothes.

When they'd set off, the temperature had been in the high twenties Celsius. Now, four hundred plus miles farther north, as she came out in goosebumps, Nessa regretted her shorts and T-shirt. Even so, she paused to admire the pier and an odd folly perched high on one of the neighbouring hills. The overall effect was picturesque, and utterly unlike anything she'd grown up with. They might still be in the UK, but Scotland was a foreign country. Nessa couldn't decide whether she was more discomforted or excited.

On the road again, they passed through swathes of forests, rough pasture, and small, scattered settlements. Eventually, as they drove into something almost large enough to be called a town, Dad pointed out a school. "That's where Finlay goes."

That must mean they were closing in on their destination. To make sure, Nessa asked, "How much further?"

"Another twenty minutes, give or take."

They were almost home.

*

The last leg of the journey took them along a narrow road scarcely better than a track. There were small, unmarked lay-bys peppered along its edge, which Dad told her were passing places. He pulled over to let a delivery van pass, as if to illustrate the point. If not for that, Nessa would have found it easy to believe they were totally cut off from civilisation.

Dad parked in a lay-by in front of a pair of... Were they cottages? What was the difference between a cottage and a house? He turned off the ignition and stretched. "Well, here we are."

Nessa opened her door and unfolded herself out of the car.

Dad had sent her pictures of the house before, but now, for the first time, she saw how it fitted into its surroundings.

The houses, along with a field on the opposite side of the road, nestled between two hills. A moss-covered dry-stone wall and a lot of brambles amidst other scrub edged the field and enclosed the flock of sheep within.

The houses were one-and-a-half storeys high. They had white walls and black paintwork, and there were dormer windows set into the slate roofs. Their house was accessed via three steps, a wrought iron gate, and a footpath, which bisected a small front lawn. A tiny storm porch, its doors currently open in welcome, led into the main body of the building.

"C'mon. We'll get your things out of the car later."

"At least let me have my small case. I need to put on something warmer."

Dad rummaged around the boot and pulled the case out. He lifted it effortlessly, and Nessa followed him up the path.

Someone had hung a banner over the inner front door: "Welcome Home Nessa!" Nessa found the gesture as unsettling as it was sweet.

Cindy appeared, Finlay lagging a few steps behind. He was almost as tentative as Nessa, which made her feel marginally better.

Cindy ushered Nessa into the house, talking too fast for Nessa to take everything in. Something about a lasagne and garlic bread in the oven, table settings, dessert, freshening up before dinner, unpacking...

A wave of disorientation crashed over Nessa. How come Cindy welcomed her into the house Nessa was supposed to share with Dad in the same way Cindy might welcome a guest? "Here's the bathroom...the bedroom...clean towels on the bed...dining room down the stairs and turn left...see you in five minutes..."

Nessa's room was tiny. There wasn't enough space to open her case on the floor, so she put it on the bed, on top of the clean linens, where it left a dirty mark. She ferreted out a pair of jeans and a hoodie. The clothes were familiar and cosy. She pulled the sleeves over her hands and hugged herself for comfort.

Nessa took her time finding the dining room, peering into the various rooms she passed en route. Some of the furniture was familiar, some not; some old and worn, some new. Some pieces had come from Cindy's house, and some, possibly, from one of those gargantuan warehouse stores ubiquitous to urban ring roads.

The bedspread in Dad and Cindy's room was immaculately smooth, scatter cushions arranged perfectly, slippers neatly paired and tucked under the bed. Finlay's room was messier, which wasn't surprising. He was a boy, and he'd clearly been interrupted mid something. Whatever game he'd been playing, it was unfamiliar to her.

Although Dad and Cindy's room smelled of fresh paint, as did Finlay's and the living room, the decorating had yet to reach the rest of the house. Pots of paint and rollers at the bottom of the stairs suggested the hallway might be next.

By the time Nessa wandered into the kitchen, Cindy was getting things out of the oven, and Dad was transferring a salad to the dining table. The food smelled great. Unfortunately, Nessa was too travel-worn to be hungry.

Cindy smiled at her and asked her to call Finlay to the table, giving Nessa an excuse to have a closer look at the living room, where Finlay sat cross-legged on the floor, watching something animated on an enormous television which was too large for the space.

The family convened around the dining table. Cindy dominated the conversation, summarising the work she and Dad had done on the house so far and the plans they had for the future.

Cindy was making an effort, but Nessa wished she wouldn't, at least not tonight. After all the time on the road, stressing about the new house and unfamiliar family dynamics, Nessa didn't have the energy to reciprocate. She worried she came across as surly or moody, and she wasn't like that. Was she? If she was, she didn't want to be.

It didn't help that Finlay wouldn't stop staring at her.

As soon as was polite, Nessa made her excuses and headed to her room. Except for the suitcase stain, the bed linens were crisp and fresh, and the duvet was lofty and airy. As she lay in bed, she heard sheep bleating, and was that an owl?

*

Nessa woke up disorientated. Light flooded her room, the flimsy, cotton curtains no match for the sun. The sheep were still bleating, or were they bleating again? Sparrows chirped loudly in the gutters, and other birds she couldn't identify squawked with tuneless enthusiasm. For somewhere so quiet, this place sure was noisy!

Had she slept in? She rolled over and scrabbled for her phone, which she'd left on the windowsill. She squinted at the screen and flopped onto her pillow in disgust: 5:50 am!

She closed her eyes; the light turned the backs of her eyelids orange. She rolled over and tried pulling the duvet, followed by a pillow, over her head, but she felt smothered by them.

Could she ask Dad for new curtains? Or a blind? Or even for one of those sleep masks people wore on aeroplanes?

In the end, she gave up trying to escape the light, popped her headphones on, found some music to listen to, and fell asleep anyway.

*

Cindy woke Nessa as she chastised Finlay, and Finlay, in his prepubescent, high-pitched voice argued back. Something about a cat? Did they have a cat? Nessa didn't think so. Nobody had mentioned one, or if they had, it must have been sometime over yesterday's dessert. By that point, she'd pretty much zoned out.

Deciding it was bladder-emptying o'clock, Nessa got out of bed, found her washbag, and padded downstairs to the bathroom.

Maybe, if she left her toothbrush with the others and used the communal toothpaste, she'd feel more at home. But she found she wasn't ready to take such a momentous step, and she replaced her things in her bag. As a compromise, she left the washbag on a shelf and her towel over the top of the shower screen, the towel rail already being full.

By the time she appeared in the kitchen, Cindy was supervising Finlay, who was guzzling a bowl of cereal topped with fruit as though eating was an Olympic sport. "Slow down! You'll choke yourself!"

Finlay's only response was a brief lift of his eyes.

Cindy shook her head indulgently. "That swing isn't going anywhere. A couple of minutes extra won't hurt."

Apparently, patience wasn't a virtue Finlay was familiar with.

Nessa dispensed with any greetings. "Where's Dad?"

Cindy glanced around. "Outside. I think he's trying to figure out where to put all your stuff."

Nessa told herself Cindy wasn't making a veiled criticism, but she heard one anyway. It wasn't Nessa's fault she'd had a carload of belongings to bring home at the end of term, and it wasn't her fault Dad and Cindy had bought a house too small to accommodate everyone.

"Do you want some tea? Or is coffee more your thing?"

"Tea's fine." Beyond the weakest, milkiest, most insipid lattes, Nessa had never developed a taste for coffee, but she didn't bother to tell Cindy that. As an afterthought, as Cindy reached for the kettle, she added a "Thanks."

Nessa hovered. Should she sit? Help herself? She would have happily seen to her own needs, but she didn't know where anything was, and Cindy's presence discouraged her from exploring.

Cindy solved her dilemma by pointing out various things: bread; toaster; crockery cupboard; cutlery drawer. She ended her litany by saying, "Milk, sugar, butter, and marmalade are on the table." Making the tea was as far as Cindy's waitressing service went.

Finlay scraped the bottom of his bowl noisily and leapt to his feet before he'd completed his final swallow.

"Bowl. Dishwasher."

Albeit with a hint of hurt in his eyes, Finlay obeyed. Nessa made a mental note of where the dishwasher was hidden and what was expected.

"Good boy." To Nessa, Cindy said, "When you've eaten your breakfast, I'll give you the rest of the tour."

Hadn't Nessa seen everything the house had to offer already?

She fixed herself some toast and marmalade, the latter apparently a gift from their next-door neighbour. Cindy cheerfully explained that Moira had also given them some bramble jelly, which had been to die for, and which they'd polished off in short order.

Would Nessa ever get used to hearing about things she'd missed out on?

"Finlay and I are going into town later. Do you want to come with us?"

"Sure." Nessa plastered something which might have passed for a faint smile on her face. She didn't want to go, but there wasn't much else to do, and it would be good to get to know the area, wouldn't it?

Cindy's answering smile was wider. Nessa had given the right answer.

Nessa ate two slices of toast and drank two mugs of tea. If this had been school, she'd also have pocketed a banana for later.

What was Cindy's take on snaffling snacks from the fruit bowl? Would it be accepted, tolerated, or frowned upon? It was a crazy thing to worry or ask about in your own home.

Which was the point: Nessa didn't feel as though this was her home. Even the rules at Meg's house were clearer than the rules here.

*

Cindy's tour made Nessa feel as though she was going through ori-entation, and it reminded her of when she'd joined the boarding house. "If you use something, put it away afterwards. No outdoor shoes to be worn indoors. Don't leave the door open, else the neighbour's cat will get in."

Ah. At least that explained the earlier argument.

"If you finish anything, either replenish it, or if we've run out, add it to the shopping list. If you break anything, let us know. You make a mess; you clean it."

Nessa had been right; she had seen everything the house had to of-fer, at least indoors. She hadn't, however, seen the outbuildings. These comprised a wood store and a "workshop" full of bicycles, garden equip-ment, and plastic boxes packed with things, including her belongings, which didn't fit indoors.

"You've seen how tight we are for space. We couldn't unpack it all for you, and we thought it best to leave you to decide what you wanted."

By the time they'd finished the tour, Dad had started to add the con-tents of the car to the collection of stuff in the workshop.

"How much of this will you need while you're here?"

Nessa resisted the urge to say, "All of it." It would be nice to have all her things around her; however, realism overtook comfort. "I suppose some books. Some clothes. I can manage without my mugs and linens, and I don't suppose I'll be needing my winter coat. Or my favourite boots."

"Let's hope not. We'll keep the stuff you don't need here. As for the rest, if we need to, we can clear some space in our room, or maybe Fin-lay's. Safer in ours though."

Dad must have read something in her expression. "I know it's not ideal. But it won't be forever. We've got an architect working on plans for the extension, and by this time next year…"

This time next year, Nessa would be getting ready to head off to university, and she'd have practically left home. How often would she come back after that?

Then she would be a guest.

*

The nearest shops were ten miles away, so there was no nipping out on a whim for a chocolate bar, and shopping lists were essential to make sure nothing got forgotten. Thus, after lunch, armed with a dozen shopping bags and a list that ran over several pages, Cindy, Finlay, and Nessa climbed into Cindy's small hatchback and set off on their quest.

Nessa sat in the front. Finlay sat behind Cindy, engrossed in a video game.

Cindy tried to engage Nessa in conversation, but Nessa was too busy taking in details she'd missed the day before to pay much attention.

The Scottish landscape was a far cry from the rolling hills with their patchwork quilt of fields and hedgerows she'd grown up with. It was rougher and wilder than she was used to. There were fewer crops and cows, and many more sheep. And there was more water. No matter where they went, they were never far from the sea. Or was it freshwater? Nessa's inability to read the landscape at a glance left her confused and uneasy.

Everything about the town, from its population, the supermarket, and the swimming pool, was small.

If Nessa had been there with Meg, they'd have made an adventure out of the new experiences. They'd have been lost and confused together, and they'd have made a game of it. It would have been fun.

But this! This trailing around after Cindy, who had meticulously planned her shopping list in the order the produce was shelved, made her feel like a spare wheel. Even Finlay, who pushed the trolley, had more purpose here than she did.

*

Moira was having an Awful Day. Capital A. Capital D. It was worse than an off day or a bad day. It was the kind of day people should put in their diaries, right up there with Christmas, Easter, and the occasional birthday. It was the kind of day where the level of awfulness was so high it deserved to be recognised.

Moira's Awful Days weren't new. She'd had them on and off throughout her adult life, most particularly in the aftermath of the crash and burn of her pop career. She'd tried therapy, but she'd drawn the line at her doctor's suggestion of antidepressants. She'd turned down the medication partly because she'd seen the damage drugs did and partly because she didn't believe they would tackle the root causes of whatever problem she had, only mask its symptoms. Therapy hadn't helped much either. Talking had been pleasant enough, but the therapist hadn't offered much in the way of advice, preferring to tell Moira to find her own answers.

Both had been a long time ago. Moira told herself things were better now, although Covid had forced her to take a good, hard look at her life and had brought her perilously close to the abyss once again.

The pandemic had brought home to her exactly how isolated she was; how unable she was to bond with the people around her. She had never considered herself to be lonely until she was forced to accept she was alone.

Everyone had had immediate family to spend time with, or if they hadn't, they'd formed extended household bubbles. Everyone except her.

Nobody, not even her closest friends, had invited her to bubble with them, and she hadn't invited anyone to bubble with her for fear of getting in the way of their domestic obligations.

She'd told herself she was fine without a bubble, and she was fine, until someone told her they'd assumed she didn't want to be in a bubble, and they'd linked up with someone else.

Moira hadn't known what to say, so she hadn't said anything. But it had hurt.

By God, it hurt like hell.

"You didn't want to bubble with me."

How the hell had Rosalind come to that conclusion? They hadn't even talked about it.

These days, they barely talked at all.

Other people had told Moira she was resilient enough to cope on her own; she didn't need the support a bubble might have given her. In a way, that was a compliment, albeit one so backhanded it verged on triple jointed.

Covid restrictions had ended, people were mixing again, but scars remained. Possibly they would never go away, not entirely.

The shop was getting back on its feet, but Moira struggled to reconnect with her business associates. Before, she might have called them friends, or at least friendly acquaintances, but they'd forgotten about her swiftly enough during the pandemic, and now she found it hard to pick up where they'd left off. She felt hollow when engaging in small talk, and angry at the fair-weather nature of their relationships. On her Awful Days, dealing with them was agony, and she hated that what they had, at best, was a symbiotic relationship.

Once she would have had sympathy for those people who struggled to do their shifts because they had childcare responsibilities, or caring responsibilities, or were ill themselves and didn't feel up to taking the turns in the shop required by the contracts they'd signed. Once she would have leaned over backwards to help.

Once.

Now she was angry and twisted, and this was what Covid and the Awful Days had done to her.

Others had things far worse, which made her hate herself even more for being so resentful. Other people had lost their lives, their loved ones, their health, their businesses. Yes, she'd had to dip into her savings, but she was still standing. She should be grateful.

Twenty-nine days out of thirty she was grateful.

But that thirtieth day?

That was an Awful Day.

*

After dinner, and after the dishwasher had run through its cycle, more because she wanted an excuse to avoid the "family" and to nose around the kitchen than from a genuine desire to be helpful, Nessa unloaded the dishwasher, put everything away, and withdrew to her bedroom. To her relief, Meg was online and available to chat. It was good to see a familiar face!

Nessa waved at the computer screen. "Hey!"

"Hey, yourself. How's it going?"

"Okay. No worse than expected anyway."

"That good, huh?"

"Finlay doesn't know what to make of me. Which is fair. I don't know what to make of him either. Cindy wants me to spend time with him. She says she wants me to, ugh, bond with him, although I think she wants me to keep him out of her way. But he's perfectly capable of entertaining himself; he doesn't need me. We're in the middle of nowhere. There's nothing to do. Wanna see my room?"

"Of course!"

Nessa picked up the laptop and turned it around in her hands so Meg could look. There wasn't much to see. There was a small window to the right of the bed's headboard, and a sloping ceiling. The bed, which was higher than normal, but not high enough to be called a bunk, had cupboards beneath the sleeping platform and ran almost the full length of the longest wall. There was the door onto the hallway, closed now, which had a row of laden coat hooks on it, a single bookshelf fastened high on the wall opposite the bed, and a thin strip of carpet. Nessa had put up a couple of pictures and a string of fairy lights, but there wasn't much more she could do to make it her own.

"Wow. Small."

"Yeah."

"Like a TARDIS in reverse; I bet it looks larger from the outside." Meg had gone through a major *Dr Who* phase a few years before. Nessa assumed she'd mostly grown out of it, but times like now, when she made references to the Whoverse, made Nessa wonder.

She caught a glimpse of her beloved Piggle-Iggle lying on the pillow; maybe you never grew out of things you loved. You put them aside from time to time and picked them up again when needed.

"I want to say, it's awful. But I don't want you to feel bad."

"It's okay. You can say it. I'll get a decent bedroom when Dad and Cindy build the extension, but for now..."

"I'm sorry."

"To be honest, I'm grateful to have space that's mine, even if it is smaller than the room I had in Hobby."

"So," said Meg, "there's something I want to talk to you about."

"Do tell."

"I want to make a podcast."

"You do? Why?"

"I was thinking. You know this big project thingy I have to do next year for media studies?"

"Vaguely." Meg had mentioned it a few times, but the details escaped her.

"We're not supposed to start it until well into our second year, but I want to be prepared. If I make a podcast, I'll be able to hone my skills, ready for when I need to use them in earnest."

"That sounds uncharacteristically diligent and sensible of you."

"It'll be fun. Plus, think! My own podcast. How cool would that be?"

"Um, very?"

"Of course, very!"

"Are you in?"

"Me? In? In what?"

"I thought it might be something we could work on together."

Nessa laughed. "That sounds suspiciously like you getting me to do your homework. And you swore, after you gave up physics, you'd never do that again."

"I never got you to do my homework."

"No, but you copied mine."

"I did not copy it."

"Oh, really?"

"Really. I simply checked mine robustly and changed anything I'd done wrong."

"And filled in the gaps of the parts you couldn't do."

"That too," Meg conceded. "But this would be different. For one thing, I'll do the planning and the techie bits, which are the bits that matter. The rest of it? We can present together. It'll be fun. And a partnership. And extra curricula. C'mon, please?"

Nessa had never been able say no to Meg's schemes. "Okay. I'm in."

"Great! Now all we have to do is figure out what it's going to be about."

*

N essa frowned. Something was different about the mugs in the cupboard. Someone had rearranged them since last night. The crockery was arranged just so, all mug handles pointing the same way.

It was unnerving.

What kind of person redid another's tidying?

Cindy was methodical. Almost pathologically organised. It showed in everything she did. The fridge was arranged according to a food hygienist's dream, with cooked meats on the top shelf and uncooked below. The tea towels were hung to dry without a crease or a wrinkle, the chopping boards aligned perfectly, and the drainer had been polished free of water marks. Everything was intimidatingly perfect, meeting an exacting set of standards Nessa could never live up to.

The tidiness was all Cindy. Dad had never been so precise. How did Dad stand it?

*

T he warm welcome Nessa received on her arrival lasted barely forty-eight hours.

"Are you going to spend all summer lounging around here, doing nothing?" Cindy asked.

"I'm not doing nothing. I've been cramming for my driving theory test, catching up on my reading, and doing my prep for next term."

"And when you've done your homework? What are you going to do then?"

"I'll find stuff to do." Nessa had no idea what. If she grew bored enough, she might end up watching make-up tutorials on ViewHoo.

"Like what? You spend most of your time shut away in your room."

"What do you expect me to do? We're miles from anywhere, and I don't know anyone."

"Get a job. I did when I was your age."

"Doing what? Where? There's nothing here, not even in cycling distance."

"What about at the hospital?"

Nessa found herself speaking through gritted teeth. "It's not in cycling distance." That wasn't strictly true. Someone fitter, faster, and keener than Nessa might have relished the commute. It was only ten or twelve miles. Each way. With hills. Nessa crossed her fingers that Cindy wouldn't fault her argument.

"Your dad and I can give you lifts."

"What about Finlay?" Nessa hated herself for asking. It almost sounded like she was volunteering to babysit him, and goodness knew she didn't want to.

"We manage when you're at school. I'm sure we'll manage if you go to work."

Nessa's instinct was to resist and look for reasons why not, but a job did have a certain amount of appeal. She'd meet people. She'd get out of the house. It would help to pass the time. And some extra money might be nice.

If only there were decent shops to spend it in.

Chapter Four

Moira found the girl behind the shed.

Moira called it a shed, but it was grander than that. It was an insulated pod she'd had built in the garden the previous year. There had been a time when she had been happy to craft in her house and sell through the shop but, when Covid forced the shop to close for extended periods of time, she'd found product accumulating in her spare room. As circumstances forced Moira to change her business model and put more effort into selling online, she grew to resent the way work invaded her home.

After the pandemic, knowing online was never going to go away, she had reclaimed her house. Thus, she'd made an investment of a few grand, moved her craft studio into the garden, and, voilà, work and home were separated, even if only by a few metres.

Moira was standing in front of her computer and sifting through the morning's emails when she smelled burning. It wasn't the smell of bonfire, or even chimney smoke from next door's wood burner. It was the nose-wrinkling scent of a cigarette, and it came through the small window set high in the pod's rear wall.

Moira pulled a disgusted face and went outside. She sniffed the air. In front of the shed, the smell wasn't as strong, but there was enough of a whiff to lure her around the corner, and there the girl squatted, her back resting against the wooden slats.

The girl was too engrossed in her phone to hear Moira approach, so Moira observed her for a few seconds. Moira's first impressions were of ripped and faded black denim jeans, canvas ankle boots, shiny black jacket, and lots of straight, dark hair, which fell in a sheet, hiding her face in a way that made Moira think of Cousin It from *the Addams Family*.

The girl held phone and cigarette in her left hand while she scrolled with her right. The burned part of the cigarette was long; she hadn't been smoking it, preferring to let it smoulder to ash. Why had she bothered with it at all?

"Ahem!"

The girl startled and leapt to her feet. The ash broke off the cigarette as she fumbled it and the phone. "Shit!" she exclaimed.

She flicked her hair over her shoulder and Moira saw her oval face for the first time. She had thick, perfectly executed eyebrows of the kind that don't occur in nature; she had taken time and care over her appearance, even if her make-up made her look like she'd stepped off a vaudeville stage.

Sixteen or seventeen, Moira guessed. Maybe younger, although Moira hoped not. Moira didn't want the smoking to be any of her business.

"Who are you? And what are you doing in my garden?"

Even under her heavy make-up, Moira saw colour flare in the girl's cheeks.

"I, uh..."

Moira cocked her head, folded her arms, and waited.

The girl bit her lower lip, which didn't do her immaculately applied lipstick any favours. She gestured to the house next door. "I wanted to get away, and this is as far as the Wi-Fi stretches."

During polite chit-chat over the fence, Moira had learned that, in the middle of the last lockdown, Cindy and Joe had vowed to get married and to move somewhere new. They needed a change of scenery and a fresh start. So far, they'd made the move and had put an engagement ring on Cindy's finger, but they had yet to make concrete plans for the wedding.

Theirs wasn't the only family to move into the area. While Argyll, after years of population decline, welcomed new blood, Moira doubted many of the new migrants would settle. There was rural and rural, and you didn't get much more rural than this.

Moira took an odd sort of pleasure in knowing the statisticians at Scottish Government defined the area as "Very Remote Rural". They were an hour away from the nearest large supermarket, and upwards of two hours from the nearest city. Some people couldn't hack the lifestyle. Others moved in and couldn't tear themselves away again. Time would tell which the Clarksons were.

In the chat, Moira had gathered the fourth member of the blended family attended boarding school, something to do with the Scottish and English education systems being so different, Joe's daughter working towards her A levels, and it being less disruptive for her to complete her schooling down south. Moira had paid only enough attention to make sure she nodded in the right places.

"Ah. You must be Vanessa."

"Nessa." Apparently, it was important Moira lost the first syllable.

"Moira." Moira waved vaguely at herself.

Moira didn't know what made her say it, but, instead of chasing Nessa away, she said, "If you're going to skulk around in my garden, please don't smoke while you do it." Path of least resistance probably.

Nessa tilted her head, and Moira saw something approaching curiosity in her eyes. "You're not mad?"

"Should I be?"

Nessa scuffed her feet. "I dunno."

"You're quiet. You're not disturbing me. Or you wouldn't if you lost the cancer stick. Don't smoke, don't make a mess, and we'll get along fine."

*

Nessa hid out for as long as she dared, but eventually she returned to the house, switched on her computer, and opened the application form for a job she doubted she wanted.

Several hours and a lot of procrastination later, she stared at her laptop screen, frustration eating away at her. She had no idea what to write. Filling in her qualifications had been easy enough, once she'd figured out how they fitted into the grand scheme of things. Why did Scotland have to be so complicated? Why did it have Nationals and Highers when it could have good old GCSEs and A levels? And how did Standard Grades, Intermediates, and Advanced Highers compare?

It hadn't taken her long to list her GCSEs. Give it another few years, and hopefully she'd have a lot more qualifications to mention. But she had no idea what made her qualified to do "the job", particularly when she had no idea what "the job" might involve. As far as she could determine, the hospital wanted a general dogsbody, someone to do whatever they were asked to do, but that didn't help her much.

"What's up, love?" asked Dad.

Nessa startled. "Jeez, Dad! Way to sneak up!"

"Sorry. I came to see how you're getting on."

Nessa pulled a face. "I don't know what to write. I'm struggling with the whole why do I want the job thing. I'm guessing it's not appropriate to say I don't have anything better to do."

"Can't you borrow from your UCAS statement?"

"I don't think so. That's all about why I want to get into microbiology. Hardly relevant to an admin job. And this bit about previous experience? I don't have any."

"Sure, you do. You can work to deadlines. You can manage your time. You know how to use word processing programmes and spreadsheets."

"Doesn't everybody?"

"You'd be surprised. There are plenty of people who remember life before computers."

"Yeah, I know." But she found it easy to forget. She'd barely had to learn how to use a computer; they'd always been a part of her life.

"Tell me again why you want to get into microbiology?"

Nessa resisted the temptation to roll her eyes. How was that relevant? Besides, Dad already knew why. "I want to get into vaccine research. I want to help people, but I don't want to be a doctor or a nurse. I don't think I'm cut out for medicine. But I want to do something to support the delivery of good health care."

"And where does most health care take place?"

"In hospitals?"

"And?"

"Health centres?"

"And?"

"The community?"

"And where is this job going to be?"

Nessa considered.

"So, I want the job because I will be working in an office in a combined care unit which supports the delivery of health and social care, and it will give me an insight to how this works in practice, not the theoretical one I'll get in university?"

"Attagirl! Remember, all you need to do is get through the door. Once you've got the job, you can prove your worth. Plus, next time you apply for a job, you'll have real work experience you can cite in your application."

"Thanks. I think I've got it now."

*

Soft summer rain fell outside, and Finlay, engrossed in cartoons full of explosions, was hogging the television, so Nessa sequestered herself in her bedroom with a book she borrowed from the shelves in the living room. She would have preferred something by an author who wasn't obsessed with the details of rotting flesh and forensics, but the thriller held more appeal than some of the alternatives, notably chick lit novels from the 1990s. The only plausible reason Cindy could have had for keeping those was the colours of the spines, which contrived to form a rainbow across the shelves.

Nessa, lying on her bed, was halfway through chapter seven, when Dad knocked perfunctorily on her door and, without waiting for an answer, poked his head into the room. Nessa had barely opened her mouth to protest when he said, "The architect has sent the plans for the extension. Do you want to see?"

Nessa swung her legs over the side of the bed, shrugged an unenthusiastic "Why not?" and dropped to the floor. She followed Dad downstairs and into the kitchen, where he scooped up a cardboard tube and pulled out the plans with a flourish worthy of a mediocre stage magician. He smoothed the plans out, and Cindy put some of her cookery books onto the corners to stop them curling.

Together, the four of them leaned over. Dad pointed out the most pertinent features of the plans to Nessa and to Finlay, neither having been involved in the discussions leading to their creation.

The extension would replace the old workshop and wood store with one-and-a-half storeys of additional space comprising a new kitchen, living room, and master bedroom with an en suite. The existing living room would become a dining room, and the current kitchen/diner would become a snug, whatever that was.

Nessa would move into Dad and Cindy's room, and Nessa's room would become an office. There had been talk of converting it into an upstairs bathroom, but the current layout of the plumbing didn't easily lend itself to that, and an office would be useful.

Nessa got caught up in the excitement, at least until she found out how long it would take to get the extension built. They had to get planning permission, and there was the time it would take to do the construction. From the way Cindy and Dad were talking, they'd be lucky to have it completed by the following summer.

So long as the work took place during the school year, when most of Nessa's stuff would be down south and the rest was stacked in her room, it might even be manageable, but what if something went wrong? Cindy didn't do chaos, and Nessa decided not to ask where she was supposed to be sleeping during the holidays if her room was being used as a store.

*

Moira ran across Nessa again three days later. She might have been back in the meantime, although given the amount of rain they'd had, Moira doubted it. However, as Moira hadn't looked, she didn't know for sure. If Nessa had been back, she'd respected Moira's request to make no mess.

As before, Nessa squatted behind the shed, but this time she'd left the cigarettes at home, and her make-up looked less like a pantomime dame. Hopefully, both had been nothing more than fleeting experiments born out of rebellion or boredom.

Nessa gave her an uncertain smile. "Hey, Moira."

"Guess there's not a lot to do around here, huh?"

Nessa lifted a shoulder, which Moira interpreted as teenager for no.

"You want some tea? I'm about to put the kettle on."

"Yes. Thank you."

Moira retreated.

When, a few minutes later, she returned, carrying a tray, Moira found Nessa standing in the middle of the lawn, looking unsure as to what she should do. Moira inclined her head in the direction of a picnic table and invited Nessa to sit.

Moira placed the tray between them and handed a mug to Nessa. "I didn't know how you'd like it, so I brought milk and sugar. You can add your own."

She'd also brought slices of banana loaf. The recipe was a good one, although Moira had gone off it for a while, a side-effect of Covid lockdowns. At least she'd never tried to make sourdough bread, so the pandemic hadn't managed to put her off that.

Nessa helped herself to milk, didn't bother with the sugar, but spent an excessive amount of time and nervous energy stirring the mug anyway.

"Cake?" Moira offered.

"Thanks." Nessa took a plate and helped herself. She broke off a small corner with her fingers, popped it in her mouth, and chewed laboriously. Moira pretended not to notice that Nessa had trouble swallowing, guessing it was a manifestation of nerves, instead of something being physiologically wrong.

Moira sipped her tea and helped herself to a slice of the cake. What on earth were they going to talk about?

She was on the cusp of resorting to the lame gambits of, "What's school like?" and "What are you studying?" when Mr Gillespie deigned to appear. He moseyed to the table and brushed against Moira's left calf, en route to investigating their guest.

He twined around Nessa's ankles, making sure to grab her attention.

Nessa offered her fingers for him to sniff. In return, he bumped his head against the back of her hand, looked up, and gave her the universal cat expression which meant "I demand attention."

Nessa grinned. The tension in her shoulders dropped away.

Nessa stroked under Mr Gillespie's chin, causing him to stretch his neck to give her better access. "Hello! Aren't you gorgeous!"

"And he knows it," agreed Moira.

"What's his name?"

Moira told her and, as she'd done for Finlay, gave Nessa a potted version of his backstory.

Nessa sat upright again, returning her attention to the refreshments.

Mr Gillespie gave a plaintive miaow and glared at her reproachfully.

He poised, readied himself, and jumped beside her. He leaned against her thigh and head-butted her elbow, demanding her to refocus her attention on him.

"He likes to be scratched behind the ears," offered Moira.

"Oh. Okay."

Nessa managed to eat and drink with her left hand, while her right worked its magic on Mr Gillespie's head. "He's purring!"

"He likes you."

They limped through the next few stages of getting to know you conversation, but it wasn't, thanks to Mr Gillespie's timely intervention, as painful as it might have been. Moira learned school was fine, boarding was okay, Nessa missed her friends, and she would apply to university in the autumn. In return, Moira explained to Nessa she managed a shop and sold crafts online, including hand-spun, hand-dyed yarn, and knitted items. Other than that, the garden kept her busy and, in a good year, well supplied with fruit and vegetables.

Above them, house martins and swallows swooped and chittered, and a black and grey bird landed on the roof of Moira's house. It let out a loud caw.

"Is that a crow? It looks weird."

"It's a hooded crow. Nothing weird about it at all. But I suppose you'd be used to the other kind. We don't often get carrion crows here. We get the hoodies instead."

"It looks nicer than the ones we get at home." Nessa looked embarrassed, as though she'd said something she shouldn't have. "I mean down south."

Moira didn't comment on Nessa's slip. Referring to the crow, she said, "You're only saying that because of its novelty value."

"Maybe."

Talking about the crows gave Moira an idea for another conversational gambit. "What do you think of all this?" She waved her hand around, taking in the gardens, the houses, and the countryside surrounding them.

Nessa considered her answer carefully. "It's different."

"Different good or different bad?"

Nessa shrugged, which meant either she didn't know, or she didn't want to say. "Everything's different. Well, not everything, but lots of things, and it feels foreign. Do you know there's red Cheddar in the supermarket? Cheddar isn't supposed to be red. It's supposed to be a nice, creamy white. Anything else is not Cheddar. And there are so many places with names I don't even know how to pronounce: Ardrishaig. Some place beginning with B I can't even remember. And the news! What's a procurator fiscal? And who's the sheriff?"

Moira smiled. "You'll get used to it. I remember how odd things were when I first moved here. I was shocked when I discovered haggis wasn't just for tourists, and you can buy it in the supermarket."

"For real?" Nessa's eyes were round.

"You can buy haggis, neeps, and tatties in the frozen meals section in the supermarket."

"Neeps and tatties?"

"Mashed swede and mashed potatoes. It's a delicious combination. Great comfort food."

Nessa looked sceptical.

*

Twenty-four hours after pressing Send on her application, Nessa received an invitation to interview. Nessa would have liked to think she was irresistible but, more likely, the centre was desperate. Frowning, she asked Cindy, "What 'm I supposed to wear?"

"Something smart."

That didn't help. Nessa didn't do everyday smart. She did uniform, casual, which meant jeans, trainers, and T-shirts, with or without accessories, or on rare occasions, party wear. She didn't think she had anything suitable for an interview, although she'd been hoping to go shopping sometime over the summer in readiness for university open days.

"You can wear your school skirt with an open-necked blouse, and accessorise with a scarf and earrings," suggested Cindy.

Nessa's grimace clearly showed her opinion of the idea, but she failed to come up with anything better.

"It'll have to do for now, and if they offer you the job, we can order some other stuff online."

Slightly mollified, Nessa ventured out to the workshop to dig around one of the suitcases into which she'd packed the freshly laundered clothes she hadn't expected to need until September.

Chapter Five

Moira carried her first coffee of the day over to the window and peered out. Joe and Finlay were in their front garden, enjoying the fine weather. A few fluffy white clouds speckled an otherwise blue sky, and the leaves on the trees were twitching in a light breeze. A runner, dressed in leggings and a tight-fitting black T-shirt that flattered his physique, came into sight. Runners, this far up the road, were unusual. The occasional cyclist doing a loop around the lanes passed this way, but runners, not so much.

The runner slowed and, moving only enough to keep warm, he exchanged a few words with Joe and Finlay. Possibly he wanted directions, although Moira struggled to imagine how anyone could end up out here by accident. There weren't any wrong turnings to take.

Joe moved to usher Finlay into the house, waving at the runner in a perfunctory manner as they went.

The runner's eyes followed them for a few seconds before he looked around more widely. He glanced across at Moira's house and waved when he caught her staring at him. She waved back, embarrassed. She must look like a right ol' curtain twitcher.

He grinned at her and took off up the road. Moira was still at the window when he returned, barely two minutes later.

Moira drained her mug and moved to get on with her day.

By the time she'd rinsed the mug, fixed herself some breakfast, and planned what she was going to do for the rest of the morning, the runner and his odd behaviour had slipped her mind.

*

Nessa didn't know whether her makeshift interview attire had influenced the decision, but the care centre offered her the job, and the following Monday, Dad dropped her off at the hospital entrance, ready for a nine o'clock start. Nessa walked up the drive, noticing how full the car park was and how a few vehicles had been forced to park half on, half off the kerbs. She saw a woman emerge from one of the poorly parked cars.

The first thing Nessa noticed about the woman was her hair. She had a buzz cut, which was beginning to grow out. The second thing Nessa noticed was her backpack, which had a rainbow pride patch sewn onto it. She wore a white T-shirt, a dark miniskirt with thick tights, and high-tops.

Nessa followed the woman through the double entry doors. If that was standard attire around here, Nessa was woefully overdressed. Maybe by the end of the week she'd feel confident enough to wear her favourite jeans.

Nessa wasted precious moments watching the woman disappear down a corridor.

How brave would someone have to be to shave their head?

If people like that woman worked at the hospital, how bad could it be?

Heartened, Nessa went to the reception desk, and as she'd been instructed, asked for Eilidh MacVicar.

*

Eilidh was only a few years older than Nessa, but she had children, plural, around whom 75 per cent of her conversation centred. She also talked about her divorce, the challenges of being a single parent, her on-off boyfriend, her mortgage, and shopping. She did not wear T-shirts or high-tops. Instead, she wore a flouncy dress, with a scooped neck in a hideous flower pattern, and strappy sandals. She'd painted her fingernails and toenails a striking shade of turquoise. They coordinated surprisingly well with her arms and legs, which were an alarming shade of tangerine. Her eye make-up and lipstick left dramatic in the dust.

Sometimes, Eilidh managed to rein in her runaway tongue long enough to tell Nessa about the job she was supposed to be doing. Maybe because Eilidh spent so much of her time around young children she gave instructions in the same encouraging tone she might have used to persuade her five-year-old that "Broccoli is delicious, Freddie. Honestly it is. You only think it isn't. Now, if you'll try some, you'll see I'm right. There's a good boy."

The work Nessa was expected to do was not difficult, and Eilidh soon discovered she only needed to tell Nessa once what needed to be done. As a result, to Nessa's relief, Eilidh soon left her alone, and Eilidh moved on to regale her older colleagues, who appeared genuinely interested, with her stories of little Freddie's, Molly's, or Laurence's misadventures.

How did Eilidh get any work done?

*

"**Y**ou the summer student?"

The voice behind her made Nessa jump. She spun around and found herself face to face with someone about Eilidh's age.

"Sorry. Didn't mean to startle you. I heard we were getting someone. Good job too. There's always loads to do around here, and we can use all the help we can get." The voice's owner grinned. "Welcome to the madhouse. I'm Emily, by the way. What's your name?"

Nessa found herself smiling. This was the woman with the backpack from earlier. Nessa's heart beat faster than usual. Emily had bow-shaped lips, grey eyes, and faint crinkles in her skin that made her look as though she was going to laugh at any second.

"Anyone show you where the kettle is yet?"

Nessa shook her head.

"C'mon. This way."

Nessa wasn't sure whether she should leave her filing, but Emily quickly brushed away her concerns. "Ach, it'll be fine for five minutes!"

Emily showed her along a corridor and into a small room equipped with a sink, fridge, microwave, kettle, a few cupboards, a small table, and a couple of chairs. To Nessa's surprise, there were already people in the kitchenette: Eilidh and two of her cronies.

"Oh! Nessa! I forgot about you!" said Eilidh, attempting an apology for not inviting Nessa to join them.

Emily made sure Nessa saw her roll her eyes, and she pushed the others out of the way to get at the kettle. Judging from the low-tide marks in their mugs, they'd been there for some time. Nessa frowned. With all the work Emily said needed to be done, why did nobody seem to be doing any of it?

Eilidh noticed Nessa noticing and said, "I guess we'd better get to our desks."

"Good idea," said Emily blandly. When Eilidh was out of the door but almost certainly not out of earshot, Emily smiled at Nessa. "Don't let her dump all her work on you." She turned towards the door, raised her voice, and continued. "She's a right scrimshanker, that one."

Nessa's eyebrows flew up.

Emily laughed at her consternation. "My, you are fresh, aren't you!"

Feeling reckless, Nessa said, "You don't like her much, do you?"

Emily wrinkled her nose. The expression looked cute on her, like a rabbit twitching its whiskers.

Emily leaned in, making the air in between them radiate with heat. "Not much, no. We went to school together, and we didn't get on. I went to uni. She got a job here and started producing babies. Imagine her shock, mine too, when one day I turned up in the office next door. If we're not careful, I might end up being her boss, and I don't know which of us would hate that more."

Should Nessa take Emily's confidence as a warning sign she risked getting caught up in the kind of office politics Dad groaned about? If Eilidh was supposed to be supervising her, how wise was it for her to hang out with Emily, even if Emily was the more friendly and helpful of the two?

"Now. Tea."

Emily told her where things were, and how the kitty for milk, coffee, and teabags worked. "We don't have a kitty for biscuits. We work on a buy your own basis around here. Certain people have sweet teeth and communal biscuits wouldn't last five minutes!"

Emily's hands were unadorned, her nails short and unvarnished, trimmed, not bitten, and, unlike Nessa, she had no ragged skin around her cuticles. She filled the kettle and made the tea, moving with minimum fuss and maximum efficiency, and managed to cut the time normally required for such a mundane task in half.

Nessa, armed with her drink, returned to work, and spent the rest of the morning letting her mind meander as she filed a pile of paperwork which couldn't have been especially important to start with; if it had been, would anyone have allowed a six-month backlog to build up? In fact, who even used paper these days, anyway?

Nessa's thoughts kept circling round to Emily. Emily, who wore a small rainbow pin on her jacket, and who had a larger patch on her backpack. Emily was one of the most audacious people Nessa had ever met, what with the extreme hair, the pride accessories, and the rainbow laces she wore on her high-tops! Emily didn't care everyone knew she was gay. Or bi. Or something that fell under the LGBTQ+ umbrella.

Had she always been like that? Had she ever doubted herself? Agonised about coming out? Nessa desperately wanted to know but had no idea how to frame the questions, or even whether it would be appropriate to ask at all.

Emily fascinated Nessa, and Nessa wanted to get to know her better.

*

Hotel by name, more bar with rooms and food by nature, Moira stopped by Murdo's for a quick lunch. The food was wonderful, the ambience welcoming, and the building as in need of investment as ever. Moira was one of Murdo's regulars.

Murdo had given her a tour of the rooms once. Like the bar and customer toilets, the bedrooms were drab, worn, and a throwback to the 1980s. None of the locals cared about the decor; after the pandemic, they considered themselves lucky the hotel had survived at all. People who'd seldom come in before had become regulars since, wanting to support the local business. Murdo welcomed old and new customers alike, and he looked less drawn now business had picked up. He'd even found the confidence to take on more staff.

Murdo brought her coffee over to her table and, uninvited, sat down. "Can I have a word?"

"Sure." Whatever he wanted to say, it was important enough for him to have abandoned whatever chore he had been doing.

"There's a man staying in the village." Murdo leaned forwards, keeping his voice low. "He's been asking questions. About you."

It happened from time to time, and Murdo knew the drill. Don't say anything that might be construed as a story, warn everyone to keep shtum, and wait the stay out. Either time on a holiday rental would run out, or the visitor would get bored. Either way, they went away eventually.

"Thanks for the heads-up."

"He's smoother than usual, this one. Came in a few days ago with his family, when he asked some questions about the area, but he waited until last night before asking about you. He's booked into one of the holiday lets until after the gala." The gala was a week on Saturday.

Although Covid restrictions had eased over the spring and summer of the previous year, community events had been slow to restart. The gala, a cross between a fête and a show, would be the first one in three years, and it would bring the community together with games, raffles, stalls, and demonstrations. Its reinstatement in the calendar of local events had generated quite a buzz. No doubt Moira would put in an appearance, not because she enjoyed those kinds of events so much as to be seen to be supportive. Murdo, who pulled the gala together, would never let her forget if she didn't.

Moira struggled valiantly not to sigh as she asked, "What's his name? What does he look like?"

"Ryan Walker-Price. Tall. Long, thin face, but not gaunt. I'd guess somewhere around forty. Dark, curly hair. Keeps fit. I've seen him running past here most mornings."

Moira remembered the unlikely sight of the jogger passing her house earlier and kept her unprintable thoughts to herself.

Murdo frowned. "You won't let him keep you away from us on Friday, will you?"

The post-Covid resumption of normal service included the reintroduction of weekly live music nights. These were relatively informal affairs. Most weeks, Murdo brought in a local band, but the third Friday in every month was open mic night, designed to encourage new talent. Moira made a point of coming along as often as possible. Sometimes, if Murdo was desperate, she'd let him persuade her to perform. More often, she was happy to listen, applaud, and encourage. This week, two of her favourite performers were graduating from open mic night to performing a full-blown gig.

"Nah. I wouldn't miss the Elephant Twins for the world."

Gordon and Billie a.k.a. the Elephant Twins weren't anything like elephants and they weren't twins. As youths, they had been skinny boys. Since they were in the second year at university, Moira supposed they were young men these days, and hadn't they grown up fast? Their studies notwithstanding, they still liked to make music together when they had a chance.

Moira had known the boys from the cradle. They were talented, self-deprecating, and fun to spend time with, full of tall tales and taller ambition. After not seeing them for more than a year during the pandemic, she'd been shocked to discover they had grown into their lanky bodies at last.

She had given them encouragement and advice when they were younger, and she still liked to support them, even though the only support they needed from her these days was moral.

Murdo got up and patted Moira's arm on the way past. "Good."

*

"I like your hair," said Nessa shyly. What did it feel like? Soft? Bristly? Her hand twitched as she resisted the urge to touch.

"Thanks." Emily had spotted Nessa eating a sandwich at her desk and had invited her to join her outside. "I had it shaved off after the first lockdown, and I liked it so much I bought a pair of clippers, and I've kept it this way ever since. I'm saving a fortune on hairdressers! Mind you, if my hair had ever looked as good as yours, I'd have left it alone."

Nessa felt unexpectedly bashful in the face of the compliment.

Emily popped open an orange and blue can and took a swig of its contents. Nessa watched, fascinated by the way Emily's neck stretched as she lifted her chin.

"You new around here?"

Nessa nodded.

"From down south?"

Nessa nodded again.

"Whereabouts?"

"Somerset."

Emily made a weird movement with her head, indicating she'd heard of the county but didn't know enough about it to say anything intelligent. "What's it like there?"

"Different." No, that wouldn't do. She tried again. "Green. Fertile.

Rolling hills. Lots of fields and hedgerows. A few garden centres and nurseries. A smattering of towns. It's rural, but there's loads more people there than here. More roads. And they're busier." Sometimes, when the wind was in the right direction, she could hear motorway traffic from the school grounds.

"Huh." Emily took another slug of her drink. "Lots of people have been moving here since Covid. You think you'll stay?"

"I don't know. I doubt it. I'm still going to school back ho—down south. And I want to go to uni afterwards. The rest of the family might settle, but for me, this feels temporary."

"Huh," said Emily again, but in a way that suggested she understood.

On a whim, as they went back into the building, Nessa paused at a vending machine and bought herself a can of whatever it was Emily had been drinking earlier. She told herself it was curiosity, and not because she wanted to mimic Emily's cool. When, mid-afternoon, she tried it, she discovered it was not to her taste. Why would anyone want to drink something that tasted like bubblegum? On the other hand, maybe she'd get some for Meg.

*

"So!" said Nessa that evening as she video chatted with Meg. "Tell me what you've been up to!"

"Oh, not much," Meg said in a breezy way which meant she'd been doing a lot. "I've been out with Jez is all."

"Jez? As in townie Jez?"

"Yep. He's now six feet tall, wears contact lenses, and is gorgeous! He looks like a god in a tight tee and jeans! Muscles in all the right places."

"Aren't you into Kai?"

"Oh, I am. Jez and I aren't serious. At least I'm not. But he's a laugh, and we have fun together. Plus, this way I get to hone my kissing skills before I move on to the real thing, right?"

"If you say so."

"We're going to the cinema on Friday."

"What are you going to see?"

"Does it matter? It's a date. We get to eat popcorn and hold hands."

That didn't sound much fun to Nessa, but as she hadn't met the god-like reincarnation of speccy, freckly Jeremy, maybe she couldn't judge. "Send me a picture of you both, okay? I want to see what you look like as a couple. I want to know how cute you are."

"Will do." Meg's face filled so much of Nessa's screen her features appeared distorted, and her nose was out of focus. Nessa caught sight of a blob of mascara on her lower eyelashes, where Meg hadn't applied it perfectly. Nessa tried not to stare. "What's new with you?"

"I got a job, and I've had my first driving lesson."

"Okay." Meg settled herself into a more flattering position. "Job first. How, what, where, and why?"

"How: I applied. Cindy's suggestion. What: clerical work, so basic admin, answering phones. Boring stuff. Where: at the hospital. Why: gets me out of the house, gets Cindy off my back, keeps me busy, and I get to earn some money, which is nice."

"Do you like it?"

Nessa tilted her head. "Makes me doubly determined to go to uni; I'd hate to do it for the rest of my life, but I guess it's okay for a few weeks. The work's dull, and so are some of the people. You wouldn't believe how much they talk about babies and mortgages! But it's experience, and one of the people I've met seems cool." Nessa's face warmed. She hoped Meg, through the webcam, couldn't tell. "She's called Emily, and she's invited me to join her for lunch a couple of times, and some of the others invited me to go to the pub with them on Friday after work. I think it's someone's birthday."

"Are you going? To the pub, I mean?"

"If Dad comes to collect me, I might. Otherwise, I can't. No way to get home afterwards. He seems pretty cool about it, but Cindy says I'm too young. She says she remembers what she was like at my age, but I don't think she does. She wants to keep me on the straight and narrow, but it's not like she's my mum, and I won't drink alcohol anyway. I keep telling her I'm not like her, but it doesn't make a difference."

"How are you getting on with her otherwise?"

Nessa curled her upper lip and frowned. "Things are okay, I guess, but it's taking some getting used to. Dad, Cindy, and Finlay were all settled in by the time I got home, and I feel, I don't know, like an outsider."

"Poor you."

Nessa, who had passed her theory test the day after her birthday, was regaling Meg with an exaggerated version of the horror which had been her first driving lesson, when she heard noises out on the landing and the door to Finlay's room being pushed open.

"Finlay!" exclaimed Cindy. "What's the cat doing here?"

Nessa lifted her head to listen. "Uh, oh," she murmured, her voice full of delighted mischief.

"What's up?"

Nessa shook her head, signalling Meg to be quiet while she eavesdropped unashamedly.

"Sleeping?" suggested Finlay.

"If I've told you once, I've told you a hundred times, don't leave the door open! I don't want that cat in the house!"

Finlay must have protested his innocence because, exasperated, Cindy snapped, "How did he get in? Climbed the drainpipe, I suppose!"

Nessa laughed even as she turned her attention away from the argument.

"What's going on?" demanded Meg.

Nessa looked at her computer screen. "Finlay's got Moira's cat in his bedroom. Again." She briefly described Mr Gillespie and his history. "Cindy isn't happy, but Finlay wants a pet, and I think he's trying to woo Dizzy to move back here. Trouble is, I think Dizzy wants to be wooed, at least on a part-time basis. He's happy enough to go next door for his dinner."

"What does Moira think?"

"I think she's sitting somewhere between exasperated and highly entertained. Anyway, the podcast?"

"Yeah." A pall of gloom fell over Meg. "I've been doing some research, and I still haven't got a clue what it should be about."

Nessa, whose brain had stalled happily at the mention of research, said, "What have you got so far?"

Meg ran through her findings, which she'd organised into a couple of lists: what format the podcast might use; what genre it might fall into. "Scripted fiction and comedy are out. Too much like hard work. I ruled out in-depth journalism for the same reason. Also, anything involving lots of guests is a no go, so that pretty much leaves us talking to each other. I've started thinking about genres."

"Genres?"

"You know. Themes. Types. Topics."

"Oh, yeah."

"But none of them grabbed me."

"Why not?"

"Celebrity gossip is out. I don't know any celebrities. Politics is too boring. Religion is a no go because boring and also you can't make a whole podcast out of nope."

"What's left?"

"Health."

"Might be interesting?"

"To you, maybe. Not to mere mortals like me. True crime, game shows, pop culture, investigative journalism, drama, which we already ruled out with the whole nothing scripted thing, and the news. Everything is either too difficult or too dull."

"There has to be something not on your list."

"I sure hope so. Why is this so hard?"

Interlude

"Who do you fancy?"

I wasn't sure what Sarah meant.

"You know," Sarah persisted. "Who do you like?"

"C'mon. You must like someone," Jayne said. "Everyone does."

I thought about it. I didn't think I liked anyone in the way they meant, but I had to say something if I wanted to fit in. I gave the name of an obscure actor who had appeared in a short-lived detective series. My classmates frowned. "Him? Honestly?"

I'd chosen wrong, but I didn't know why. So, I defended my choice. "I love the character he plays."

That night, when I went home, I did what the others did. I wrote my actor's name all over the cover of my rough book. I drew his name in big, blocky letters, which I outlined in black and coloured in with felt-tip pens. I drew a few love hearts, and I scrawled aspirational statements about our impending marriage.

I went to bed, and as I fell asleep, I daydreamed about the character my obscure actor portrayed, sketching out the crimes we would solve together.

*

My brother, who's four years older than me, found my rough book, and he wrote on its cover, making fun of my crush. "Why do you fancy a fictitious prick of a private dick?" He made me feel small, stupid, and confused.

If I didn't fancy him, I wouldn't fit in at school, and I would be teased.

I didn't want to be teased.

But I was being teased at home anyway.

I couldn't win, and I couldn't find the words to explain how confused and torn I felt.

Chapter Six

Nessa had seen the pub from the outside, a long, two-storey building with white roughcast walls, black-painted window frames, sills, doors, and guttering, and a slate roof. A covered arch, halfway along the frontage, hinted at its origins as a coaching inn.

By the time Nessa arrived, a fraction after five thirty, the bar was halfway to heaving. She looked around for the rest of the party, spotting them on the far side of the room. She wove her way through the customers and tagged herself onto the edge of the group, most of whom were already well into their first glasses of the evening. In a fit of uncharacteristic helpfulness, Eilidh introduced her to the people she hadn't met previously.

Nessa thought Eilidh was being nice until she explained how they'd set up a kitty and held out her hand expectantly.

One of the other women took pity on Nessa. She glared at Eilidh and told Nessa to buy herself a drink and, once she'd done that, put the balance into the pot. "It's only fair since we're already one ahead of you."

Grateful, Nessa went to the counter, taking in more details of her surroundings as she did so. Half of the pub's lower floor was given over to the bar, and the rest was used as a restaurant. The upstairs was accommodation for the manager and bedrooms for guests.

The bar room had bare stone walls, a flagstone floor, and an open fire, unlit at this time of year. A pair of incongruous, oversized, white leather sofas with sagging cushions flanked the fireplace. The rest of the furniture, comprising stools, tables, and settles, was made of dark wood. A pool table and a dartboard towards the rear of the room, and a one-armed bandit close to the toilets, attracted small crowds of games players.

By six o'clock, the place was teeming, and loud music blared out of speakers, making it necessary for people to shout over each other to have a conversation. Even so, most of the talk was unintelligible. After a while, Nessa gave up trying to listen to everything and settled on nodding politely whenever Mhairi, the helpful woman from earlier, asked, "You okay, hun?" in a grandmotherly way.

*

The reassurance she'd given Murdo notwithstanding, Moira almost backed out of going to see the Elephant Twins.

She had been a pop star for about twenty minutes during the eighties. At the tail end of punk, outrageous ragged hair, excessive make-up, attitude, and enthusiasm had been more important than musical ability. She'd had raw talent, and she could sing in tune, although the Diptych's earliest songs had involved more shouting and deliberately discordant noise than easy on the ear melodies. Moira had never had any formal training, but she'd had a knack for lyrics and tunes, and she'd penned songs not only for the Diptych but also for some other bands. The royalties she'd received from her songs had been a useful supplement to her income over the years.

In the beginning, she'd played the guitar badly and keyboards with two fingers, but it hadn't mattered. Their producer had polished everything to perfection, and they'd mimed on *Top of the Pops*. Plus, Moira had worked hard to learn and improve, and she'd become almost proficient by the time she left the biz behind.

For years after leaving London, she'd only played for her own pleasure, nobody else's, and she'd continued to improve. The Diptych became a memory, bittersweet and slightly embarrassing, and Moira never ceased to be amazed when someone dug up the past. Why in the world did anyone care anymore?

Sometimes, in the supermarket, they'd play "Will You (Ask Me Out)?" over the radio, and she'd stop in the aisles, somewhere between the tinned soup and the dried pasta, and she catch herself humming along, or slipping into the ridiculous dance routine, head jerking like a chicken pecking at the ground, shoulders, arms, and hands contorting in ways not natural to the human body, and for a moment she'd be transported to black, wide-legged trousers, over-sized, white frilly shirts with billowing sleeves, lacy cuffs and collars, and huge hooped earrings. If she was unlucky, someone would see her, and if she was extremely unlucky, they'd try to join in, and she'd have to smile and pretend not to be mortified.

One of the Sunday papers, in the noughties, had run a *Whatever Happened To...* column. They'd tracked down Nikki and Robin; she had been divorced, living in Devon, and he'd been eking out a living singing on a Mediterranean cruise ship. The paper claimed not to have tracked Moira down, preferring to rehash old, libellous stories to admitting

Moira hadn't wanted to be interviewed.

She'd threatened to take legal action if they didn't print an immediate retraction. Hers wasn't an empty threat: in the wake of the band's break-up, she'd infamously sued Julia Walker and the tabloid employing her, and the jury had found in Moira's favour.

Moira had fought for what she'd believed was right. She'd fought to clear her name, their names. And it had been exhausting. The experience had left her battered, jaded, and disillusioned.

The courts might have found in her favour, but there were still people who believed there must have been a grain of truth in the stories, and the tarnish clung. Her youthful idealism had been replaced by cynicism.

In the years since, she had tried to keep her head down, and any activism she'd got involved in had been limited to signing the occasional petition or fighting for causes that mattered to the local community but wouldn't change the world. She missed the firebrand she'd hoped to be when she was nineteen or twenty, before life had happened and she'd given in to commercial interests.

There had been other papers and other journalists over the years, any of which could have used long-lensed pictures and "outed" her. Instead, possibly inspired by her neighbours, friends, and acquaintances who respected and guarded her privacy, they settled for describing her as "the forgettable one on the right-hand side" of ancient photographs.

Occasionally, though, there'd be a new flurry of rumours or speculation, usually when Nikki tried to stage yet another comeback. The old allegations would resurface; Moira never failed to be astonished by what the papers got away with, so long as the stories used the word "allegedly" every other sentence.

But an evening with the Elephant Twins was tempting, and she shouldn't have to hide herself away. She'd have to keep her fingers crossed Ryan Walker-Price didn't like live music.

By the time Moira arrived, it was standing room only at Murdo's, and getting to the bar involved lots of shoulder tapping and excuse-mes. The noise level made conversations difficult, but nobody cared, or if anybody did, they hid it well.

In the same way that during the Covid crisis she'd sometimes found herself waiting in supermarket queues and questioning how the wearing of masks had become part of everyday life, Moira caught herself marvelling this type of gathering was permitted again. The first time, post-pandemic, the pub had filled up, people had been twitchy, at least until alcohol had removed their inhibitions. Nobody had any qualms now!

Waiting to be served, Moira found herself next to a familiar face. She raised her voice loud enough to be audible. "Hi, Emily. Don't see you in here often."

Emily turned to face her. "There's a work do tonight, and the girls were planning on going to my local. Couldn't stand the idea of it, so I came here to avoid them. Besides, I thought it would be fun to come see the lads. I remember them from school. They were a few years below me, but they still managed to leave a lasting impression."

"Oh? Do tell."

"They were clowns. If there was any trouble, they'd be in the thick of it. But they were never mean, and they were always the first to volunteer for anything." With the condescension of someone who had been three years older at a time when age differences mattered, she said, "They were nice kids."

Emily's assessment sounded about right. Gordon and Billie had always been quick to get into scrapes, but equally quick to get out of them. Helpful, outspoken, and silver-tongued, they were easy to like.

Some twangs, hisses, and clattering from the room next door

indicated the Elephant Twins were getting ready to perform. A particularly loud whistle from the mic made people wince in the manner of a Mexican wave passing through the bar at the speed of sound. As the pair riffed on their instruments, people drifted through to the function room. A few, Emily and Moira included, stayed in the bar.

They found room at a vacated table, where they stacked an array of empty glasses towards one end, clearing space for their own. Moira leaned against the high back of a settle and smiled contentedly as, next door, to whoops and cheers, the Elephant Twins launched themselves into a rousing version of "Donald, Where's Your Trousers?"

"They're good!" Emily sounded pleasantly surprised. From the applause at the end of the song, the rest of the audience agreed.

"Next," said Billie, "here's something we wrote called "Everyone is Angry Now"."

Moira couldn't make out all the words, but she got the gist, and the tune, especially the chorus, had all the makings of an earworm. By the last chorus, Emily and Moira were belting out the words, muscle-aching grins plastered on their faces.

> *There's no discussion,*
> *Just assertion,*
> *Vitriol and aversion.*
> *Half-read threads.*
> *Everyone is*
> *Two-hundred-and-eighty characters of angry now.*

The Twins switched tempo to perform a melancholy song about unrequited love before gathering pace again and launching into a sea shanty.

There followed a five-minute break, which resulted in a crush at the bar.

As the queue waned, a man holding a pint came to stand over Moira and Emily's table.

Ignoring Emily, he said, "Hello. You're Moira Cavendish, aren't you? Let me introduce myself. Ryan Walker-Price." He forked a business card out of an inner pocket and held it out. Moira pointedly didn't take it or answer.

Emily grabbed the card and glanced at it. "Well, Ryan Walker-Price, we were in the middle of a private conversation, so if you wouldn't mind..."

His eyes narrowed as he caught the lie. They hadn't been talking much at all, preferring to focus on the entertainment. Nonetheless, he took the hint and moved away, but not far enough to be safely out of earshot.

Moira muttered, "Dammit!"

A glint flashed in Emily's eyes, and she said louder than necessary, "So, I was telling you about Felicity's haemorrhoids," and went into excruciating detail about the entirely fictitious Felicity's predicament. From there, Emily moved on to regale Moira with tales of the equally fictitious Annette's female problems, and as she and Moira launched into a discussion about periods and menopause, Ryan Walker-Price edged away.

They managed to contain themselves until he'd left the room. They had to stuff their fists into their mouths to muffle their guffaws.

"You, Emily, are evil! Brilliant, but evil. I am officially in awe!"

"At uni, my nursing friends and I used to do that to get rid of boys in bars. Works every time!"

*

All told, Nessa found a great deal to hate about her first work do. Unlike everyone else in the group, she was too young to drink alcohol, and the more everyone else drank, the lewder and louder they got, and the more uncomfortable Nessa grew.

Nessa had been privy to plenty of talk about boyfriends and girlfriends, dating and kissing at school. In the lower years, the conversations had mostly been theoretical. Nobody had any practical experience.

Just when they might have begun to get some, Covid came along and cramped everyone's style. Dating and social distancing hadn't gone well together.

Since restrictions had been lifted, her peers had been trying to make up for lost time, desperate to have all those first experiences they'd been denied. Pent-up puberty.

Gossip was rife. Sinead and Sebastian had been caught snogging behind the bike sheds. Wendy and Martin might have gone all the way; Wendy had gone out of her way to fuel the speculation by brazenly waving some condoms around in the dining hall as though they were some kind of trophy.

But none of her experiences had prepared Nessa for the way the women, especially the married ones, talked about who they would sleep with, given the chance. Plus, there were the gestures, the miming, and the raucous laughter.

Nessa felt young and uncomfortable. Were these lewd and crude conversations the normal stuff of adulthood? Not wanting to look bad, she resisted the urge to sneak into the ladies and text Dad to see if he could collect her early.

A rush of relief washed over Nessa when he sent a message on the dot of eight to say he had picked up a takeaway and was waiting outside. She made her goodbyes hastily and slalomed through the melee as fast as possible, grateful to escape.

After several hours in the bar's gloomy interior, the evening sunlight dazzled Nessa as she emerged from the pub. A fresh breeze blew off the loch, and Nessa allowed herself several seconds to savour it while her eyes adjusted. Her shoulders relaxed.

She glanced up and down the street, and spotted Dad's car, parked fifty yards away, outside a charity shop. She jogged down the road, opened the passenger side door, and slid in. The smell of Chinese food hit her and made her stomach growl.

"Good evening?" Dad asked hopefully.

"Fine." Even to her own ears, she sounded unsure.

"Want to talk about it?"

She shook her head. "No, I'm good." In her head she screamed, *No bloody way am I telling you about everything that happened in there*!

To her relief, he switched on the indicator, checked the road was clear, pulled out, did a U-turn across the carriageways, and headed home.

*

In the next room, the Elephant Twin's music gave way to a playlist being pumped out through the speakers. The boys were taking a break, and they, along with half their audience, piled into the bar.

"Sandwich!" yelled Gordon as soon as he clapped eyes on Moira.

"Sandwich!" agreed Billie, and before she had time to react, Moira found herself being pulled to her feet and squeezed tightly between them, her left ear scrunched painfully against Gordon's chest.

Moira flinched at the ebullient greeting of the Elephant Twins, even as she savoured the emotions engendered by the hug.

"C'mon, boys! Enough. I can hardly breathe!"

"Ah, but you love it." Gordon loosened his hold on her but didn't let go. He ruffled her hair with his knuckles.

Moira didn't answer. Instead, she laughed, itself an admission. "C'mon you two. Let me get you both a drink."

At the welcome invitation, they let go, if only so Moira could get to the bar. They followed close behind her, like an honour guard.

The boys, armed with pints, squeezed themselves around Moira and Emily's table, where, with half an eye on the time, they caught Moira up on their news while they downed their drinks. Their studies were going well, and they were home for the holidays. Gordon was studying forensic psychology, which sounded terribly grand, and, as far as Moira knew, hadn't existed as a degree when she was their age, while Billie planned to make a career out of engineering. But nothing was going to stop them making music together. They didn't want to make a career of it; they wanted to have fun and a few thousand followers on ViewHoo.

Lubricated and rejuvenated, the boys returned to the stage, retuned their instruments, and launched into the second half of their act. Two songs in, Gordon startled Moira by reappearing at their table, mic in hand.

"Come and join us!" he belted into the mic, loud enough to ensure everyone on the premises heard.

Moira shook her head.

Gordon stuck out his bottom lip in an exaggerated pout, tilted his head to one side, and clasped his hands together. "Pweese?"

"C'mon, Moira!" Billie shouted from the next room.

The crowd joined in. "Moira! Moira! Moira!"

One of the regulars grasped Moira's right hand and pulled, trying to yank her to her feet. She could have resisted him, but now Murdo joined in. She gave in to the inevitable, touched by their enthusiasm.

Blushing slightly, she joined the Elephant Twins. "And now we're triplets!" Gordon joked into his mic.

That the boys had planned this became obvious when they suggested performing one of the Diptych's songs, which they'd clearly rehearsed.

No wonder Murdo had been so keen she came tonight!

The song wasn't one of the band's hits, but something buried on an album, where only true fans would find it. Moira kind of loved the Elephant Twins for that.

Gordon handed Moira a spare guitar, and the crowd waited expectantly as Moira fiddled with the microphone stand, adjusting its height.

Across the function room, Moira caught sight of Ryan Walker-Price. She wasn't sure whether he was trying to hide behind a pillar, or whether he was using it as a convenient thing to brace himself against as he pointed his mobile phone in their direction.

She turned around far enough to catch Murdo's eye and gesture discreetly in Walker-Price's direction. Murdo nodded infinitesimally before he lifted the hatch in the bar's counter and dodged out of the front door. Seconds later, he reappeared from the direction of the kitchens and stood directly in front of Ryan Walker-Price's mobile.

*

A couple of lights were still on in the Clarkson house when Moira got home, one in the living room, and one in Nessa's bedroom. What did the Clarksons usually do on Friday nights? Did they know about the live music at Murdo's? Perhaps Moira should tell them. They might enjoy it, and Finlay would be welcome, at least in the earlier part of the evening. Plus, it might be a way for Nessa to meet a few more people closer to her own age.

She climbed out of the car and nodded to herself as she locked the door.

Yes. She'd mention it. And maybe they'd come along sometime, and hear the Elephant Twins sing.

Maybe she'd tempt them by showing them the Elephant Twins' ViewHoo channel.

Before she'd left, Gordon and Billie had had a quiet word with her.

"We wanted you to know. We were taping the set. We're going to edit the recording, and we'll take your part out if you want, but it's up to you."

She should have told them to take it out. She valued caution. But it had been fun, and she'd found herself saying, "You can keep it in, if you want. But don't credit me, okay?"

It was a risk, but sometimes risks were worth taking. Besides, an anonymous ViewHoo appearance was hardly newsworthy, was it?

*

As Nessa lay in bed, she recalled the conversations that had made her so uncomfortable. How had those women come up with so many potentially shaggable men?

She tried to think who, in her year, she'd want to snog. No one sprang to mind. They were all too young, too pimply, except for Tarone, who was too male.

Not like Emily, who made her feel tingly, nervous, and tongue-tied.

So, this was what a crush felt like!

Nessa had known she liked women for a while. The knowledge had grown from a niggling suspicion into a question and, later, into a certainty. But until she'd met Emily, knowing she was lesbian had been academic.

Lesbian.

She let the word wrap around her brain like a gentle caress.

Nessa fell asleep thinking about short hair, grey eyes, and bow-shaped lips.

Chapter Seven

Moira was covering someone else's shift. Again. Callum and Bethany had messaged her to say they were unable to work this Saturday, despite having agreed to the date over a month ago and confirming they would do it two weeks previously. They'd made a vague reference to sniffles and sore throats, but that was balderdash. She'd seen the social media posts announcing their presence at a craft fair in Helensburgh.

Moira had messaged around, asking for a volunteer to step into the breach, but nobody had come forwards. A few people pleaded previous commitments, but most kept quiet. Although Moira had signed the lease and managed the paperwork and rotas, the business was supposedly a co-operative. Nobody would have known, though, as cooperation was in desperately short supply, and as usual, it had fallen to Moira to pick up the pieces.

Moira unlocked the door, disarmed the burglar alarm, and tried not to think about all the things she'd been planning to do today. She had fleece to card, yarn to spin, and skeins to dye. Every extra shift done was time and earnings lost, and she resented the way her business associates took her for granted. At least she'd brought some knitting to occupy her during any slack time.

She switched on the lights and the till, replenished stock on a few shelves, and on the dot of 9:30, flipped the sign on the door to open. She waited hopefully for customers to pour in.

They didn't pour, but there was a steady trickle, and a few of the trickle deigned to buy. Moira sold some ceramics and greeting cards to an elderly couple, who insisted on telling her they were visiting from Edinburgh for the weekend, and a wicker basket to a German woman who spoke better English than Moira did.

Moira was giving Mrs McCrossan, who'd popped in to stock up on knitwear for yet another great-grandchild, her change when a quartet of familiar faces, in the form of her next-door neighbours, turned up.

Cindy cooed excitedly as she flitted between stands, unable to focus on any single one for long, Joe looked quietly impressed by Callum's wood-turned bowls and spurtles, Finlay managed to combine boredom with wanting to pick up and touch everything, and Nessa made a beeline for the costume jewellery.

For all their touching and browsing, only Nessa found something she liked enough to buy. She put the necklace she had chosen on the counter and gestured towards Moira's work in progress. "Nice."

"Thank you."

Nessa pointed towards the array of shelves at the rear of the shop. "That your stuff too?"

"Some of it."

"Some of it is yours, or it's some of your stuff?"

Moira's lips twitched. "Both. Some of the things on the shelf are mine, and I have a lot more things at home. I sell online, as well as through a few other shops." With practiced ease, she wrapped and rang up the necklace while she talked.

"Cool." Nessa handed over a twenty-pound note.

Moira didn't see much cash these days; Covid had changed people's behaviour. Like many others, she barely carried cash anymore, preferring to swipe a card. At what age did teenagers get their first debit cards? If she didn't have one already, Nessa was surely on the cusp.

Moira scrabbled around the till. "Sorry about the shrapnel."

"'S okay," muttered Nessa, pocketing her change. She looked straight at Moira, stopped mumbling, and said more clearly, "Can you teach me?"

"Teach you?"

"To knit."

Cindy, overhearing the request, interjected. "Nessa! Don't put her on the spot!" To Moira, she added, "I'm sorry."

"No need to apologise. And I don't mind. I'll show you if you want."

Nessa's face lit up. "You will? What do I need?"

"I've got spare needles and plenty of yarn, so you don't need anything. Call around, and I'll get you started. You free tomorrow afternoon?"

If anything, Nessa's face grew even brighter.

*

The politicians and the statisticians claimed Covid infection rates were at a low level, and they must have been, because Public Health Scotland had long since stopped publishing daily statistics and the pandemic no longer dominated the news. The experts had yet to claim the risk was entirely gone, however.

Unrestricted indoor visits had been allowed, if not recommended, for over a year now, but Moira still tended to sit outside with her guests if she could, midges be damned. Thus, Nessa sat across from Moira at the picnic table, her tongue poking out of the corner of her mouth as she concentrated. She scrunched her forehead up and she squinted as she poked her righthand needle through the first stitch on her left.

Moira had found some self-patterning yarn, wanting Nessa to start with something pretty enough to hold her interest as she learned. She'd helped Nessa to cast on, and now she was showing her how to form knit stitches.

"That's it. Now, wind the yarn over. Good. Pull the loop through, and let the old stitch drop off the needle. Now, again. In. Over. Through. Off." Moira supervised as Nessa ploughed her way through the rest of the row. Nessa's movements were slow and ham-fisted, but she would improve in time, assuming she stuck with it. Given the amount of determination Nessa showed, Moira hoped she would.

"You'll want to check you have the same number of stitches you started with."

Nessa counted and nodded. "What would I do if I hadn't?"

"We'll worry about that when it happens. For now, keep practising."

After another couple of rows, Moira picked up her own knitting, happy to let Nessa continue with minimal supervision.

After a few more rows, Nessa grew confident enough to try talking while she worked. "How are you so fast?"

"Years of experience. Once you've got the hang of how the stitches are formed, we'll work on finding ways for you to hold the needles more efficiently, so you'll get faster too. All you need is time and practice."

Nessa liked to talk economics and politics.

These days the news bulletins were full of war, climate catastrophe, nationalism, separatism, independence, trade deals, the dire straits of the economy, and how it was going to take decades to get the country back on track. Moira could hardly bear to listen, but she couldn't bring herself to ignore it either. Forewarned was forearmed, and all that.

By contrast, based on their conversation, Nessa lapped the news up, and liked to talk about it at length. At a similar age, Moira had also been earnestly idealistic and had wanted to save the world.

As the first fat raindrops fell, Moira suggested they retreat inside. They hastily gathered their bits and pieces together and ducked in through the back door.

*

Moira's house was a revelation.

They went into what Moira called the lobby, which was the equivalent of Cindy's utility room. An elderly chest freezer, which was humming noisily, dominated the space.

Moira still had a couple of face coverings hanging on a hook, and she had hand sanitiser sitting on top of the fuse box. It had taken long enough for the Covid precautions to become second nature; it was taking even longer to readjust now they were no longer necessary. Or maybe Moira couldn't be bothered to tidy things away.

As they hung their jackets on a row of coat hooks, Nessa took in the pile of shoes and boots, and a pair of waterproof trousers which had been left in a heap next to them. She spotted a couple of dusty cacti in terra-cotta pots in the wide window recess; they looked almost as old as the house.

Nessa followed Moira into the kitchen, and what a kitchen it was! The room didn't pretend to be a dining room; it was all kitchen, with a massive range in the fireplace, and a large, utilitarian table in the middle. There were units and shelves, a washing machine and a butler sink with wooden drainers, a large dresser against one wall, and a Sheila Maid hanging from the ceiling. The overall effect was old-fashioned and homely.

Best of all, there was clutter! There was even a faint sheen of dust on the shelves. Nessa found it a relief to be somewhere with less than A-star level cleaning.

"Go on through to the living room and make yourself at home while I make us some tea."

Nessa assumed the downstairs layout of Moira's house would be like the one next door, albeit without the extension which housed Cindy and Dad's bedroom. She exited the kitchen, passed the bathroom and front door, and found the living room where she'd expected.

A two-seater sofa backed against a wall, a recliner in one corner, and a modestly sized television in another were all focused on the fireplace. In the middle stood a small, low coffee table. Around the edges of the room, shelves overflowed with books and CDs. A dated hi-fi system squeezed into a tiny nook behind the door.

Nessa took a closer look at the books, an eclectic mix of fiction and non-fiction. The books had been grouped approximately by theme, not by size and colour. This wasn't pretty; it was practical!

Why did she feel more at home here than she did next door?

*

Moira carried a tray and her knitting bag through to the living room, where she found Nessa kneeling on the floor, rooting through her CD collection, an extensive assortment of classical, pop, film soundtracks, and folk. There were even a few birdsong CDs, bought on impulse at least two decades before, when Moira had had ambitions to tell species apart by listening to their calls. She'd listened to the CDs a few times, but they had proved to be a source of frustration, not education.

She put the tray on the coffee table, invited Nessa to help herself, and, armed with her own mug, sat in the recliner.

Nessa scooted over to collect her tea and a biscuit and on her knees, shuffled back to the CDs. She put the mug on the floor, held onto the biscuit with her teeth, and returned to her rummaging.

"You like music?"

"Some." Nessa stopped long enough to take the biscuit out of her mouth with her left hand. She took a bite.

"What kind?"

"No particular genre. Bits of this and that." Another couple of bites, and the biscuit was history. Hands free again, Nessa returned her attention to the CDs.

What did Nessa find so fascinating about them?

"Hey, Dad's got this too. And this." Nessa had reached an area of the shelf where lots of eighties music had amassed together. "Oh, and this!" She brandished one of the discs and gave out a raucous laugh.

Moira raised her eyebrows. "What's so funny about the Diptych?"

"Nothing. Only..." Nessa laughed again. "Aunty Helen told me once that Dad had a huge crush on the lead singer. He had posters on his bedroom wall and everything. I guess it's funny because it's Dad, you know?" Nessa took a closer look at the CD. "Mind you, she was pretty."

"Yeah. She was. She was on a lot of bedroom walls back in the day."

"You make it sound like you knew her."

"You might say that."

"You knew a pop star? Before or after she was famous?"

"Before and during. We were in the band together."

"No way! You were in the band?"

"I don't usually tell people." Why had she told Nessa?

"Why not? It's so cool! I'd tell everyone if it was me."

"It's complicated. Plus, it's in the past. Not important."

"Not important? But it's huge! Were you on telly? You must have been. You had hit records."

"It was only for a few years. Over three decades ago."

"That's, like, almost twice as old as me ago."

"Yes."

The way Nessa said, "Wow," made Moira feel old.

"What did you do in the band?"

"Guitar, mostly. A bit of singing. Sometimes keyboards."

"Do you still play?" Nessa looked around, confused, as well she might be. There was no evidence of any instruments on display.

"My guitar's upstairs. I've got a keyboard too, but I don't often get it out."

Nessa sat on her heels and drank from her mug. "What was it like? Being in a band, I mean."

"Maybe I'll tell you sometime." She didn't mean it. "Okay, tea break is over. You want to try again?"

Nessa perched on the edge of the sofa, got her needles out, and worked a few stitches before saying, "Cindy can't knit."

"Lots of people can't. In the days before the internet, most people would have learned from an older relative. If you didn't know someone who knitted, you wouldn't learn. Plus, knitting went out of fashion in the nineties when fleeces became popular. Now it's making a comeback, but I think it skipped a generation."

"Cindy's not much younger than you."

"Nice of you to think so."

"Have you always knitted?"

Moira shook her head. "My mother tried teaching me several times before I decided I wanted to learn."

"What do you mean?"

"She believed it was something I should know how to do but, in hindsight, she was a terrible teacher."

"Why?"

"For one thing, she hated knitting. She was good at it, but she considered it a chore. Boring. And she complained about it. How was I supposed to be inspired, when she made it clear knitting was something to be endured, not enjoyed? For another, she tried to start me on making doll scarves and dishcloths. I didn't play with dolls much, and what child wants to make dishcloths?"

Nessa laughed.

"Also, I couldn't hold the needles the way she did, and I didn't find out until years later there were other ways to hold them."

"There are?"

"A few. What works for me mightn't work for you. We'll have to experiment. See what suits you best."

"What made you learn in the end?"

"Pretty much the same thing as you. I went into a craft shop and was inspired. I was about your age. Gaudy sweaters were the height of fashion, and I fell in love with some particularly fine examples. Mum and Dad told me I could have one as my main Christmas present if I wanted. I didn't; I never liked clothes as presents. Too utilitarian. Not special enough. Instead, I asked Mum if she'd teach me to knit, but only if it was something interesting."

"Not dishcloths."

"Not dishcloths," agreed Moira.

*

Nessa reappeared on Tuesday evening, having added several inches to her scarf along with two extra stitches.

"Mr Gillespie tried to give me a mouse on my way in," Nessa said as she struggled to follow what Moira was doing to correct her mistakes.

"One of his less endearing qualities. But if he's giving you gifts, it means he holds you in high esteem."

"I'm honoured."

"As you should be. There. That's you sorted."

"Thanks." Nessa flashed Moira a smile. "You mind if I hang around for a while?"

"You're not needed at home?"

"I doubt they'll even notice I'm gone. I needed to get away. Finlay was being a pain. I mean, he's always a pain, and it's like he's every-where. But he was being more of a pain than usual. The only place I can avoid him is my cubbyhole."

"Your cubbyhole?"

"It's too small to be called a room. The only way they could squeeze me, my stuff, and a bed in it was to give me a captain's bed, which might have been cool when I was ten, but not now. Dad and Cindy have the master bedroom, Finlay got spoiled, and I got the cubby."

Ah. Nessa was referring to the twin to the small, upstairs room that, since she'd acquired the shed, Moira had been using for storage.

"I thought my room at school was small, but it was huge compared to the cubby. Dad and Cindy are talking about building an extension, but until they do, we're squished into the house like sardines, and they say it doesn't make sense for me to have the second room when I'm away most of the year. It wouldn't be so bad if Finlay kept to his room, but he doesn't. I go into the living room; he's there before me. I go into the kitchen; he comes in, demanding snacks. His mess gets everywhere too. It drives Cindy crazy."

"It sounds like it's driving you crazy too."

"Well, things were way better when Dad and Cindy sneaked (snuck?) around—"

"Sneaked. We're not American."

"—pretending like I didn't know. But then they started talking about blending the family, and they decided to move here."

"What's boarding school like?"

"It's okay, I guess."

"Nikki, the other half of the Diptych, went to boarding school. She rarely talked about it, and I often wondered." Nikki had never mentioned any friends either, which always struck Moira as odd since she had been such a friendly, outgoing, kind of person.

Moira caught a glint of something almost calculating in Nessa's eye. "How about a trade?" Nessa said. "I'll tell you if you tell me."

"Tell you about what?"

"Nikki. And the band."

Chapter Eight

Nessa's work did not get any more interesting as the days went by, but the novelty of being paid to be bored, weekly driving lessons with a middle-aged instructor called Lesley, the lunches she had with Emily, and the things she learned about her new home and its culture offset the tedium of the job.

The language she heard every day was different to the English she knew. Nessa started keeping notes of the unfamiliar words she learned, words like braw, gallus, thall, and outwith. Scots said things differently too. They did not like the words "to be" and, too impatient to use the extra syllables, missed them out in sentences. Things never needed to be done. They needed done.

Scottish culture wasn't something the Scots played up for the benefit of tourists. It was real and distinct. People wore kilts and ate haggis in non-ironic ways and were loyal to the local pipe bands. The English thoughtlessly considered themselves to be British; the Scots knew the difference, and many of them felt their identity was lost in, or irrelevant to, the union.

Nessa had been to Scotland before but visiting and staying were different things. She'd known the Scots had different bank notes, but she hadn't appreciated they were in everyday circulation, and the English notes she occasionally came across were unusual. The signposts were bilingual, in both Gaelic and English, though she had yet to hear any Gaelic spoken. Would she recognise it if she did?

The first few times she espied oval stickers with the word yes in white against a blue background, she didn't know what they meant; she eventually asked Emily and felt foreign when Emily laughed at her and explained.

Nessa grew used to seeing the saltire flying on the flagpole on the esplanade of the nearest town, seeing indyref2 stickers on cars, and hearing the frustrated mutterings of her colleagues every time someone in Westminster brandished a Union Flag or talked about patriotism.

*

"Ugh!" Emily plonked her bag on the top of the picnic table and sat opposite Nessa, who had already broken into her lunchbox and opened her packet of cheesy corn puffs.

"Everything okay?"

"Don't you hate meetings where you suggest something, nobody comments, but five minutes later someone else says the exact same thing and presents it as though they came up with the idea, and you had never spoken at all? And they get the credit!"

"That happens?" Nessa didn't have much experience with meetings.

"More often than you'd think."

"Why?"

"Office politics? Nepotism? Casual misogyny? Possibly a combination of all three? Who knows?"

"That's awful."

"Yep. Sometimes I think it's time I moved on."

"Would you? Move, I mean."

"Maybe. I want to change jobs. Maybe I should be open to moving to the Central Belt too. Plus, the dating pool'd be bigger there, you know?" Emily huffed. "My first two years at uni were brilliant. But along came Covid. The teaching suffered, what with everything going online and access to the libraries being restricted. I got through it, but the social side of uni was f—ruined. I was, I dunno, short-changed, and I'd like to go to the Central Belt and go to all those gigs and shows I never got a chance to see when I should have."

Nessa understood, at least a little. Her home schooling and online learning had been restrictive too. She changed the subject. "I was disappointed not to see you at the pub on Friday."

"Oh, God! You didn't go, did you?"

Nessa quirked an eyebrow.

"Poor you." Emily grimaced. "Was it hideous?"

"Um." How tactful did she need to be? "It wasn't great."

"If that's your answer, you must be the mistress of understatement. I'm sorry I didn't warn you to give it a miss."

A rush of relief surged over Nessa. She wasn't weird for hating that kind of thing, after all! She laughed. "It's okay. I survived, and now I'll know exactly what I'm missing out on if they ever ask me again." She ate another corn puff. "What did you get up to at the weekend?"

Emily told her about the pub and the Elephant Twins, and how they'd persuaded Moira to get on stage.

While she whipped out her phone, accessed the video Gordon had uploaded, and forwarded the link on to Nessa, Nessa asked, "You know Moira?"

"Everyone knows everyone around here. Or, if they don't, they'll know someone who does."

That sounded scarily like school. Were all small communities like that? What would it be like to go to a big city where nobody knew your name, and where you could reinvent yourself without having to answer any awkward questions? Would it be liberating or terrifying? Would she be brave enough to arrive at university as a ready-made queer, out and proud?

"Penny for your thoughts," said Emily.

Were they worth that much? Maybe they were worth more.

Nessa shook the questions off. Hoping to distract Emily, she asked, "Did you know Moira used to be a pop star?"

Around a mouthful of sandwich, Emily said, "O' course." She swallowed. "Everyone knows."

"Do they? Nobody's mentioned anything."

"She doesn't like to talk about it, so we don't. But we know."

"Do you know why she doesn't talk about it?"

"No. I think something happened, but whatever it was, it's ancient history, so I think a lot of her keeping it quiet is habit. Or, maybe, it happened so long ago, she doesn't think it's important anymore."

"Maybe." Nessa didn't believe it, and after what Emily had said, Nessa felt flattered and singled out that Moira had told her anything at all about her time in the limelight.

They lapsed into silence. After a while, Emily said, "Something's bothering you."

If she couldn't tell Emily, who could she tell? Apart from Meg, of course, but Emily was more likely than anyone she'd met to empathise.

"I was wondering what it's like to come out somewhere like this. You know, where everyone seems to know everyone else's business, even before it happens. I'm not sure how I feel about that."

Emily's eyes widened at the mention of coming out. "Are you asking out of curiosity or personal interest?"

"Both," admitted Nessa. "But mostly the personal thing."

Emily smiled. "You like the lassies? Or are you bi?"

"I like the lassies." The words were unwieldy on Nessa's tongue.

"Coming out wasn't easy, but I was born here, which made things harder, I think."

"Why?"

"People knew me. They had preconceptions I suppose, and I was frightened of what they'd think when they found out they were wrong. When I came home from uni, I decided if they didn't like who I am that was their problem. Fortunately, most people don't care, and not anybody who matters."

Was that why Nessa hadn't told Dad yet? Because he mattered?

"Where did you get all your badges?"

"Like them, do you?"

"Well, yes." Nessa's face flamed. Why did she feel as though she'd been caught out? There was nothing wrong with liking them.

"I got them various places. Mum gave me this one." Emily pointed. "She must have ordered it immediately after I came out to her. She hugged me, kissed me, and told me she loved me and wanted me to be happy." Emily stroked the badge fondly. "It's my favourite."

"That sounds wonderful." Nessa tried to imagine Cindy or Dad doing something similar and failed. What did that say about them or about her?

"I got this one at Pride in Edinburgh, a few years ago, 2019. Before

Covid. Before social distancing. There were thousands of us there, all squashed together and marching up the Royal Mile. The atmosphere was fabulous. Loud and joyful."

"Have you been to a lot of Prides?"

"Some. That was one of the best. I'm hoping to get to a few this summer, now they're being held again."

Nessa felt an odd kind of yearning mixed with fear. What would it be like to go to a Pride event?

"There's a local LGBT+ group. I'd take you along, but it's not meeting over the summer."

"Pity," said Nessa, although a tiny, treacherous part of her was relieved she wouldn't have to meet a roomful of strangers when she hadn't come out to most of her family or friends.

*

After the evening meal, Cindy, Dad, and Finlay ventured out on their bicycles, making the most of the long evening. Alone in the house, Nessa took the opportunity to set up her laptop on the kitchen table. Sitting upright, a glass of water conveniently to hand, made a pleasant change from sprawling across her bed as she video chatted with Meg.

Meg was mastering the technical skills she required for her podcast, but she still had no idea for a theme.

To cheer her up, or at least distract her, Nessa said, "I've got something to show you. Here: I'm sending you a link."

"What is it?"

"Moira. And a couple of local lads. Apparently, the guys were playing in one of the local pubs, and they persuaded Moira to sing with them. You'll need to scroll forwards to fifty-two minutes, seven seconds."

"Okay." Meg leaned towards her laptop. "I'm opening it. Oh, wow.

So that's the Moira you've been talking about so much!"

"Yep."

"With two hunkalicious guys!"

"I'll take your word for it."

"You do that. They're in a similar league of godlike lusciousness to Jez, right down to the sweaters!"

Nessa laughed.

Meg pressed Play, and Nessa listened to the music second-hand, coming via the mic on Meg's phone. Meg nodded her head in time to the beat.

After about half the song, Meg pressed pause. "I'll listen to the rest later. They're good."

"I know. Moira wrote the song."

"Did she! Wow. I'm impressed."

"Yeah. Says she doesn't do it anymore, but I bet she could, if she wanted. She just needs to get her mojo back."

Meg snorted, as if the idea was unimaginable.

Archly, Nessa asked, "Did you know 'Last Christmas' got to number one thirty-six years after it was released? And what about Kate Bush? 'Running Up That Hill' got to number one thirty-seven years after it first came out!"

"Your point?"

"She could be cool again. Sorry, wrong words. She's already cool. She could be popular again. Moira says, when she was at school, there was only the one chart. You followed it or you didn't. You were cool or you weren't. It wasn't like now, where we have all these different genres, and you have more choice about where or how you choose to fit in."

"Now there are more ways to not fit in at all."

"True. Overall, I think now is better, though. There are so many places you can find your niche. ViewHoo, SayMate, PicBlast..."

*

Moira was attacking the soil around a vigorous dock, excavating with an energy verging on manic, when Nessa interrupted her.

"Do you have a minute?"

"Do I look like I have a minute?" Moira glanced up in time to see how her uncharacteristically brusque response forced Nessa to step backwards.

Nessa clutched her knitting tighter to her chest and blurted out an apology. "I'm sorry. I'll come back another time."

"No. No! I'm sorry. I'm having an off day, but there's no excuse for me taking it out on you." Moira rolled onto her heels and looked at Nessa. "I wanted to keep myself busy, and this bu—beggar has been on my radar for a while. If I don't get all the tap root out, it'll grow healthier and more stubborn than before." Moira wiped her forehead with the gloved hand holding the trowel and left a smear of soil on her skin.

"Come on." Moira clambered to her feet. "It can wait for later. I'll put the kettle on." She peeled her gloves off, and as they passed through the lobby, she dropped them along with the trowel onto the top of the freezer.

Nessa followed Moira into the kitchen and watched as Moira puttered around. Unable to resist temptation, she tilted her head to one side and asked. "Do you have a lot of off days?"

"No. Sometimes."

"My dad says if you're having a bad day you should talk about it, not avoid it."

"That's not always possible."

"Why not?"

Moira couldn't bring herself to say talking required someone to talk to and an ability to open up enough to let the words out.

"Isn't that what therapists are for?"

Moira glanced at her. "What do you know about therapists?"

"Dad went to see one. After. He told me it helped."

"After? Sorry. None of my business."

"After Mum left. And again later. After Covid."

"Ah." Moira had known he was a doctor. She hadn't liked to ask what it had been like for him when Covid hit, and he'd never said. Now Nessa was telling her, and it wasn't pretty.

"He was a consultant in A&E. It almost broke him. He considered giving up medicine entirely. Instead, he decided to retrain as a GP. Coming here was supposed to be a fresh start. For all of us."

"And is it? A new start, I mean."

"It's not perfect, but nothing is, right? And Dad's happier than I've seen him in ages. He's more relaxed, and he looks younger. I don't know the half of what he went through. Cindy does, though. They talk about it sometimes, but they shut up whenever Finlay or I are around."

"Maybe they don't want to worry you."

"I know people died. More than is normal for doctors to have to deal with. And it must have been harrowing. I used to want to be a doctor. But I saw what it did to Dad, and I watched the news, and I decided I couldn't do it. I guess that makes me a coward, right?"

"I think it makes you human."

"So, I'm going to be a scientist. Help in other ways. I'm applying to Oxford because that's where they made the vaccine."

Moira was impressed. Even to apply, Nessa had to be bright.

Chapter Nine

A fter a week of high pressure and record-breaking hours of sun, the television weather forecaster on the breakfast show took far too much pleasure in warning viewers of an unseasonal storm heading in from the Atlantic, impending gale force winds, and torrential rain. He showed viewers a graphic of the warm front, currently hovering somewhere off the west coast of Ireland, pointed out the tightly packed isobars, and with a level of joy worthy of a lottery winner, warned people to cover their garden furniture, protect their runner bean plants, and secure their kids' trampolines. How much self-restraint was the forecaster applying to resist an urge to gleefully rub his hands together like a 1970s cartoon villain?

Moira scooped up a spoonful of cereal as she listened to the forecast and resolved to spend the morning in the garden. At least the storm was coming twenty-four hours too late to ruin Murdo's gala.

Moira mowed the lawn, checked the bamboo wigwams the beans

and sweet peas trailed up, and moved a few of the lighter plant pots into sheltered spots lest they blow over. She also laid her wheelie bins on their sides, so the wind didn't get a chance to send them flying. Bitter experience had taught her how scary wheelie bins could be, under the right conditions; she'd had the narrowest of escapes once when an empty bin had flown over her car's bonnet.

"Is that necessary?" Cindy called over the fence, sounding worried.

Moira straightened and turned to face Cindy, who held a laundry basket full of freshly dried linens. "The wind can blow something fierce up the glen. Better to be safe than sorry."

The breeze was already picking up. A bank of lead-grey clouds loomed across the western sky, and the smell of moisture hung in the air.

Cindy thanked her for the warning.

When Moira looked out later, next door's bins lay on their sides too.

*

Providing a sanctuary from the weather, Moira's living room was even cosier than usual. Mr Gillespie lay stretched out on the windowsill, and Moira had put out slices of yet another variety of cake, one of several she'd bought from the bake stall at the gala. What was Moira going to do with the rest?

Nessa perched on the edge of a sofa cushion, sitting upright with her right-hand needle secured in her armpit as she tried to master a more efficient way of knitting. The motions still didn't feel smooth, but she was picking up speed and she had developed enough muscle memory that she no longer had to consciously think through the formation of every individual stitch.

The lights and music cut off around three, making Nessa startle and drop a stitch, and plunging Moira's living room into semi-darkness.

"I wonder how long the power will be off this time." Moira made it sound as though outages were a regular occurrence.

"Does the power go off a lot around here?" asked Nessa.

"Often enough. Mostly in the winter. I keep candles and torches ready, and a camping stove. That way, I have light, heat, hot water, and can make a cup of tea. Oh, and I have a corded landline upstairs. The cordless phones won't work, and sometimes mobiles don't either, if the mast gets damaged."

Nessa fished out her mobile and checked for a signal. Nothing. Not that it proved anything; thanks to the thick, stone walls, getting reception indoors was challenging at the best of times.

Outside, the storm roared vengefully, the wind pushing curtains of rain up the glen. The deluge turned the landscape into a hazy blur of grey silhouettes, and rain splattered against the double glazing, streaming down the windows in rivulets.

"Have you got any more stories?"

"Aren't you bored of hearing about the Diptych?"

Nessa quickly reassured her. "No! It's exciting."

The future, and the wider world, stretched out ahead of Nessa, and she felt the joint lures of independence and adventure. She hoped in the next few years she would have experiences as exciting as the ones Moira described. Meanwhile, she would make do by living vicariously through Moira's memories. She liked the anecdotes of struggle and squalid venues, of sticky floors and clapped-out Bedford vans, of adoring fans and celebrity.

What Nessa hadn't managed to work out was why, when everything had been going so well, Moira had turned her back on it all, choosing to retreat into obscurity.

"I like hearing your stories about the old days." Nessa finished the row, turned her knitting, and started to purl.

Why were purl rows so much more awkward and slow than knit rows?

"Not so old," said Moira, who was toiling over a complicated lace pattern Nessa could only aspire to. Moira's hands stilled for a moment, and the way she peered over the top of her spectacles made Nessa uncomfortable.

"Way before my time," said Nessa uncertainly. "I bet you even remember the last Labour government."

Moira harrumphed and shook her head.

*

Moira puttered around the kitchen, clearing away the debris left in the aftermath of Nessa's visit. Outside, the rain finally stopped, the sun inched out, and the wind dropped to a breeze. Water dripped from the eaves, and the grass glistened wetly.

Maybe Nessa had meant her comment about the last Labour government as a joke, but Moira felt as though she'd been hit over the head with a two-by-four.

As she put the last of the crockery away, Mr Gillespie twined himself around her ankles, letting her know it was time for his dinner.

"All right, all right. I haven't forgotten you."

Moira retrieved a tin from the cupboard and opened it. She eyed it, sniffed it, and wrinkled her nose. "Couldn't get your usual this week, so salmon in gravy it is. It looks and smells disgusting, but hopefully you won't mind too much. It's too bad if you do. This is all there is."

She did some rapid calculations. Nessa would have barely been old enough for primary school when Gordon Brown lost the 2010 general

election, and she'd have been a pre-teen at the time of the Brexit refer-
endum. Both things felt painfully recent to Moira, but they verged on
ancient history for Nessa.

Never had the generation gap been so big. Big? It was a chasm!

Moira had only hazy recollections of Jim Callaghan and Ted Heath,
but she had vivid memories of Thatcher's early years. The nightly news
programmes had enumerated job losses in the same tone of voice news
anchors had more recently announced Covid cases, deaths, and vaccina-
tion numbers. Then there had been the Falkland's War, and the miners'
strike.

She and Nikki had gigged around student unions where, in the mid-
eighties, Socialist Worker's posters hung on noticeboards, impotent ral-
lying cries for radical change.

She'd been idealistic, hopeful for a better, more egalitarian tomorrow, but the eighties and nineties had been a procession of political dis-
appointments and personal let-downs only occasionally punctuated by
beacons of hope.

Mr Gillespie mewed, demanding that Moira stop wool gathering.

She scraped the last of the cat food from the tin and onto Mr Gillespie's dish.

Moira had cried with joy when Tony Blair had been swept into
Downing Street, but the winds of change had proved to be disappoint-
ingly weak.

All those things had happened before Nessa was born. Before she'd
even been a twinkle in her parents' eyes.

The conversation with Nessa had made her feel aeons older than
seeing the grey in her hair every morning in the mirror did.

Moira put the dish on the floor and moved to fill Mr Gillespie's water bowl.

"I'm not old. Merely more experienced."

Mr Gillespie ignored her in favour of the food.

When had she lost her ideals and her optimism? When had she stopped believing in a better world? When had she started to look back instead of forwards?

"Huh." Moira put the water down. "If you like that muck so much, I'll have to get you some more, eh?"

*

When Dad got home from a trip to buy yet more paint and rollers from one of those large DIY warehouses beloved of everyone who had a mortgage, the power was still off, and Cindy was scratching her head as she tried to work out what she could rustle up for tea.

His shoes were caked in mud and his trousers were soaked up to mid-calf. "There're some massive trees down in the lane. I had to leave the car near the road end and walk the rest of the way." He turned to Nessa. "We'll have to allow plenty of extra time tomorrow, if we want to get to work on time."

Moira came to their rescue with a couple of vacuum flasks of hot water and the offer of a loan of her camping grill, which Cindy and Dad accepted gratefully.

For a short while the lack of power was an exciting novelty, but the novelty soon wore off. An evening without Wi-Fi or internet dragged beyond belief, especially when Dad insisted on setting up a board game.

*

Morning brought cooler temperatures and light drizzle. There was still no electricity, and the contents of the hot water tank had gone cold.

Dad and Nessa walked together to where he'd left the car the night before, although walk was too tame a word to describe their trek.

Dad hadn't been joking when he had warned Nessa she would need her wellingtons. They had to leave the road in several places to get around the fallen trees. Leaving the road meant dodging into, and trudging through, waterlogged fields, and where there weren't gates to move between fields, climbing over barbed wire fences and dry-stone dykes.

The walk started as an adventure, and Nessa found herself thinking about how she would tell Meg about it. She compiled some words: intrepid; bold; adversity.

By the time they reached the road end, her collection had grown to include slog, painful, zonked, and shattered.

On the plus side, their arrival coincided with that of a yellow council van and a quartet of men in high-vis clothing, armed with chainsaws. Dad and Nessa gave the work crew a grateful wave. Thank heavens, come evening, they would not have to do the walk in reverse!

*

Moira's garden had escaped the storm mostly unscathed, although one of the bamboo wigwams listed at a forty-five-degree angle, a couple of flowerpots and a ball had miraculously materialised in the middle of the lawn, and the removable plastic door from the compost bin had vanished.

Next door hadn't been so lucky. The wind had uprooted a lanky silver birch tree. It had landed on their fence, where it had brought down a couple of panels, before coming to rest in the middle of Cindy's nascent vegetable patch.

Moira put her own garden to rights with an efficiency borne of experience and, when she spotted Cindy looking overwhelmed and despondent, offered to help.

To Cindy's surprise and Finlay's delight, within five minutes of her offer being accepted, Moira, armed with a small chainsaw, joined them in their garden. The three of them got to work cutting, sorting, and stacking and, by the end of the morning, they had created what would, when seasoned, be a satisfying supply of free firewood.

Around noon, when they went inside for a breather, resolving to recharge their batteries before tackling the vegetable plot, they found the power had been restored. Finlay made a beeline for the television, while Cindy put the kettle on and suggested an early lunch of bacon butties, which she served with lashings of ketchup.

Three-quarters of an hour later, while they were on their second mugs of tea, Moira heard an engine. She sat straighter and cocked her head. "They must have cleared the road."

The noise crescendoed outside the house before it cut off. A door slammed. Moira and Cindy exchanged glances, silently managing to convey that neither of them was expecting visitors.

The front-door bell rang. Cindy got up and answered.

Moira couldn't make out all the words, but she got the gist of the conversation taking place at the front door: two strangers, an exchange of introductions, and a "You'd better come in."

Cindy returned to the kitchen, and a familiar face followed her.

"This is Ryan Walker-Price. He's a journalist, writing a piece on the impact of yesterday's storm."

Moira tensed. "I know who he is."

Cindy raised her eyebrows at the prickles in Moira's tone.

Ryan Walker-Price heard them too. Something—surprise, maybe, or annoyance—flashed in his eyes, but he recovered swiftly. "Moira

Cavendish! What a surprise! How lovely to meet you! May I say how much I enjoyed your performance the other night?"

"Performance? What performance?" Cindy asked.

Moira opened her mouth to answer, but Ryan Walker-Price got in first. "At the pub. She joined a couple of boys on stage. Performed one of her old songs. The crowd went wild."

"I've known Billie and Gordon since they were small. They were doing a gig. They asked me to join them for a song. One song. That's all. They were being nice."

"That can't be all. Your performance was too polished. You must have practiced. Go on, admit it. You had it all planned."

"No," said Moira through tight lips. "Not planned. No premeditation. Anyway, I thought you wanted to talk about the storm."

"Oh. Yes. But first, tell me, what made you settle all the way out here?"

Moira and Cindy exchanged glances. Cindy, bless her, said, "I only have a few minutes, so if you want to talk about the storm, you'd better get on with it. Otherwise..." She left the sentence hanging, a polite threat hovering in the air.

*

"I wish I hadn't invited him in," said Cindy, five minutes later, after Ryan Walker-Price had left. "Something about him was off. He told me he wanted to talk about the storm, but he wasn't interested in anything we had to say about it. He was far more interested in you, but if that was the case, why did he come here, and not next door?"

Moira chose her words carefully. "I think he was using the storm as an excuse. He's been sniffing around for the last week or so."

"Sniffing around? Whatever for?"

"Dirt. On me."

"What? Why?"

"I was famous for five minutes, and that makes me a target, especially when my former band mate is in the news, or if it's a slow news week."

"The Diptych was a few years before my era, but Joe was impressed when Nessa told him you'd been part of the group." Cindy paused and frowned. "Is there dirt to dig?"

"No. But people like him never stop looking."

"Must be horrible," said Cindy sympathetically.

"Do you remember the Leveson Inquiry?"

"Phone hacking? That happened to you?"

"Yeah." Moira had felt violated when she found out she'd been on a list of victims. "Must have been boring for whoever monitored my calls, given I only had the mobile in case of emergencies; there can't have been much news value in my calling the AA that time I got a double puncture at the top of the Rest! I'm told phones are secure these days, and journalists don't come poking around so often anymore, one of the advantages of getting older, I guess. Plus, most people around here are great, protective, even. Someone usually gives me the heads-up if anyone's snooping around."

"Is that how you knew about him? Someone tipped you off?"

"Murdo," agreed Moira.

Cindy looked disillusioned. "Do you think that's why he tried his luck here? Because we're new to the area?"

"Probably," admitted Moira. "I'm sorry. I'm sure you didn't think you'd have to deal with paparazzi when you moved next door to me."

"Not your fault."

Moira was grateful Cindy viewed things that way. "Now, what say you we go sort out those vegetable beds of yours?"

*

Back in her own garden, Moira whipped out her mobile phone and sent Gareth a text. "Call me. Urgent."

If that didn't get his attention, nothing would.

Five minutes later, her phone rang.

"What's up?" Gareth asked.

"The usual. There's a journalist making a nuisance of himself, and I want to know how worried I should be."

"Do you have a name?"

"Ryan Walker-Price. Mean anything to you?"

"I don't think so. Give me ten, and I'll see what I can find out for you."

Moira thanked him, ended the call, and waited with increasing impatience through the twenty-five minutes that passed before the phone rang again.

Moira swiped right to answer, put the speaker against her ear, and wasted no time on pleasantries. "What did you find out?"

"You're not going to like this. He's Julia Walker's son."

Moira squawked and paced. "What!"

"He's not like his mother," Gareth placated her desperately.

"You sure? Usually, these guys give up after a couple of days, but he's been hanging around for well over a week. He seems more tenacious than usual." She gathered up her courage. "Do you think his mother put him up to this?"

"His mother barely talks to him and, from what I can gather, this isn't his kind of story. He's carved himself a niche as a serious political commentator in the broadsheets. Don't take this the wrong way, but going after you seems beneath him. Too tabloid. Too lightweight."

"So, what's his angle?"

"My guess? His Achilles heel is his mother. He's a grown man, but he still wants her approval. I suspect he thinks if he can get this story he'll prove himself worthy."

"And will he? Be worthy, I mean."

"I doubt it. Julia has ignored him his whole life. She's not going to change now. In fact, he might even make things worse, if he manages to get the story his mother so spectacularly failed to."

"Except, there is no story."

"You know that. I know that. They don't."

Moira sighed so gustily with frustration that Gareth couldn't help but hear it at the other end of the phone.

"Look, I'm going to tell you something else, but it's got to stay between us, okay?"

"Okay."

"The reason there might be interest in you now is word is out about *the Cats' Meow*."

"So, Nikki agreed to do it after all?"

"Yes. But the producers had to let her go after the first week of filming. She kept turning up drunk. She caused too many production delays, and several of the crew said they couldn't work with her. I don't think her manager or his dogs helped matters either."

"Dogs?"

"Huge beasts, which he insisted on bringing onto the set with him."

"Oh." Moira groped for a seat. "And drugs?"

"Not as far as I know."

Which meant there was room for doubt. Moira's stomach churned.

"How have I not heard anything about this?" Moira didn't expect anyone to have let her know, but she hadn't seen anything in the media.

"Everyone's done their best to keep things under wraps. But there are rumours—"

"Aren't there always?"

"—and Nikki cost the production company thousands, five or six figures, if you believe the stories because they had to scrap the entire first show."

Interlude

At break, we'd huddle around the latest issue of Jackie, *and I would do my best to join in with the oohing and aahing over the pin-ups and problem pages.*

The problems didn't vary much from week to week. Every unsure letter writer who asked about kissing was given the same answer: Don't worry about it. It will come naturally when you try it.

Why was everyone so obsessed with kissing? Nobody ever wrote in to ask that. Apparently, everyone else knew. All they wanted to ask about was how to do it, or how to do it better.

Chapter Ten

Nessa scrutinised the selfie Meg had sent her. Meg had scraped most of her hair away from her face, leaving a couple of strands hanging in front of her ears to soften her appearance. She'd even made an effort with her make-up, augmenting her minimal mascara by shading her brows and applying eyeliner, eyeshadow, and lipstick. She looked pretty; most of all, she looked exultant.

Jez appeared beyond happy too, and nothing like the child Nessa remembered. He had stubble and cheekbones, and contact lenses allowed her to appreciate the blue of his eyes. She understood why Meg might find him appealing, even if she didn't feel anything herself.

Meg and Jez.

Could Nessa persuade Emily to take a selfie with her? What would Meg see, if she looked at a picture of Nessa and Emily staring into the same camera lens? Would they look as natural as Meg and Jez did?

Nessa could dream, but she and Emily weren't a couple, and

assuming she plucked up the courage to ask, and Emily didn't refuse, no matter how close they squeezed together in a photo, they wouldn't look as together as Meg and Jez did in that selfie.

*

The wooden surface of the bench warmed the backs of Nessa's thighs, and she revelled in the sun's heat against her bare legs and sandalled feet. Next to her, Emily leisurely ate a hummus and cucumber sandwich, a baseball cap pulled forwards to shade the top half of her face.

It was Tuesday lunchtime, birds sang in the trees, and the drone of distant cars was more soothing than annoying. Above them, a jet plane left a vapour trail at 35,000 feet. Nessa squinted as she counted another four contrails. Where were the planes going? How great would it be to spend an afternoon stretched out on a sandy beach, Emily by her side?

"What are you thinking about?" asked Emily. "You look miles away."

"Air travel and foreign holidays. Blue sea, water twinkling in the sun, swathes of pristine white sand."

"And sex?"

"What? No!" Nessa blushed.

"There's nothing wrong if you are. Perfectly natural. The four *S's* of a perfect summer holiday: sea, sand, sun, and sex." After a beat, Emily added, "I could kiss you if you'd like?"

"Wha—?"

"So you know what to expect, if you ever do find yourself on that perfect beach. Or anywhere else, for that matter."

Kissing Emily would be a dream come true.

"I'll be gentle. No tongues."

Oh, wow. Emily thought she needed coaxing, but the only thing giving her pause was surprise. She had imagined what it would be like to kiss Emily. She'd imagined it a lot. But never in her wildest dreams had she imagined it would happen in real life, and the idea her daydreams were about to come true...well.

"Go on." Dammit! She should have come up with a more romantic response!

First, Emily touched Nessa's cheek with her fingertips. Next, she cupped Nessa's jawline with her palm.

Nessa trembled.

Emily leaned in, moving in slow motion. Or maybe Nessa's brain was playing tricks. Someone had once told her being in a car crash was like that; you saw the impact coming, but you could do nothing to stop it, and fractions of a second stretched out, torturing you with the knowledge of what was to come.

Not that being kissed by Emily was going to be a car crash. Or torture.

Nessa's senses kicked into overdrive. She instinctively moved her head to one side, and she found herself closing her eyes. Emily's exhalation brushed her skin.

Emily's lips were warm and soft and, yes, as gentle as advertised. They brushed her own, and Nessa worried fleetingly whether she had been using too little or too much lip salve, but her worries evaporated as she succumbed to sensation.

A light pressure.

Tenderness.

Sweetness.

Emily pulled away gradually. Nessa leaned forwards, trying to prolong the contact. Her lips tingled with the echo of the kiss. She yearned for more. Involuntarily, she lifted her fingers to her mouth, a gesture of surprise or want or something she couldn't define.

Nessa had nothing to compare it to, but she knew the kiss had been far more chaste than it might have been, than she would have liked it to be.

Nessa blinked her eyes open.

Emily watched her with her customary amusement. "Good?"

"Good," agreed Nessa. She licked her lips, and she tasted echoes of Emily on them. "Very good."

Emily grinned. "Excellent. I'd hate to have been a disappointment."

"I can see what all the fuss is about."

"In that case, my work here is done."

"It doesn't have to be." Where had those words come from? When had she become so bold, so brazen?

Emily's expression shifted into something far more serious. "Yeah. I think it is."

"But I like you. I mean, I *like* you. Attracted like." And she needed to shut up. Right now. Before her words got any more tangled.

Emily shook her head. "I think you are more intrigued by me than attracted."

"Why can't it be both?" Nessa asked slightly desperately.

"It can be, but the thing is I made a mistake. If I'd known you felt that way, I wouldn't have offered."

"But I—"

"I didn't mean to lead you on."

Dammit! Nessa wanted to be led!

*

Despite feeling a mix of somethings that included disappointment, embarrassment, confusion, and flickers of other, more nebulous emotions which came and went like quicksilver, shifting too fast for her to pin down, Nessa sternly told herself her heart wasn't broken.

She wanted to talk to somebody, so she tried to call Meg, but Meg didn't answer. When she sent a message, Meg replied: *Am with Jez. Full deets tomorrow.* The words were followed by a string of emojis: an aubergine; two of hands which, when put side by side, left no doubt something had been put into a hole; a horny devil; fireworks. The emojis were followed by a legion of exclamation marks.

Wow.

Nessa had assumed her kissing Emily would be the big news.

The realisation Meg's initiation as a sexual being was going to trump everything else came as a body blow. Nessa felt small and alone. She wanted to cry.

*

Nessa's mixed-up emotions plagued her over the next few days and into the weekend, blindsiding her every time she let her guard down. Perhaps that was why, when she went for her next knitting lesson with Moira, she blurted out, "I'm gay!"

"Uh-huh?" Moira, who was executing a tricky decrease, didn't look up. "That's nice."

"You don't seem surprised."

Stitch completed, Moira lowered her needles and gave Nessa her full attention. "Should I be?"

"No," said Nessa doubtfully.

"Anyone would think you wanted to shock me. Sorry to disappoint you."

Had she wanted to shock Moira? If so, why? Wasn't Moira's unquestioning acceptance better? "I didn't want to shock you, exactly, I don't think. But I did expect a bit more of a reaction." Her eyes narrowed. "Did you already know?"

"No, I didn't know. But I'd wondered."

"Why?" Did she have lesbian tattooed across her forehead, or was she giving off some weird vibes she didn't know about?

"Emily mentioned she'd been hanging out with you. She doesn't do that with just anybody."

"You know Emily?" Stupid question. Of course Moira knew Emily. Nessa knew that, had known since Emily had told her about the Elephant Twins. Besides, there was the whole everyone knew everyone else thing which went on around here. Nessa had known, but the implications hadn't registered.

"She paints."

Nessa knew that too.

"I sell some of her things in the shop. Greeting cards, mostly. A couple of mugs. Emily's good people. I like her."

Was that Moira's way of saying she approved?

"We're not, you know, seeing each other." Nessa glanced at her hands. "We've been hanging out. She's been helping me with a few things." Or, she had been helping, until she'd given Nessa an entire raft of new things to have to figure out. "I thought I knew about lesbianism." Perhaps that needed a bit of explanation. "We learn about it in school."

"You do?" Moira quirked an eyebrow.

"LGBT stuff is included in our SRE classes."

"SRE?"

"Sex and Relationship Education." SRE had tried to normalise same sex relationships, but it wasn't all the way there yet. If it were, Nessa wouldn't need to worry about what other people might think, or how they might react.

"Good grief!" exclaimed Moira. Her tone made it clear her reaction was born out of disbelief and envy, not disapproval. "We didn't have any of that in my day."

Now it was Nessa's turn for disbelief, so Moira elaborated.

"They were beginning to bring in Sex Ed when I was in secondary school, but my cohort was a couple of years too old to be offered the classes. In my year, we got the bare minimum of information we needed to pass biology O level, and not everyone got that because biology wasn't a compulsory subject."

"Wow."

"So, we were sent out into the world full of misconceptions and woefully unprepared for what we were going to meet."

"Wow," said Nessa again.

"What's in your SRE course, anyway?"

"All sorts of things. Different types of family. Various orientations. Sexual health, from menstruation to menopause. What we've learned is helpful, as far as it goes. But the lessons don't prepare you for the experiences. Plus, the lessons are dry. It's like we're standing on the outside, looking in, especially the way Mr Gibson teaches. You can tell he finds the lessons incredibly awkward, and some of the people in my class don't help. They go out of the way to ask questions that will send him into a tizzy of stammering, and they laugh at him."

"That's cruel."

"Yeah," agreed Nessa.

"So, you're saying, lessons haven't prepared you for the real world."

Nessa admired the way Moira had managed to sum up her ramblings so succinctly. "Have you ever liked someone who didn't like you the same way?"

"When you say liked?"

"I mean liked. Really liked. Were attracted to."

"Ah. You're talking about fancying someone." Moira meant Emily but was tactful enough not to say.

"Yeah."

"And this person doesn't fancy you?"

Nessa shook her head. "No. She's been clear about that. I thought she liked me, but she doesn't, at least not as much as I like her."

"Ah. I can kind of relate."

"You can?"

"It's not the same thing, but I had a best friend. She and I... What's the phrase people use now? Oh, yes. We were going to be BFFs. Best Friends Forever. But everything changed when she met Robin."

"You're talking about Nikki."

"We met in our first year at uni and for a while we were inseparable. I'd never felt so close to anyone before. Never had a friend like her. We joked about how we were going to grow old and grey together and have adjoining rooms in our nursing home. But, underneath the joking, I thought we were being serious. Apparently, she didn't, because when someone better came along, she dropped me, and spent all her free time with him."

Nessa frowned. "You didn't like-like her, did you?"

"Fancy her, you mean?"

"Yes."

"No. There was nothing romantic between us. But she was a special friend."

Nessa and Meg had been besties for years, but Nessa couldn't imagine them living out their old age in the same nursing home. Nessa wanted to grow old and grey in the arms of a special someone, even if that special someone wasn't Emily. How could Moira have not like liked Nikki, but still liked her enough to want to spend the rest of her life with her?

"Now," said Moira, "are you ready to learn about Fair Isle knitting?"

*

That evening, Nessa sat cross-legged on her bed, her laptop resting on a pile of pillows in front of her, and searched Nikki Thompson, curious to learn more about the woman Moira missed so much.

Nessa found a wiki page, official and unofficial SayMate pages, an old-fashioned website that hadn't been updated since 2013, an official Yapper account, and a selection of old interviews on ViewHoo, which had been uploaded by a handful of die-hard fans.

According to the website, Nikki had been born in 1975, which was clearly inaccurate because that would have made her about ten years old at the height of her fame. More plausibly, the wiki page suggested she'd been married twice, both marriages ending in divorce.

The Diptych might have split because of Nikki's relationship with Robin, but Nessa couldn't find any information to suggest their relationship had led to marriage. In fact, when Nessa tried to search him, she found no sign of Robin anywhere on the internet. Either he'd changed his name, or he was a nobody. But even most nobodies left some kind of digital footprint. Robin was a dead end.

Maybe he was actually dead.

Nikki had tried to revive her career several times. She'd also tried to diversify into acting, as evidenced by a scathing review of a television dramedy wherein the critic had written, "I'm giving this show one star because the family's dog tried so hard to please."

Nikki, having failed at acting, had subsequently turned her attention towards reality television, and she had appeared on several of the more obscure programmes beloved of minor celebrities trying to boost or rehabilitate their public profiles. She had never got far in any of them; she couldn't cook, knew nothing about antiques, and couldn't keep her balance on ice. The footage of the ice fiasco had been viewed several hundred thousand times on ViewHoo.

Nessa watched incredulously as Nikki, in the space of three memorable minutes, managed to fall forwards, fall backwards, get herself wedged on her skating partner's shin, and as a finale, get her hair caught in his costume. Nessa had to stuff her fist in her mouth to stop herself screeching with laughter. She watched it three times. Nikki was lucky it hadn't been viewed several *million* times.

Interlude

A persistent rumour circulated around the school, frequently whispered in bus queues at the end of the day: the girls' grammar had the highest rate of teenage pregnancy in the country or the county. Nobody was ever clear about the specifics, and I wasn't sure I believed any of it.

Why would anyone want to have sex, anyway? It sounded incredibly messy and unappealing.

Chapter Eleven

N essa was video chatting from her bedroom again.

As promised, Meg had provided Nessa with details of her close encounter with Jez. Meg's detailed description had been informative, even educational. It had also been graphic enough to be embarrassing.

Still, Meg had been bursting to spill, and listening was what good friends did... Wasn't it?

Nessa didn't go into equally lurid details when describing Emily's kiss. For one thing, the kiss had been too chaste for the details to come anywhere close to lurid. For another, that amount of sharing made Nessa uncomfortable. Did her reluctance to share every intimate detail make Nessa a worse friend? Or did it merely mean she had a better filter?

Meg nodded in the right places and made appropriate platitudes, leaving Nessa feeling, if not better, at least calmer and more resigned to her fate.

Once the topics of their personal lives had been exhausted, Nessa asked, "Have you had any ideas for the podcast yet? Or have you ditched the idea in favour of other things?"

Meg made a face, a noise, and a hand gesture that combined to indicate ambivalence or uncertainty.

"If you're going to do it, you'd better get a move on. The summer's half over already."

"Don't," groaned Meg. "I haven't even started on my prep yet!"

"Knowing you, you'll leave the prep until the evening before term starts, pull an all-nighter, and yawn your way through your first day."

"And I'll hate myself for it."

It happened every holiday. Nessa was used to Meg's last-minute panics before work had to be handed in. Meg always managed to muddle through, though, and Nessa had long since given up trying to persuade Meg to improve her study habits.

"I haven't given up on the podcast, exactly. I've been messing around, recording myself talking complete drivel, or reading out of books, and I've been getting used to the sound of my own voice and the hang of using a mic and the editing software. I've even had a go at video in case I decide to go down the ViewHoo route, instead. But I still have no idea about actual content."

"Maybe I can help you there."

Meg perked up. "You can?"

"Maybe. It might be a terrible idea."

"Or it might be brilliant. Tell me."

"I was thinking... How about we do an investigation?" She held up her hand to forestall the inevitable protest. "I know you ruled an investigation out before, but that was when you didn't have a story to investigate."

"And you do?"

"Yeah. You know Moira?"

"Not personally, no."

"Don't be funny. You know who I'm talking about."

"Yes, I know. Your knitting neighbour."

"That's the one. I told you she was in a band? The Diptych?"

"Yeah. So?"

"So, I went online last night. They were a big deal. They had five top ten hits. Three number ones."

"So?"

"The band split, and nobody knows why."

"You think you can find out? From Moira?"

"Not exactly, no. She doesn't talk about it."

"What's our angle, then?"

"Our angle is she misses her band mate. They fell out. Drifted apart. But it's obvious, Moira misses her like crazy. So, my thought is, we could do a proper investigation. You know, like those cheesy TV shows that reunite lost families and make your mum cry."

"My mum cries at everything. Dad says it's the change of life, though what that has to do with anything, I don't know."

"Well? What do you think?"

"I think, how are we going to do it?"

*

"Nessa's been spending a lot of time at your place." Joe stood on the lane, next to where Moira was tidying the verge.

Moira glanced up. "Is that a problem?"

"I don't know. Is it? I want to make sure she's not outstaying her welcome."

"No."

"Good. I wanted to be sure."

Moira stood and looked directly at Joe. "She's welcome to call around any time. If I'm busy, I'll tell her. Okay?"

"Okay."

He hovered. Clearly, he had something else on his mind. Moira put her hands on her hips and resisted the urge to tell him to spit it out, whatever it was.

"I... We're... Look. This is going to sound odd, but does Nessa talk to you?"

"Talk to me? Of course she talks. Why wouldn't she?"

"Because she doesn't say much at home. I'm worried something's bothering her, and I hate to think she doesn't feel she can come to me or Cindy about anything."

Moira didn't know what to say, so she said nothing.

"What do you talk about?"

"Knitting. Life, the universe, and everything. Whatever we feel like talking about."

"Has she confided in you?"

"If she had, wouldn't that be between us?"

"So, she has mentioned something."

"I didn't say that."

"You didn't need to. There's something bothering her, but we don't know what it is, and we want to help. She won't talk to us."

"Maybe that's what's wrong. You're not you anymore. You're part of an us. You've worked so hard to make Cindy part of the family, you've made Nessa feel like she can't talk to you anymore. To you, her dad. Not you-and-Cindy."

"That's rubbish!"

"Is it? Maybe I don't know what I'm talking about. But think about all the changes you've been going through from Nessa's point of view. You move here. You leave her behind—"

"Because she needs to finish school in England. She's too far through the system to switch now, and she knows that."

"—and when she does visit, she gets the smallest room—"

"Because Finlay's here all the time, it made sense to give him the larger room. Plus, we're going to build an extension. Nessa knows that too."

"—and you don't spend time with her, only with her, like you used to."

"She told you all this?" he asked, hurt, defensive, and verging on angry.

Moira shook her head and held her hands in a placating manner. "She didn't need to. She's mentioned a few bits and pieces in passing. Most of it, I put together. You, Cindy, and Finlay have had more time together to get used to the way things are now. Nessa's been at school for most of that time, so it's taking her longer to adjust. She needs time to get used to this new version of family."

"I see." He shrank in on himself as his puffed-up anger deflated. "I hadn't considered that."

"Well. Consider it now. And another thing. She worries about you. It might help if you didn't try so hard to protect her. She knows you and Cindy have been through some terrible things. Not talking to her about them isn't helping. I'm sure you have good intentions, but it's making her fear the absolute worst she can, and, in turn, she wants to protect you."

"But I'm her father. Of course I want to shield her from everything horrible in this world. It's what parents do."

"She knows that."

"Oh."

Moira held out an olive branch. "She loves you. But she's confused. She's trying to make sense of where she fits in with this new normal you've got going. My advice, for what it's worth? Think about what I've said. Talk to her. And if, after all that, you still can't get her to talk to you, or there's something else bothering her, then maybe you have a real problem."

Thoughtfully, Joe turned away.

Moira returned to her tidying, but her heart was no longer in it. Her mind whirled with questions and concerns. Even without broaching the topic of Nessa's sexuality, had she said too much? Betrayed too many confidences or suspicions? How much did Cindy and Joe know, anyway?

If Nessa needed to talk, Moira wanted her to have someone to talk to, and, if that person wasn't Joe or Cindy and could no longer be Emily, maybe she should ready herself for the task. Just in case.

How much should she tell Nessa about this conversation? And how would Nessa react? She'd overstepped a mark. More than overstepped; she'd leapfrogged over a baker's dozen worth of marks.

*

On Saturday, Dad took Nessa to Oban. On her own. The idea he wanted some quality time with her was weirdly unsettling. Freaky, almost.

Although Oban was only forty miles away, the journey, thanks to hills, bends, a scattering of narrow bridges, and signs warning of oncoming drivers in the middle of the road, took almost an hour. Despite the new L-plates on the car, Dad had told her she couldn't take the wheel.

She had whined but, with hindsight, she was glad Dad hadn't let her drive. Seen through the hyperaware lens of a nascent driver, Nessa noticed a myriad of hazards that would previously have escaped her. Plus, being in the passenger seat afforded her the luxury of taking in the views which were, in places, stunning.

Oban was small, but seeing the ferries passing through the bay and thinking about where they might be going was cool. One day, Nessa would go to see the Hebridean islands. How amazing would it be to go so far west you'd look across the Atlantic, knowing the next land was North America?

They went to an eatery on George Street, which buzzed with noise and bustle, for lunch. A harried server escorted them to a table. Dad sat on a cushioned bench positioned against a stone wall; Nessa sat opposite, where she had to rely on a mirror above Dad's head to see what was happening in the rest of the restaurant.

The server took their drinks orders and returned a few minutes later with a ginger beer for Dad, a cola for Nessa, and menus.

Nessa spent too much time reading the menu, partly to avoid having to find something to talk about, and partly because the range of options bemused her. Once she'd finished reading, Nessa toyed with her glass and paddled her right index finger in the condensation dripping down its sides. Taking courage in both hands, she asked, "What are we doing here, Dad?"

Dad rested his forearms on the table and leaned in. He was so serious Nessa found herself swallowing, bracing herself for whatever he had to say. With an expression like that, it couldn't be good.

"I've been worried about you."

"About me? Why?"

"I want to check you're okay. And I decided it would do us good to have some time together. Just the two of us."

Nessa searched his face for anything that might make her question his sincerity. She saw nothing.

She bought some more time by taking a gulp of her cola and replacing the glass carefully on the wet ring it had already left on the tabletop. "I'm fine," she said at length.

"Fine?"

"Cool. Without problems. Hunky-dory, even."

"You don't have to overdo it."

"I'm okay, Dad. Seriously, I..."

"You, what?"

"It's a new place. It's taking me a while to get used to everything, I guess."

"It's new for all of us."

"I know." Did telling a half-truth count as a lie?

"It'll get better."

"I know that too."

A few seconds passed. Nessa drank some more, even though she wasn't thirsty. At this rate, she'd have finished the glass by the time the server returned to take their food orders.

"How are you finding the job?" He'd asked about it before, but this time Nessa thought he was asking more out of genuine interest than a desire to keep the conversation going at the dinner table.

"Honestly? It's awful! Not I-can't-stand-it-awful, but... Ugh! If I hadn't wanted to go to uni before, I would now! I had no idea work could be so boring!"

"Welcome to the real world."

Nessa knew his job wasn't all sunshine and roses, but she'd never considered it might be dull. "Isn't your job all excitement, stress, and helping to save people's lives?"

"Not anymore. That's one of the reasons we wanted to move here. Sometimes tedium is a luxury."

"Huh. I never thought about it that way."

"Excitement and stress are okay for a while. But eventually they're exhausting. And they wear you down."

Something tight and hard in Nessa's chest unfurled. Dad had never spoken to her like this before, and it made her feel hopeful. She listened avidly to everything he had to say.

The server reappeared, notepad in hand. Nessa almost ordered the haggis wrapped in Yorkshire pudding to find out what that might look, let alone, taste like, but common sense won out, and she ended up ordering fish and chips, which she knew she would enjoy.

"Dad?" said Nessa later, as they embarked on their desserts, "can I ask you about the Diptych?"

"What can I tell you about them that your new friend, Moira, can't?"

"Aunty Helen once told me you used to fancy the lead singer."

"I'll kill her. I wanted to take that secret to my grave."

"Too late." Nessa took a ridiculous amount of delight in embarrassing him. She gave him a pitying smile. "I've known for years. What was she like?"

"The lead singer? Slim, punky hair, trademark short skirts, long legs in an era before photo editing gave everyone long legs, and oversized shirts with excessive amounts of lace trim."

"Do you remember anything about her?"

"Like what?"

"I dunno. Interests. Gossip. Where she was from."

"I don't think I ever knew any of that."

"Isn't that the sort of thing people know about their crushes?"

"Is it? I only remember caring about what she looked like. And she looked fine."

"Dad!"

"What?"

"Nothing."

"Why are you asking me about the Diptych?"

"Moira won't tell me, and I can't help wondering: Why did they break up?"

"It was a long time ago. I don't remember exactly. Artistic differences? That was the official line, but the tabloids ran some stories about personal issues."

"Do you remember what?"

Dad shook his head. "It's too long ago."

"Almost two of my lifetimes ago," murmured Nessa, remembering what she'd said to Moira.

*

After lunch, Nessa and Dad walked around Oban together, exploring a few shops before heading to McCaig's tower, a folly that dominated the skyline and from which visitors got stunning views over the town's buildings, the bay, the boats within it, and the surrounding area, including the islands of Kerrera and Mull.

Nessa felt closer to Dad than she had in months. What was happening? He was the person he used to be, the dad who'd been missing since he and Cindy moved in together. Someone had sprinkled fairy dust on their relationship, helping to make everything a little, or a lot, better.

"You know," Dad said, as he held her in a one-armed hug while they watched a ferry disappear into the Sound of Mull, "I'm going to tell you the same thing I told Cindy."

Nessa tried to twist her head to get a better look at him, but unless she pulled out of his embrace, she couldn't. She stayed put and focused on listening.

"Everything will turn out fine. You need to relax and let it happen."

Nessa didn't know what to say, so she said nothing.

Maybe Dad heard doubt in her silence because he said, "I know it hasn't been easy on you, and moving here must be a huge adjustment. Cindy's been trying hard. Too hard, maybe. The two of you have been tiptoeing around each other but, I think if you both stop worrying about what the other thinks, you might get on."

Nessa nodded against his shoulder. He'd given her something new to think about. She'd been too busy thinking about herself to see that Cindy had been going out of her way to try to be the perfect partner and almost-stepmother. It had never crossed Nessa's mind that Cindy had been on her best behaviour too.

*

They did a grocery shop before heading down the road, the back and boot of the car brimming with toilet paper, kitchen roll, detergent, and enough food for the rest of the summer, although Dad told Nessa they'd be lucky if it lasted the week.

Nessa slouched in the passenger seat, idly gazing out the window as the scenery passed by. The atmosphere was different to earlier. It was more relaxed. More companionable. More Dad.

The time was right, so, before Nessa thought herself out of it, she said, "Dad? Can you pull over when you get a chance? There's something I want to tell you." Her heart pounded in her chest.

"Sounds ominous."

"It's not. At least, I don't think so."

"Can't you tell me now?" he asked as he steered around some tortuous bends.

"I'd prefer not to," answered Nessa, not wanting him to split his attention between driving and listening.

Dad spotted a sign for an upcoming stopping place, so he slowed, signalled, and pulled into a lay-by on the banks of a sea loch. He switched off the engine, pointed at a picnic table, and asked whether Nessa wanted to get out.

The smell of seaweed hung in the air as Dad, seated across the table from Nessa, said, "You know you can tell me anything, right?" Worry lines creased his forehead. "You're not in trouble, are you?"

Nessa gasped as she grasped what Dad was getting at. "No!" She waved her arms in a scything motion across her chest to reinforce the negative. "No. It's nothing like that! In fact, given my preferences, that'd be nothing short of a miracle."

"Your preferences?" Dad tried the words on for size, letting their meaning sink in.

Nessa made sure to look him in the eye. "For a long time, I assumed I was straight. When I felt the first pull of attraction towards girls, I wondered whether I might be bi. Or confused. Until it dawned on me, I never feel the same way about guys. So, lesbian it is."

Dad didn't say anything immediately, and Nessa feared she had done this wrong. Was he shocked? Upset? Disappointed?

"I knew you were worrying about something. I should have guessed it was more than the move."

Nessa shook her head. "It was the move, mostly. But this... It's taken me a while to work things out."

"I wish you'd told me sooner. Maybe I could have helped."

Nessa shook her head. "I'm not sure you could have. This is

something I needed to figure out for myself."

"Am I the first person you've told?"

Something in his tone made Nessa suspect her answer mattered to him, so she regretted having to admit he was not. "I told Meg." Dad's expression shifted towards something that might have been understanding. "And Emily."

"Emily?"

"At work."

Dad looked more surprised at that, so Nessa justified herself. "She's been helpful. She's the first out lesbian I've ever met, so it's been good to have her to talk to. And I told Moira."

"Why Moira?"

"I don't know. I was upset, I think. And she was there. And she was sympathetic."

"That's good," said Dad, possibly with more hope than certainty.

"Are you okay with this? You're not upset?"

"Yes, I'm okay. No, I'm not upset. Were you worried I would be? Silly question. You must have been, else you wouldn't be asking."

"I didn't think you would be. But I didn't know. And I've read stories."

Dad smiled sadly, fondly. "I love you. You know that, don't you?"

Nessa nodded jerkily.

"Nothing's ever going to change that, and definitely not this."

Once they were on the road again, Dad said, "Are you going to tell Cindy, or shall I?"

"Tell Cindy?" Nessa hadn't planned that far ahead.

"She won't mind, either, if that's what you're worried about."

Was it? "Can we keep it between us for a while longer? I'll tell her when I'm ready."

Chapter Twelve

The next time she visited, Nessa quizzed Moira again about her time with the Diptych.

"How did you become a pop star?"

"I suppose I fell into it."

"How do you fall into becoming a star?"

"Surprisingly easily." A hint of a smile played around Moira's lips.

Moira's resolve to keep her secrets collapsed at last, and Nessa barely managed to restrain herself from gleefully punching the air.

"Nikki and I met at university. We were in the same hall of residence. It was a rambling, soulless building with multiple wings, floors, and common rooms, and one enormous dining room, which doubled as a function room for big events."

Nessa put her knitting down, preferring to focus every gram of her attention on Moira's story.

"The summer before, I'd bought a guitar and a teach-yourself book from a charity shop. I practiced a lot, which must have driven my neighbours demented; I had way more enthusiasm than skill."

Moira paused to drink some tea. Nessa waited impatiently for her to continue.

"About halfway through the first term, someone on my corridor organised a talent contest to raise money for the miners' strike, and she put my name down to enter. I think she did it out of spite, but she might have been desperate. Anyway, in a fit of hubris, I tried to write a song, and it wasn't terrible."

Nessa wanted to rip the mug out of Moira's hand as she stopped to drink more tea. Moira spent an age putting the mug down again.

"Go on," Nessa demanded impatiently.

"Nikki won the competition. She had a great voice, and she accompanied herself on the piano. She sang some godawful cover of a seventies ballad. Not her taste at all, and different from everything else she ever sang, but she made it sound wonderful. She came looking for me after the show. I'd seen her around before, but that was the first time we met properly. She told me my song had potential and, if we worked together, we could be great. I thought she was crazy, but I couldn't say no. She had that kind of personality. Plus, I was a first-year student, I was shy, and I was desperate to make a new friend."

Nessa tried and failed to imagine Moira as a young, socially awkward student, only a year older than herself.

"Nikki was technically brilliant, and she knew more about music than I ever would. But she couldn't create music. What she could do, though, was take my rough ideas and polish them into gold, so we turned out to be a pretty effective team. One song led to a whole bunch of others. Nikki suggested we do a gig. I had no stage presence or experience, but she made it seem easy, and that first gig, to twenty underwhelmed undergraduates in the seediest student bar on campus, turned into a regular booking."

Moira had mentioned the gigs before, but hearing about them now as part of a bigger picture, made Nessa feel more invested than ever.

"We spent the summer between our first and second years touring England in the oldest, rustiest Bedford van you can imagine. It broke down more times than I can remember, and I got to know my way around her engine. We played in whatever pubs and clubs would have us, and I had the most fun I've ever had. It was just us, the open road, and the shows. We got better, and by the time we started second year, we were surprisingly good.

"Word got around. We pulled in bigger crowds, and we didn't have to beg for bookings, or play in the grottiest venues anymore. People sought us out, and we got invitations from other colleges and universities."

"What was touring and gigging like?"

"Hard work. Grubby. Noisy. Smelly too. The stink of tobacco got into all our clothes."

"You make it sound rank."

"It was. It was also exhilarating. We got to meet people and do things most people only ever dream of. Then, one day, everything changed."

"Why?"

"A talent scout from one of the record companies found us. He'd heard about us, and he came looking. He offered us a deal and the rest, as they say, is history."

"Sounds like a dream come true."

Moira made a noise vaguely like a snort. "Maybe, in the beginning. But gradually everything I enjoyed about playing with Nikki got stripped away. I liked things when it was the two of us, but once we signed the contract, other people got involved, and we couldn't do what we wanted any longer. We had to do what our manager told us. I still wrote the songs, but Nikki stopped working with me, happy to turn up, sing, and lap up the adoration, and the record company produced the music to death. Yes, it was exciting. But it was also hard work and not at all what I imagined a glamorous lifestyle would be like."

"How do you mean?"

"We didn't have groupies or private jets. Instead, we had a lorry, a few roadies, and a handful of men who sent us fan mail from jail, a lot of it from Strangeways, for some reason."

"Sounds charming!"

"Very," said Moira wryly.

"And you turned your back on it all," Nessa said in a way she hoped would invite Moira to tell the rest of the story.

Moira didn't accept the invitation. "Yes," she agreed. "But at least I had something to turn my back on. Most people never have that."

"Do you ever wish you'd carried on?"

"No. It was an adventure. I'm glad I had the chance. But, these days, it's enough to play in Murdo's."

*

The memories were closer to the surface than they'd been in years. Too many things had happened in the last few weeks: Gareth's mention of Nikki and the television show; the appearance of Ryan Walker-Price; all Nessa's questions.

Moira couldn't ignore the past.

The conversation with Nessa sent Moira off on one of her rare nostalgia kicks. With half a mind to show Nessa its contents next time she visited, Moira pulled a trunk out from the storage space in the roof. She dragged it into the small room which, until she'd relocated most of her business activities to the shed, had served as an office but now was a cross between an archivist's nightmare and a dumping ground for clutter.

Moira unpacked the trunk with the same care a museum curator might use to unwrap treasured objects. Minus the white gloves.

The Diptych years hadn't all been bad.

Moira smiled sadly as she worked her way through the stash of old mimeographed programmes and posters. She lost herself in the memories of evenings spent in student unions with sticky floors, cheap beer, and plastic tables, and nights spent sleeping on bedroom floors in cramped halls of residence or in lumpy beds in seedy bed and breakfasts. There had been one place in Leicester where the kettle was chained to the floor, guests hadn't been provided with towels, and the water in the shower, a half-landing away, ran cold.

It had been fun.

Nikki had made it fun.

Moira had loved doing things with her, being with her. Moira had never had another friend like her.

Moira delved further into her collection.

The posters and the programmes became fancier. They used more colour, and the posters were on thicker, glossier paper. That must have been around the same time as she'd fully appreciated they could afford individual rooms in decent hotels. In the wake of signing with the record company, they'd been on the up, on the cusp of fame and glory, and she and Nikki had moved into a shared house in London.

The first number one single had come soon after, followed by appearances on *Top of the Pops*, the first album, and other hits. They'd returned to the studio to record the second album, and they'd been sent to Elstree to film pop videos.

Then Nikki had met Robin, and things fell apart.

Moira was almost at the bottom of the trunk now, where the things she never looked at were buried, things relating to the aftermath of Nikki's overdose, the police investigation, and the court cases. The infamous articles were in there too, the cheap newspapers discoloured and friable with age.

Why did things that happened so long ago still have the power to hurt?

Moira put everything away in a hurry and closed the trunk's lid. The past was the past. Over with. Done. Dusted. She would forget it. She'd told herself that many times before, but this time she meant it.

Like she always meant it.

She decided not to show Nessa, after all.

*

Having returned the trunk to the eaves, Moira desperately needed a distraction, so made good on her intentions to find out what she should do to support Nessa.

When she'd been Nessa's age, Moira had occasionally heard mention of lesbians, gays, and bisexuals, and there had been an LGB society at her university. There had been whispers of transsexuals, too, but mostly in the perplexed way of how does that work? She shuddered, acutely embarrassed at her younger self's utter lack of awareness and empathy.

In her first year at university, rumours had circulated in hushed, scandalised voices over dinner in the refectory and under the cover of the *Eastenders* soundtrack in common rooms. Dominic was homosexual. He had propositioned Bertie Blythe, who was bisexual.

Rumours had also been rife about heterosexual pairings. They'd never been spread with the same salacious horror, although Moira had found them equally baffling and almost as shocking.

Moira was honest enough to admit she'd arrived at university with baggage and prejudices, although she'd managed to shed the worst of them by the time she'd started to brush shoulders with the pop stars of her age. Being brought face to face with real people turned out to be a terrific way to challenge ill-informed preconceptions and stereotypes.

Even so...

Where had that baggage come from? Some of it, undoubtedly, she'd picked up at home. Her parents had struggled to accept their children were reaching maturity in a world different from the one in which they had come of age.

Moira's mother had placed far greater emphasis on Moira's coming of age at twenty-one than she had at eighteen, when Moira had been allowed to vote for the first time and to buy alcohol. Moira had never understood that.

More baggage would have come from her schooling. She'd been to an all-girls school where the headmistress had viewed sex education as distasteful and unnecessary. Much of what she'd learned as a teenager had come from the occasional racy books, stolen from a mother's bedside drawer, and passed from girl to girl, magazines, and conversations during recess. Every shred of it had normalised heterosexual relationships. Anything else was, at best, exotic and, at worst, wildly deviant.

Homosexual acts had been decriminalised in England and Wales in 1967, but the age of consent would remain at twenty-one for another twenty-seven years. The higher age of consent sent a message: homosexuality was different, on the fringes of acceptability. The reporting around the AIDS crisis hadn't helped, leaving behind an impression of a counterculture characterised by anonymous hook-ups and risky behaviours. The same things went on in heterosexual communities, but they were never highlighted in similarly censorious ways, and nobody mentioned the possibility same sex couples could have long-term, happy, stable relationships.

She had learned to look in windows of pubs to check the gender mix before going in, knowing some venues were favoured by a gay clientele. She told herself she didn't want to intrude, although maybe it was her own fears and prejudices which kept her away.

At least Nessa lived in a time with greater acceptance than there had been in Moira's day, and she had access to resources Moira had never dreamed of. What resources there were too!

Moira searched the internet, and the first thing that struck her was the veritable alphabet soup of letters, some for things she'd never heard off.

LGBTQIA.

As Moira read, she learned the word transsexual was now outdated and disliked, with trans or transgender being preferred terms. There were new, at least to her, terms and concepts aplenty: ally; spectrums and umbrellas; pansexuality; polyamory; asexuality.

Asexuality.

She'd always envisaged LGB culture as being focused on sexual behaviour and activity, and yet there, amid the extended alphabet soup lurked something different.

Something that resonated, like the outsized gong the Rank Organisation used to employ at the start of cinema adverts.

Reading the definition of asexuality came with a lightbulb moment of clarity which upended all her previous assumptions.

Her interior world underwent a seismic upheaval.

Was this what it was like to be born again?

*

Nessa's holidays were almost over, and she found herself trying to cram as much as possible into her final days of freedom.

On her last day at the care centre, her co-workers presented her with a bouquet of flowers, some chocolates, and a gift voucher for the independent cinema in Tovington. Someone must have put effort into finding out about the closest cinema to her school.

Emily, with whom Nessa had made her peace, waited until they were alone to give her a Pride mug, a pin, and a fabric patch. Emily said, "Look me up on SayMate. Keep in touch."

At five o'clock, when she walked out of the doors for the last time, Nessa came close to regretting her departure.

In the remaining days, she spent as much time as possible on her knitting. Despite having mastered several methods of casting on and cables, learning how to read knitting patterns, the first principles of Fair Isle, how to correct basic mistakes, and some simple lacework, she was determined to squeeze in as much learning as she could before she lost ready access to Moira.

Nessa started to gather her school stuff together, contemplated the new academic year's living arrangements, and worried she was running out of time to find the information she needed to progress the investigation.

*

Nessa chewed and swallowed.

She frowned.

"What's wrong?" asked Moira.

"Nothing. It's..." Nessa didn't want to lie, but she didn't want to be rude either. "This cake's not your usual standard."

"Good."

"Good?"

"I didn't make it. It's one of the ones I bought at the gala. It's nice to have confirmation that mine are better."

"At the gala! How old is it?" Nessa shoved her plate away.

"Don't worry. It has been in the freezer."

"So, it was this bad when you bought it?"

"Apparently. Is it awful?"

"It's not good."

Moira picked up her slice, took a bite, and grimaced. She whipped the plates off the table. "I'll find something else."

When she returned, she brought some biscuits and a long, thin parcel. "Here. A small going away present."

"You didn't need to do that!"

"I wanted to. Go on. Open it."

Nessa tore at the paper wrapping, and her eyes widened when she discovered several pairs of knitting needles like the ones Moira used, the ones favoured by true aficionados. "Moira! They're—" Fabulous? Wonderful? Too much? "—brilliant!" She leapt out of her seat and hugged Moira before she could stop herself. "Thank you!"

"You're welcome. Most of the popular sizes are there."

Nessa leaned back on the sofa. "What'll I do if I get stuck?"

"You won't." Moira complimented Nessa on her diligence and the progress she'd made over the summer. "Or, if you do, there's lots of good stuff on ViewHoo."

"You use ViewHoo?"

"Sometimes."

"Can you recommend anyone to follow?"

"Sorry. No. I don't follow anyone. I rely on the search function to find what I want."

"But what if you find someone you like? Don't you subscribe?"

"Like to a particular channel or something?"

"Yes."

"I've never gone down that particular rabbit hole. And I'm too old to see ViewHoo as an alternative to television."

"Television will be dead in twenty years," said Nessa with certainty. "Nobody under thirty watches it anymore."

"At least with television, you know what you're getting. Not like some of the things on ViewHoo. There's no quality control, and I'm still at a loss as to how anyone makes money out of it."

"If you're popular, you get money from adverts. Plus, there's influencing."

"And that's another thing. What do influencers do? Nothing worthwhile, I'm sure. They don't make anything. They don't produce. They're parasites on society, getting free stuff simply because enough people are stupid enough to listen to their opinions. They encourage the sheep mentality, instead of letting people make up their own minds about things. Advertising is bad enough, but influencers take it to a whole new level."

Moira offered Nessa the chance to look through her stash of paper patterns. "You might find something you like. Follow me."

Nessa trailed Moira up the stairs and into a part of the house she had not visited before. Moira led her into the room equivalent to the one

Nessa had been using as a bedroom. Moira's version was every bit as cramped. It was also cluttered, being used as a mix of office, dumping ground, and store.

Moira stretched to pull a couple of box files from a shelf and handed them over to Nessa. "Help yourself."

"Thanks."

"While you browse, I'll make some more tea."

As Moira retreated down the stairs, Nessa glanced around.

Maybe she'd find more clues in here.

She pulled out a pile of patterns to make it look like she was doing what she'd been invited to do; then she glanced around again. She felt sneaky, guilty, and underhanded. She shouldn't snoop around her friend's stuff, but she tamped down her qualms, telling herself it was in a noble cause.

She ran her eyes along the shelves. Nothing helpful there, only a plethora of tattered books. On the disused desk was a landline phone, reams of paper, printer cartridges, a couple of notebooks, and a pile of blank invoices.

Nessa rapidly moved on.

In the desk drawers, she found pens, more printer cartridges, spare staples, and some screen wipes.

Nessa's heart pounded. How long had Moira been gone? How much longer did she have?

She wasted a couple of precious seconds as she moved closer to the open door to listen. Moira was moving around in the kitchen.

Filing cabinet. Locked.

Cupboard.

Notebooks! Lots of notebooks! Some had dates on them. Nessa took one out. She flicked it open.

Moira kept a journal? If Nessa found volumes from the eighties, they would be gold dust!

She searched. And searched some more. The earliest volume she found was dated 2003.

She was running out of time.

Nessa shoved home the journal she'd picked up and rummaged to see what other treasures lived in the cupboard.

Jackpot!

There was an address book. And, from the look of it, it was several decades old. Its spine was broken, its covers dented and worn, and its pages brown with age.

Nessa's breathing grew shallower, quicker, as she flicked through the pages. Several addresses were crossed out, with newer ones written in beneath. Some, the earliest ones, judging from their positions on the pages, had been written neatly; others, scrawled hastily, verged on illegible.

Nessa ran her finger along the index tabs until she found the letter T. She flipped to the correct page.

There!

Nikki Thompson.

And an address.

Which had been crossed out, not with the two neat, diagonal lines used elsewhere, but with deep slashes. The page radiated anger or hurt.

The landline rang. Nessa jumped and fumbled the address book. She struggled to catch it and lost her place. She scrambled to reshelve the book before Moira came to answer the phone.

Moira picked up and spoke into the handset in the living room.

Nessa swallowed and exhaled. She shook out her hands and arms to calm herself.

How much extra time had the phone call bought her?

She refocused her attention on the address book.

Nessa couldn't find an updated address for Nikki. She checked under Nikki's married names to make sure. She even checked under "Nikki" in case an address had been filed under her forename.

Nessa flicked through the pages to where she had seen the scored-out address, whipped out her phone, and took a photo.

She couldn't hear the muffled noises of Moira's conversation anymore. The telephone call had ended.

"Nessa? How are you getting on? The tea's ready."

Nessa was out of time.

Moira was coming up the stairs.

Nessa thrust the address book into the cupboard. She hoped the cupboard's contents had been untidy enough that, if she had replaced anything incorrectly, Moira wouldn't notice.

Heart thudding, and feeling flushed, Nessa picked up the pattern lying on the top of the pile, opened it, and prayed she looked engrossed.

*

"It was bloody close!" said Nessa to Meg.

"What happened next?"

"I put the book away, closed the cupboard door, and grabbed a pattern. When Moira came in, I pretended to be fascinated by a complicated pattern for a baby cardigan!"

"Oh, no!"

"Moira was surprised I was interested in it but said baby cardigans are good practice pieces; you can learn a lot of new techniques in a small amount of time. And so..." Nessa leaned over, picked up her latest knitting project, and waved it in front of the camera. "I'm knitting a lace cardigan for a newborn."

"Oh, my God!" Meg guffawed.

"I couldn't think of a way to get out of it fast enough. It gets worse though. When Cindy caught sight of what I'm working on, she wanted to know if I had something to tell her! She might have been joking, but I don't think so. What is it with her and my dad? He thought I was pregnant too! As if!" Nessa laughed excessively loudly and derisively.

"What did you tell her?" Meg laughed so hard she had to wipe tears from her eyes.

"I repeated what Moira said."

"And she bought it?"

"Thankfully, yes. And I told her I'm a lesbian. Anyway, going back to the address... It's an old one. It's crossed out. But it's the only one I could find. I'm thinking, it's so close to the start of term now, we might have to give up the whole idea."

Meg disagreed. "We've come this far; no way am I giving up now."

Interlude

Sixth form was a challenge. I didn't fit in, and I soon stopped trying. There were too many parties with excessive amounts of home brew and people getting off with each other. People would say, "I must have had a wonderful time. I don't remember anything after nine o'clock!"

I didn't like the taste of the alcohol, I didn't find drunk people entertaining, and I didn't want to snog.

I didn't fancy any of the boys I met, but I still clung to the idea there was someone out there, waiting for me. I believed the problem, or issue—I need a non-negative word here, but I can't think of one—lay with them. I never considered the common denominator was me.

Chapter Thirteen

Forty-eight hours after meeting Poppy Crystal for the first time, Nessa knew the meaning of roommate from hell.

Poppy was a new girl. She was a year older than Nessa, and she had a suite of failed A levels under her belt. Her parents had sent her to St Drogo's to retake Year 13, get into university, study a "sensible" subject, improve her life chances, and as Poppy told it, dripping with resentment, "Make them proud."

Poppy decorated her half of the room with an excess of pastel-shaded plushies, cushions, and afghans, and lectured Nessa on how she, Poppy, wasn't going to waste her time studying when her life chances were mighty fine, thank you very much. She planned to make her way in the world as a reality TV star, or maybe a ViewHoo influencer. She had yet to work out the specifics, but she had enough confidence in her destiny to say, "I think celebrity is a valid career choice and I don't see the point in qualifications. I mean, I'm sure they're fine for some people who have nothing else going for them, but I'm a lot more than brains."

Nessa swallowed her instinctive scorn. She wanted to be nice and give Poppy every chance going. She had been the new girl only the term before and knew how rotten it felt.

Poppy droned on about her favourite influencers. Nothing, not even Meg's unfathomable love of all social media, had prepared Nessa for the litany of names and avatars of people she'd never heard of.

Nice did not come easily.

*

Now Nessa had left, Moira found she had plenty of time to think about asexuality, although dwell, obsess, or wallow might have been more appropriate words for what she was doing.

Moira found books! People had written about this! People were talking about it too. She found ViewHoo videos and podcasts, and she discovered online forums and offline events, and she discovered activists who were working hard to raise awareness and to educate people.

Moira learned there were words for things that had previously been nebulous concepts in her mind, and she learned sexuality and romantic orientations weren't merely personal. They were political.

BOGOF offers in the supermarket, the family packs which were too large for her alone, single-room supplements, the way businesses prioritised flexible working practices to accommodate working mothers, bereavement leave arrangements that honoured relations but not close friends, tax breaks for married couples and pension arrangements for widows were all products of a world which took "compulsory sexuality" for granted.

She struggled to think of anything she got as a single person which married people didn't, and the only thing she came up with was the 25 per cent reduction on her council tax.

She'd long been resentfully aware of these things. She'd also felt guilty for feeling resentful. She'd seen her resentments as things she needed to get past.

She'd felt out of step with the rest of society.

She'd believed her values were wrong.

But maybe they weren't wrong. Maybe she wasn't the problem.

Maybe society was wrong.

Heteronormativity. Allonormativity. Amatonormativity.

The words rolled around her mouth like poetry.

There was a song in those words, waiting to burst out.

Maybe she would have a go at writing it.

Probably not.

*

E veryone had to go to the first and last services of term. The school roll had long since outgrown the chapel, so now the services for the preparatory, lower, and upper schools were carried out separately, phased throughout the first week. Even so, everyone had to scrum and squeeze to get in.

Meg stood and waved frantically to indicate she had managed to save Nessa, who had ditched Poppy, a seat.

Nessa elbowed her way through the throng and greeted Meg with a hug and a "How's Jez?"

"Fine," said Meg, as Nessa slid into the pew. "But I'm thinking of dumping him."

"Why? I thought you were getting along great."

"We are. But he's got a Saturday job. I've got classes and homework. It's hard to juggle everything. Plus, there's Kai."

"Who's never spoken to you."

"No. But being in school with him again... All that attraction has come flooding back."

Nessa shook her head.

"How're things with you?"

"My new roommate is a nightmare!"

"Oh, dear. What's wrong with her?"

"What's right with her? She's shallower than an April puddle."

Meg snorted.

"She has nothing worthwhile to say but she can't stop talking. We've been rooming together for barely three days and she's already driving me nuts!"

"Poor you." Meg drew Nessa into a loose, one-armed hug.

Mollified, Nessa said, "If I kill her, will you appear in court as my character witness?"

"Of course. But it won't come to that."

"I wouldn't be so sure. Did you know the third of July is Compliment Your Mirror Day?"

"I did not. Did I need to know that?"

"You did not. Nobody needs to know that. Nor the proper way to celebrate it. But Poppy told me anyway. She asked me when my birthday was. Before I had time to answer, she put her fingertips to her forehead, went all mystical, and said, 'No, don't tell me. Let me tell you.'" Nessa mimicked the gesture and exaggerated Poppy's voice. "'You're a Libra!'"

"What did you say?"

"I lied and agreed with her. She went into ecstasies. I've never seen anyone so happy about anything so stupid. Apparently, she's Aquarius, and Libra and Aquarius are highly compatible signs."

"Well, that's good," Meg said doubtfully.

"She asked the exact date. Thankfully, I'd had enough time to look up when Libra is, so I made one up."

"Which was?"

"Sometime in October. Ninth or tenth, I think."

"Won't your real birthday show on your social media?"

"Won't matter. We'll be out of here by July. So long as I don't friend her, she need never know."

The chapel continued to fill.

Chapel, Nessa had long ago concluded, was an anachronistic hangover from a bygone era when people believed the Christian God would guide and protect.

God, if He, She, or It existed, was supposed to be merciful, wasn't He, She, or It? Nothing about the current state of the world was particularly merciful. Nessa had grave doubts about God, and she worried the planet was trying to re-establish a new balance to compensate for all the damage humans had done. How else was she supposed to account for wars, plague, fires, and floods of almost biblical proportions?

Meg nudged her.

"What? Sorry. I was miles away."

"I said, it won't be long now. The teachers are coming in."

The service followed the same format every year. A reading. A homily about how the students should embrace the opportunities open to them, knuckle down and study, and prepare for their great and glorious futures. Then they'd sing the school hymn before the head made a few announcements and dismissed everyone. The school bell would ring, and there'd be a scramble to get to first lesson on time.

"I'm fairly sure I know the whole service off by heart. I don't know why we bother. It's boring."

"It's tradition," said Meg. "It's part of the pomp and ceremony our parents lap up. Makes 'em think they're getting value for money.

"That's silly. I'm here for the education. End of."

"Same here. But some people want the good ol' English public-school polish, the one that gives us all confidence, an air of entitlement, and entry into places other people can only dream of."

"That doesn't sound like you. Where's all this coming from?"

"Jez, mostly," Meg admitted. "He's a socialist."

"That must be hard around here. This constituency is true blue, through and through." Dad had sometimes spoken nostalgically of a hint of liberal-democrat orange in the nineties, but it had withered and died before Nessa had been born. Had part of Scotland's appeal been the possibility, no matter how remote, of a move away from the increasingly right-wing politics of successive Westminster governments?

Nessa's musings were interrupted by a voice to her right. "Budge up. Make room."

Meg shifted along until she pressed against the girl on the other side of her. The girl turned and scowled as she hit the wooden end of the pew. Nessa pressed against Meg, and Tarone and Tim squeezed in on her other side.

Tim made some heartfelt mutterings about how his right buttock dangled off the seat. "Dunno why we have to bother with this shit anyway."

In unison, Meg and Nessa chorused, "Tradition," and giggled.

"Fuck tradition," muttered Tarone. "Up the revolution!"

"Don't tell me you're a socialist too," said Nessa.

"Who's a socialist?" asked Tim, twisting around in a way that almost unbalanced him. He braced himself against the pew in front.

"That'll be between me and the ballot box," said Tarone, but Tim had stopped listening.

Tim whistled softly. "Oh, wow! Who is that?" He pointed indiscreetly towards the chapel entrance, where a girl in an obviously new uniform hovered uncertainly, trying to spot a seat amid the melee.

"Oh, wow!" was right! Nessa felt her presence like a gut punch, even from ten metres away. The girl was tall, but not too tall, slender, but not thin, curvy but not buxom, and had short, chestnut brown, curly hair, which she wore in an unfashionably natural style. Her skin was tanned, as though she'd spent the whole of the summer in the sun, and if she wore make-up, she wore it lightly.

"Another new girl. Must be."

"She's gorgeous!" Tim salivated.

Nessa agreed with him, but she kept her salivation to herself. She'd felt like this about Emily, only now her feelings were magnified a thousand-fold.

The girl found a free chair on the opposite side of the chapel, one of the ones that had been placed along the aisle to create extra seating. The seats were unpopular with the students since there was no chance of playing with your phone without being seen. Nessa appreciated her good fortune; she got a good look at the new girl, top to toe, as she sat, ankles crossed daintily beneath her chair.

The head swept in, academic gown billowing impressively around him.

Suddenly Nessa was grateful she knew the service by rote. She didn't have to think as she stood and sat as required, all the while incapable of taking her eyes off the new girl.

Maybe chapel wasn't so boring after all.

*

"**W**hat's wrong with you? You were like a zombie in there!" said Meg twenty minutes later, as they emerged into fresh air.

Nessa waited until they had descended the steps and were clear of the crowd before she answered. "Can I tell you something?"

"Anything. You know that."

"It's about the new girl."

"Your roommate?"

"No. The other new girl. The one in chapel."

"The one you were staring at all the way through the service. What about her?"

"I think she's... Well. She's hot!"

"The way the guys were drooling, I'd say that's pretty obvious."

Nessa grabbed Meg's sleeve, pulled her to a halt, and turned her around, so they were face to face. "No. You aren't listening. I," she emphasised the I and pointed ferociously at herself, stabbing her chest repeatedly, "think she's hot."

"Oh. Oh! You think—!"

"Yeah."

"Because of the gay thing."

"Uh-huh. If I'd had any lingering doubts, seeing her would have dispelled them. For all eternity. You're shocked, aren't you? I can tell. I've shocked you, haven't I?"

Meg didn't reply.

Had she made things uncomfortably real for Meg? Had she ruined their friendship? Surely not, but this silence couldn't be good. "Say something!"

Meg cackled gleefully and almost doubled over with laughter. "You are so easy! I could tell you liked her from the way you were ogling her."

"Oh, God. Was it that obvious?"

"Oh, yes," she said between bursts of mirth. "To me, anyway. I doubt anyone else paid enough attention to notice."

"Phew. That's a relief. But what am I going to do? And will you stop laughing!"

"Okay." Meg pulled herself together. "First things first. We've got to find out who she is. It's a small school. It won't be hard." She hooked her arm through Nessa's. "To the library!"

"You think she'll be there?"

"No." Meg rolled her eyes. "But we've got a free period, and I've still got to finish the last of my summer prep."

*

"**D**ammit! I've lost my—" muttered Meg five minutes later, trying to keep her voice down while she futilely rummaged around in her bag.

"Looking for this?" asked Tarone, interrupting them. He held out Meg's pencil case.

"Yes! Thank you!"

"You dropped it as you were leaving chapel."

"Thank you!" Meg said again.

"What was it yesterday, Meg? Your phone? I'm amazed you have any possessions left, the way you keep dropping them!"

"I can't help it. No matter how hard I try, I keep losing things."

"Try harder," said Nessa, not entirely unsympathetically. "Closing your bag properly would be a start."

Meg stuck her tongue out. "Yes, Mum."

Tarone moved around the table to sit opposite them and plonked a large, fat book down. From its cover and the glossy illustrations within, Nessa guessed Tarone had to research some artist or other.

Next to her, Meg got down to work on the French translation she could have finished in July. Her disgruntled mutterings suggested it was a particularly tricky one.

Nessa turned her attention to her chemistry book and chewed on her lower lip as she tried to get her head around a thorny calculation.

Five minutes later, Tarone nudged her hand with his sketchbook, his eyes dancing with mischief. She took the sketchbook to get a better look at his work.

Tarone hadn't got as far as looking up his artist, preferring to focus his attention on creating a cartoon, which he'd expertly executed with felt-tips.

The image showed a girl with bouncy red hair. She wore a short skirt and a shirt two sizes too small, and she shed possessions from a gaping bag as she ran. Nessa did her best to contain her laughter by covering her mouth with her hands, but she attracted Meg's attention, anyway.

Meg demanded a look, recognised the truth of the joke, and laughed at herself.

Tarone was gratified by their reaction. "Seriously, though, Meg, you need to learn to take more care of your possessions. We won't always be around to pick up after you."

*

Moira lost herself in a morass of angry comments on Yapper, where activists spread with evangelical zeal the news that being single wasn't an undesirable state which needed to be corrected as soon as possible. Being asexual and aromantic didn't lead inevitably to a life cursed with sadness and loneliness. Aroaces lived rich, fulfilled lives, full of different kinds of love. Romantic love shouldn't be set on a pedestal against which all other kinds of emotional connections were found wanting, and, by the way, many romantic relationships fell short of that ideal too.

Moira believed it all.

She did.

She told herself she did.

To believe otherwise invalidated her whole existence.

But.

There were times when she was sad. There were times when she was lonely. Yapper's unremitting self-righteousness made her feel as though those emotions were moral failings on her part. They made her feel broken, but in a different way to how she'd felt before she'd found out about asexuality.

She needed to recognise the emotions. Accept them. And move on. She wasn't broken.

She was capable of love. She was sure of it. She simply hadn't had much opportunity to show it, especially in the last few years during which Covid had shrunk her world and social circle and shown her how much of a grip amatonormativity, or was it allonormativity, had on the people around her.

She simply needed to find her own people and forge connections.

Easier said than done.

*

The first few days of term were summer warm, and Nessa shed her blazer as she sat in their favourite spot and waited for Meg to join her. The concrete balustrade atop the wall had been cooked by the sun, and Nessa's skin soaked up the heat.

Meg, beaming, plonked her bag on the wall and vaulted upwards with more than usual vigour and dexterity. She brimmed over with excitement, and her excitement translated into exaggerated movements so flamboyant as to verge on camp. "What's up?" Nessa quirked an eyebrow.

"Francesca Nightingale," said Meg, as though that explained everything.

"What?"

"Your new favourite person. You know. The new girl. She's called Francesca Nightingale."

A flush of something hot ran through Nessa's body. "Francesca Nightingale."

Meg nodded.

"Fran...ces...ca... Night...ing...gale..." There were so many syllables, and they rolled around Nessa's mouth. Six glorious syllables, each one to be savoured like the finest, darkest, chocolate. Delicious.

"Jeez, you've got it bad!" Meg's tone veered from self-satisfied towards amused.

"Sorry," murmured Nessa, embarrassed. "Okay, what else can you tell me?" She leaned forwards like a puppy eager for a treat.

"She's in Year 12. Transferred from one of the local academies to do her A levels. She's insanely bright and she got a scholarship. Big into English and drama, and she wants to go to Cambridge."

"How did you find all that out so fast?" asked Nessa, impressed. They might be drawing a blank on the Nikki front, but perhaps Meg had a future as an investigator, after all.

"She's also in Beaver, so I accidentally on purpose bumped into her in the corridor outside the loos, and we got chatting. She told me she talks a lot when she's nervous."

Nessa leaned back, bracing herself with her hands, and closed her eyes against the glare of the sun. She sighed absentmindedly, and even though her mind still focused on Francesca, she said, "This feels good!"

"Didn't you have sun in Scotland?"

"What?" Nessa's brain had to rush to catch up with the conversation. "Oh. Yeah. Some. But not often as warm as this."

"I don't know how you stood it."

"It was all right, in the end. I think I might even miss it."

"By the way, your roommate? I think she's in both my media studies and English classes. Pouty blonde? Long hair and longer nails? Thinks she's one of the popular kids?"

"That's the one."

Meg wrinkled her nose. "She's a proper 'mare, isn't she?"

"Yep."

"The rest of us hate her already. What's her name again? Something to do with Popsicles?"

"Popsicle! I love it!"

"Seriously, though, what is her name?"

"Poppy Crystal, a.k.a. the Popsicle forever after!"

*

Nessa had never considered Tovington to be large before; there was nothing like spending a summer in Argyll to change your perspective.

As much to avoid Poppy as to enjoy the good weather, Nessa spent Saturday afternoon wandering around town, rediscovering old haunts, and thinking through her current preoccupation. She had never felt this way before. She had so far resisted the impulse to scrawl Francesca's name all over her jotter because that would be weird. Wouldn't it? Over the top, even, and verging on stalkerish?

The mega crush Meg had on Kai? Nessa got it now.

Big into drama, Meg had said.

Which meant Francesca Nightingale was bound to take part in St Drogo's Christmas show.

Nessa didn't sing, couldn't dance, and, other than in the ubiquitous Year 1 nativity play, she'd never tried to act. Even then, in light of her singular lack of talent, she'd been cast in a non-speaking role, as a sheep.

Nessa was overcome by a sudden urge to audition.

Chapter Fourteen

The temptation to write a song made Moira remember the ones she'd written before, and driven by a blend of curiosity and nostalgia, she dug through a pile of ancient boxes, searching for notebooks she hoped she hadn't thrown out.

She found them in a large shoebox, which, according to the label had once housed a pair of knee-length boots made by a long-gone high-street brand.

Moira carried her prize into the kitchen, where she set it down. She found some paper towel and wiped layers of dust and cobwebs away. There was a hole in one of the box's bottom corners; not surprising, given mice sometimes liked to move into the eaves during the winter.

She threw the towel into the bin, rinsed and dried her hands, and settled herself at the table.

The notebooks were tired, old, and worn, their pages scuffed at the edges. Over the years, the ink from the cheap biros she'd used had soaked deep into the paper, casting a blue shadow around each letter and note.

There were songs she remembered, and more she'd forgotten.

Some were finished, most were not.

Songs. Lyrics. Chords.

Some of the melodies weren't bad. She smiled, pleased. But she shook her head when she read the snatches of half-formed verses she'd tried to put alongside them.

Most of her abandoned lyrics were about love and relationships. Relationships gone wrong. Relationships gone right. The words were hollow, empty, insincere.

Her mother had once asked an old family friend a question about classical music. They'd been listening to St Cecilia's Mass by Gounod. It was the first time Moira had heard of, let alone heard, the Mass, and she'd fallen in love with it at first sound.

"How do you reconcile listening to religious music with your faith?" The friend was Jewish.

He'd shaken his head. "It doesn't matter. It's music. The words are in a foreign language I don't understand. All that matters is the melody. I don't hear anything else."

Is that what she had done all these years? Tuned out the words because romance and attraction were foreign languages to her?

Surely it wasn't that simple. She'd tried to write them, and she had sung them.

But she had seldom been invested in the words, even the ones she'd written herself.

It was the melody that mattered. That spoke to her soul.

Why had she tried to write about these things?

Because that was what she was supposed to do? Because that was what people wanted to hear?

No wonder she'd abandoned them, although, with a bit of tweaking and a change of perspective, maybe some of them were salvageable.

Halfway through the third notebook, she stumbled across the first draft of "Will You (Ask Me Out)?" A torrent of long dammed memories burst free.

When they'd made the video, the record company had insisted on a high-end production story about a woman, Nikki, seeing a man, Robin, across a crowded club and how they were instantly attracted to each other. They'd turned "Will You (Ask Me Out)?" into a song about romantic love, new beginnings, and coming of age.

Moira had hated the video shoot for lots of reasons, only one of which was it was where Nikki and Robin had met.

The song hadn't started out as a romance. Telling a love story had been the furthest thing from her mind when Moira had penned her initial words. They had been about a single person questioning the existence of a soulmate she had yet to meet. Did that magical person who was supposed to make life complete and transport her into the world of adult love exist?

Moira had grown weary of watching everyone around her pair up, while she hadn't found anyone who came close to filling the partner-shaped hole she'd been indoctrinated to believe existed inside her. The original song hadn't been happy: it had been about self-doubt, confusion, and yearning, none of the things it later came to be.

Her peers had played "Will You (Ask Me Out)?" at weddings, and, in their speeches, they had talked about how it reminded them of the first time they'd set eyes on their partners. More recently, it had become popular at significant wedding anniversaries.

Over the years, she had almost forgotten about the coda the record company and the producer had forced her to take out, but she read the words again now and she felt as though all the air had been sucked out of her lungs.

> *I want to feel*
> *Like others feel.*
> *I need you*
> *To make me*
> *Feel*
> *Real.*
> *But you can't make me feel*
> *Because you're not real.*

The confusion, pain, and desperation from all those years ago leapt off the page, along with the self-doubt and the certainty something was wrong with her.

Dammit.

Damn the producer for saying the words of the coda didn't fit with the rest of the song, that they weren't commercial enough, that they were unrelatable. And damn her for going along with what everyone else wanted, and for accepting what they said was true.

If only she'd known then everything she was learning now.

She wanted to weep for the person she'd been all those years ago.

*

"Nessa Clarkson. This is a surprise," said Ms Markides, as Nessa took her place at the front and centre of the stage. From the way she spoke and the way she eyed Nessa dubiously, Nessa gathered

the surprise wasn't a particularly welcome one. "Why the sudden interest in theatre?"

Ms Markides had taught drama and history since the early noughties. A large woman with an ample bosom, olive skin, dark eyes, and hair
a brassy colour which didn't exist in nature, she'd always had her favourites, and Nessa had never been one of them. That was one reason why
Nessa had never enjoyed either of Ms Markides's subjects. She had
dropped them both as soon as she was allowed.

According to rumour, Ms Markides had been an extra in one of the
1990s major film franchises, but nobody knew for sure. Nessa suspected
it wasn't true; Ms Markides was the kind of person who would have
boasted about it forever if she had been in the films. By keeping quiet,
she maintained an air of mystery that would have been destroyed by a
flat-out denial.

Nessa, the last person to audition, had rehearsed her answer. She
straightened her shoulders, hoped she'd sound at least semi-convincing,
and said, "Because of my father's work, I could never come to the rehearsals before, but now I'm boarding, I'm able to commit. It's something to add to my personal statement, and this is the last chance I'll
have to try this before I leave St Drogo's."

Huh. Maybe she should have restricted herself to one reason, instead of making a list. She hadn't found herself convincing, so she wasn't
surprised when Ms Markides sniffed and pursed her lips. "Very well.
Read. Then you can sing."

Nessa didn't think she did too atrociously. At least she didn't flail
her arms around like Becca, or flick her hair away from her face like
Poppy, and why, oh, why did Poppy have to be here too? Nessa even
managed not to stumble over her words like Alicia, or speak in a slum-
ber-inducing drone like Alex. Plus, while her singing voice lacked power,

at least she could hold a tune.

The only people at the auditions with any noticeable talent were a spotty Year 11 called Mickey, Kai, and Francesca.

As soon as Nessa finished, Ms Markides gathered everyone around and told them who had been given which part.

Nessa had neither expected nor wanted a leading role, but she had hoped for something a fraction more interesting than being relegated to the ensemble; however, lacking in talent, experience, and not being a favourite of Ms Markides, perhaps she should have been surprised to have been given a part at all.

Nobody, other than Poppy, was surprised when Ms Markides announced Mickey had been cast as Seymour, Kai as Orin, and Francesca as Audrey.

*

"**Y**ou want to be in *Little Shop of Horrors*?" exclaimed Meg.

"Shush! You'll get us thrown out!" Nessa hissed. They were in the library again, and Nessa regretted choosing to have the conversation there.

Mindful of Nessa's warning, Meg crammed a fist in her mouth to plug her incredulous laughter. Her eyes bulged and her face reddened, as though she was about to rupture something.

"What's wrong with me being in the show, anyway?"

Meg removed the fist and tried to pull herself together enough to be coherent. She wasn't entirely successful; her voice still shook with laughter. "What's right with it, don't you mean? You've never wanted to be in a show before. You used to get tongue-tied every time you were called on to read in English. You only ever put your hand up in science."

"That was years ago." Before the pandemic, before home school and online classes. Before Nessa had learned the universe held bigger threats than her looking foolish in front of her peers.

"You've never done it before. What makes you think you can even act? Need I go on?"

"Way to be supportive! Anyway, if Moira could get up on a stage without any training and perform, why can't I?"

"You're going to do this?"

"I've already done it."

"You're kidding."

"No. I put my name down. And I auditioned."

"What has got into you?"

"Would you believe me if I told you I wanted something to do in the evenings?"

"No."

"How about, I wanted to get away from the Popsicle?" Nessa pitied Poppy's parents, who were throwing good money after bad by sending her to St Drogo's, unless they considered it good value to have her out of the house; as Poppy's litany of uncensored resentments and inanity wore Nessa down, Nessa would have paid good money to get rid of Poppy too.

"I might have done, except, in English this morning, she boasted about being in the show."

"Yeah. That's unfortunate. I honestly did want to get away from her."

"So, what's the real reason?"

"It gives me something else to put in my personal statement for my UCAS application?"

"Nope. Ms Markides might believe that, but you already told me you wrote your statement before we broke up for the summer."

"You're going to make me say it, aren't you?"

"Yep." Meg popped the *p* happily and grinned. Meg had known the real reason all along.

"It gives me an excuse to maybe get to know Francesca—Frankie—better."

"Did Francesca—Frankie—get a good part?" Meg waggled her eyebrows at the nickname.

"Yeah. One of the leads. Audrey."

Meg brayed with laughter again, earning the pair of them glares from some of the students as well as the librarian, who was halfway out of her seat. Nessa put her finger to her lips. The librarian sat down again, and Meg managed to get her laughter and volume under control. "That's the part Poppy wanted. She boasted about being in the show on the one hand and made out she'd been unfairly overlooked on the other. You should have heard her! 'Of, course, I would have made a perfect Audrey. Far better than the girl who got the role'." Meg parodied Poppy with uncanny accuracy.

Nessa shuddered. "Of course she'd make a perfect Audrey! She is Audrey. In the flesh. Ugh!"

"What do you mean?"

"Audrey is blonde, pretty, and, according to the script, has a tacky taste in clothes."

"Aha! And she aspired to that?"

"It's the female lead. Anyway, she still landed a fairly decent part. Ronette, I think."

"Who else is in the show?"

"Let's see. Besides Frankie, of course—"

"Of course," said Meg wryly.

"There's a Year 11, Mikey or Mickey or something, playing

Seymour." Mickey, who was gangly and several inches shorter than Frankie, had a great singing voice; he was the perfect choice for Seymour. Nessa had a hunch he would morph into a hunk when his final growth spurt kicked in, he put some more meat onto his bones, and the acne cleared up. "Kai is playing an evil dentist, who—spoiler alert—gets eaten in the first half." Nessa continued running through the list of cast members, sure she'd forgotten a few people. It didn't matter. Meg's limited interest waned rapidly.

Nessa made the radical suggestion they get on with some work.

*

The cast and crew met two days later for what Ms Markides described as a pre-rehearsal. She got everyone to introduce themselves, name, house, year, what kind of animal they would like to be, and why. Nessa cringed. Why couldn't Ms Markides simply hand out the scripts and let them go?

Nessa's fellow thespians came up with the usual range of dogs, cats, rabbits, and other cute, furry creatures, although Frankie announced with a remarkably straight face she would like to be an amoeba; she would most likely be invisible to humans and would be able to make herself into pretty much any shape she wanted. "Think, with those pseudopod thingies, I'd be like autonomous silly putty."

Tarone, who had an important backstage role, leaned over and whispered in Nessa's ear. "Someone's given this way too much thought."

"Or has had to do way too many of these icebreaker thingies before."

When it got to her turn, Nessa said, cringing inwardly, she'd settle for being one of the koi in the Hobby fishpond; they had a fantastic life, none had been eaten by herons in the last three years, and the school fed them well and made sure the pond water was clean.

Poppy prefaced her choice by taking a deep breath as though she was going to make a grand pronouncement. "I would like to be one of those adorable tiny handbag dogs, a Papillon, maybe. Something nice and fluffy. It would be wonderful to be dressed in cute outfits, carried around in designer luxury, and fed tidbits from the fingers of my own personal celebrity."

Nessa was so busy trying not to wretch, she almost missed Tarone saying he'd be a tiger because why not?

If things didn't exactly improve after that, at least they didn't get any worse.

There were more performers than parts in the musical, but Ms Markides said they could fudge that easily enough by doubling up on doo-wop girls and having a decent-sized ensemble of winos, prostitutes, customers, and dental patients. "We wouldn't want anyone to miss out, would we?"

Nessa second-guessed herself for a moment, but she caught sight of Frankie, reminded herself why she wanted to do this, and along with everyone else, shook her head.

Nessa nearly third-guessed herself when she caught sight of the rehearsal schedule. Three times a week! That was a lot of rehearsals, and the number rose to four the week before the performance. She would also need to allow time for costume fittings and learning lines. Then again, Nessa didn't have much to do, so hopefully the learning bit wouldn't take long, after all.

The pre-rehearsal ended with cast and crew signing what Ms Markides described as a commitment contract. Nessa read through the document and dubiously eyed the red pen being circulated alongside it.

We, the undersigned, pledge ourselves to give special priority within our lives to the endeavour of producing and performing St Drogo's production of Little Shop of Horrors and do hereby pledge:

1) To show up on time for all rehearsals.

2) To show up on time for all performances.

3) To show up on time for all wardrobe fittings.

4) To show up on time for all other related activities as deemed necessary to ensure the success of our endeavour.

The document had been printed on coloured A3 paper in a gothic font. Nessa presumed it was supposed to look intimidatingly impressive.

After everyone had signed, Ms Markides produced a label that mimicked a wax seal and stuck it to the bottom of the page. "I'll bring this along to every rehearsal," she declaimed in sepulchral tones, "and put it on display. It will be a reminder of the commitment we have all made to this show and to each other."

"Does the theatre crowd always take things this seriously?" Nessa asked Tarone quietly as they filed out of the hall amid everyone else's excited chatter.

"Yes. The contract is part of the ritual. So is the blood-red ink."

"Huh. I thought this was supposed to be fun, but now I'm worried I've signed my soul away."

Chapter Fifteen

When Nessa read through the script, she discovered she had even less to do than she'd suspected. She had one spoken line, and she was lucky to have that. She got to pose on stage a couple of times as Prostitute Number 3, would help to move a couple of bits of scenery, had a dance number in a dental surgery, and got to sing in the finale, where she'd stand in the audience, holding up one of Audrey Two's tendrils.

The show was not going to turn her into an overnight sensation.

On her side of the bedroom, Poppy was also reading the script. Her brows were drawn close together in a scowl, and she was chewing on her lower lip. "Why," she lamented loud enough to make sure Nessa heard even though she was pretending to talk to herself, "do I have to share my limelight with these extra doo-wop girls? The original script only asks for three. These others will detract from my performance. Steal my lime-light."

Poppy had more to do than Nessa, but her part wasn't enough to make her happy. Nessa put on her headphones, volume turned up high, and tuned Poppy out.

*

The Cats' Meow premiered in the second half of September. Out of morbid curiosity, Moira tuned into the first episode. The producers had found another washed up duo to play the adversarial roles originally proposed for Moira and Nikki, and the show's dynamic was even more ghastly than she'd anticipated.

Moira switched off after a quarter of an hour. She despised the way the male judge picked at his former partner and loathed seeing how much the former partner hated every second of it.

There but for the grace of God.

*

The realisation hit Moira while she was showering. She was lathering herself up, standing under the spray of hot water, letting her mind wander.

I was in love!

I have been in love.

With Nikki. That's why I'll never stop worrying about her, no matter how much I try.

And it's why everything hurt so much.

I'm not an unemotional, dried-up husk of a human being.

Moira had assumed true love was romantic, characterised by terms of endearment, bunches of flowers, and boxes of chocolates. She'd assumed there would be flutterings, tinglings, and yearnings. And she'd assumed there would be a man because the world she'd grown up in was heterosexual by default.

She hadn't recognised her feelings for Nikki for what they were. She hadn't had the language or been equipped with the concepts, and she'd confused a deep platonic love with close friendship.

She had looked forwards to spending time with Nikki. She'd liked the feeling someone "got" her, sharing inside jokes, doing things, and making plans together.

Maybe Nikki had liked her, but she hadn't loved Moira, not the way Moira had loved Nikki.

Moira had loved, been in platonic love with Nikki, and that's why everything had hurt, and why Moira's memories of Nikki remained sharp, whereas those of other friends she'd lost over the years were blunt and faded.

She'd known she'd been upset. She'd assumed she'd been over-reacting because nobody should feel that bad over a rift between friends.

But now she saw things with a new clarity.

Nikki had dumped Moira, although neither of them had been equipped to understand it at the time, and Moira's heart had been broken.

With her new understanding came forgiveness. She forgave herself for the depths of her pain, and she forgave Nikki for unwittingly causing it.

*

At the first *Little Shop of Horrors* rehearsal the entire cast sat in a circle and read through the script, supposedly to familiarise themselves with it. However, everyone had already read it, so Nessa wasn't sure what the session was going to achieve.

To one side, Mr Clements, one of the music teachers, sat at a piano, ready to play accompaniment whenever necessary. Frankie already knew all the words to her songs and belted along to the music with the confidence of a seasoned performer. She reminded Nessa of a wren, a tiny bird that sang with amazing power.

Poppy hadn't managed to learn all her lines, but she only needed to glance at the score a few times, and she didn't do too badly. As the rehearsal schedule didn't require the cast to be off book for another couple of weeks, nobody, except Poppy, who feared she had been shown up by Frankie, minded.

Nessa didn't have much to do beyond listening to everyone else and joining in a few choruses. When she'd studied the script and score, she had struggled to remember what she'd learned about reading music when she was younger, but she picked up the melodies easily enough when she heard them.

*

"She had a go at Francesca." Meg filled Nessa in on Poppy's latest fit of temper, which Nessa had missed because she'd stayed after chemistry class to clear away the debris from an unfortunate accident that had scattered glassware and chemicals across the workbench and floor.

Not only had Nessa arrived too late in the cafeteria to hear the argument, but she'd also missed out on her favourite fish pie. Nessa poked at her curry unenthusiastically while Meg continued her account.

"The Popsicle, hand on hips like so, asked her, 'What have you got that I don't?' Francesca looked uncomfortable, but Tarone came to her rescue. He said, 'Talent!' The Popsicle was furious!"

Nessa laughed, albeit uneasily. "Tarone's right though. Frankie has more talent in her pinky finger than all the doo-wop girls combined."

"All the what now?"

"Not important." Nessa brushed the question away and took a bite of her meal. On any other day she'd have been happy with curry, but, oh, to have missed the pie!

"How are the rehearsals going, anyway?"

"Honestly? Pretty boring. I've got so little to do in the show, I spend most of my time sitting around."

No excuse was good enough to miss a session. When one of the day pupils said her dad would be out of town and she had no transport, Ms Markides told her she'd arrange for a member of staff to take her home.

As Nessa boarded, no excuse was ever going to wash, and so she found herself stuck at the rear of the great hall for hours on end, watching other people go through their paces. "But at least I get plenty of time to work on my prep or my knitting. And Tarone's doing work on the stage sets, so I get to hang with him a fair amount too."

Were it not for the chance to admire Francesca, being in the show would have had no redeeming qualities.

"By the way, did you know the school is going to livestream one performance from each of its productions this year?" said Meg.

"What? No! Why?" Nobody had mentioned that at rehearsals, had they? She didn't think so, but maybe she hadn't been listening. Maybe someone had said something while she'd been hanging out with Tarone.

"Because so many of the boarders' parents can't get to the shows. It'll give 'em a chance to see their darling poppets on stage. And we, as in the Year 13 media studies class, are going to set everything up. It'll be fabulous experience."

Livestreaming? Wow. That sounded way more serious than appearing on stage in front of a couple of hundred people, who would have forgotten about it by new year.

"I'm going to be stuck with whatever lame production the lower school are doing, worse luck." Meg changed the subject. "Meanwhile, while you've been busy waiting around for things to happen, I've been having another go at looking for Nikki."

"Any progress?"

"Not much. But I'm working on some leads."

They were interrupted before Nessa could press for details.

"Ah, hah! We've tracked you down!" Tim, flanked by Tarone, had arrived.

Tarone waved a greeting.

Meg said, "Hey guys."

Nessa, mid-mouthful, settled for glancing up at them.

Tim and Tarone sat down.

"We've been looking for you," said Tarone.

"Why?" asked Meg.

"Actually, it's Nessa we were after."

"I'll try not to be offended," said Meg.

"Don't take it personally," said Tim. "It's always a delight to see you. However, today, I have business with your better half."

"She's not my better half. I'm hers."

Nessa swallowed and said, "Charming. What do you guys want?"

"Besides the pleasure of your company?"

"Besides that."

"You room with Poppy Crystal, don't you?"

Nessa suppressed a shudder. "Yes. What's it to you?"

"It's—" Tim broke off.

Tarone said, "Tim, here, wants you to put in a good word for him. I've told him not to bother, but his mind's made up."

"She's gorgeous," said Tim happily.

"Her brain is emptier than a vacuum flask." Nessa bit her lip.

Tarone poked Tim in the ribs. "Told you."

"And I told you, it's not her brain I'm interested in."

"Ugh," muttered Nessa.

"I'm in the mood for some recreational snogging, and she's most definitely—"

"Snoggable," said Tarone.

"Ugh," said Nessa again.

"Don't knock it until you've tried it," said Tim.

"Who says I haven't tried it? Not with the Popsicle, obviously, but I've done my share of kissing." Okay, so she was exaggerating but she had kissed Emily once, and that had to count for something.

"Oh, yeah? Who's the lucky guy?" demanded Tim.

"That's none of your business."

"Because it didn't happen."

"Yes, it did," said Meg.

"How do you know? Were you there?"

"No. But Nessa told me about it. It happened over the summer." Possibly to take the pressure off Nessa, she added, "I've kissed too. Lots of times."

"Yeah, we know. You've posted enough about it on your social media. There's such a thing as oversharing."

"You complain Meg shares too much, but you don't believe me because I don't share enough?" Nessa asked.

"You don't share at all."

"That's because it's nobody's business!"

"You're the one who mentioned it."

*

Moira tried to hold on to the revelatory clarity she had found in the shower, but it slipped in and out of focus as she found new questions to ask and new doubts to ponder.

Had Moira been comparing all her subsequent friendships against Nikki and finding them wanting? Certainly, they'd never been as vivid, as vibrant. They'd never made her feel so alive.

But was that because they couldn't match up, they hadn't been the same, or because she hadn't let herself grow as close to anyone else?

She needed to appreciate her friendships for what they offered, not judge them against what they lacked.

How had it taken her so long to see this? If only she'd had the words, the insight!

She'd long questioned conventional wisdom and societal conditioning, and she was ready to throw them aside. Why had she waited until now? Why had she needed to read what others had to say to give her the strength, the permission, to do it?

She felt better about herself than she'd done in years. She hadn't needed medication or therapy to "cure" her; all she had needed was a change in perspective.

Even so, she still had questions.

If she had loved Nikki, did that mean she wasn't aromantic, after all? Was she homoromantic, grey romantic, quoiromantic, or some other label she had yet to stumble across?

But no. Aromantic felt right. She'd never wanted to kiss or cuddle or hold Nikki's hand. She had been in platonic love. There had been nothing romantic about it. And platonic love was as valid as any other kind.

She wished she didn't have so much time to think. More accurately, she wished she didn't have so much alone time to think. Perhaps it would be nice to have someone to talk this over with.

Maybe none of it mattered. Maybe all she needed to take away from this was that love came in a myriad of forms and was even more complicated and messy than the media, with its preference for binary pairings, portrayed.

Maybe it was enough to know she had loved, could love, and if she was lucky, would love again.

*

Nessa was putting the final touches to a pair of mittens, which might make a decent stocking filler for Dad, when Tarone sat down beside her. He watched the stage for a few minutes, where Francesca and Kai were blocking out a scene with the help of Ms Markides.

He nudged her gently with his elbow. "Who was the lucky guy?"

"What?" asked Nessa absently, snipping off a tail of yarn and re-threading her needle, ready to weave in the next loose end.

"The one you kissed over the summer. How'd you keep something like that quiet in a place like this?"

"By not telling anyone. Plus, it happened in Scotland."

"In Scotland. So, nobody I'd know."

"Nope."

"Even so. Details, please."

"Why do you care? It's not like we did anything much. Nothing gossip-worthy, anyway."

"Okay." Tarone was suddenly serious. "I admit, I'm curious. Not so much about who, what, and how, but more about the why."

"The 'Why'?"

"Tim got me thinking. He doesn't care about Poppy as a person, and I don't get it. I can't imagine being with someone without getting to know them first, so I've been asking myself, am I the odd person here? Or is Tim?"

Tarone had a better idea what coming out was like than most people at school, not because he'd come out himself, but because of his mums. His credentials as an ally were impeccable, so maybe telling him wouldn't be completely terrible.

"Okay." Nessa put aside the knitting and gave Tarone her full attention. "First, if I tell you, you must promise me you'll keep it to yourself. Swear you won't tell anyone. Not even Tim. Especially not Tim."

"What's the big deal?"

"No big deal. But Tim's a blabbermouth, and I'm not ready to broadcast this to the whole school."

"Point taken." Tarone made a sloppy cross-my-heart gesture with his right hand. "I swear."

Nessa leaned closer. "You know the way you aren't attracted to guys... You aren't attracted to guys, are you?"

"What? No!"

"Right. The point is, I'm not attracted to guys either."

"What? You mean you...?"

"Like the lassies?" Nessa unthinkingly used Emily's phrase. "Yes."

"Oh. I had no idea."

"Not surprising. It was pretty much theoretical until the summer."

"What did happen in the summer?"

Nessa hesitated.

"You might as well say. It's not that big a deal, is it? Particularly given what you've told me. So, was it an impulse? Instant attraction? Or was it more of an after three dates kind of thing?"

"To be honest, it was..." Nessa struggled to find the words. "Emily's a friend. We met at work—yes, I got a job during the hols, and the job wasn't totally awful—and we got to talking. She's a few years older than me, and she asked if I wanted to kiss her. To know what it was like."

"What was it like?"

"Nice."

"So, you kissed her as, what, an experiment?"

"I guess so."

"So, you get where Tim is coming from?"

"Not really. I wanted to go out with her. Unlike Tim, I do care about a person's personality. I was up for doing it again, but it turned out I was way more into Emily than she was into me. She was trying to be helpful."

"And left you with a broken heart?"

"Not broken, exactly, but slightly battered. Or maybe that was my ego. I haven't helped you much, have I?

"So, you didn't sign up for the play to be near me?"

"God, no! What gave you that idea?"

"Something Meg said. About you doing the show to be near your crush."

"And you assumed it was you."

"I'll have you know, I'm extremely crushable."

That was true. Tarone was one of the Year 13 hotties, and Nessa knew a few students who liked to doodle his name when they were supposed to be studying.

"Besides," Tarone continued, "there're only three Year 13's here, so the odds were in my favour."

That was also true. "You're not disappointed, are you?" Nessa hoped not, because how awkward would that be?

"Nah. My ego might be a bit bruised, but I'll live." He paused. "If you're not into blokes..." Tarone trailed off and considered. He clicked his fingers. "You're into Frankie!"

"Shush!" Nessa blushed. "Someone'll hear you!"

"You are! You like Frankie!" Tarone exclaimed, but at least he tried to quieten his glee.

"Doesn't everybody?"

Tarone grinned. "She's gorgeous, all right. But she turned me down. Kai scored a date with her though."

"Kai? Meg's Kai? Dammit!" hissed Nessa, partly on her own account and partly on Meg's.

"What do you mean, Meg's Kai?"

"Oh, come on! She's only been crushing on him since forever! Everyone knows that!"

"Will you two hush?"

Whoops. They'd attracted some unwelcome attention.

"Sorry, Ms Markides." Nessa hoped Ms Markides had heard nothing more of their conversation than unintelligible whispers.

They managed to be silent for five seconds before Tarone whispered, "Kai's date ended badly. He won't say why, so it's got to be something embarrassing, and Frankie's not talking. I can only guess what went wrong." He nudged Nessa and waggled his eyebrows. "Maybe she's into the lassies too."

Interlude

At some point, I gave up wondering. I gave up trying, but I was content. I didn't feel as though I was missing out on anything.

If anything, I considered myself lucky. I watched people marry and divorce. I saw people desperate to be a part of a couple, as though they couldn't survive by themselves. And I couldn't understand why being unhappy with someone was better than being alone.

Chapter Sixteen

"I'm giving up the shop." The words sprang out of Moira's mouth. She hadn't planned to say them, but now she had, she felt lighter. Liberated. Relieved, bordering on ecstatic.

For a generous quantity of seconds, the other crafters stared at her.

A surge of noise followed their stunned silence as everyone expressed shock, dismay, regret, or anger. Someone went so far as to use the word betrayal.

Any lingering doubts Moira might have harboured vanished. Her eyes narrowed, and she pointed at Callum, incredulous. "Did I hear you say I betrayed you?"

"Yes?" His intonation reflected discomfort at having been overheard, rather than contrition.

Moira let rip. "How dare you! I struggled to keep this place going during the pandemic. When we fully reopened again, and I asked for someone to help me out on a more regular basis, none of you came forwards. And you, Callum, you haven't done a shift in three months; I've covered more than half your sessions. You're behind on your rent. You do nothing but moan and snipe on SayMate. I need a break. And the only way I'm going to get one is if I walk away from this. I've tried and tried to keep this place going, but I'm sick of trying! I'm chucking in the towel. We're paid up until the end of the next quarter. After that, I'm not going to renew. One of you can take it on if you want, but you'll find it a thankless task. I'm washing my hands of the lot of you."

Before she knew it, she'd marched out of the shop, run a hundred yards down the street, and had come to a grinding halt in the middle of a pavement.

She took deep gulping gasps of air.

Tears pricked her eyes and ran down her face, but she wasn't sad, and her chest felt open, as though a huge knot had unravelled. She hadn't known until that moment how blocked and twisted she'd been, or how weighed down by resentment.

"Moira?"

She turned.

Emily stood next to her, looking worried. "Are you all right?"

Moira swallowed her emotions, determined to get a grip on herself. She wasn't mad at Emily, who was one of the good ones.

"They sent you after me, did they?"

Emily shook her head slightly. "I volunteered."

Moira didn't trust herself to say anything.

"We talked about it." How long had Moira been out here? Must have been a while if they'd had time to discuss the situation. "They didn't know." Moira noticed Emily hadn't included herself in the collective noun.

Didn't think, translated Moira. Or if they had thought, they had thought only of themselves.

"And they're sorry. They should be shouldering more of the burden."

Burden. That was the perfect word.

"You do your share," said Moira flatly, putting the emphasis on the you.

"Callum pushed you over the edge, and you lashed out in the heat of the moment."

"He did. And I did. But I've been thinking those things for a long time. He gave me the push I needed to say them out loud."

"And you truly want to walk away?"

"I've tried to get help. I've asked and asked, and nobody except you has listened."

"But now everyone has seen how desperate you are…"

"You shouldn't have needed to see. You should never have let me get so desperate." Guiltily, Moira added, "I mean the collective you, not you personally. You've done more to help than all the others combined."

"Things'll be different from now on. Now they know."

"Maybe for a few days. A few weeks at most. After that, they'll revert to how things are now."

"You're wrong."

"I'm not."

"Maybe you'll feel differently after you've slept on it?"

"I'm not going to change my mind."

Emily considered Moira's words for a few seconds. "Whatever you decide, I'll support you, 100 per cent."

"Thanks."

"Are you going to finish the meeting?"

"No."

"What shall I tell the others?"

"They can go home. If anyone wants to take over the co-op, they can get in touch, and I'll talk them through what's involved. I'll carry on with the admin until the lease ends, but then I'm out. And I'm not covering anyone else's shifts. If it means the shop doesn't open some days, tough. What all of you do after that is up to you, but I'm not going to be a part of it anymore."

Emily braced her shoulders as she prepared to report to the ungrateful horde.

*

As soon as Saturday morning lessons were over, Nessa piled into Meg's car. Meg cranked up the volume on the radio, and by the time they left the school grounds, they were singing as loudly as they knew how.

As promised, Meg had been given a car for her birthday. It wasn't the shiny new red model she'd been hoping for but a second-hand, navy-blue supermini, which she had instantly fallen in love with anyway. Meg named it Nelly.

Nessa was going to stay with Meg's family for the weekend, and she didn't have to be in school until Monday morning. Whoop! Whoop! They'd planned the visit over the summer, and it had been approved by the school at the beginning of term.

Nessa had loads of homework to do, and she hoped Meg would let her get at least some of it done, but hopefully they'd have plenty of time for fun too. They still had so much to catch up on.

Nessa had missed hanging out with Meg over the summer. Moira was cool, but she had to be closing in on sixty, and spending time with her wasn't the same as hanging around with someone closer to Nessa's own age. Plus, Meg and Nessa had been friends for so long, they'd developed loads of in-jokes and shorthand ways of talking.

Nessa had first visited Meg's family farm when she was seven and she had been in love with it ever since. Nestled in the Blackdown Hills, there were barns to play in, tracks and fields to explore, and a host of crops and animals to look at. Ever since her first sleepover, she had revelled in listening to the tawny owls calling in the night, rising early to watch the morning milking, feeding orphaned lambs, and collecting eggs from the hen house in the orchard.

Nessa knew, because Meg told her often enough, that although Meg liked life on the farm, she didn't understand Nessa's fascination with it, possibly because Meg had grown up with, and took for granted, all the things Nessa delighted in. Meg was also vocal about her relief her older brother wanted to take over the business and she wouldn't have to; she wanted a different life for her adult self, one that would take her closer to the bright lights of a city. Any city would do. In fact, she would settle for anywhere with street lamps.

Nessa didn't know when the farmhouse had been built, but it was old enough to have wooden beams, huge fireplaces, two staircases, three reception rooms, and flagstone floors in the working parlour, where the Aga, which powered the central heating, burned day and night. There were nooks and crannies to explore and hide in, and clutter left from bygone ages. The landline phone in the kitchen even had a cord, and how often did you see that, these days?

Like Moira, Meg's parents kept it in case of power cuts. In the noughties a storm had knocked out both the landline's cordless handsets and the nascent mobile network, and Meg's parents, Ted and Liane, had never forgotten. They were "just in case" people, and they lived by the Scouts' motto of "Be Prepared".

The farmhouse's furniture was old too, passed down through the years and kept because it was solid and serviceable. The table in the working parlour sat twelve with ease. It was covered with oilcloth and flanked by benches, a throwback to an era of big horses and labourers. Another, only slightly smaller table stood in the kitchen. There were immovable sofas and chairs throughout the house; their upholstery and scatter cushions got replaced from time to time, but their wooden frames remained, chipped and dark with ancient varnish. Nessa had been amazed when she'd discovered an old-fashioned washstand, complete with basin and ewer, in the best spare bedroom, next to the room Liane put her in.

Photographs of several generations of the family, some blurred and faded and rendered sepia with age, hung along the walls in the long hallway, which ran through the middle of the house. Nessa liked looking at the people dressed in old-fashioned clothes, cloth caps, and hob-nailed boots.

The modern era had not extended beyond the office, the cutting-edge machinery in the yard, and the superfast broadband Meg relied on so heavily to keep up with her social media.

In the days before Covid, everything about the house had made Nessa's suburban existence feel dull by comparison. During the pandemic, there had been a couple of years during which visits had been impossible, and Nessa had fretted until they'd been allowed once more.

This visit, she was struck by how much the place felt like home.

Ted and Liane made her feel at home too. She hugged them both warmly, grateful such things were allowed again, and thanked them for letting her stay.

"You're welcome, dear. Must be nice to get away from school, at least for a bit."

"It is!"

"Her roommate's a nightmare," said Meg cheerfully.

Over the lunch Liane had prepared, Nessa regaled Meg's parents and brother with exaggerated stories of Poppy's flaws and foibles.

"In that case, it's a good thing you're here, isn't it?" said Liane. "Have some more cake."

Nessa grinned. The only other person who made cakes this good was Moira, and she said as much. That led to a lengthy conversation about how her summer had been, and what Scotland was like.

Nessa wasn't able to answer any of the questions Ted asked about the cattle or sheep she'd seen; all she knew was they were different to the ones she'd grown up with in the West Country.

After the tea, cake, and chat, Meg dragged Nessa up to her bedroom.

Nessa had always envied Meg her room, even before her parents had installed secondary glazing, when it had got cold enough in winter for ice to form on the inside of the windows. The room was large enough to house a double bed, a wardrobe, chest of drawers, desk, and chair, and still have floor space enough to walk around.

They flopped onto the bed, lying on their backs, lower legs and feet dangling over the edge of the mattress.

Sounds of mooing cows and chirping birds drifted in from outside, and the music from Liane's radio seeped up from downstairs.

Nessa sighed contentedly. "It's peaceful here."

"Is it?"

"Hmm."

At that moment, as though to prove her wrong, a tractor engine fired up from somewhere beneath Meg's window. Meg and Nessa burst out laughing and sat up again.

The rest of the weekend stretched out ahead of them. "What are we going to do?"

*

They spent most of the afternoon and evening watching ViewHoo videos. If anyone had asked, they'd have said they were researching presentation skills. What looked and sounded good?

One person spoke eloquently and stared straight into her camera, but she held and drank from an oversized novelty mug, which she passed from hand to hand, allowing her free arm to windmill and pump, drawing the viewers' attention away from what she was saying. Someone else had a distracting habit of flicking her long hair away from her face every thirty seconds.

Nessa and Meg stared into too many bedrooms, saw too many blank walls, and listened to too many people reading in stilted monotones and to too many people who dispensed with script altogether, saying in a thousand words what they could have said in a hundred.

They learned as much about production values and delivery from what ViewHooers didn't do as from what they did.

When they tired of watching talking heads, they did searches for cute puppy videos and tiny houses, which kept them occupied long after they heard Ted and Liane go to bed.

They rose late on Sunday, binge-watched sci-fi on a streaming service, went for a walk, ate lots of Liane's home cooking, and got next to no homework done.

Going to bed on Sunday night, Nessa reflected, even though she would return to the school in a mild state of panic over her backlog of prep, panic was a worthwhile trade-off for the weekend she'd had.

Interlude

I wrote "Will You (Ask me Out)?"

The record company and the producers weren't happy with the original version. They wanted to make it more commercial. So, I changed it. At the time, I was convinced it was the right thing to do. But now I want to tell you what the song was meant to be about, and I'm going to play it the way it should have been.

Chapter Seventeen

"**W**ould you like to come to the cinema with me?" Nessa had asked shyly. "I have some gift vouchers, so my treat. And, maybe, we can go for a meal after? Get to know each other better?"

Surprised and pleased, Frankie had bashfully said, "Yes."

Thus, on the first Saturday in October, as soon as lessons were over, Nessa and Frankie changed out of their school uniforms and, in Nessa's case, applied some light make-up.

Together, they walked into town where they grabbed a snack and did some window shopping until it was time to queue outside Tovington's cinema in readiness for a matinee.

The window shopping was fun. Nessa learned Frankie wasn't interested in make-up, would never get bored of browsing around bookshops, and was adept at sniffing out bargains in charity shops.

Which was great because it meant they had at least a couple of things in common.

As they waited on its front steps for the cinema to open, Nessa revelled in Frankie's conversation, liking Frankie's voice, liking the way Frankie's voice made her feel, and liking what Frankie had to say.

The film was a blockbuster, not ideal for a romantic date, but the cinema only had one screen, and it was a case of take it or leave it. Frankie didn't seem to mind. In fact, Frankie turned out to have an encyclopaedic knowledge of all things superhero and explained enthusiastically why the film was a big deal.

The cinema was small and old, a far cry from the state-of-the-art multiplexes on the edge of the nearest city. Squeezed in between two terraces of houses, its frontage only hinted at the Art Deco delights of its interior, which had managed to survive almost intact, despite the cinema having been refurbished sometime in the 1990s. The only things which had not survived, so the older townsfolk claimed, were the toilets, but nobody mourned the loss of the rusted-out cisterns with pull chains that barely worked.

But the 1990s were a long time ago, and the cinema was overdue another refurbishment. The grout in the current washrooms was stained, a couple of the sinks were cracked, and the toilet seats wobbled.

Because it was so small, the cinema had escaped the trend for subdivision into multiple screens, and the original arrangement of stalls below and circle above remained.

Seats in the circle were more expensive than those in the stalls. Nessa didn't know why. She preferred the stalls and being closer to the screen, but she splashed out for the circle, wanting to impress.

In return, Frankie insisted on buying drinks and popcorn for them both, saying it was only fair if Nessa was providing the tickets.

They accessed the circle via a sweeping staircase which hugged against the building's outer wall. There was no lift. They entered through heavy, painted, wooden doors at the rear of the auditorium and made their way down to the front row, where they could see over the balcony onto the stalls below. There were still ashtrays on the backs of the seats, which had been bought second-hand for the previous refurbishment, a legacy of a time when indoor smoking was allowed. The velour upholstery was crushed and worn.

Nessa didn't hate the film, even though it should have been shortened by a good forty-five minutes. She enjoyed sitting next to Frankie and the way Frankie's arm radiated heat next to hers. She liked the way Frankie laughed and gasped in all the right places. As a first date, Nessa couldn't have asked for better.

The lights came on halfway through the final credits, and Nessa moved to stand.

Frankie put a hand on her forearm to pull her into her seat, and Nessa, delighted by the casual touch, obliged. "They often put something after the credits," Frankie said. "Can't miss that."

They were duly rewarded by a fifteen-second teaser for the next film in the franchise, and Frankie exuded satisfaction because they, unlike most of the audience, hadn't missed it.

They gathered up their empty popcorn cartons and cups and headed towards the exit. They binned the rubbish and clattered down the stairs, emerging into the late afternoon.

"What now?" asked Frankie. They still had a good hour to kill before they could eat, and the shops were beginning to close.

"We can go for a walk," suggested Nessa doubtfully. "Have you ever been to the park?"

Frankie shook her head.

"Come on."

They chattered as they walked, dissecting the movie and, in

Frankie's case, speculating on what it meant for future ones.

Nessa knew the back lanes and footpaths around town in a way Frankie, who lived eight miles away, did not, so she acted as guide. They skirted around the local academy, silent and empty for the weekend, with whom St Drogo's had a less than friendly rivalry. They passed in front of some pretty houses, which were almost as old as the town itself, and then a nursing home, and finally came to the archway which, with its open gates, marked the entrance to the park.

"It's not much," said Nessa, as they went in, "but it's pretty."

Could she...should she...dare she take Frankie's hand? Was it too soon?

Yes, it was, so her fingers itching, she kept her hands to herself, thrusting them safely into her jacket pockets.

They walked around the meandering paths. They lingered by the ornamental pond where they watched the fish. They discovered the public toilets had, at some point, been converted into a café; the café had closed for the season but still had a sun-bleached menu board for ice creams in its window.

They sat on a covered bench where they talked about school and plans for afterwards, books, films, and ViewHooers. They talked about Frankie's family, and about Nessa's, and about the truly execrable reality series that had become a must-see Saturday night phenomenon.

The sun set, and it was time to head to the restaurant.

Someone had locked the gates, so after a few minutes of horror followed by a few more of hysterical laughter, they climbed over a wall and dropped onto the verge next to a minor road. There, clutching each other's shoulders in relief, they howled hysterically some more.

*

They'd recovered themselves by the time they arrived at the Taj Mahal. Taj Mahal wasn't an inventive name for an Indian restaurant, but Tovington wasn't an inventive kind of place, and the name fitted the location well enough.

A smiling waiter showed them to a window table, which offered a view across the high street. The restaurant was at the edge of the shopping area, so there wasn't much to see: pavements, an occasional passing car or dog walker, and on the opposite side of the road, an optician's and a chiropractor's.

Soft, twangy sitar music played from the restaurant's speakers. Nessa did her best to ignore it.

The waiter brought them poppadoms, mango chutney, and mint raita, and took their orders for their main courses: two garlic naan, chicken rogan josh for Nessa, and chicken and mushroom balti for Frankie.

They ate the poppadoms, and if their hands brushed as they reached for the dip, it wasn't planned.

Other customers arrived, and gradually the restaurant filled. There were a large, loud birthday party made up of three generations of a single family (the tweenagers looking uncomfortable in their best clothes), and a couple of couples, one of which held hands across the table even while they were eating.

"Hardly a practical arrangement, is it?" Frankie observed, as one half of the couple tried to cut a pakora with the side of a fork, and half the pakora skidded off their plate, onto the floor.

"Maybe not, but they're cute. And so much in love!"

Frankie might have grunted, "Ugh," but maybe Nessa imagined it.

They were too full of curry and naan to want dessert, so they lingered over too-strong tea until the time came to head to the stop from where Frankie was to catch the last bus home.

They stood next to the shelter, underneath a street lamp, in a spot of white light. A screen with pixelated letters told them the next bus would be for Gudmellingham, leaving at seven thirty. Ten minutes to go.

They'd talked all afternoon, apart from when the film was on, but now Nessa could think of nothing to say.

Was now the moment? How was she supposed to do this? She lacked experience in the rituals of dating, and everything she'd ever read had told her things would happen naturally or the boy would take the initiative. But what if there was no boy?

She'd been the one to ask Frankie out, so should she be the one to take the next step?

"You don't need to wait with me," said Frankie.

"What if I want to?"

"I guess it'd be all right."

Now. Don't miss your moment.

Nessa reached out and, as Frankie said, "Thanks for—" their fingers touched. Nessa curled her hand to capture Frankie's palm and tried to pull her closer. She leaned in, her eyes half-closed and her lips puckering.

Frankie flinched and jumped backwards, out of the lamplight, yanking her hand free. "What the hell!" she yelled, outraged and horrified, and Nessa had no idea what she'd done wrong.

Nessa and Frankie stared at each other. Nessa tried to make out Frankie's expression, but the dusk made it impossible.

"Was this supposed to be a date?" Frankie demanded.

Nessa stared. Hadn't it been obvious?

"Oh, my God. You thought we were on a date. Didn't you?" Frankie looked and sounded appalled.

"Didn't you?" asked Nessa.

"No! Why would I?"

Nessa felt as though she'd been stabbed in the gut. When she'd learned Frankie hadn't been interested in Kai, she'd been so sure, so confident Frankie would be at least open to the possibility of a same sex relationship. She'd put herself out there, and Frankie was horrified.

Nessa felt sick to her stomach, and beyond, deep into her intestines.

"I want you to go now." Frankie's voice was cold. "I'll wait on my own."

Nessa swallowed. She mumbled something. She had no idea what. An apology, an excuse? She didn't know.

She backed away from the heat of Frankie's anger. As soon as she was sure she'd been swallowed up in the shadows, she broke into a run.

*

How had she managed to make such a mess of things? And where did the impulse to scream so many sweary words come from?

Tears of hurt and humiliation pricked at her eyes. She wiped them away fiercely with the back of her hand.

Frankie hated the idea this had been a date.

Hated the idea of dating her.

Hated her.

Frankie's reaction had been homophobic. But Frankie wasn't like that.

Was she?

Nessa needed to calm down before she headed to school, so she detoured onto the network of back streets and lanes which hid behind the town's main thoroughfares.

She found a garden wall, topped with large, flat slabs, to sit on.

There, the stone cold against her thighs, feet swinging above the ground, sitting hunched over, she put her head in her hands and allowed herself to weep.

Her crying jag didn't last long, only a few seconds, but long enough to leave her feeling as though someone had scooped out her stomach and heart. Did she look as ashen as she felt?

She found a tissue in one of her pockets, wiped away the last of the tears, and eased herself off the wall, dropping the six inches to the ground. She hoped she didn't have panda eyes from the tiny bit of mascara she'd bothered to use.

As she walked through the town's industrial estate, its businesses dark and shuttered, she caught sight of two people, one with a distinctive and familiar platinum ponytail, the other a bearded man.

Poppy dragged the man behind a tree as Nessa approached.

Poppy obviously didn't want to be seen, which was fine with Nessa. Nessa wasn't in the mood for small talk either.

Knowing Poppy was out and she'd have their room to herself gave Nessa courage to return to Hobby, where she signed in, bypassed the common room, and headed upstairs.

She showered, removing the vestiges of her ruined make-up, put on some fresh pyjamas, drew the curtains, turned the light off, and crawled into bed. She curled up under her duvet, her face to the wall and her back to the world.

*

She was still lying in the dark when Poppy came in, less than an hour later. Poppy turned the key in the lock and pushed the door so hard it banged against the side of Nessa's desk.

Startled, Nessa squawked, which made Poppy scream in surprise.

Poppy flicked the light on. "What the hell are you doing, lying here in the dark! You scared me!"

"You scared me first!" protested Nessa. "Banging around like that!"

"My bad. Seriously, though, what are you doing, skulking around in the dark?"

"I wasn't skulking. I was lying down. In my bed."

"In the dark. At a quarter past nine on a Saturday evening. It's not normal behaviour. Why aren't you downstairs with the rest of your cronies?"

"Migraine," lied Nessa. "I wanted some peace."

"Didn't know you got migraines."

"I don't. Not often. It's better now."

"Huh."

It wasn't a good lie. Weren't migraines supposed to last for hours? Sometimes days, even? No wonder Poppy was sceptical.

"Who were you with earlier? Your boyfriend?" Nessa didn't care, but she wanted to change the topic.

"Who did you think it was? My dealer?" Poppy acted as though she'd said something hilarious.

"Is it serious?"

"As a Covid outbreak in a nursing home." That wasn't funny either.

"He looked older than you."

"So?"

"So, nothing. Just an observation. You two serious?"

"Nah. He's convenient."

Nessa shook her head. Why would anyone settle for convenient?

Chapter Eighteen

N essa was in the middle of confiding in Meg when Tim and Tarone joined them at lunch the following Monday.

"Well, aren't you two rays of sunshine?" asked Tim blithely, as he slid into his seat.

"Read the room, mate," said Tarone.

Meg and Nessa gloomily prodded their food. Nessa knew why she wasn't hungry, a bruised heart did that to you, but she didn't know what had got into Meg.

To Meg and Nessa, Tim said, "Cheer up, it might never happen!"

"It already did," said Nessa. "Or didn't. That's the problem."

Tim and Tarone leaned in. "Do tell," said Tim.

"Only if you swear on all your mothers' lives this won't go any further," said Nessa, forgetting she hadn't wanted Tim to know about her sexual orientation.

The guys swore.

"Frankie and I went to the pictures on Saturday. And to the Indian afterwards."

"Movies and a restaurant! Nice!" Tim leered. "Sounds almost like a date to me!"

Tarone swatted Tim around the head.

"What? Oh! You're serious! Like it was a date for real? I didn't know you were—"

Tarone moved to swat him again, but this time Tim managed to dodge out of the way. "Oi! Stop that!"

Nessa made a weird motion with her head; it started out as a nod but swiftly turned into a shake of resignation or disapproval at their antics. "I put myself out there. Frankie shot me down. Viciously. We won't be going out again. I'm not sure we'll even be talking to each other."

"Don't take it personally," said Tim blithely. "She doesn't talk to Kai either."

"What's Kai got to do with anything?" asked Meg, lifting her head and focusing in the same way a hungry dog does when it gets a sniff of dinner.

"He asked her out at the beginning of term. They had one date and..." Tim made a cutting-his-throat gesture and a squelching noise.

"And Jez dumped me yesterday, so, you know, misery loves company and all that," said Meg.

Nessa found it hard to sympathise. "Weren't you going to dump him at the beginning of term?"

"I considered it. But better to have a boyfriend than not, right?"

"A bird in the hand?" asked Nessa quizzically.

"Exactly."

"I'm not sure that's how relationships are supposed to work," said Tarone.

Tim asked, "Why are you so gutted if you wanted to dump him anyway?"

"Nobody likes to be dumped."

"So this isn't about him so much as about your wounded pride?"

"Exactly. Hey, Tim, you don't happen to know whether Kai needs someone to cheer him up, do you?"

*

The biggest gifts Moira's research into asexuality gave her were the realisations there were other people who didn't obsess about sex, and not everyone was preoccupied with relationships or believed in "the one" with more fervour than many people believed in God. She wasn't an outlier in the human condition. She simply didn't fit into the mould society liked to portray as normal.

With fascination, she read other people's accounts of wanting neither sex nor romantic connection, and she found them validating. She also read about people who didn't want sex but still yearned for romance, kissing, and cuddling, although she found those stories harder to relate to.

She read about the split attraction model, which was a new idea to her, and one that came with new language. She struggled to get her head around it. It challenged the way she'd been conditioned to believe romance and sex were inextricably linked.

How many times had she heard humans needed both sex and romance to reinforce a relationship? And she knew plenty of people who made rituals of their anniversaries and of Valentine's Day, scheduling romantic trysts in their diaries months ahead of time.

She also found challenging the idea you could be asexual and still have sex, although she almost got that. Sex was a gift you gave your partner. It wasn't about the physical act so much as about love for another person. And if, like her, you'd been brought up to believe sex was inevitable and expected...

What she struggled most with was, how could you be asexual and seek sex out? How did that work?

Where were the lines between being ace and allo? Did lines even exist? Being on a spectrum suggested there weren't any, but if there weren't lines, what was the point of the concept of asexuality at all? In her darkest, most doubtful moments, she questioned whether it was even real.

But that was nonsense.

Wasn't it?

All these shades of ace.

In the effort to be inclusive, and inclusivity was surely a good thing, was the fundamental idea of what it meant to be asexual being diluted into nothing? Was that why so many people were inclined to discount its existence, to discount as "normal" the thoughts, feelings, and behaviours associated with asexuality?

Was asexuality simply a reaction against the pervasive dominance of a societal model that emphasised sexual appetites, heterosexual pairings, and the importance of children?

Asexuality, along with homosexuality, bisexuality, pansexuality, and other labels made it possible for minorities to say we're different. We're here. Recognise us, and don't model society in a way that leaves us out.

Maybe that was all Moira wanted, no, *needed* it to do.

Moira was still new to this. Too new and uncertain to voice her questions.

The only things she knew for sure were: she wasn't attracted to other people; she was on the extreme end of the aroace spectrum; if she'd known there were people like her when she was younger, she would not have spent so many years feeling broken and disconnected from the world around her.

She embraced the concept of asexuality because it gave her a route towards self-acceptance and self-forgiveness.

She would have to work on the rest.

*

Wanted to check u r okay.

Moira was so touched by the text from Emily that tears pricked her eyes.

I'm fine, she replied, which wasn't true but, as she wasn't broken or bereft, fine was as good a description as any.

As an afterthought, she added:

Thanks for asking.

Her phone dinged a minute later.

Fine as in Freaked, Insecure, Neurotic, and Emotional?

A tsunami of conflicting emotions flooded over Moira: wry amusement; surprise Emily had questioned her answer; gratitude that she had. She stared at her phone as she tried to frame an answer.

Her phone dinged again, while she was still thinking.

Want to meet for coffee? I'm free after 3 this pm. Bothy Tea

Room?

Moira keyed her answer.

See you then.

She added a smiley face for good measure.

*

The Bothy Tea Room was a small café housed in a low slung, single-storey building, located in the tangled lanes behind the town's main street. Despite its name, it had never been a bothy; possibly it had once been someone's workshop, or maybe an animal shed.

The exterior walls were white with limewash. Inside, the interior walls were roughly hewn stone, and the lighting was dim. Under certain circumstances, some might even have described it as intimate. At 3:15 on a Tuesday afternoon, when the Bothy was particularly popular with young mothers with buggies and women of advancing years, the atmosphere leaned more towards informal and friendly.

As she wove her way across the room to bag a table, she waved at Murdo's mother and said hello to one of Mrs McCrossan's granddaughters, whose baby was wearing a cardigan Mrs McCrossan had bought from her.

She seated herself at a table for four, from where, with her back to the wall, she had an unobstructed view of the entrance.

One of the staff, who didn't look old enough to be out of high school, shuffled shyly forwards to take her order.

Moira was halfway through her first coffee, a decaf cappuccino, when Emily, full of gushing apologies for her tardiness, arrived. Moira waved her apologies away with a flap of her hand.

The shy waitress returned and took Emily's order for a pot of tea.

Emily settled herself, and after a couple of minutes of bland small talk, said, "You haven't reconsidered your position?"

"No." Moira felt an upwelling of disappointment and betrayal. Had Emily arranged the meeting in the hopes of changing her mind? "Did you expect me to?"

"No. It's good you're sticking to your guns."

Moira was surprised, pleased, and confused by her yo-yoing emotions. She didn't need Emily's approval, but she wanted it anyway. To make sure she had heard correctly, she said, "You are?"

"I am. And I'm sorry. I should have recognised how bad things had got before you exploded."

Moira protested weakly. "You have a full-time job." The implication was clear. The others didn't. Crafting was a retirement hobby for most of them; they'd had time to help in the shop. What they hadn't had was the inclination.

"Doesn't matter. I made a commitment."

Moira didn't want to have this argument. She tried tactfully to change the subject. "Cake?"

"I'm trying to apologise."

"I know. Apology accepted. Let's move on. So, I'm in the mood for another cappuccino. And a slice of the coffee and walnut."

Emily gave up on her apologies and put too much effort into vacillating between a fruit scone and a slab of chocolate tiffin.

Moira waved at the waitress, who came over and laboriously inscribed the details of their order onto her pad before heading off to fulfil it.

While Moira had a clear view of what the waitress was doing, Emily had to look over her shoulder. She rapidly either grew bored of watching or got a crick in her neck.

Emily turned around. "What are you going to do if you're not doing the shop? I can't imagine you sitting around, doing nothing."

Moira resisted the urge to shrug and toyed with her teaspoon instead. "I've still got my online shop. But honestly, it will do me good to have some time to myself. To regroup. I've been going through some stuff."

"Nothing serious, I hope."

"That depends on what you'd call serious. It's nothing life threatening, but I've been..." Moira didn't know how to start or whether she even wanted to.

Emily leaned forwards. "Go on. You've been...?"

"I've figured out a few things recently. About myself. More accurately, I suppose I've been forced to face stuff I've never allowed myself to think about before."

Emily waited. Her stillness and patience were in equal measure inviting and unnerving.

Moira bought herself some time by scraping the leftover milk foam from the side of her coffee cup and eating it off her teaspoon. She swallowed.

"There wasn't a word for it when I grew up. Leastways, not one I ever heard. So, when I didn't meet anyone I wanted to be with, I buried everything deep, deep down. Ignored it. But stuff like that doesn't go away. It affects you. Eats away at you, even if you don't know that's what it's doing."

"Go on," said Emily, gently.

Encouraged by Emily's lack of judgment, Moira continued, more boldly this time.

"I realised recently I'm ace. Asexual. And I've been remembering all sorts of things that have happened to me. Reliving them, almost, and I've been seeing things in a different light. It's been a lot."

The waitress returned with Moira's second coffee and their cakes. Moira waited until the waitress had removed the dead cup and had left again before saying, "I don't know why I'm telling you this."

But that wasn't true, was it? Moira knew exactly why. She needed someone to talk to, if only to get her thoughts in order, and she had nobody else to tell.

She took a sip from her new cup, put it down, and fiddled with its handle. "You're the first person I've told."

"I'm honoured," said Emily as though she meant it. "Coming out's a big deal. Thank you for trusting me."

Moira felt stupid for not realising it before, but here was another reason for telling Emily. Emily would have had her own experiences of coming out; she'd understand the import of it in a way many people could not.

"I feel stupid. How did I not know this about myself before? Now I do know, what am I supposed to do with the information? I'm still the same person I've always been, but this is new and different, and I don't know how to tell people I've known for years about it, or even if I should."

"Forget should. Do you want to?"

"I don't know."

"Why not?"

"Because..." she trailed off, unable to finish the sentence. "What would you do if you were me?"

"I'm not you. And our situations aren't the same."

"I know. But I'd like to hear someone else's perspective on this."

"All right. If you're sure."

"I'm sure."

"First, you don't have to come out all at once. I didn't. I'm out now, obviously." She gestured in the direction of her backpack. "But it was a gradual process, not some grand big bang. I did it in stages. First, my best friend. My brother next. Then my parents. I went to university and, at some point, I... I was going to say, I stopped hiding it, but I don't think I ever hid, so much as I never went out of my way to be obvious. Anyway, the rest of the family gradually cottoned on, especially after I took a plus one to my cousin Jacinta's wedding." Judging by her tone and the expression on her face, Emily's memories of the occasion were amusing ones. "Just because you haven't told anyone today, other than me, obviously, doesn't mean you can't tell them tomorrow. Or the day after. Or not at all."

Moira pondered but came to no conclusions. She'd have to consider it some more, later.

"What do you want to do with it?" asked Emily.

"What do you mean?"

"For me, being out helps me to meet people. The right kind of people, I mean. Women. I want to attract attention. I'm advertising my wares, so to speak. So, do you want to meet someone?"

"Why would I?"

"There are all kinds of ace."

Moira had read enough to know that, but she was impressed Emily did too.

"My point is, if you don't want to meet someone, there might be less reason for you to tell anyone. Unless it would make you feel better, you know, for yourself."

Would it? Moira didn't know.

"Look, tell me if I'm out of order here, but I've got an idea."

"Oh?"

"There's a group, an LGBTQ+ group, that meets in Oban. Maybe it would help you to come along."

"Are there other aces there?"

"Not as far as I know, but there's plenty of people who've had to deal with similar issues. It might do you good to meet them. Talk to them."

Moira didn't know whether it was a good idea, but she didn't say no.

Chapter Nineteen

"**H**appy birthday!"

"Wha'? 'S not my birthday." Nessa winced as Poppy turned on the room lights. She tried to bury herself deeper under her duvet. Her alarm hadn't gone off, which meant it was too early to have to deal with whatever nonsense the morning was throwing at her.

"Course it is! I wrote it down." From across the room, Poppy flashed her diary so Nessa could see. "And I've got you a card and a present."

Eh?

Oh.

Oh, God.

Meg had warned her about this, but never in Nessa's wildest dreams had she believed Poppy would do anything to mark her birthday. She, Nessa, had forgotten it. Why couldn't Poppy have had the decency to do the same?

Could she brazen it out?

No. She'd already told Poppy today wasn't her birthday and, even if she managed to recover from that faux pas, there was no way to hide the fact that nobody, not even her best friends, had given her any gifts.

Better to 'fess up. But, God, how embarrassing!

"I'm sorry. But it isn't my birthday. I lied to you at the beginning of term."

Poppy's eyes bulged, and her lips narrowed. "You lied. Why would you do that?"

"I... Well... You were so happy when you guessed I was a Libra. I didn't want to disappoint you."

"You. Lied." Poppy wasn't going to let it go.

"Yes. But, when you think about it, it was a teensy white lie. Done with the noblest of intentions." And that was another lie, wasn't it? The only intention she'd had was to get the conversation over with as speedily as possible.

"When is your birthday?"

"Twentieth of July."

"Cancer! That explains everything! I've tried and tried to get on with you! I couldn't understand why nothing worked. I mean, everybody likes me, except you! But now it makes perfect sense, you...you *crab*!"

Nessa couldn't help herself. "What's my being Cancer got to do with anything?"

Poppy huffed. "Don't you know anything? Me, Aquarius. You, Cancer. Ours are the least compatible star signs out there."

"Oh."

"Yeah. Oh."

Poppy folded her arms across her chest, flounced across the room, and onto her bed.

"For what it's worth, I'm sorry. I honestly didn't think it was a big deal."

Poppy sniffed and didn't accept her apology.

*

"**W**hat are we doing up here?" asked Tarone at the next rehearsal. They were sitting in a small balcony at the rear of the great hall, killing time until Nessa had to be on stage.

"We're hiding. Leastways, I am. You're keeping me company."

"Who are you hiding from?"

"The Popsicle."

"Any particular reason why?"

"Does there need to be a reason? Other than the usual, I mean?"

"You tell me. I know you don't like her much, but you don't usually go to these lengths to avoid her."

"You're right. She's angry with me. I mean positively, incandescently angry."

Tarone's lips twitched. "That angry, eh?"

"And then some."

"Care to tell me why?"

"Would you believe me if I said because I'm Cancer, not Libra?"

"No?"

Nessa told him the whole story.

He struggled not to laugh.

*

Later, during a break between scenes, Nessa sought Frankie out, hoping to clear the air. "Hey, Frankie. Can we talk?"

"I don't have anything to say to you."

"Please?"

Frankie tried to squeeze past, but Nessa danced in front of her, blocking her way.

"I need to get on stage."

"Not for another couple of minutes you don't. They're still setting up for the next scene."

Frankie's eyes narrowed. "What, you're going to keep me here against my will? You want to try to kiss me again, is that it? Can't take no for an answer?"

Did Frankie see Nessa like that? That was an appalling notion! "No! I wanted to apol—"

Frankie, on a roll, didn't let her finish. "What is it with everyone around here? First Kai. Now you. Why does everything always have to be about sex? Why can't people simply be friends? Romance ruins everything, but it's all anyone around here seems to think about!"

"Frankie, I—"

"Get out of my way." Frankie shoved Nessa into a wall, her anger and upset putting unexpected force behind the push. Nessa staggered, tottering three steps before she managed to grab hold of a handy shelf and steady herself.

By the time Nessa had regained her balance and brushed herself down, Frankie was long gone.

But Poppy was standing in front of her, a malicious gleam of victory in her eyes.

*

Poppy feigned the onset of menstrual cramps and pleaded her way out of rehearsal twenty minutes early.

Dinah was waiting for Nessa on the front steps of Hobby House when Nessa returned. She caught Nessa by the arm. "You might not want to go in right now."

Nessa groaned. "What's Poppy done?"

"What makes you think Poppy's done anything?"

"She walked in on the tail end of me trying to apologise to someone, and from the look on her face, I knew she was going to make a big deal out of it."

"You want to tell me your side of the story? Then I'll tell you what Poppy's been saying."

"Ugh! Okay. First, I've been tempted to tell you this for a while. But it's awkward and embarrassing and..."

"Spit it out. Thanks to Poppy, it's safe to assume I've already figured some of it out."

"That I'm gay?"

"Yeah."

Nessa took some comfort from the matter-of-fact way Dinah spoke. Clearly it wasn't a big deal for her.

"There's this girl I like. I mean, like-like. I've been crushing on her since the beginning of term and, last week, I plucked up the courage to ask her out. And we had a great time until..."

"Until?"

"I tried to kiss her at the end of the evening. She freaked. I've been trying to apologise ever since, but she's been avoiding me. We were both at rehearsal, so I took the opportunity and I... I cornered her. I wanted to make her listen. But it was a stupid thing to do. She lashed out. Said some things. Pushed me and ran off. And Poppy overheard the whole thing."

"You need to know, the way Poppy's telling it, you tried to assault Frankie and got mad when you didn't get your way."

The twenty minutes Poppy had bought herself had been all the time she'd needed to spread her latest gossip around Hobby. By now, the entire common room had heard about how lesbian Nessa had pressed her unwanted attentions on an unsuspecting Frankie, and how Frankie was so traumatised she couldn't bring herself to look Nessa in the eye.

"What! No! It wasn't like that at all!" Unless... Was that how Frankie had seen things too? She'd screwed up epically, hadn't she?

Dinah pulled Nessa into a quick hug. "I believe you. And most people will take your side. Poppy has had it in for you the last day or so."

"Yeah, and that's also my fault."

"You want to tell me about that too, before we head in?"

*

There was a full-blown, ding-dong fight going on when Nessa and Dinah arrived at the common room. Nessa hung back, unsure whether to be horrified or gratified at the number of people, Dhriti included, who were on their feet, out-shouting Poppy, letting her know in no uncertain terms that whatever Nessa might have done, Poppy's outing her was bang out of order.

"Plus," said Dhriti, chin thrust forwards and pugnacious, "We've only got your word for any of it, and why should we believe you?"

"Why don't you ask her yourself?" Poppy snarled. "She's right over there." She pointed to where Dinah and Nessa were lurking at the common room's entrance.

All heads turned in Nessa's direction.

Nessa gulped. Had there always been this many girls in Hobby?

She stepped forwards. Lifted her chin. "What do you want to know?"

A multitude of voices clamoured.

Dinah stepped around Nessa, held up her hands, and cried out, "One! At! A! Time! Dhriti, you first."

Dhriti glanced around and into the abrupt silence said, "Why don't we let Nessa tell her version of the story?"

The telling was no easier this time around. In fact, it was harder. Previously she'd told friends who, while they mightn't have approved of everything she'd done, liked her well enough to stand by her anyway. She was less certain where she stood with some of her housemates, especially those who were watching the evening's spectacle with avid fervour.

Nessa told them everything, trying to be open and honest instead of defensive. She told them she was a lesbian, which set the context for her asking Frankie out. She said she'd misread the signals, that none of this was Frankie's fault, and she'd handled things badly, both on Saturday and since.

"She's lying!" yelled Poppy. "Once a liar, always a liar!"

"I'm not lying," wailed Nessa. "You're mad at me because of the birthday thing, and I've already apologised to you for that. But, if it makes you feel better, I'll apologise again." The birthday debacle was, as far as Nessa was concerned, the only thing she'd done wrong that was any of Poppy's business, and she regretted it.

"What birthday thing?" asked Elspeth.

Nessa told them. Some people laughed. Others were bemused. A couple were appalled. Overall, the reaction was better than Nessa had feared.

Nessa started to relax, but Poppy, sensing the atmosphere shift in Nessa's favour, shouted again. "She's a liar! She's a queer! And I have to share a room with—"

*

"What! Is! Going! On!" The foghorn voice of the Head of House blared over everyone else.

The room fell silent, and everyone turned to face Ms Breckenridge, who stood in the doorway, fisted hands on her hips.

"Well?"

Nobody spoke. Nessa, like everyone else, tried not to catch Ms Breckenridge's eye.

"Dinah? Perhaps you would like to enlighten me."

"Um. Poppy or Nessa could explain better."

Nessa took in Ms Breckenridge's thin lips and narrowed eyes, and gulped.

"Poppy?"

Poppy did not gulp. She lifted her chin. "Ask Vanessa Clarkson. She started it."

There was uproar. Even amid the cacophony of raised voices, Nessa could make out several people protesting Nessa hadn't even been in the room when the argument broke out.

Ms Breckenridge turned to Nessa. "Is that true?"

"Um. Yes, Ma'am," but the doubt in her voice was her undoing.

"Nessa?"

"I—" She felt like a small, furry creature caught in the headlights of an enormous pantechnicon heading along the road at a steady sixty-four miles an hour. Ms Breckenridge's stare was more than usually stern and barely banked fires of furious anger flickered behind her pupils. "I didn't mean to. It was an accident."

Maybe Ms Breckenridge read something in Nessa's expression. Fear? Embarrassment? Confusion? Uncertainty? Her demeanour softened slightly. "Come with me."

Nessa followed Ms Breckenridge through to a small room that contained little more than scratched tables and plastic chairs which had been salvaged from a classroom upgrade in the main school. The students sometimes used it as a meeting room for study groups, or, if the common room was particularly busy, to play board games.

Ms Breckenridge closed the door behind her and gestured for Nessa to sit. She pulled out a chair from the adjacent side of the table to Nessa's and sat at an angle meant to be as unthreatening as possible, one that didn't put the table between them. "Why don't you tell me what happened, from the beginning."

Where was the beginning? Was it her fateful first meeting with Poppy? Or asking Frankie out on a date? Or the ridiculous birthday fiasco, or... "I'm gay."

Ms Breckenridge's eyebrows lifted. "That's what they were arguing about? That you're gay?"

The suppressed outrage in Ms Breckenridge's voice mollified Nessa.

"No. At least, I don't think so. I think they were angry at Poppy because she," Nessa stared at her hands, "outed me. And they were angry because I lied to Poppy, not about my being gay, about something else, and I don't even know any more."

Ms Breckenridge inhaled deeply and exhaled slowly. "I see. Let's take this one step at a time. Why did Poppy out you?"

"Spite?" suggested Nessa. "She's angry with me."

"For any particular reason?"

"I did something stupid. At the start of term. And when Poppy found out, she was hurt."

"What did you do?"

"It's silly."

"Maybe. But if it has caused this much trouble, it also sounds serious. Don't you think?"

Yet again, Nessa had to explain how she'd lied about her birthday, a white lie that had come to haunt her in a big way. She told Ms Breckenridge about asking Frankie out, about the way that had ended, and how, when she'd tried to make her peace this evening that, too, had gone horribly wrong. She finished by saying, "Poppy overheard. She left rehearsal earlier than I did, and when I came in…"

"I see," said Ms Breckenridge. "Very well. You may go for now. Send Poppy in."

Nessa didn't know how the conversation between Ms Breckenridge and Poppy went, but Poppy reappeared a while later, looking mutinous. She glared at Nessa and told Dinah she was next.

*

When Dinah re-emerged, Ms Breckenridge behind her, she gave Nessa a discreet thumbs up. Ms Breckenridge shooed the students to bed and said she'd continue her investigations—investigations!—the following day.

How had the disagreement between Nessa and Poppy escalated into an affair that required a full-scale enquiry?

Going to their shared room was beyond awkward. Tense, Nessa had no idea what to expect. But Poppy didn't say anything, just stormed around until she buried herself under her duvet cover.

Nessa lay in bed, rolled onto her side, eyes open in the darkness, too wired to sleep. Across the room, Poppy was also awake. Nessa could tell from the unnatural silence and the lack of slow, steady breathing.

*

A t lunchtime the following day, Nessa braved the school cafeteria where the bright, overhead lighting made her feel as though she was under a spotlight.

Rumours were spreading. Nessa felt them like physical things, hot and itchy between her shoulder blades. Even if only 10 per cent of the students were noticing or talking about her, it was 10 per cent too many.

She tried to keep her head bowed and she narrowed her attention onto the tuna pasta bake she'd selected but for which she had next to no appetite. She skewered a bit of fusilli with her fork, lifted it to her mouth, and chewed. How did something so small feel large enough to choke her? She put her fork down and pushed her plate away.

Meg watched, concerned. "You have to eat something."

"I know." She'd barely managed toast at breakfast, and her stomach was sending her mixed messages of hunger and revulsion. She pulled her plate closer again and had another go, this time scooping up some tuna and sweetcorn, which she hoped would be easier to cope with.

"Uh-oh," muttered Meg.

Nessa followed the direction of Meg's gaze.

"Have you any idea—" The cafeteria suddenly fell silent as Tarone's voice carried across the room.

Nessa spun around, ducked her head, and tried to be invisible. Then, compelled by some force she couldn't control, she turned to watch the drama unfold.

Two tables over, Tarone, his arms braced against the back of a chair, glowered at Poppy.

Now Tarone had everyone's attention. "Have you any idea how crappy what you did was?" Behind him, Tim stood tall, arms crossed over his chest, nodding in an exaggerated manner.

Poppy looked up. All Nessa could see was the back of Poppy's head, but she had no trouble imagining the sullen, defiant expression on her face. Poppy put her cutlery down and said something Nessa couldn't hear.

Tarone scowled. He moved closer, leaning over the table and invading her personal space, forcing her to lean back as far as possible in her chair. "That's no excuse for what you're doing. You're not in nursery anymore. Don't behave like it." He curled his lip at her and, to Nessa's surprise, earned himself a hearty round of applause.

Tim and Tarone collected their meals before coming over to sit with Nessa and Meg.

"Bitch," muttered Tarone as he unloaded his tray. Nessa didn't need to ask who he was talking about.

"Pity we don't have scold's bridles anymore," said Meg.

Nessa shook her head. She wouldn't wish that on anyone, not even Poppy. Although, on second thoughts, maybe she would. It was a nice daydream.

Tarone had a similar idea; he whipped out his sketchbook and a couple of felt-tips. Between forkfuls of pasta bake he drew a caricature. When he finished, he held up the cartoon for the others to see. Nessa laughed along with the rest, and the people further along the table craned their necks to see what was happening. A small crowd gathered around, and the laughter grew.

"Please," said Nessa, her laughter turning to misgivings, "put it away. You'll make things worse."

Tarone closed the pad. "Sorry, guys. Show's over."

"Thanks."

Tarone, either by way of apology or justification, said, "She was bang out of order. You know that, right?"

"She was angry with me. Lashing out."

"Don't make excuses for her. You might forgive her if she'd done it once and had apologised afterwards. But she's still doing it. Still talking."

Tim agreed. "I heard her in history. Bitch." He paused. "I'd still do her, though."

Nessa, Meg, and Tarone rounded on him in disbelief.

"What? I'm only saying. She might be a bitch but she's a hot bitch!"

*

Only partly because of the deliberately public stance Tarone had taken, the gossip spread through the school like wildfire, almost as fast as Thomas Mitchum's expulsion, suspension, banishment, or whatever it was called, had done the year before. Nessa hated being the focus of attention, especially as what they were talking about wasn't worth talking about, shouldn't have been anyone else's business, and people she barely knew were looking at her with curiosity, sympathy, or pity. Nonetheless, she was relieved the student body was far less interested in her orientation than outraged by what Poppy had done. The consensus appeared to be that, no matter the provocation, Poppy had gone beyond the limits of acceptable behaviour when she'd outed Nessa.

Poppy, who had never been nearly as popular as she'd believed herself to be, was suddenly persona non grata.

"What I don't get is why, if people are so outraged about what Poppy did, they still talk about it," said Nessa gloomily to Meg. They were sitting in their favourite corner of the library, doing their best to hide out.

"Huh?" Meg glanced up from the Shakespeare sonnet she was covering in highlighter.

"They can't pass on the gossip about Poppy outing me without outing me. So, in a way, they're as guilty as she is, but they still act outraged. It's..." Nessa groped for a word, didn't come up with one, so said,

"Ugh!" instead.

*

Nessa's mind spun with all the things she could have done differently. She could have been honest with Poppy. No doubt there would still have been some tension, but it wouldn't have been so bad. Poppy wouldn't have been so angry and would have had no reason to bear a grudge.

Nessa could have come out earlier. Would that have been better? She could have come out on her own terms, instead of being so abruptly, cruelly outed by someone else. But she hadn't been ready. So, no, maybe she couldn't have done that differently.

She could have been more explicit with Frankie, instead of assuming Frankie was on the same page as her. Did other people have to set out every particular when setting up a date? She didn't think so. She didn't know. Maybe she needed to live with her hurt and embarrassment for a while longer, before chalking that one up to experience.

She wished she had someone to talk to about this besides Meg. Meg was a good listener, but she couldn't relate, not when she lived up to society's expectations and norms. How much easier would it be to be straight in a straight world? Or, how much nicer would it be to live in a world where queer relationships were the norm, and the heteros had to go through this kind of grief, instead?

But no. Nessa wouldn't wish this kind of confusion on anyone.

She wished she had a place where she could talk about this stuff.

Which gave her an idea.

Was it a good idea?

Given how many bad ones she'd been having recently, she wasn't sure she trusted her judgement. Maybe she needed to nurse the idea for a while, to be sure.

Nessa barely got through the days that followed. She wouldn't have done, were it not for the staunch support from her friends and a few un-expected allies, and the promise that, come Saturday, she'd be travelling to Scotland for the half-term break. Hopefully, some of the craziness would have died down by the time school recommenced.

On the plus side, Poppy wasn't speaking to her anymore.

Chapter Twenty

The train journey north took as long as the one by car, but Nessa didn't mind. She dozed, listened to music, watched films, and read, and it saved Dad from making the drive. Plus, there was something novel about making the trip on her own.

At least Dad didn't expect her to get the bus from Glasgow. Instead, he collected her from Central Station, and Cindy and Finlay came with him. They had made a day of it and, before picking Nessa up, they'd done some shopping, acquired a few things for the house, and been on a tour of the abandoned platforms underneath the train station.

After stowing Nessa's suitcase in the car, they went to a restaurant that specialised in fancy burgers.

Halfway through their meal, Nessa became aware of a silent conversation going on between Cindy and Dad.

Cindy lifted her eyebrows in a non-verbal question.

Dad gave the tiniest of nods.

They smiled softly at each other.

"Nessa—" said Dad.

"Finlay—" said Cindy.

"We've got something we want to tell you."

Finlay stared at them, wide-eyed, even as he continued to eat a chip, rodent-style, nibbling his way along its length. Nessa put her burger down.

"We've set a date for our wedding!" Cindy and Dad finished together.

"Did you rehearse that?" said Nessa. "You must have rehearsed that. I mean, congratulations!"

"Thank you," said Cindy.

"We didn't tell you before because we wanted to wait until we'd got the both of you together," Dad said.

Nessa smiled, warmed by the consideration. They'd gone out of their way to include her. "Thanks," she murmured. "Tell us more. Like, when is it?"

"The last Saturday in June, next year. Your exams will be over, and you'll have finished school." Cindy nodded at Nessa. "We're going for a civil ceremony, with only closest friends and family. We'll have a bigger evening do separately at Murdo's. Nice and informal."

"We want to focus more on the celebration than the ceremony," said Dad. "More knees-up, less pomp."

Finlay, bored with the conversation, asked, "Can I have pudding?"

*

This time of year, night came early, and it was dark by the time they left Glasgow. Other than rain splattering the windscreen, the swish of the wipers, taillights of the cars in front, and headlights of oncoming traffic, there was nothing to see. Next to Nessa, Finlay watched a video, listening to the soundtrack through headphones.

Cindy, Dad, and Nessa ran through their plans for the next fortnight. Nessa had booked a couple of driving lessons as well as her practical test, which she was to take the Thursday before her return to school. She also hoped to squeeze in as much driving practice as possible with Cindy and Dad, wanted to catch up with Moira, and with a groan, admitted she had a heap of homework.

"Sounds like you'll be busy," said Dad.

"Tell me more about the wedding." Nessa glanced at Finlay, who had fallen asleep. His mouth hung open, and he looked like he was about to drool.

"We're going to have the ceremony at the Loch View Hotel."

"Nice," murmured Nessa, thinking of the hotel she'd seen on the road to Oban. She'd never been inside, but she knew the hotel commanded spectacular views down a sea loch, along the coast of the mainland, and across to several islands. On a fine day, visitors could see as far as Islay.

"We'll take you while you're here," said Cindy.

"Maybe combine it with some driving practice?" suggested Dad.

"Sounds good," said Nessa.

"We've still got loads of details to sort out," said Cindy. "Even a small wedding requires a huge amount of organisation."

"Let me know if there is anything I can do to help." Nessa wasn't sure whether she meant it or not. She couldn't imagine what she might give in the way of assistance, particularly since she wouldn't be around much.

Cindy appreciated the offer, anyway.

"Next year's going to be a big one. It'll also be your eighteenth," said

Dad. "Any ideas what you want to do for it?"

Nessa made a noncommittal noise. Some people at school threw lavish parties, but she wasn't sure that was her kind of thing. Plus, her birthday fell in July, and her friends would have scattered for the summer. Would it be possible to gather enough people together to have a decent celebration? Might it be easier to throw a reunion bash when she got to university?

Dad quizzed Nessa about school.

"This term's been crazy busy. The teachers are piling on the work, like they've suddenly remembered we've got A levels at the end of the year. This year's much more demanding than last. Plus, I've been fitting in a driving lesson each week, and I signed up for the show."

"I admit, I was surprised when you told us," said Dad. "I didn't think you were into theatre."

"I'm not," admitted Nessa. "But it seemed like a good idea at the time. Now I'm stuck with it."

"If you hate it so much, can't you get out of it?"

"I don't think so. They made us sign a contract. To be honest, it's not too bad, and I don't have much to do. At rehearsals, I spend more time waiting around, doing my homework and knitting, than I do rehearsing. Plus, I get to hang out with Tarone a lot, which is fun."

"Speaking of knitting, Moira's started teaching me too."

"That's great, Cindy!" Nessa's response was more enthusiastic than the news warranted, but she was relieved the shift in the conversation meant she didn't have to skirt around some of the more embarrassing aspects of the last couple of weeks. She still hadn't decided how much, or indeed *whether* to tell them.

"What can I say? You inspired me. I'm nowhere near as good as you though. Moira never says anything, but I can tell she thinks I'm slow."

*

They made a dash through the rain into the house. Cindy packed Finlay off to bed, while Dad rustled up tea and biscuits for everyone else.

Nessa, asking herself how travel could be so exhausting when all she'd done was sit while others did the work, retreated to her room as soon as the mugs and plates had been loaded into the dishwasher. She tried to look outside as she drew her bedroom curtains, but she couldn't see anything other than unremitting black.

She pulled the curtains across, climbed into her bed, and snuggled under her duvet. It was good to be home.

The last thing she was aware of before she fell asleep was rain splattering against her window.

*

The rain must have stopped sometime before dawn because when Nessa woke up soon after eight, although she heard water dripping heavily from the guttering, the sun was shining.

Nessa eased herself out of bed, stretched, and peeked outside. The landscape had changed dramatically in the few weeks she'd been away. Autumn had taken hold, and the leaves on the deciduous trees were turning from shades of yellow, through vivid orange, to warm rust. The bracken had withered, and the grass was no longer lush and green. The east-facing hills were glowing gold as the sun rose. The overall effect was both beautiful and bleak. The only thing that looked the same were the sheep grazing in the field opposite the house.

Nessa pulled on a dressing gown, slid her feet into her slippers, and headed downstairs.

She fixed herself some cereal, which she ate at the kitchen table, looking out across the rear garden. The swallows and martins were gone, but there were lots of thrushes and blackbirds. There were some species she didn't recognise, and she looked them up in a bird book someone had left alongside a pair of binoculars on the windowsill.

*

Moira was tidying away the last of her lunch things when there was a perfunctory knock on her back door and a voice called out, "Hello! Anyone home?"

"Nessa! Back already? Seems like you only just left."

"Six weeks. It's been an age."

Moira waved Nessa inside and led her into the kitchen, where, without asking whether Nessa would like a drink, Moira put the kettle on. While the water heated, she got out plates, the ubiquitous cake, mugs, teabags, and milk. They chatted while Moira worked. "How long are you home for this time?"

"A couple of weeks."

"Add that to the weeks you had over the summer. Hardly seems worth your while going away at all!"

Nessa laughed uncertainly, as though she wasn't sure whether Moira was serious or not. Slightly defensively, she said, "They work us hard while we are there though!"

Placatingly, Moira said, "I'm sure they do."

Mollified, Nessa brightened. "Finlay's jealous. He's figured out I get more holidays in a year than he does. And Dad jokes the more you pay for education, the less education you get. I get more than three weeks off at Christmas. Same at Easter, although I'll be swotting for exams, so maybe that doesn't count, and you should see the pile of work I had to bring home with me this time!"

"And next year you'll be at university, and none of it will matter."

Nessa changed the subject. "Cindy says you've been spending time together."

"Yes. Is that weird for you?"

"Maybe a bit. But that's my problem. Not yours. The two of you are here all the time. I'm not. It's good you both have someone to hang around with. Right?"

"Right."

"See. I'm learning to share. First Dad. Now you."

"Maturity suits you." Moira made the words sound mocking, but she meant it.

"Shut up." Nessa ducked her head, embarrassed.

Tea made, they headed into the living room, made cosy by the red glow coming from the fireplace. Mr Gillespie sprawled on the hearthrug, lapping up the heat. Nessa crouched to scratch the top of his head, and he deigned to purr.

Once they were settled in their seats, Moira asked, "How is school?"

"Okay. Busy. I told you I'd signed up for a show, right?"

"*Little Shop of Horrors*, isn't it?"

"Yeah. There are loads of rehearsals, but as I've only got a couple of lines in the whole thing, I spend most of the time hanging around. After the second week, I started taking my knitting along. At the rate I'm going, I'll have knitted Christmas presents for everyone by the end of term."

"Good for you!"

"Things are much better in the house too."

For a moment, Moira thought Nessa was talking about next door, but based on what Nessa said next, she was still talking about school.

"I've made more friends, so that's good. Can I ask your advice?"

"Of course."

"I screwed up."

Moira put her mug aside and leaned forwards to show Nessa she had her full attention.

"There's this one girl. I liked her. I mean like-liked her. You know?"

"You're talking attraction, I take it."

"Yes."

Moira doubted she'd be able to help Nessa, but she could at least listen. Besides, sometimes the clearest head was the one most detached from a situation. "Go on."

"I asked her out. We went to the cinema and for a meal. Everything was great until..."

"Until?"

"Until the end of the evening when, while we were waiting for her bus, I tried to kiss her."

"What happened?"

"She got angry. Asked me what the heck I was thinking and told me to leave."

"What did you do?"

"I left. But I tried to apologise later, only we ended up having a blazing row. She did all the blazing, but you get the picture. And now she won't talk to me." Nessa hadn't gone into gory detail, but she had revealed enough for Moira to get the gist of what had happened. Words had been exchanged, voices had been raised, and Frankie hadn't spoken to Nessa since. "And, to make matters worse, The Popsicle overheard the argument, and she couldn't wait to spread the news around Hobby. The news spread like wildfire, of course—"

"That's awful!"

"—and now the whole school knows I'm gay."

"How did people react?"

"Surprisingly okay. Most people have been great. Supportive. Tarone laid into Poppy for outing me. The worst thing is a boy called Godfrey Manning hitting on me because he sees me as a challenge."

"Godfrey Manning sounds like a right numpty."

"I was pretty upset when it happened. Nobody wants to be outed like that, and it was a sh— awful thing for the Popsicle to do, although I kind of get why she did it, and that's a whole other story. I guess everyone would have found out eventually. At least this way, it's out of the way."

"I don't think I'd be as forgiving as you."

"Yeah, you would."

"How can you be so sure?"

"You wouldn't have any choice. Plus, I'm not forgiving. I'm dealing. It's not the same thing. Anyway, I'm getting off topic. I wanted to tell you, ask you, about Frankie."

"The one you went out with."

"Yeah. Only, she says she didn't know it was a date. But it was dinner and a show, and just the two of us. How was it not a date? It wasn't like when I do things with Meg. Frankie and I don't have a track record of being friends. Of course it was a date."

Moira nodded, more an acknowledgement she was listening than actual agreement.

"Tell me more about your Frankie."

"Such as?"

"What is she like? Likes? Dislikes?"

"Clever. Pretty. Gorgeous. Short, curly, dark hair. Nice teeth. Not as tall as me. Big into drama. That's why she switched schools. She wants to get into Cambridge Uni, and she's got her sights set on joining the Footlights. She's focused on her work and the play. She's also weirdly obsessed with cake. You'd get on with her." Nessa pointed at her half-eaten slice of lemon drizzle.

"Cake?" asked Moira. "She likes baking?"

"I—" Nessa frowned. "I don't think so. But she's got stickers of cake on her laptop and a badge on her schoolbag."

"What do the stickers and badge look like?"

"Does it matter?"

"It might."

"It's slices of cake. Cartoon drawings. A sponge, maybe? Several layers thick. Iced."

"Any other emblems or badges? Like an ace of spades, for example."

"Yeah! How did you know?"

"I suspect your Frankie might be asexual."

"What?"

"Do you know anything about asexuality?"

"Not much, no. I've seen a slogan: 'The A is for Asexual.' That's about it."

"It's not mentioned in those SRE classes of yours?"

"No. At least, not that I remember."

"That's disappointing. I was led to believe you kids were being given all the answers these days, but apparently not."

"Will you tell me?"

Moira shook her head. "Go home. Do some research. And if you want to talk about it some more, drop by again. Of course, you're welcome to drop by, even if you don't want to talk about it."

*

On Monday, Dad let Nessa drive him to work, where she rendez-voused with Lesley, the driving instructor who had given Nessa her first few lessons in the summer. Together, they worked their way through the various manoeuvres Nessa would need to complete for the examiner, and they drove the test route.

Nessa gave way at a junction, turned left, and drove along the main street. Two hundred yards further on, at Lesley's command, she turned left again. Driving around here was a breeze compared to down south, and Nessa worried taking her driving test in a town with no filter systems, bus lanes, or dual carriageways, and only one set of traffic lights was possibly a cheat. The test centre closest to St Drogo's was in a town whose population was larger than that of the whole of Argyll and Bute put together.

Lesley must have read her mind. "Now, don't you be getting complacent, just because you think you know the roads!"

Nessa swallowed and reined in her meandering wits.

"If you stay focussed, you'll do fine."

Lesson over, Lesley dropped Nessa in the centre of town, and Nessa found herself with a few hours to kill before the next bus home.

There was little to do in the town on a drizzly day in October. Nessa walked around some of the back streets Lesley had taken her along. She found herself looking at the houses, some old, some not so old, and a few new, and the derelict remains of a primary school, which had been abandoned about ten years before. The real estate should have oozed potential. Instead, it made Nessa feel sad. The redevelopment on the main streets and loch side, with its new pavements, railings, playpark, and landscaping, was never going to penetrate this far into the settlement. What would become of this site in the future? Already, broken glass littered the car park, and bottles, cans, and even a desk chair, lay abandoned in the undergrowth. Crude graffiti had been daubed on the walls, and buildings were decaying, their windows boarded, and the wooden detailing softening from its exposure to the elements.

The damp had soaked into her jeans, so Nessa made her way towards the shops, where she hoped to find shelter.

She had no need of a pharmacy, wasn't interested in fishing tackle, and hadn't been commissioned to pick anything up from any of the food shops. That left an ironmonger's, some gift shops, an art shop, a book shop, a couple of charity shops, and a quartet of cafes as potential places to visit.

Nessa went into the art and book shops, where she browsed but didn't buy. She had more luck in one of the charity shops, where she found a couple of scruffy paperbacks, which she carried with her to the cafe nearest the bus stop. There, she worked her way through one fruit scone, two mugs of tea, and five chapters before she paid and left to catch her bus.

The bus stop leaked and was barely drier inside than out. She nodded politely to the two other people who were waiting. They obviously knew each other, and Nessa found herself eavesdropping on their conversation, which was about the care and maintenance of goats. They had a lot to say on the topic, which they continued once they'd boarded the bus. They were still going strong when the driver dropped Nessa at the road end.

Nessa walked the last two miles to the house. The drizzle had turned into full-blown rain, its drops battering against the fabric of her umbrella.

By the time she got home, Nessa was chilled and in desperate need of warmth, a change of clothes, and more tea.

*

The rain was still lashing when Nessa called Meg that night.

"I'm bored!" Meg moaned. "I've even done some of my prep!"

"Seriously? You've started your homework already?"

"Your incredulity isn't flattering."

"Do you blame me, given your track record of leaving everything until the last minute?"

Meg made a gesture that indicated reluctant agreement. "Prep's helping me to keep my mind off Jez. I really miss him. I can't help it. If we were still together, even if we couldn't have seen each other every day of the holidays, I'd still have been able to message him. And I could have fantasised about him. Nice fantasies, I mean. Not heartbroken, I miss you fantasies. I need you to cheer me up. Distract me."

"Only if you do the same for me. I'm still a bit battered after everything that happened with Frankie and the rest."

"Deal. We'll cheer each other up. You go first."

Nessa did her best. She told Meg about the train north, the hamburger restaurant, and Cindy and Joe's wedding plans.

"Have you seen Moira?"

"Yes."

"Did you find out anything new? Any idea where we should look for Nikki next?"

"To be honest, I haven't given it any thought, what with everything else that's been going on."

"But you'll try, won't you? You've got almost two weeks to find something out."

"I don't know, Meg. If I didn't find anything before, I don't think I'm likely to now." Besides, Nessa wasn't sure she wanted to. She didn't know why, but the shine had gone off the idea.

"Oh, well. If you can't dig anything up at your end, maybe I should try harder at mine."

"How?"

But Meg either didn't know, or she wouldn't say.

After ending her call with Meg, Nessa deep dived down a virtual rabbit hole. She read her phone screen under her bedclothes until gone midnight.

Chapter Twenty-One

Driving with Dad was more enjoyable than going out with Lesley. While Lesley was working hard to prepare Nessa for her test, Dad took her places as much for fun as for practice. Plus, they got to spend time together.

On Tuesday, while Finlay spent a day with a friend, and Cindy stayed home to catch up on chores, Dad let Nessa drive to Oban where they did a big shop, wandered along the esplanade, walked past the craft co-operative's premises, and had another meal in the restaurant they'd visited in the summer. This time, Nessa braved the haggis in Yorkshire pudding wrap, which proved to be surprisingly good.

*

Nessa didn't beat about the bush when next she visited Moira. "Are you ace?"

"Yes."

"Why didn't you tell me before? On Sunday, for instance. Or in the summer when I came out to you."

"I didn't tell you last summer because I hadn't figured it out for my-self. And on Sunday the conversation wasn't about me. It was about you and Frankie. You needed to work things out for yourself, not have me spoon-feed you the answers."

"What do you mean, you hadn't figured it out? How could you have not known?"

Moira quirked an eyebrow.

"Sorry. I didn't mean to sound so harsh."

Moira nodded to show she'd accepted Nessa's apology. "How can you identify as something if you don't even know it exists? You told me you know next to nothing about asexuality. Now imagine what it was like for me, growing up and not even knowing the word. All I knew was I never found that mysterious, special person, the one the media would have us believe exists for everyone."

It had never crossed Nessa's mind there might not be a special someone out there for her. Even as a child, she'd assumed there must be. Because of all the fairy stories where the princesses got swept off their feet by princes, she'd assumed her one true love would be male. These days, she still assumed she would meet someone. The only things that had changed for her were she knew she wanted her person to be female and she wasn't going to wait around for the other person to do the sweeping.

"Does that mean you're not only asexual? You're aromantic too? Or do you have a romantic orientation and haven't found someone?"

"My. You have been doing your homework!" Nessa caught a whiff of wry approval. "I'm also aromantic, yes."

What must it be like to not feel the pull of a future where there was someone to kiss, cuddle, and pledge to share your life with?

Moira pulled Nessa away from the unasked question. "How many films or franchises can you come up with that don't include a romantic subplot?"

"Um."

"Do you remember *Sex and the City*?" Moira didn't wait for an answer. "No. That would have been before your time."

"I know of it. There's been a reboot. I haven't seen it."

"Me neither. And I don't want to. The original show was popular in the noughties. I wasn't interested in the sex aspect of the storylines, which maybe should have told me something, but the series was a rare thing: a showcase for strong, single women. Being single myself, that was empowering to see. But what did Hollywood do when the series came to an end? It paired all four main characters off in a fit of...of..." Moira shook her head. "Apparently, the producers thought there was only one acceptable happy ending. All the women found true love and rode off into a romantic ever after. And suddenly the series was no longer empowering or inspiring. It was like every other show out there. The ending sucked."

Nessa swallowed a laugh. "Sucked" sounded incredibly incongruous, coming from Moira's mouth.

"My point is, imagine living in a world where everything you see reinforces the idea you must be with someone. Everything emphasises that: stories full of Prince Charmings, *Jackie* magazine, another thing from way before your time, even the chat on the school bus. Articles about love, romance, and sex in glossy magazines. The way horoscopes focus on romance. All those things condition you to think the only acceptable outcome for an adult is to be in a meaningful, monogamous, heterosexual, relationship. Usually, one which results in kids."

Nessa didn't think the picture these days was as bleak as the one Moira painted, but the portrayal of same sex relationships was still unusual enough to be worthy of comment, and she'd had to cast off some assumptions of her own before she'd accepted that she was gay. She understood the concept of conditioning.

"Now, imagine you don't feel all those things which seem to come naturally to everyone else. What would you think? How would you feel?"

"I would feel isolated."

Moira nodded.

"Frightened?"

"Sometimes."

"Confused?"

"Definitely."

"Excluded."

"Yes."

"I said confused already. But really, really confused. And maybe, with all that buzzing around in my head, ready to explode."

"Add a sprinkle of broken in there, and you'll have covered everything. But life goes on. You earn a living. Get up in the morning. Eat. You push your doubts and insecurities aside and ignore them. Until one day, your neighbour comes out to you, and you want to be an ally, so you do some research into LGBT themes only to find LGBT has grown some extra letters since you last looked, and one of them is A."

Nessa stared. "Is that honestly how you found out?"

"Pretty much, yes."

"Wow."

"If you are aromantic and asexual, everything you see around you is everything you're not. From what you say, Frankie is lucky; she has the words she needs to understand who she is. But all those emotions are still going to be there to some degree. I doubt Frankie realised it was a date. From my own experience, and from what I've read, aces are often ill-equipped to read the signs. My guess is Frankie wants a friend, some-one who'll treat her as a person worthy of spending time with, not a so-cial stopgap until someone better, more romantic, comes along. Now, I have some work to do. You're welcome to stay and help if you want."

More out of curiosity than genuine enthusiasm, Nessa followed Moira out to her shed, where, under Moira's tutelage, Nessa helped to dye some wool. Dying was messy, satisfying work, and Moira promised to pay her for her time in skeins of Aran-weight yarn, which made Nessa's fingers tingle with anticipation.

*

They were clearing everything away when Nessa said, "Dad and I went past the shop, but it was closed."

"Was it?"

"You don't sound surprised." If anything, Moira sounded amused.

"That's because I'm not."

"Are you laughing?"

"Maybe a bit."

"Um, why?"

Moira gave Nessa an edited version of what had happened with her co-workers, ending with "And I told them to go jump in a loch."

"You didn't!"

"No, I didn't. Not exactly. But I told them I'm not covering anyone else's shifts. If they don't turn up, the shop stays closed."

"Good for you!"

"We've been losing trade, and there have been some stinking reviews online, but as I'm resolved to give it up come the end of the quarter, I can't say I care. Nobody has come forwards to take it on. I didn't appreciate how much of a burden it had become until I stopped trying to hold everything together. A couple of the crafters have asked if I'll change my mind and renew the lease. But I won't. They can sort themselves out, if they want to, but I don't think they will."

*

"**W**hat have you been up to?" asked Meg on Friday evening.

"Driving practice. Prep. Moira's been showing me how to spin. Finlay's off school this week too, and Cindy had some errands to run today, so I spent most of this afternoon playing games with him. It wasn't horrible."

That was the closest Nessa was prepared to go towards admitting she'd had fun. She'd even felt her heart swell when, between games, Finlay had grinned at her and said, "It's good to have you home." Of course, he'd ruined the moment immediately by qualifying the statement with, "You're way better at this than either Mum or Joe!"

"How about you?"

"Mum says I've been spending too much time on the computer."

"Have you?"

"No more than usual. And it's not as though I've got much else to do."

*

The second week of the holiday was quieter than the first. Finlay was at school and Cindy was at work. Dad took a day off so he and Nessa could explore the Kintyre peninsula together, but most of the time Nessa found herself left to her own devices.

She didn't mind. Something had changed over the last few months. She no longer felt left out, sidelined, or isolated. This was the rhythm of the household, and she was content to fit in with it. She read, watched too much rubbish on TV, finished the last of her prep, and knitted.

She also visited Moira, who continued to try to teach her to spin. Nessa managed to produce something that was too lumpy and bumpy for her to confidently call yarn, but Moira told her to treasure it. Nessa, impatient to achieve perfection, wasn't encouraged when Moira told her how many hours she'd have to put in before she would produce anything fine, smooth, and even.

They didn't talk about asexuality again, and Nessa, even though Meg would be disappointed if she found out, didn't ask about the Diptych either. Nessa recognised Moira's asexuality and the Diptych were inextricably linked, even if she didn't know how. She tactfully resolved not to pry, but she hoped Moira knew she'd be happy to listen if ever Moira wanted to talk.

Nessa did, however, run an idea past her, which over the course of half-term, had grown from a pie-in-the-sky, hare-brained scheme, into a concrete ambition.

"I'm considering setting up a club at school. Or a support group. I think it would be good for queers and allies to have a place to go where we can talk about things, learn from each other. Find our people and make friends. It'd be like a safe place to get together."

"We didn't have anything like that in my day," said Moira wistfully.

"Would it have helped if you had?"

Moira considered the question more carefully than Nessa expected; Nessa had assumed the answer would be a straightforward yes.

"I don't know. I'd like to say yes, but when I was your age, I didn't know enough to understand it would have been useful."

"What do you mean?"

"I knew I wasn't gay. Or bi. At least, I assumed I wasn't. I assumed I was straight. So, even if we'd had something like you're suggesting, I'm not sure I would have joined. I don't think I'd have realised it was for me. I'm ashamed to admit this, but I'm not sure I would have wanted to join. These days, you'd call it internalised homophobia or transphobia, I suppose. But we didn't have those words either. It was the way things were."

"That's terrible."

"I know."

"You wouldn't even have come along as an ally?" asked Nessa, unaccountably disappointed, and already knowing the answer.

Moira shook her head sadly. "Things were different. I hope they're better now. Your club, groups like that, can only be forces for good." Her lips twitched in something approaching a smile. "It's a lovely idea. You should do it."

*

Nessa returned to school with a bag of completed homework, a freshly minted driver's licence, two jars of Moira's legendary bramble jelly, several skeins of the yarn she'd helped to dye, a greater understanding of what Frankie might be going through, a conviction about what she needed to do next, and hope that whatever the rest of the autumn term threw at her she would manage to get through it.

Chapter Twenty-Two

"**W**hat do you think?" Nessa, having outlined her plans for a club, looked expectantly at Tarone.

They were in the great hall, where the first rehearsal, post-holiday, was not going well. The mechanical parts of one of the Audrey Two puppets had seized up the first time the puppeteer had tried to work it, sending him into a tizzy of despair. Already, more than twenty minutes had passed since disaster had struck and Ms Markides had called for a fifteen-minute break.

The other performers milled around aimlessly, waiting for something to happen, while Ms Markides flapped her hands uselessly, and several of the technical crew, screwdrivers and spanners in hand, tried to get the carnivorous plant's maw, stuck halfway to open, to move.

"It's a great idea. Here. You might as well make yourself useful while you're waiting." Tarone held out a roller and gestured towards a tray containing dark grey, matt paint.

Nessa took the roller tentatively. "What do you want me to do with it?"

"I need all these painted with undercoat." Tarone made a sweeping gesture that took in an array of oddly shaped bits of chipboard. "After, I'll draw the outlines, and you, along with anyone else I can rope in to help, can colour in the details."

The last time Nessa had done any painting had been in Year 9, before she'd dropped art in favour of pursuing as many sciences as possible, and she had never been good at it. Still, how hard could it be to cover some wood with grey emulsion? She dipped the roller in the paint, experimented a bit, and with only a small amount of dribble and splash, set about her task.

"How are you going to do it?" asked Tarone.

Nessa frowned fleetingly. What was he talking about?

The proverbial penny dropped. "Oh! The club, you mean?"

Tarone grunted an affirmative.

"Ask for permission to use a classroom. Put up a few posters. Word of mouth. To be honest, I haven't got much further than 'Wouldn't it be great to have somewhere for queer kids and allies to meet?' If you have any ideas, I'd love to hear them."

"Maybe what you said is enough. Invite people along and see what they want. And who is prepared to help."

"And you? Would you be prepared to help?" Nessa glanced across at him.

Tarone grinned. "I thought you'd never ask!"

On stage, someone screamed for a can of lubricant.

*

Having been shushed one too many times in the library, Nessa and Meg were trying, not entirely successfully, to get out of a biting November wind by hunkering down against one of the walls that flanked the chapel steps. On the plus side, they had some privacy, and they were unlikely to be disturbed. The downside was they were freezing.

"You know I told you Mum said I spend too much time on the computer?" Meg was brimming with excitement.

"Yes?" said Nessa cautiously.

"Well, it turns out, it's time put to good use!"

"How?"

"I've found Nikki!"

"You have?"

"Found might be a bit of an exaggeration, but I'm close. I know she's been living in Devon, at least until recently. She has a Bichon Frise called Winston, and she is 'in a relationship'. She has a ViewHoo channel that hasn't been updated since 2015, and someone called Derek manages official fan accounts on SayMate and Yapper for her."

"Where did you get all that from?"

"The internet."

"I know that! I mean, how'd you know how to find all this out? I searched a lot over the summer, and I didn't find out any of that."

"I've watched way too much *Catfish*?"

Nessa raised her eyebrows. She had seen a few episodes of *Catfish*, mostly when she'd been staying at Meg's, but the novelty of watching them had soon worn off. She didn't get why people invested so much time and energy into duping each other, and she had a much lower appetite for watching people being nasty to each other than Meg did. It hadn't crossed Nessa's mind anyone could learn useful skills from the show.

Unable to help herself, Nessa asked, "Have you found out anything about what happened between her and Moira?"

Meg shook her head. "I've inquired in a few fan spaces. There's lots of speculation, but nobody seems to know anything. I even found some real person fanfic about the Diptych. Some of it is wild! Slash. Threesomes."

"Ugh! No! Don't tell me! That's my friend you're talking about!" Thinking about what people might have written, even if it was entirely fabricated, made Nessa queasy. The idea of real-person fiction made her uneasy, anyway, but knowing it had been written about someone she knew personally!

Did Moira know about it? She couldn't imagine Moira reading fanfic of any kind. In fact, she had a hard time imagining Moira even knowing fanfic existed.

"Maybe we should cut our losses. We're never going to get to the bottom of the mystery, and I'm not sure I want to anymore. If Moira had wanted me to know, she'd have told me by now."

"Hey! This was your idea, remember? And I'm not ready to give up yet. I've reached out to a few people, and there's an internet forum waiting to be helpful. I still have hope we can pull this off. All we need is a bit of good luck."

"If you say so."

Was Nessa wrong to hope the only luck they had was bad?

*

The pub, a stone's throw from the esplanade, was located on a quiet side street notorious as the haunt of parking wardens. Called the Sgian-Dubh and Sporran, the pub occupied the ground floor of a three-storey building, the upper floors being given over to a solicitor's office and a short-term holiday let.

The pub's front door was made of heavy wood with stained glass panels depicting thistles and a saltire. Although heavy on the Scottish imagery, the pub's landlord was a Mancunian.

An A3 poster had been put into one of the windows advertising a drag show, showcasing the fabulous Molly Jellysnake, every third Thursday of the month. Manchester Mitchell was working on expanding his customer base beyond the more gullible breed of tourist.

Moira paused on the pavement. Her stomach twisted and clenched, bringing to mind memories of the Diptych's early days, when she and Nikki turned up at unfamiliar venues for their gigs. She would worry nobody would turn out to see them, or the audience would hate them, or they had got the day wrong, the hour wrong, or they had arrived at the wrong address.

They'd done that once. They'd been booked to play in Bradford-on-Avon, but they'd gone to Bradford-on-Tone instead. They'd asked the landlord of the only pub in the village where the Lion's Head was. The landlord had been by turns confused, surprised, amused, and sympathetic, and he'd ended up inviting them to stay and do an acoustic session. Moira took courage from the memory of how the customers, predominantly male, with an average age of sixty-three, had cheered them on and offered to buy them drinks afterwards and had turned a disaster into a wonderful night.

She pushed the Sgian-Dudh and Sporran's door open and stepped inside.

Her first impressions were of blood-red velour upholstery, brown wooden tables and settles, a swirly carpet that either dated back to the 1970s or was charmingly retro, and a crowd of people who were milling around in a way that suggested they all knew each other. There was a mix of ages and genders, voices raised in the unintelligible hubbub common to crowded bars the world over, and conversations punctuated by volleys of laughter.

She didn't recognise any faces, which was unusual. Normally, when she went out for drinks or a meal, she would see at least one or two she recognised. The unfamiliarity of the clientele added to her anxiety.

This had been a bad idea. No, not bad. Terrible. And terrifying.

She turned around to leave and bumped into Emily.

"Come on," said Emily. "They won't eat you. And I'll introduce you around."

Moira allowed Emily to pass in front of her and followed her to the bar.

Emily leaned over the counter and waved at the staff. They greeted Emily with smiles that were more than customer friendly. They spoke of friendship.

"Hey, Em. What can I get you?"

"A pint of your guest draught ale and...?" She glanced at Moira.

"Um. Orange juice and soda."

"You don't want something stronger?"

"I'm driving." That was a rare downside to living so far up the glen. Not only was the closest bus stop to her house two miles away, but the last of the three a day passed the road end around five thirty in the afternoon. She'd learned early that nights out had to be teetotal by necessity, and it was never much fun to watch people get louder and drunker as evenings progressed. For that reason, unless the main purpose of an evening out was something other than inebriation, she tended to avoid the area's hostelries.

"Of course." Emily didn't press.

Moira listened idly as Emily made small talk with Mitchell, while a bartender, who sported a name badge that identified him as Malkie, prepped their drinks. Moira let her eyes wander and take in details which had escaped her previously.

The pub's walls were stone and mortar, and the low ceiling was comprised of gloss-painted plasterboard and wooden beams. Wall decorations were comprised of mirrors advertising long-extinct brands of beer or unfashionable beverages such as vermouth.

Although, hadn't Moira read an article recently that lauded the renewed popularity of vermouth? Maybe it was in again.

Someone had put two small rainbow flags on the mantelpiece, a tiny gesture towards claiming the room as an LGBTQ+ space.

Emily paid for the drinks and pushed Moira's glass towards her. Moira thanked her and, as she lifted the glass to take a sip, made a promise the next round would be on her.

Emily picked up her drink and stepped away from the bar.

Moira again followed and, together, they moved into the melee.

Emily worked the room with ease, greeting, schmoozing, air-kissing, hugging, and making introductions with enviable nonchalance.

Emily introduced Moira to Dave and David, who in turn introduced them both to Fearn. Emily's hand lingered in Fearn's longer than was strictly necessary, and Fearn's eyes sparkled in response.

The five of them splintered off from the wider group and found a small table in a corner to gather around.

Moira had never encountered getting to know you small talk like it. She was used to fielding *What do you do for a living? Are you married?* and *Do you have any children?* questions. This was the first time she found herself being asked about her preferred pronouns or how she identified. Under other circumstances, she might have found the questions discomforting or intrusive. Here, she found them, along with the unquestioning acceptance with which her answers were received, liberating.

"How did you hear about our group?" Dave, or maybe it was David, asked.

Moira gestured towards Emily. "Emily suggested I come."

"How do you two know each other?"

The question led to a five-minute conversation about the shop and crafting more generally.

Fearn squealed with delight and said to Emily, "Those rainbow pictures are yours? I have one in my bedroom, and I've got one of your mugs too!"

Emily beamed and sidled along the bench seat to sit an inch closer to Fearn. Fearn edged along to meet her halfway.

"How did you learn about us?" David asked Fearn.

"What?" Fearn looked as though she'd momentarily lost track of the conversation, but she rapidly replayed the question in her head. "Say-Mate."

David turned to Dave. "See?" he crowed. "I told you creating the page was a good idea!"

Dave didn't argue.

"For what it's worth, I'm glad you did." Fearn gazed at Emily.

Moira had nothing to contribute as the conversation moved on, meandering through people's experiences of Pride, and how close the rest of the group had come to bumping into each other at various marches over the years.

Dave took note of their rapidly emptying glasses and offered to get the next round in.

By the time he returned, carrying a tray, the conversation had moved on again.

"Who do you see most of, growing up?" Fearn asked as Dave distributed the glasses, put the empty tray on the next table, and sat. "Your parents. So that's going to normalise the family. I had a bachelor uncle, and, yes, it was a euphemism, but he was never a central part of the family, so I didn't have him as a role model. I assumed he didn't want to be, but now I think he might have been squeezed out."

"That's awful," murmured David, while everyone else saluted Dave with their drinks by way of thanks.

Fearn carried on. "I have a brother and a sister. They're both married and have kids of their own. They get together with each other and with our parents so the cousins can have play dates, but they never invite me along. They expect me to provide presents for the kids at birthdays and Christmas, even though they have resolved that as adults we don't need to give presents to each other. It makes economic sense, but overall the dynamic hurts. And yet, I can't broach the topic without coming across as self-involved." She paused. "I'm sorry. I don't usually vent like that. But sometimes..."

"It's okay." Moira surprised herself by speaking. "I can relate. I don't see much of my brothers anymore, and usually I only hear from them when I make the first contact. But I don't like to do that too often. I feel as though I'm intruding into their lives, and I've been conditioned to accept their family units take priority over everything else. But I feel...how did you describe it? Squeezed out. I wish I could have seen my nephews and nieces grow up. Instead, they're barely more than strangers. Sometimes I get an invitation at Christmas when someone doesn't want me to be alone. The invitations come from a good place, and they're made with generous intent, but it can be lonelier to be in the middle of someone else's celebrations, not knowing the traditions that make it special for them, than to be on your own. I don't want an annual invitation at

Christmas. I want to be valued and included all year round."

"As soon as a sibling gets a partner, you're demoted from peer to extended family," said Fearn.

"Yes! That's it! Exactly!" agreed Moira.

"Which is one of the reasons why we set up this group." David spoke with evangelical zeal. "Groups like this can help. You can find people who share your point of view and will support you. And if you're lucky, you can find a new family."

A new family. Found family. Chosen family. That sounded so good!

Moira caught the twin sparkles in Emily and Fearn's eyes. A sense of isolation washed over her. "My round," she said, as much to give herself a few moments to pull herself together as because the glasses needed refilling.

*

On stage Frankie and Mickey were rehearsing as best they could without the malfunctioning Audrey Two puppet, which had temporarily been relocated in pieces to the technical science department for a major redesign. Meanwhile Nessa and Tarone, who was waiting for the last undercoat of paint to dry on the scenery, sat at the rear of the hall, quietly planning the first meeting of the new LGBTQIA club.

"Hey. This might be cool."

"What?"

Tarone turned his laptop around so Nessa could see the screen. He'd found a website devoted to those most hideous of things, icebreakers.

"I don't know, Tarone."

"Granted, some of them are awful. But there are a few in here that might get people talking without putting them on the spot."

"Okay..." Nessa tried to keep an open mind. It wasn't as though she had come up with a better idea.

They ruled out some of the questions like *What is the longest you've ever stayed in one job?* and *Where do you want to retire to?* as being aimed at older age groups. Fearing *What is the worst pick-up line you've ever heard?* and *What kind of wedding do you want?* might be difficult to answer for anyone with limited experiences of, or appetite for, dating, Nessa and Tarone ditched them too.

Tarone liked *If your home was packed full of tennis balls, how would you remove them?* and suggested he'd invite the local kennels to bring along its dogs to take them away. In the end, however, the tennis balls didn't make the final cut of about thirty questions, which hopefully would be fun to answer without being awkward.

"We'll put them on bits of paper, fold them, and put them in a bowl. Each person will take one at random. Nobody'll know what to expect, and that'll add a touch of jeopardy," said Nessa.

"Great."

"We'll pass the bowl around, and whoever is holding it must introduce themselves: name; pronouns; orientation if they're comfortable telling the rest of the group, but that should be optional. They take a question out of the bowl, answer it, and pass it on."

"Okay, so we do that for the first five or ten minutes."

"Then we can ask what people want future meetings to be like. What do they want? And take it from there."

They had a plan.

Chapter Twenty-Three

The next thing Nessa did was sound out Ms Breckenridge, who'd sought Nessa out to check how she was coping and who considered the idea a good one.

"It'll be great for students to have peer support." Ms Breckenridge nodded firmly. "School rules, policies, and customs can only go so far, as you know all too well."

Her scheme thus blessed by her Head of House, Nessa got Tarone to help her design some posters. They were careful to incorporate a range of pride flags, including the asexual and aromantic ones, and they made a point of using the full LGBTQIA+ abbreviation instead of LGBT+.

By the end of the week, Nessa had found a classroom the club could use every Tuesday lunchtime, and she spent a chunk of Friday afternoon putting posters up and posting an announcement on the student intranet pages.

Maybe Frankie would see them; maybe she wouldn't. Maybe she was aspec, or maybe she wasn't. Maybe she'd come; maybe she'd decide it wasn't for her. But Nessa had done everything, short of outright inviting her, to make Frankie feel included and welcome.

But this wasn't just about Frankie. She wanted everyone to feel welcome, and who knew how many asexuals or aromantics there were in the school who were unsure where they fitted? Maybe there were students from other minority orientations too, but because of Frankie and Moira, Nessa couldn't help thinking more about aces than anyone else.

*

Nessa hadn't been in the geography classroom since she'd dropped the subject, but it didn't seem to have changed much in the intervening years. There were still maps, diagrams of meanders and the insides of volcanoes, and population pyramids on the walls. If they had been changed or updated, she couldn't tell. Nor did she much care. Geography had never appealed to her in the way the neat logic of chemistry and maths did.

She and Tarone had bolted their lunches to ensure they arrived early. Nessa had invited Meg to join them, but Meg had declined. Meg had also bolted her lunch because she had a media studies essay, due at three o'clock, to finish. She'd promised to come another time.

Nessa extracted the questions from her bag. She hadn't found a bowl, so she'd put them in a plastic box she usually kept hair accessories in instead. Now she worried nobody would show.

"They'll come," said Tarone. "Don't worry."

"How can you be sure?"

"I'd come, even if I wasn't your friend. And I'm sure I'm not the only one."

He wasn't. At that moment, a couple of students Nessa didn't know shyly entered the classroom. From the look of them, they appeared to be in Years 10 or 11 and were terrified. Tarone beamed at them. "Come in! Welcome!"

They were soon followed by a Year 11, who Nessa did know, thanks to the show. Becca smiled sheepishly. She sat in the row behind the other two. Nessa was delighted when they introduced themselves to one another without prompting.

Maybe this club idea was going to work out just fine.

Dinah and Dhriti came in and waved at Nessa. Dhriti said, "We want to know how to be good allies."

Numbers swelled until there were twelve of them, which wasn't bad for a first meeting.

When everyone was seated, Tarone shut the classroom door, and Nessa got out her box. "To help us get to know each other better, I've brought along some questions. What I want is for us to pass it around..." She outlined the instructions. "To prove it's not so scary, Tarone and I will go first."

"I'm Tarone. Pronouns: he or him. I'm an ally. I have two mums, one of whom was assigned male at birth." He put his hand into the pile of questions and pulled one out. "*Who would you want on your team in a zombie apocalypse?*" He glanced around the room. "People who can't run as fast as me, obviously. And all the Avengers."

Nessa took the box from Tarone. "My name's Nessa. Preferred pronouns: she and her. I'm a lesbian. Or gay. I'm still a bit hazy about my preferred label. I'm leaning towards lesbian. And I'm babbling. So if any of you are nervous, you're not alone. And if you're worried you're going to look stupid doing this... Hey, I've already been there, done that." She unfolded her square and read. "*Is it ever okay to waste time?*" She put her hand to her heart. "God, yes! I just wish I had time to waste! It's like this school hates us to have a single moment to ourselves!"

The rest of the group laughed. Some of the laughs were hesitant, but any laughter was good, right?

Out of the corner of her eye, through the glass panel in the classroom door, Nessa caught sight of someone hovering in the corridor, apparently trying to decide whether to come in.

Nessa passed the questions on to Becca.

"Hi." Becca waved half-heartedly. "I'm Becca. Pronouns: she and her. Um, I'm questioning. But I might be bi. Or pan. Yeah, so questioning." She nodded a few times to reinforce her answer. She read her question to herself, laughed, and read it aloud. "*Would you prefer to fart or burp glitter?*"

This time, the group's laughter was wholehearted, and it banished the last of the tension inside the room.

The door handle dropped. The door edged open, and Frankie sidled in.

Nessa beamed as Frankie slipped into a seat.

Tarone summarised what was going on, and Becca helpfully reread her question before she answered it. "Tricky. I like the idea of seeing something bright and beautiful coming out of my bum, but unless I was naked, wouldn't all the glitter get caught up in my underwear, so nobody would see it? Also, it could be kind of scratchy, sitting in a pile of glitter all day. So, yeah. I'll go for the burping. Definitely the burping."

To Becca's gratification, her answer earned her a round of applause.

Dhriti's question was *Would you prefer to be funny or clever?* She replied archly. "Why do I have to choose? I'm already both!"

The two students who'd arrived first, Phil and Sam, both from Year 10, struggled to answer their questions: one gay, one questioning. One he/him, one shyly admitting they'd like to go by they/their but hadn't mustered the courage to tell the school yet.

"Would you like to be they and their in here?" asked Tarone.

"Could I?"

Sam flushed happily when everyone chorused variations on "No problem!"

When faced with the question, *If you could be a kitchen appliance, what would you be, and why?* Sam said, "An Aga. I'd be warm and welcoming, and at the heart of my home."

Nessa pictured the range at Meg's. "Good answer."

In response to his question, Phil admitted he'd dreamed of being a superhero when he was six. "But when I found out something horrible usually had to happen for you to get the powers, if you hadn't been born with them, I decided I'd prefer to be a spy."

"Do you still want to be a spy?" asked Becca.

"I haven't ruled it out."

Dinah's question was *What is the worst food you've ever eaten?* "That's an easy one. The weird stew the cafeteria used to serve with the orange-brown sauce and the lumps of sheep meat in it." She gave a theatrical shudder. "No wonder the students revolted! The students *were* revolted!"

Nessa laughed. She had also been scarred for life by the goulash. Some of the younger students hadn't been around during the "Great Lunch Uprising", but even they had heard about it. No doubt the GLU would live on in school legend for decades to come.

When her turn came around, Frankie drew herself upright, apparently gathering courage to say, "Name: Frankie Nightingale. Pronouns: she and her. Orientation: Asexual. Aro too."

Nessa didn't miss the way she glanced around warily, worried about what reaction she'd get. When everyone smiled at her, the tension in her shoulders lessened, and she moved on to her question, which was: *If a volcano formed on Exmoor, and you got to name it, what would you call it?* Frankie sucked on her upper lip for a moment before answering. "It would depend how close I was to it. If I was right next to it, I'd call it AAAARRRRRGGGGGGHHHHHH!!!! Otherwise, I'd call it Terence."

There was another round of applause, this one mostly for the way Frankie had committed to the scream.

All in all, the meeting was off to a promising start.

*

To Nessa's surprise, Frankie hung around as everyone else exited the room in a flurry of eager chatter and promises to come back next week.

Nessa wasn't sure what to say as she and Frankie faced each other.

"Thank you for com—"

"Thank you for organ—"

"You first."

"No, you."

"I'm sorry," said Nessa. "About what happened between us before. I should have made it clear what I had in mind, and I'm sorry."

"So am I. I'm sorry I got so angry with you. And I'm sorry about what happened afterwards."

Nessa guessed she was referring to what Poppy had done. "Not your fault."

"I know. But even so..."

"Seriously, it wasn't your fault. Poppy was already angry with me. If she hadn't outed me, she'd have found some other way to get her own back."

"What was she— Sorry. None of my business."

Nessa told her anyway.

Frankie laughed. "Horoscopes? Seriously? I'd have lied too! I mean, you have to share a room with her, and poor you, by the way. She's a nightmare! How do you cope?"

"By spending as much time away from our room as possible, at least when she's in it. Almost broke my heart when I found out she'd signed up for the show as well, but I'd already committed myself, so..." She made a what-can-you-do gesture with her hands.

"Yeah. Once you've signed Ms Markides blood contract, there's no escaping with your soul intact!" Frankie rolled her eyes.

Nessa found herself warming towards Frankie again. The attraction was still there, but she could deal. More than that, she wanted to deal. Hopefully, she said, "Friends? Just friends."

"That's the thing, isn't it? 'Just friends.' That's how people say it, like friendship's less important than a romantic relationship."

"I didn't mean it that way."

"I know you didn't. I got the context. But that's how language works, isn't it? When you're a kid, it's okay to say you're friends with someone. Or BFFs. Or besties. But somewhere along the line, the word 'just' comes into it. You're no longer friends, or best friends. You become just friends because somewhere else there is something better, or something more, waiting for you." Frankie was frustrated, bitter, and quietly resigned, all at once.

"I get that now."

"I'm sorry, but I don't see how you can."

"Because I don't have the lived experience?"

"Maybe."

"Maybe I don't, but I have a friend back home who's asexual. And

I've done some research. I do get it, at least a bit. And I like you. Not just as a possible romantic partner. Not even, now I know where you're coming from. But as a friend. We got on well, didn't we, before I screwed everything up? I liked spending time with you. Talking to you. And I'd like to do it again."

Frankie regarded her. "That's a lot to take in."

"Is it?"

"You know another asexual?"

"Yes."

"I've never met one in real life," said Frankie enviously.

"I don't think Moira has either." For a moment, Nessa was tempted to ask whether Frankie would like an introduction, but maybe it was too soon for that. Plus, it would be presumptuous to speak for Moira, without checking in with her first. Nessa was relieved when Frankie didn't ask.

"As for the other, yeah. We had a good time. Before." Frankie held out her hand. "Friends."

Chapter Twenty-Four

M eg was waiting on Hobby's drive by the time Nessa appeared, dressed in civvies and weekend case in hand. The case filled up almost all of Nelly's boot. Nessa jumped into the front passenger seat and strapped herself in.

Music blared out of the speakers as, in high spirits, they headed towards a roundabout where, instead of heading east, towards Meg's family's farm, they joined the motorway, and headed south, towards Exeter.

Nessa leaned back contentedly. Two nights away from St Drogo's and Poppy! Time with her best friend! Freedom of the open road!

"Do you realise," said Nessa, as they sped along the M5, "this'll be my first time shopping in a city since..." *The previous February when Dad and I spent a day picking up everything I needed for the boarding house.* It hadn't been much fun; she hadn't said all the things she'd wanted to say, and Dad had been in a rush to get everything done as swiftly as possible.

"What? I can't hear you!"

Nessa turned down the music. "I said, this'll be my first time shopping in a city since last winter!"

"And I get to drive you. Yay! Girls' day out!"

*

They left the car on the outskirts of Exeter and used a park and ride bus to get into the city centre. There, they sauntered around, dodging in and out of shops as the fancy took them. They stopped for hamburgers from one of the major chains, a guilty pleasure that prompted Nessa to say, "These are good, so long as you don't think of them as actual food." She savoured a bite from her burger. "Would you believe, there're no burger bars in Argyll and Bute?"

"After everything else you've told me, yes, I'd believe it."

Fortified with not-food, they walked around some more. They mourned the passing of shops that had vanished during Covid, their premises still standing vacant and depressing, and they poked their heads inside the cathedral because that was the kind of thing you did in Exeter.

They were in a bookshop, where Nessa wanted a quick look at the LGBT+ section before they headed to the park and ride, when Meg's phone pinged. That wasn't unusual, but her reaction was.

"Oh, my God!" exclaimed Meg. "I've got an address! And it's on our way home! Leastways, it could be if we take the scenic route."

"An address for what?"

"Nikki!"

"What! You're kidding me!"

Meg shook her head vigorously.

"No, seriously. She's still here, in Devon!" She tapped her phone, putting the address into her maps app. "Look! It's barely five miles out of Tiverton! We can go there on the way home!"

"I don't know, Meg." It was too quick, too sudden, the sun had already set, and Liane and Ted would be waiting on them to eat. "How'd you get the address, anyway?"

"Social media."

"I don't know," said Nessa again. "I mean, doesn't this feel a bit stalkerish to you?"

"Rubbish. Don't tell me you're getting cold feet now. Not after we've come so far."

"Maybe I am. Or maybe I'd like more time to prepare. Plus, your folks are expecting us."

"Mum and Dad know me well enough to know we'll be late."

"That's true," Nessa admitted grudgingly.

"And when are we going to get another chance like this?"

Meg had a point. They couldn't get together often; who knew when the next time would be? Not this side of Christmas; that was for sure. And maybe it would be an adventure.

Meg sensed Nessa's hesitation and went in for the kill. "C'mon. It'll be a lark! Plus, I've got the keys. You can't get home without me!"

*

The shortest route would have been to drive into the city and out again on the Barnstaple road, but shortest didn't necessarily mean easiest, so Meg retraced their steps along the more familiar M5 as far as junction 27. There, relying on Nelly's sat-nav, she turned off the motorway, heading west along a dual carriageway and into less familiar territory.

They turned off the dual carriageway at Tiverton, a small town

Nessa might have visited a long time ago with Dad. The sat nav guided them through a one-way system, and soon they were out into the countryside again, this time squeezing their way along narrow lanes. Even if it had not been dark, there wouldn't have been much to see as the lanes were flanked by high hedgerows which blocked the views of the countryside on either side.

At least at night oncoming headlights gave some warning of other traffic. As Meg dodged into a muddy gateway to allow another car to pass, Nessa said, "In Scotland the lanes have proper passing places."

*

Even with the sat nav, they missed a couple of turns and had to backtrack. Via a circuitous route, which took much longer than they'd expected, they managed to find their destination.

Upper Slaughter was a tiny hamlet, a "blink and you miss it" kind of place, comprised of nothing more than an old-fashioned and iconic red telephone box, a wooden bench, a terrace of five houses, a church, and a pub, which was currently closed and up for sale.

Meg parked in the pub's empty car park. Nessa got out while Meg checked the handbrake one last time.

Meg exited the car, locked the doors, and dropped the key into the top of her shoulder bag.

"Dark, isn't it?" said Nessa. There were no street lamps, and the clouds that had been gathering all day blotted out the moon and stars. "I think it's going to rain."

They walked past the phone box, where Nessa spotted an A3 poster: something about the kiosk being scheduled for removal and a six-week consultation period which had ended in 2019.

People had mobile phones now. It was amazing payphones had

lasted as long as they had. Dad had taught her how to use one, in case of emergencies, he'd said, when she was in primary school, and for a long time, she'd carried coins around with her. She'd never needed them.

"The house is called Ye Olde Place of Worship," said Meg, reading off a screenshot she'd taken earlier.

"Seriously?"

"It's a converted church. I'm guessing the one we passed on the way in. There." Meg pointed.

They walked along the road as far as the church that wasn't a church any longer.

"Are you sure this is the right place?" Nessa doubtfully eyed the building. She shivered as she spotted headstones in the graveyard. She wouldn't want to live alongside the earthly remains of other people's relatives.

There were lights on inside the building, which showed off stained glass windows and suggested someone was home.

"It must be," said Meg.

Someone had hammered a "For Auction" sign with a December date into the verge next to a six-foot-tall wooden gate.

Nessa hesitated, one hand on the gate, which had been augmented by a Beware of the Dog sign, and the other on the latch. "We're going to do this?" Her mouth was dry, and her stomach was full of butterflies.

"Yeah. We've come this far. We can't back out now."

"If you say so." Committed at last, Nessa released the latch, pushed the gate open, and stepped through.

*

Nessa held the gate for Meg, then let it swing to behind her. Meg led the way up the path. A bright light, triggered by their movements, flashed on.

The original church doors, solid, wooden, and covered in a glossy black paint that glimmered where they caught the light, were still in situ. Nessa searched around for a doorbell, eventually finding one mounted on the stonework. Next to the oversized doors, it looked small, insignificant, and incongruously new.

Nessa hovered her right forefinger over the button.

Meg urged her on.

She pressed.

Nessa didn't hear anything. Was the bell broken? Or was it so far in the house, it was inaudible from outside. She tried again.

Nobody came.

"We should go."

Meg shook her head. "Not yet."

She pushed past Nessa and leaned on the bell, pressing hard for at least five seconds.

Again, they waited.

Nessa was turning away, about to pull Meg with her, when the heavy clunking sounds of bolts being pulled back came from the other side of the door.

The door opened noiselessly on well-oiled hinges.

They heard dogs barking from inside the house. There was more than one, and possibly several. Meg had mentioned a Bichon Frise called Winston, but Nessa doubted Bichon Frises barked baritone or bass.

Nikki Thompson leaned against the edge of the door, which she'd opened to a forty-five-degree angle. She had a tumbler with several fingers of an amber-coloured liquid in one hand, Winston under her other arm, and a scowl on her face. "If you're carol singing, you're a month early, and if you're collecting for anything, you can piss off. Not like we have any money to give you." She made a poorly coordinated gesture in the direction of the For Auction sign and caused the contents of the glass to slosh.

Behind Nikki, Nessa glimpsed piles of cardboard boxes, some made up, and others lying flat, with a parcel-tape dispenser lying on top of the heap.

Where would Nikki go when she moved out? What would she do with all her possessions? Take them with her? Sell them? Store them? Give them away?

"We're not collecting for anything," said Meg earnestly, stepping forwards. "We wanted to ask you some questions."

"You're too young to be journalists." Nikki's lips curled disdainfully. Nessa didn't know whether the disdain was for journalists, in which case Nikki still had something in common with Moira, or for Nessa and Meg. "And you don't look like Jehovah's Witnesses." Maybe Nikki was disdainful of life in general.

Nessa swallowed, trying to find the words and courage to broach the reason for their visit.

Meg had no such problem. She ploughed straight ahead. "We want to talk to you about Moira Cavendish."

"Moira? You're here because of Moira?" Nikki yelled, outraged and loud and so drunk Nessa knew the glass in her hand was not her first, second, or third of the evening.

Nessa and Meg recoiled. Nessa wished they hadn't come. "She doesn't know we're here," said Nessa weakly.

Nikki blinked owlishly. "She left me, and when I needed her, she wasn't there. Has never been there."

"The way I heard it, you dropped her when you got yourself a boy-friend," said Nessa.

"What? No, I didn't. I was right there. Like I'm right here. But I won't be for much longer. All she had to do was say she'd be on that stupid show, and I could have saved the house but, no, she's too effing good for TV these days."

"What TV?" asked Nessa.

"*The Cats' Meow*, of course! Should have been us, not those pretty boy posers, although they're not so pretty anymore."

"My mum said the same thing about them! She loves that show!" said Meg.

Nikki sneered. Winston yapped and wriggled, demanding to be put down, and Nessa tried to keep up with the conversation.

"You were invited to be on *the Cats' Meow*? You and Moira, both?" Why hadn't Moira mentioned anything?

"Well, duh! I said yes. Moira said no. They tried it without her. But it didn't work, and they told me they didn't want me after all, and Bloody Moira!" Nikki's expression crumpled, and she shifted from resentful to wretched in the space of a microsecond. "We used to be friends." She dropped Winston, who yelped and ran into the house.

Nikki's raw and unpredictable emotions were making Nessa twitchy. She glanced at Meg who looked equally unsettled.

Tears flowed down Nikki's face. "She left me. How could she leave me?"

"But I thought—" Nessa broke off.

"What did you think?" The anger was back, fiercer than before.

Nessa flinched and stammered. "I...I don't know. Only you...and Robin... You shut her out..."

"Bullshit!" Nikki's denial was automatic. Instinctive. A hint of rationality entered her tone. "Well, maybe I did. Robin and I were involved. But that's how it is at the beginning of a new relationship. It's normal. Moira should have been happy for me, not resentful. She threw a tantrum, and the band was finished. Bloody selfish!"

"That's not the way I heard it!" said Meg. "She left because she overheard Robin saying you and he didn't need a third wheel, and you were going to branch out on your own."

That was news to Nessa. Where had Meg got that from?

"Talk. It was idle talk."

Suddenly all the clues and hints, and all the things Moira had left unspoken, came together to form a picture so clear and ugly Nessa was outraged on Moira's behalf. "You agreed with him?"

"It didn't mean anything! Flirting. Chit-chat."

"You got a boyfriend, and you no longer made time for her. You left Moira ages before Moira left you."

"What is going on here?" a voice from behind Nikki demanded.

Nikki turned around and murmured something which might have been, "Oh, Derek! Make them go away!"

The newcomer pushed in front of Nikki, revealing himself. Unless he was much older than her, the years had been unkind to him. Initial impressions: thin, bristly, tired, worn. There were pouches under his eyes, and thread veins covering his nose.

"Get the fuck off our property!"

"We only wanted to—"

"Did Moira put you up to this? Using kids to get to Nikki? That's low!"

"We're not kids—"

"Moira didn't put us up to anything! We—"

"Go! Or I'll set the Dobermans on you! And I'll call the police! You've got thirty seconds to get off our land!"

Nessa and Meg stumbled over themselves as they hurried to leave.

"Boris! Churchill! Thatcher! C'mere boys!"

One step. Two steps. Faster, and they were legging it down the path, Derek screaming vitriol until they'd passed through the gate, making sure to close it behind them. They blended themselves into the shadows beyond.

They bent over, panting as the worst of their panic leached from their bodies.

When Meg managed to catch her breath again, she said, "That was..."

"Yeah."

"You don't think the dogs can jump over the gate, do you?"

"I hope not."

Nervously, Nessa glanced towards the converted church, where the Dobermans were prowling around, barking desultorily, and casting black shadows the size of horses.

What had Moira ever seen in Nikki? How had she ever been friends with someone like that? It didn't make sense.

"We shouldn't have come."

"No," agreed Meg. "Let's go home."

*

"Oh, shit!"

"Oh, shit?"

"I've lost the keys."

"What do you mean, you've lost the keys?"

"I didn't fasten my bag. They must have fallen out."

"Meg! How many times—?" She broke off. What was the point of saying anything now?

"I know! I'm sorry. Oh, God. They could be anywhere."

"Okay. Deep breaths. You need to calm down." Nessa needed to calm down too. Her heart hammered in her chest. Her brain felt as though it was floating about six inches to the left of her body. How come her voice sounded so normal when, in her head, it was loud and squeaky and verging on hysterical?

Meg pulled her phone out of her pocket and switched on its flashlight. She scanned the ground. Nessa copied her, desperately hoping they'd catch a glint of metal.

No luck.

"I must have dropped them in the churchyard."

"And we can hardly go and look."

Meg switched off the flashlight and held her phone close enough to her face for her to see the detail of the screen. "I haven't got a signal."

"Nor have I."

"What now?"

Nessa hated the hopelessness and panic that tinged Meg's words. She hated that Meg was looking to her for answers.

She couldn't afford to be angry or frustrated.

She needed to figure out what to do.

She had an idea. "Follow me. And hope."

She jogged to the phone box, pulled open the heavy door, and stepped inside. The box had an odd, stale smell. Was it from damp? Disuse? Something else?

Nessa shook the questions away. She didn't want to know the answers. Instead, she scrabbled around her pockets for coins. To make a call, she needed sixty pence made up of a maximum of four coins, and all she had was one twenty and two tens.

Meg squeezed into the box beside her. "What are you doing?"

Nessa resisted saying, "What does it look like I'm doing?" Instead, she lifted the receiver and heard a dial tone. Glory be! "Okay. This is still working. Have you got a twenty-pence piece?"

Meg ferreted around in her bag and extracted her purse. She pulled out a coin.

"Perfect." Nessa snatched it from her. She fed the change into the machine. "What's your parents' number?"

Meg rattled off a string of digits, which Nessa punched into the keypad while she held the receiver to her ear. There was a pause before the ringing tone kicked in. "Pick up," she mumbled. "Pick up."

They were in luck. Instead of letting the call go to voicemail, Liane answered the phone.

"Hello?" She spoke cautiously, almost certainly because she didn't recognise the number.

"Liane! It's me. Nessa."

"Nessa! Where are you? Where's Meg? What's happened! Are you all right?"

"We're fine. Well, not fine. Nothing's wrong with us. But we're in a mobile black spot, Meg's lost the car keys, and, well, we need rescuing. Please?"

Nessa moved to hand the receiver over to Meg, who shook her head vehemently. She mouthed, "You talk to them!" while gesturing and pointing furiously.

Lots of questions followed, some necessary, others less so.

Where were they phoning from? (A phone box.)

Where was the phone box? (Upper Slaughter.)

Was Upper Slaughter a real place? (Apparently so. There were Lower and Middle Slaughters too.)

Where was Upper Slaughter? (Somewhere between Exeter and Tiverton.)

What were they doing there? (It was a long story, one which, please, could they save for later?)

Upper Slaughter wasn't on the way home, was it? (Um, no. That was part of the long story.)

"They're coming," said Nessa unnecessarily, as she hung up. "Your mum says to stay near the phone in case they have to call."

Meg nodded.

"You can't put off talking to them forever. You know that, right?"

"Yeah, but I also knew they couldn't get mad if you were the one to call."

"Coward." Nessa nudged Meg affectionately.

"Too right."

They stepped out of the phone box and sat on the bench.

*

Time dragged.

After what felt like an aeon, but was barely five minutes, Nessa said, "Tell me the truth. Did you genuinely get the information about this place from the internet?"

"Yes." Meg dragged the syllable out in a way that suggested she wanted Nessa to believe it, instead of it being the truth.

"Meg..."

"I couldn't have got it without the internet."

"'Fess up. How did you know Nikki was here? And be honest."

"Okay, okay. I had some help."

Nessa, worried and angry, spoke through gritted teeth. "What kind of help?"

"A woman. She friended me on SayMate."

"What woman?"

"I don't know. I got a friend request, and she appeared okay, so I accepted it."

"Meg!"

"We're not all as paranoid as you!" Meg sniffled pathetically. "This is all my fault."

Nessa didn't argue.

"She told me there wouldn't be any problems."

Had Meg asked for reassurance, or had she, whoever she was, given it unprompted? And, if so, why?

"I thought—" Meg snuffled and wiped her eyes and nose with a tissue. Nessa waited impatiently for her to continue. "—she was my friend. She said she'd help me."

"You've never met her!"

"Online friendships count!"

"Not when you don't know the person. Even I have seen enough *Catfish* to know that."

"You know I hate this trust-no-one attitude thing you've got going." For once, perhaps the first time ever, Meg's criticism wasn't laced with derision. Her words were full of regret.

Equally regretfully, Nessa said, "Better than trusting everyone."

"I won't be doing that again in a hurry."

Was that a good thing or a shame? Maybe Meg would be more cautious from now on, but one of the things Nessa liked about her was her eternal optimism. Nessa would hate for Meg to lose that.

Nessa put her arm around Meg's shoulders and drew her into a hug.

It started to rain. Cold and sleety, it added to their misery. Short of breaking a window, they couldn't get into the car, and after the encounter with Nikki, they were reluctant to rely on the kindness of strangers. Besides, lights were on in only two of the terraces. Did anyone live in the others, or were they holiday lets?

They retreated to the telephone box, where they spent the next fifty minutes huddled together, listening to the rain hammer against its roof and sides.

Chapter Twenty-Five

Meg's parents arrived in the end.

Ted pulled up next to the phone box and ushered the girls into the car, saying, "Get in before you catch your deaths!"

Ted and Liane had come armed with spare car keys, blankets, and vacuum flasks of hot tea.

As she climbed into the back of the estate, Nessa felt as though she was sinking into a hot bath. Cold, tense muscles eased. She wrapped a blanket over herself, only reaching out from underneath it to take hold of a mug. The tea warmed her from the inside out. Gradually, feeling returned to her toes.

Ted and Liane had the decency to wait until Nessa's teeth stopped chattering and she had recovered enough for relief at being rescued to give way to worry about what was coming next before they launched the inevitable interrogation. Nessa managed not to fidget in her seat, but next to her, Meg failed miserably to achieve similar self-control.

"What are you doing all the way out here!" wailed Liane. "If anything had happened to you! If we'd had to send out a search party, we wouldn't have known where to look!"

"If anything had happened? Mum! It did happen. We phoned you, and you're here! We're fine!"

"That's not the point! Why are you here?"

"We, uh, got lost?"

"Don't be ridiculous!" snapped Ted. "Nessa? Perhaps you would like to fill us in."

Nessa managed not to say no, she wouldn't. Instead, she said, "We wanted to get in touch with an old friend of Moira's."

"What on earth for?"

"Because Moira misses her. And we hoped we could bring them together." Had the idea always been as lame as it sounded now? Or did it only sound that way because of the apologetic way Nessa told the story?

"That's sweet," sighed Liane.

"No, it's not. It's foolhardy and reckless and—" Ted ran out of synonyms.

"Can you just give me the keys, so we can go home?" asked Meg.

"Absolutely not, young lady!" snapped Ted.

Liane said, "What makes you think we'd trust you to drive yourself after all you've been through! Goodness knows what kind of mental state you're in!"

Meg started to weep.

More kindly, Liane said, "This isn't a punishment. We'll talk about that later. I'm going to drive your car because we're concerned about you. You've obviously had a shock, and you're still in a state."

Nessa looked at Meg, who was using the corner of her blanket to mop her face. Liane had a point.

*

"W hatever possessed you?" Ted asked when they were seated around the kitchen table, a hearty stew, which Liane had prepared earlier and left to cook in the bottom oven of the Aga, in front of them.

While Meg had made disjointed comments about how they'd been shouted at and chased by slavering dogs, and Ted had managed to hold off asking questions, Nessa had spent most of the journey to the farm asking herself the same thing.

"It was... We were..." Meg stumbled over her words.

Liane pursed her lips impatiently as she passed around glasses of water.

"It was stupid," said Nessa.

"Go on," said Liane.

Nessa felt like she had been sent on stage to perform a leading role she hadn't prepared for. She sat straighter. Her fingers twitched and tapped against her plate. She forced them still. "I guess it started last summer when I met Moira."

"Your neighbour. The one with the cakes."

"You know she used to be in a band?"

"The Diptych," said Meg helpfully. "With Nikki. The woman we went to visit."

"Ah," chorused Ted and Liane.

"Moira told me—" Nessa frowned and cut herself off. Had Moira told her? Or had she inferred it from what little Moira had shared? She tried again. "From what Moira told me, I gathered she and Nikki had been best friends when they were our age, but they had fallen out. I assumed she regretted that and wished they could reconnect."

"You said earlier that you wanted to reunite them?"

"Yes." Nessa could have said much more about what they'd been doing in Upper Slaughter, but that was the crux of the matter, wasn't it?

"Isn't that their business?"

"I don't think Moira knows where Nikki lives," said Nessa. "At least, I didn't think she did, although Nikki suggested she knew. But most of what Nikki said didn't make any sense, so maybe I was right, and Moira doesn't. Anyway, I thought..." Maybe she hadn't thought at all.

Meg said, "It's my fault, at least as much as Nessa's."

"How? You don't even know these people!"

"No, which maybe makes my part in this worse. You know I want to make a podcast?"

Ted rolled his eyes. "You've mentioned it enough times. What does that have to do with anything?"

"I thought—"

"It was my idea," interrupted Nessa.

Meg waved at her to be quiet. "I hoped the podcast would be something we might do together, even though we were hundreds of miles apart. I didn't know what we could podcast about to make it different from anybody else's show. But Nessa met Moira and had the idea we should do an investigation. We decided it would be cool to track Nikki down and, you know."

"Don't you think that was rather presumptuous of you?" said Ted.

"Naïve too," suggested Liane.

"We know that now," said Nessa, miserable and chagrined.

"You know the house rules. You tell us where you're going and when you'll be home. You don't go off on magical mystery tours and knock on strangers' doors!"

"If we'd told you, you—"

"We would have said no? If you knew that then that should have told you something."

"But if Nikki had been nicer, it would have been great. Happy endings all round," said Meg, which did nothing to cool the discussion.

Liane and Ted were equally exasperated. "But she wasn't, was she? And you two put yourselves in who knows what kind of danger! Thank God nothing worse happened to you!"

Everyone took unenthusiastic mouthfuls of the stew to fill the uncomfortable silence that followed Liane's outburst.

After several forkfuls, Meg said, "Just so you know, today was my idea. Nessa didn't want to go, but I was driving, so I made her."

"At least one of you has an ounce of sense," said Ted grimly.

"I didn't try very hard to dissuade her," said Nessa.

"Only because you knew I wouldn't let you." Meg turned to her parents and asked, her voice uncharacteristically tentative, "What's going to happen now?"

"We haven't decided yet," said Ted.

"That's enough talk for now," said Liane. "Eat up, everybody. It's getting late."

"And I've got to get up early for milking," said Ted. "We'll talk again tomorrow and figure out what your punishment is going to be."

"Punishment?" said Meg, unnerved.

"You're not too old to be grounded. Not while you're living under this roof. And," Ted added, looking directly to Nessa, "I'll be calling your father too."

Should she try to phone Dad and get her version of the story in first? But Nessa didn't feel up to it right now, not after everything else they'd been through. Plus, no matter how angry Ted was, she trusted him to be fair.

She hoped.

*

Nessa woke in darkness which felt like the middle of the night, but it must have been well after seven because she could hear voices; Ted had finished the milking. Careful not to disturb Meg, Nessa crept past her room and along the landing towards the bathroom.

Something about the conversation made her stop and strain to hear. She tiptoed down to the half landing, careful to avoid the creaky board on the second step. She crouched in the shadows, feeling guilty for eavesdropping, but unable to stop herself.

"There's a limit to what we can do," Ted was saying. "They're both adults, and they didn't do anything illegal."

Nessa didn't hear a reply. Ted was on the phone, which meant he must be talking to Dad. She hated to think how Dad would have reacted to being woken up so early on a Sunday.

"Stupidity isn't a crime." Ted sounded disappointed. Did he think it should be?

Nessa had heard enough. She crept up the stairs, went to the bathroom, and headed to her bedroom where she crawled under the duvet and, against all expectations, fell asleep.

*

Outside, dawn had yet to break. Inside, Moira was drifting around in her housecoat and jammies, easing her way into what she hoped would be a leisurely Sunday morning, when someone pounded on her front door loudly, furiously, and franticly enough to be terrifying.

Living so far up the glen, Moira had never considered she or her house might be vulnerable to a homicidal maniac.

She considered it now.

No way was she going to the door without first checking who her visitor was.

Moira scuttled into the living room and peered through the window.

Joe must have seen movement out of the corner of his eye because he started shouting as well as banging.

"Moira! Open up! I want to talk to you!"

What the hell? Joe had always struck her as reasonable, even easy-going. What had set him off?

She went to the front door. Unlocked it. Opened it at an angle and stood in the gap between it and the door jamb.

Before she could ask what he was screaming about, he yelled, "Did you put her up to it?"

Moira stared at him.

"Did you?"

"What are you talking about?" she asked coldly. She folded her arms across her chest and wished she had something handy to defend herself with in case this argument got even nastier. A baseball bat or a crowbar would have been nice. Maybe she'd shop online later.

Joe let rip with a torrent of words about Nessa and Meg and an early morning phone call from people Moira had never heard of. Something about dogs and a rescue, and Moira was rapidly losing patience with him.

"Anything could have happened! They're damn lucky nothing did! We all are!"

Moira forced herself to stand taller and, enunciating every syllable with care, said, "I do not know what you are talking about. So, either calm down and explain yourself, or leave!" To her surprise, as well as to his, she found herself pointing an imperious finger in the direction of her front gate.

"Nessa and her friend Meg tracked down your old pal, Nikki. As if you didn't know."

"I didn't. Why in heaven's name would they do something so crazy?"

"Nessa got it into her head you'd like to reconnect with your former partner!"

Moira's mouth flapped open and shut. She managed to squeeze a question out. "Why would she think that?"

"You must have some idea!"

"Well, I don't. We talked about the Diptych a few times; that's all." That had been all, hadn't it?

"You must have said something."

Moira shook her head. She was sure she hadn't. If she had, she hadn't meant to.

Joe stared at her. Moira stared back. They had reached an impasse.

Eventually, Joe said, "Maybe you put the girls up to it. Maybe you didn't. Either way, I want you to stay away from my daughter."

He spun on his heel and stalked down the path.

Eyes wide, jaw slack, and heart pounding, Moira watched him go.

She gently closed the door. She rested her forehead against one of the frosted glass panels. It was cold against her skin.

Her heart rate gradually slowed to something closer to normal.

Had she been to blame?

If so, how?

*

Neither Nessa nor Meg were in a hurry to get up, both unwilling to face the consequences of the previous evening's adventure. Eventually, hoping Meg's parents might be out on the farm, they ventured downstairs, questing for a late breakfast.

Nessa's appetite vanished when they were ambushed by Liane, who had been lying in wait for them, but she accepted a mug of tea. Meg managed to nibble on a slice of toast slathered with homemade marmalade.

They had barely finished when Ted came in.

Instead of saying good morning, Ted said to Nessa, "You need to phone your father. He's expecting your call." He handed her the landline phone, which she eyed dubiously. Tethered to the wall, she would have no privacy. "Now. In front of me. I want to make sure you do it."

Wow. Ted and Liane must have been way more upset than they'd let on if they were playing the heavy-handed parents to this extent.

Or maybe Dad had told them to.

What was the number of the new house? It was in her contacts on her mobile, of course, but, dammit, she'd memorised it in the summer. Why couldn't she remember it now?

"Number's on the phone pad," Ted said, which was helpful, even though it sounded like a threat.

Ted and Liane lingered until they heard Nessa say, "Hi, Dad. It's me," before they signalled to Meg to follow them into the hall.

*

The first thing Dad asked was whether Nessa was all right. The second was "Did Moira put you up to this?"

"No! Of course not! She had no idea. I just…"

"You just, what?"

"I wanted to do something nice for her, after how great she was over the summer. But things got out of hand."

"It sounds like it." Dad sighed. "You'd better start from the beginning."

Nessa reminded him of how supportive Moira had been when Nessa had told her she was gay and Emily hadn't wanted to go out with her. She told Dad how Moira had confessed she could relate to Nessa's feelings and how it had felt to lose her best friend.

Nessa skirted around Moira's asexuality; that was Moira's secret to share, not hers. But she suspected Dad guessed some of what she was not telling them.

"I thought if I could bring the two of them together, they could be friends again. Once Meg and I started, we couldn't stop, even when I wanted to, and when we met Nikki, she was horrible. And the man she was with scared the heck out of us."

*

"What did your parents say?" asked Nessa when she and Meg were safely upstairs again. They were lying on Meg's bed, neither having any enthusiasm to do anything.

"I'm grounded until I'm twenty-five."

"No, really, what did they say?"

"That's what they said. I don't think they're serious about the twenty-five thing, but I can only have the car to get to and from school, and no hanging around after classes finish. Plus, I must hand the car keys over to Mum as soon as I get home. It's going to be a while before they trust me to go anywhere on my own."

"That sucks."

"Yeah. Can't blame them though."

"I suppose not."

"What did your dad say?"

"Pretty much everything your parents did, plus a few extras. What were we thinking? He thought I was more responsible than that. Had I apologised to your folks for causing so much trouble? He's disappointed in me. I'm almost an adult; isn't it time I behaved like one? Yadda, yadda, yadda. The 'rents'll have to forgive us eventually."

"Yeah. Around the time we hit thirty."

"What I don't get is what Moira ever saw in Nikki. She was ghastly!"

"Hmm."

Nessa propped herself up on one elbow. "'Hmm, I agree with you,' or 'Hmm, shut up and let's talk about something else'?"

"Bit of both, I suppose. Yeah, Nikki was horrible. Yeah, I don't see why Moira, or anyone, would want to have anything to do with her. But we're not going to find answers to any of it by going on about it, so we might as well change the subject."

"What do you want to talk about?"

"I'm not in the mood to talk at all, I don't think."

*

They spent the rest of the day in subdued awkwardness, but at least Meg's parents didn't insist on returning Nessa to St Drogo's earlier than planned.

On Monday morning, Meg drove them both to school, heading first to Hobby so Nessa could drop off her weekend bag before going to class.

As Meg made the turning onto the school campus, she had to pull over to allow a police car to pass in the opposite direction.

There was another police car parked on Hobby's forecourt, its blue lights flashing.

Chapter Twenty-Six

As Nessa pulled her bag from the car, Dinah rushed over to meet her. Delightedly, she exclaimed, "All hell's breaking loose!"

"Again?" Nessa quirked a weary eyebrow. "I'm sick of all the drama." Although, the police presence added a novel twist to things.

"It's Poppy! She and a townie got caught red-handed in the old pavilion!"

Meg wound down her window and leaned out to hear better.

"Caught doing what?"

"Drugs, of course!"

"Drugs!"

"She'll be lucky not to get expelled. The police have been here since last night. They've been crawling all over the house and the grounds. They spent a lot of time in your room. Searching it."

"What! Holy crap! They didn't find anything, did they?"

"Not in your room, no."

"Thank God!" Maybe Poppy did have a gram of common sense, after all, if she had been smart enough to keep her stash somewhere else. If so, hopefully, Nessa was in the clear.

"Nessa. A word." Ms Breckenridge had materialised behind them.

"Yes, Ms Breckenridge?"

"Follow me. And Dinah, don't you have somewhere else you need to be? You too, Meg."

Nessa allowed herself to be led through the corridors of Hobby and into Ms Breckenridge's flat. Nessa had never been inside before, and she craned her neck to see as much as possible. She spotted a small bedroom, its door ajar, double bed sloppily made, but otherwise tidy, and a small kitchenette, where an array of saucepans rested upside down on the plate rack next to the sink. There were a couple of other doors too, but they were closed.

Nessa followed Ms Breckenridge into the room at the end of the hallway, which turned out to be a surprisingly spacious living room, with space enough for a sofa and bookshelves at one end and a dining table at the other.

A uniformed police officer got up from the sofa.

*

"What happened?" asked Dinah, an hour and a half later. Apparently, the somewhere else Dinah had needed to be was Hobby's common room, where, textbooks open in front of her, she'd lain in wait for Nessa to reappear.

"They sat me down and asked some questions. Did I know the Popsicle had been taking drugs? Had I suspected? Did I know where she'd been keeping them, given they hadn't found anything in our room? I told them no. At least one good thing's come out of our feud: the police don't believe we're in it together. But you should see the mess the police have made of our room!"

By the time Nessa finished, a surprisingly large crowd, given the time of day, had gathered around them.

"She's been stashing the drugs in the fishpond," said Dhriti.

"How do you know?" asked Su Mei, curious.

"Saw the police fish something out earlier."

"Wow," said Yi Wei.

"I've seen her hanging around out there a few times," said Dinah. "I asked her about it once. She told me she liked the koi carp."

"Where's Poppy now?" asked Dhriti.

Nessa said, "Police station. Her parents are picking her up from there and taking her home. Ms Breckenridge wants me to help pack Poppy's stuff."

"She's gone?" The enthusiastic tone in which Dhriti asked the question, and the eager way everyone else leaned in to listen to Nessa's answer, spoke eloquently of Poppy's lack of popularity.

"I guess so. Zero tolerance, remember? And, unlike Thomas Mitchum, she got caught on the grounds."

*

By the time every trace of Poppy and the police had been expunged from the room, it was late afternoon. Apparently, having the police raid your room was a reasonable excuse to miss several lessons, but it wasn't enough to get out of rehearsals.

For a couple of hours, however, Nessa had time to draw breath. She expected that to be a relief but, with nothing to distract her, Nessa's worries and regrets crowded in, trying to fill the newly emptied space around her.

Eventually, unable to resist any longer, and against Dad's edicts, she telephoned Moira.

*

"Your dad won't be happy if I talk to you," said Moira. "And I'm not sure whether I am either."

Moira's spike of alarm, brought on by Joe's ire, had worn off only gradually. Afterwards, Moira had found herself pummelled by other emotions. The easiest to identify was confusion.

She'd told Nessa more than she'd ever told anyone else, except, maybe, Gareth, and Nessa had known Moira disliked journalists digging around in her private life. Why had Nessa assumed it would be any different for her? Because Moira had deigned to share a few sanitised confidences? Why had Moira's rift with Nikki mattered so much that Nessa had poked around in matters best left alone?

"Please? Will you at least listen?"

"If you make it quick."

"First of all, I'm sorry. I should never have pried. It was none of my business, even if my intentions came from a good place."

"Oh? And what place was that?"

Moira listened as Nessa tried to explain, ending with "I wanted to surprise you."

"You did that all right."

"I mean, I wanted to surprise you in a good way. I wanted to do something for you, and I hoped reuniting the two of you would make you happy."

Moira couldn't hold onto her anger. Instead, she felt profoundly touched. No matter how disastrous Nessa's actions had been, they had been well-intentioned.

"How was Nikki?"

"Do you genuinely want to know?"

"Your question is answer enough. Plus, the way your dad talked, I gather it can't have been good."

"It wasn't."

"Tell me."

*

Meg and Nessa managed to snatch a few minutes together at lunchtime on Tuesday.

"How's the show going? Are you all coping without you know who?"

"Everything's good. Ms Markides ranted on about how the Popsicle had let us down, and how inconvenient it was to recast her role. She was melodramatic, but we already had more doo-wop girls than we need. Becca got bumped up to Ronette, and that was it. Job done. Turns out Poppy was totally expendable. The only thing we're missing is her diva-like behaviour, and we're missing that in the best way possible."

The school's rumour mill had worked as efficiently as ever, and other than Nessa admitting she enjoyed having the room to herself, there wasn't much to say on the topic of Poppy which hadn't already been said by plenty of others. Thus, Nessa and Meg returned to reflecting on their own misadventures.

Meg had recovered sufficiently from her trauma to bemoan the injustice of her punishments. "I'm an adult. Old enough to have sex. Drive. Get married. Vote. Buy alcohol. Smoke. Why are we being punished for using a car that's legally mine and knocking on someone's front door? It's not like we stole anything."

"Smoking's overrated, and I'm not sure about alcohol either. I'm yet to meet anyone to have sex with, and there isn't an election in the offing for a while yet. I'm okay with putting adulting on hold and letting the 'rents do it for a while longer," said Nessa.

Meg raised her eyebrows.

Nessa scuffed her heels against the floor. "I've never made as many poor decisions as I have these last few months." The downside to having the room to herself was that Nessa had plenty of time and privacy in which to think. And she'd been thinking a lot.

"What bad decisions?"

"I lied to the Popsicle."

"Big deal."

"Yeah, it was a big deal. That lie came back to bite me big time. Plus, there was the Frankie fiasco."

"You weren't to know."

"No?"

"It's not like she told you she was asexual."

"I didn't tell her I was gay either. We both made assumptions about the other and what we were doing, and things went horribly wrong."

"But you're putting things right now."

"I'm trying to," agreed Nessa. "I also invaded Moira's privacy."

"In a good cause."

"Was it? And even if it was, it didn't give me the right to rummage through her papers."

Nessa got the impression Meg was itching to argue the point, and maybe that was fair enough. Meg had to live with her parents and her punishment every day, while Nessa was hundreds of miles from Dad. She lived with the same school rules and constraints she'd had to accept since last Easter. In some ways, other than Dad's disappointment, nothing had changed, and that didn't seem fair.

"You'll get bored of beating yourself up in a day or so," said Meg with enough confidence to make Nessa suspect she was right.

*

After the argument on her doorstep, the Clarksons and Moira avoided each other for a few days, and Moira missed her neighbours and their cheery hellos far more than she expected. Once, she would, albeit with regret, have let them drift out of her life. Now, she was tempted to fight for the nascent friendship she'd been developing with the whole family. She wanted to fight for them in the way she'd once fought for Nikki.

Two girls. A country road. At night. Joe had been right. They had been lucky.

She would never have forgiven herself if anything had happened to them.

She reflected on everything she'd told Nessa and of all the things she'd left unsaid.

She stewed and fretted. What should she do for the best?

Just as her ingrained caution was about to get the better of her, something landed with a dull thump on her door mat.

She wasn't expecting a package so, curious, she went to the front door. She bent and picked up a small, brown, padded envelope. It was addressed to her in an almost familiar hand.

She turned the envelope over. No return address.

She ripped it open and tipped the contents onto her palm: a key ring with a car key and a house key attached.

The key ring's fob had a manufacturer's logo on it, along with the address of a garage somewhere down south. Moira had never seen the keys before. She poked around inside the packaging, but there was no note. No explanation.

The handwriting.

So familiar, yet not.

*

That evening, after she'd fed both Mr Gillespie and herself, Moira went next door, taking with her both the keys and a peace offering in the form of a lemon drizzle cake, one of Nessa's favourites. Moira hoped Cindy and Joe would like it as much.

Cindy led Moira through to the kitchen but didn't invite her to sit down. Nor did Cindy offer her any refreshment. Cindy's welcome was cool, but at least it hadn't been icy enough to have left Moira on the front doorstep.

Things could have got off to a worse start.

Moira set the cake down on the counter. "I'm sorry."

"What for? Nessa told us you had no idea what she was up to." Cindy's tone made Moira suspect she was trying to convince herself at least as much as she was trying to reassure Moira.

"I didn't. But still, she did it because of me."

"Yes." At least Moira and Cindy had found something they agreed on.

"I told Nessa a story. But I didn't tell her the whole story of what happened between Nikki and me. If I had... Is Joe here? He needs to hear this too."

"He's upstairs with Finlay. He'll be down in a minute."

As if to confirm her words, they heard movement, a muffled voice, the click of a door being closed, and footsteps on the stairs.

When he entered the kitchen, Joe crossed his arms over his chest but didn't say anything.

Moira gestured vaguely. "Cake. A peace offering. I came to say I'm sorry."

Like Cindy, Joe asked, "What for?"

"I made a mistake. I treated Nessa like a child. I didn't want to expose her to how disappointing life can be. I told myself I was looking out for her, but I think I was protecting myself. And Nikki. Looking out for Nessa would have been treating her like an adult and telling her everything right from the start. It's my fault she didn't have the information she needed. If she had, she wouldn't have gone looking for Nikki."

"Maybe not, but she'd have found some other hare-brained scheme to get involved with instead."

Moira guessed Joe was attempting to comfort her, but she refused to feel better and carried on as though he hadn't spoken. "I told her Nikki had been my best friend, and we'd drifted apart. I didn't tell her why. And I didn't tell her, no matter how much I miss having Nikki in my life, there's no going back to the way things were at the beginning when everything was good and anything was possible."

"You talk about her as though you were close," said Cindy carefully. "Is that why you and Nessa get on so well? You have something in common?"

Moira snorted.

"But didn't she go out with some guy? I don't remember his name," said Joe.

Moira nodded. "You're right. She did. She got together with Robin."

Joe snapped his fingers. "Robin! That's it! Wasn't there some kind of scandal? I don't remember."

"We weren't close, not in the way you're suggesting anyway. As for the scandal..."

"A scandal. Is that what you didn't tell Nessa about? Are you going to tell us? What did happen?" asked Cindy.

Joe led them to the table where they all sat.

Moira girded her metaphorical loins as she resolved to tell Joe and Cindy the secrets she had carried with her for close to forty years, the secrets the gutter press would have paid good money to hear.

*

Moira told them the same story she'd told Nessa about how she'd met Nikki. She'd almost got to the point where they'd been signed up by the record label when Cindy rose to put the kettle on.

Cindy returned with mugs, a pot of tea, and a plate of biscuits. The Cold War was beginning to thaw, although not enough for Cindy to have unwrapped Moira's cake.

"One Saturday in November, we were rushing to pack everything into the van." The lashing rain had plastered Moira's hair to her head and trickled down her neck. Her hands had been icy cold and slick with water, and her denim jeans soaked. She'd been thinking about how much she wasn't looking forwards to the journey south, the Bedford's heater cranked up as high as it would go but still incapable of making a dent in the chill. "A talent scout from one of the record companies appeared out of nowhere. Flash suit. Huge golfing umbrella. Totally out of place. He told us he'd come to see us, had liked what he'd heard, and he wanted to cut a deal. We dropped out of university the following week. Our parents were furious. They said we were making the biggest mistakes of our lives. Went on about wasted opportunities. But we were twentyish and we assumed we knew everything."

Joe smiled wryly. "Doesn't everyone at that age?"

"We ended up living in a shared house in Islington with six other people. It needed everything done to it. It's prime real estate these days, although at the time it was barely better than a squat. But living there was exciting, you know? We cut our first single, and we recorded our first album. And we had our first hit."

"'Loved You from the First Moment'," said Joe automatically.

"That's the one. Got to number twenty-three in the charts. More followed, including our first number one and appearances on *Top of the Pops*. It was a fairy tale. And you know what fairy tales are like: there must be at least one poison apple or evil spell." She paused to sip at her tea. She took a biscuit, nibbled at its edge, and put it aside.

"I knew people in the Islington house did drugs. I got offered marijuana. I never witnessed anything else, but there were rumours about coke. Other stuff. Still, there'd been pot at university, and I'd heard similar rumours of stronger stuff there too. All I had to do was stay away from it, and it wouldn't be a problem. I believed Nikki felt the same way. She told me she did.

"I moved out when we started to make serious money. I asked Nikki whether she wanted to share with me, but she said she'd prefer to invest in a place of her own. Her house became party central. She acquired a reputation for being the fun half of the band, and the record company was all too happy to sell that image. I got stuck with being the boring sidekick." Moira spoke without rancour. She'd sometimes felt sidelined, but she hadn't much liked the limelight anyway. For the most part, being overlooked had suited her well enough.

"I went to a few of her parties, enough to keep up appearances, and I usually left early. But she stayed up late, sometimes all night, and she could barely keep her eyes open in the recording studio the mornings after. I worried about her, but we went on tour, and once she was away from London, she was her old self. Everything seemed fine for a while, but the trouble started again when we returned to the studio."

Moira shifted in her chair to ease the tension in her neck that had formed in the telling. Cindy and Joe waited patiently.

"The record company sent us to tape videos to sit alongside the tracks we were recording. Nikki met Robin on the set when we were filming the video of 'Will You (Ask Me Out)?' Nikki fell for him immediately." Moira didn't bother to disguise her distaste. "Things weren't the same after that. Her eyes were bloodshot in the afternoons. She missed sessions in the studio. I overheard her and Robin planning to set up on their own, and when I asked her about it, she wouldn't give me a straight answer. Then she announced she wanted our duo to become a trio, and the record company was up for it."

"But the band split up instead?" suggested Joe. "You walked away because you didn't like the direction the group was going in?" But Moira could tell he didn't believe it was as simple as that. She wouldn't have mentioned drugs if they weren't relevant.

She shook her head. "'Will You (Ask Me Out)?' got to number one, and Nikki hosted a party to celebrate. I went because it was expected, but I didn't intend to stay long. The party was in full swing when I arrived, and Nikki was nowhere to be seen. Someone told me she was upstairs, so I went to find her."

"And?"

"She wasn't alone."

"Ah."

"It's not what you're thinking. She was on the bed. And, yes, they'd had sex. But Robin was dressed. He was ignoring her, and he was dealing."

"Dealing."

"Coke. Heroin. God knows what. Nikki was in a bad way, but he refused to phone for help. We argued. He hit me. Belted, more like. He broke my nose, and he sent me flying across the room." The blood had dripped down her face, warm, thick, and sticky. She'd shaken, like she was shaking now.

Joe placed his hand on her forearm and pulled her into the present.

Appalled, Cindy whispered, "What happened after that?"

"I don't remember much. I got out of the room. It was too loud and crowded to find a phone in the house, so I went into the street. Found a phone box. Phoned 999. The police came. Raided the party. And it's just as well they did. Nikki had OD'd."

"You saved her life."

Moira batted the comment away as irrelevant. "I got her boyfriend arrested, and when the police investigated, they found he'd been trafficking as well as dealing. Robin was tried and I destroyed her relationship, and with it, the band. I tried to get in touch with her a couple of times, but I guess some things can't be forgiven." Moira shook her head.

Cindy and Joe sat in silence, absorbing everything Moira had told them.

"We're not in touch anymore. Haven't been since...for a long time. But I've kept track of her. We still have a few friends in common, and I sometimes read the gossip mags in the hairdressers, so I know she's been married a couple of times. She's been in rehab too. She's tried to kick-start her career once or twice with limited success. My contacts say she quit the drugs but not the drink."

"Nessa said she was drunk. She said most of what Nikki told her didn't make sense."

"Such as?"

"Something about Nikki having been on *the Cats' Meow*? But she hasn't," said Joe.

"I've been watching it," said Cindy. "It's almost as good as *Strictly*!

I'd know if she'd been on."

"It sounds as though she's delusional," said Joe.

"She's not delusional. The show's producers scrapped the episode they recorded with her. And I shouldn't be telling you that."

"Oh."

As they assimilated the information, Joe tapped the side of his mug with his forefinger, and Cindy fiddled with her engagement ring.

"Does that mean it's also true you were asked to be on the show?"

"Yes. I said no."

"Have you ever told anyone else what happened?" asked Cindy, her voice so rich with sympathy, it was almost Moira's undoing.

"Only what they needed to know. Never the whole story."

"Why not?"

"She was my friend, and I wanted to protect her."

Moira lapsed into silence and waited for one of the others to say something.

Joe said, "To think I thought this parenting lark would get easier as Nessa got older!"

"It'll get different," said Cindy. "Not easier. Nessa's learning to navigate the adult world. We need to make sure we're here when she needs us and we're ready to help where we can."

Nessa was lucky to have them both.

They were lucky to have each other.

Moira envied them the closeness, support, and advice the family gave each other, and she felt a sharp pang of something.

She felt tired.

Moira apologised again; she should have treated Nessa more like the adult she was becoming, already was. She stood up. "I've said what I came for. I'd better go."

"No," said Cindy. "Stay. Have another mug of tea, and some of the cake you brought. I've missed talking to you these last few days. Besides, I've got into the most frightful tangle with my knitting, and I'm hoping you can sort me out."

Moira knew an olive branch when she heard one.

*

When Nessa next spoke to Dad, he was so calm it was unnerving. Surely, he hadn't got over his disappointment in her so soon. He'd been so angry.

"You can tell Meg we've got her keys," he said as soon as they'd got the usual pleasantries out of the way.

"What? How?"

"Nikki sent them to Moira. Anonymously, but it must have been her. Cindy's putting them in this morning's post. They should be with you on Monday."

"Is Moira still upset with me?" Nessa's voice was small and worried. She bit her lip. Her question gave away the fact she'd disobeyed Dad, and she and Moira had been in touch.

To her surprise, Dad didn't make anything of her slip.

"More confused and hurt than anything, I reckon. Plus, she blames herself for not telling you the full story of what happened between her and Nikki. She said if she had maybe you wouldn't have gone off on a fool's errand."

"She doesn't blame me?"

"Not so you'd notice. Which isn't to say you shouldn't take responsibility. You owe her a huge apology, and the pair of you have a lot to talk about."

"I don't have to keep away from her anymore?"

"No. To be honest, I think it's better you don't. She has lots she wants you to know."

Interlude

I don't want to talk about what happened, or why the Diptych broke up. It happened a long time ago, and the details aren't important.

What I will say is my being aromantic and asexual was a factor. I didn't understand it at the time, but I was in platonic love with my best friend, and when she found romantic love...

Learning the words asexual and aromantic has given me the vocabulary I need to articulate who I am. I have words that let me define myself according to what I am, not what I lack. The words validate my existence, and the existence of people like me.

I didn't have the language. If I—we—had, maybe things would have turned out differently.

Chapter Twenty-Seven

Meg jumped in front of Nessa as Nessa emerged from Hobby House. "We need to talk!"

"Can't right now." Nessa's head was full of chemical formulas and equations, and she wasn't in the mood to deal with Meg in high drama mode. "I'm going to be late for chemistry." As if to emphasise the point, she broke into a jog.

Meg side-stepped alongside her. "It's important! I'm— We're in trouble!"

"Trouble?" asked Nessa, still jogging.

"Journalist. She wants payback for the help she gave me tracking down Nikki. She's threatening me. Us. My family."

Nessa ground to a halt. "Shit," she murmured. That sounded serious. But chemistry. Chemistry was serious too. "All right. Listen. I've got to go, but I'll come and find you as soon as I'm done. I'll meet you in the library, okay?"

"Can't you skip chem? You can say you were sick, or something. Say you've got a migraine!"

"No. I can't. And I don't get migraines."

"Say you're still traumatised from the police search! Please, Nessa!"

The panic radiating from Meg was palpable. Nessa was torn, but... "I'm sorry. I can't! This is a make-up for the class I missed on Monday. I can't miss it a second time; if I don't take the practical, I'll fail the whole course!"

"Nessa!"

"No. Now I've got to go!" Was that too abrupt and harsh? "We'll talk later." She didn't wait for Meg to agree. Instead, she broke into a full-blown run which earned her a reprimand from a passing teacher.

*

Nessa made it to class by the skin of her teeth, tagging onto the end of the line of students filing into the lab.

Meg had been in a state, but Nessa told herself that whatever had upset her could surely keep for a couple of hours.

What if Nessa was wrong?

Nessa readied her equipment, measured out the chemicals she needed, and lit her Bunsen burner. Her hands shook as she carried out the delicate procedures required by the experiment.

Afterwards, Nessa had no idea how she made it through the practical without breaking anything. Even more miraculously, judging by her results, she'd managed to pass the assessment with flying colours.

She felt wrung out as she rushed through the clearing up. Even so, Nessa was in a better state than Meg, who, when Nessa tracked her down in the library, was a quivering wreck.

"Come on. Let's go to my room."

Nessa and Meg traipsed across the school grounds, heading for Hobby House. Given Meg's desperate desire to talk earlier, her silence now was disturbing.

Meg had visited Nessa's room before, but previous visits had been almost perfunctory because of Poppy.

Nessa sat Meg at her desk and went to make some tea.

When she returned five minutes later, armed with mugs and chocolate digestives, Meg was no longer sitting. Instead, Nessa found her standing in what had been Poppy's side of the room, looking around. She'd been driven onto her feet either by curiosity or by a nervous energy that made it impossible to stay still. Nessa suspected the latter, although curiosity was merited.

The room had changed since Meg had last seen it. Nessa had done her best to disguise the void left by Poppy's departure. She had covered the unused bed with a cover and a few scatter cushions, making it look slightly more like a couch. She'd also moved a few books and ornaments onto the emptied shelves, so they didn't look so barren. She'd even dug out a few small and subtle symbols of pride, which queer coded her space in a way she would never have dared while Poppy was there.

As much as Nessa loved her newfound privacy and didn't miss Poppy, with its second set of furniture, the room felt underoccupied. Like in a twin room in a hotel being occupied by a single person, she could sit on the second bed or use it as a dumping ground for shopping and clothes, but the fact remained, it was unnecessary and unwanted.

Nessa put the mugs and biscuits down on her desk, invited Meg to sit again, and pulled over the second desk chair to use herself.

Meg wilted as she sat.

"I'm sorry I couldn't talk earlier," said Nessa, and she meant it. She hated the way Meg looked: beaten, scared, diminished. "But we can talk now."

Her voice small, Meg said, "She won't leave me alone. She's blowing up my phone. She's leaving messages all over my social media. I'm almost too scared to look at it anymore."

"Who won't leave you alone? What's going on?"

"You know all the things I told you about how I found Nikki and the house?"

"Yes?"

"And how I told you about the woman who'd friended me on Say-Mate? The one who told me where Nikki was."

"The one who didn't warn you about scary Derek or the dogs. That friend?" Nessa spoke through clenched teeth.

"Yeah. That one. Everything I told you was true, but the thing is, it wasn't the whole truth."

Nessa's pulse raced. She counted to ten in an effort to calm herself. It didn't work.

"Don't look at me like that. Things are already bad enough. I don't want you turning on me too."

"What do you mean, turning on you?"

"I..."

Nessa crouched next to Meg. She put her hands on Meg's knees. "Meg. Meg! Listen to me! Whatever's happened, I'll always be your friend. Nothing's going to change that, and nobody's turning on anyone here. Now tell me what's going on."

"My friend... She wasn't helping me out of the goodness of her heart."

"I figured. You said she was a journalist?"

Meg nodded forlornly. "She offered me a trade. Information for information."

"What kind of information?"

"She wanted the real story why the Diptych had split up."

"What on earth for? That's hardly front-page news. That's ancient history!" Although hadn't Nessa wondered herself? Maybe it was still newsworthy even after almost four decades.

"She told me she'd been after the story for years, but she'd never got the whole truth. She said she couldn't get close enough to either Nikki or to Moira to ask the questions herself, but I could. She said she'd give me the information I needed to find Nikki in return for whatever I found out."

"You must have told her about our visit."

"Yes. But she's saying that's not good enough. I thought she could write something about the dogs and the drink, but apparently they're not newsworthy." Meg's shoulders shook. "She said if I can't give her what she wants she'll come after my family."

"Come after how?"

"I'm not entirely sure. But she promised me she can do it. All it would take is a story, a rumour. She could ruin us."

Nessa stood up and paced.

"I asked you how you did it! I asked and you didn't tell me! Why didn't you tell me?" Nessa's anger wasn't helping, but she couldn't stop the words from spilling out.

Meg didn't answer. She hung her head guiltily.

"Because you knew it was wrong."

"No! Because I knew you wouldn't approve."

Nessa slapped her own forehead, a gesture of dismay. "Because it was wrong!"

Meg tried to protest, but it was a feeble attempt. "In your opinion." Her voice was barely more than a whisper, her tone unconvincing.

They stared at each other, Nessa wanting to blame Meg, and Meg clearly blaming herself.

None of this was helping.

Nessa conceded. "I should have pressed harder for answers. I didn't because on some level I didn't want to know."

"I should have told you."

Probably Meg should have, but there was no point in dwelling on the cause of the problem. They needed to focus their attention on how to solve it.

"Right. First thing: we're going to call our parents. Both sets. And we're going to tell them what we're up against."

"We can't! They'll go ballistic!"

"We've got to. We can't sort this out on our own. We need help."

Meg gave in. "Okay. But can we call your dad first?"

*

"**W**e've got a problem." Joe's breath plumed in front of his face as he spoke. Cindy and Joe were standing on Moira's doorstep, pale-blue winter sky overhead. The frosted grass behind them in the shade of the house was silvered, pallid and crisp.

From the expressions on their faces, the problem, whatever it was, was a doozy.

"You'd better come in."

Joe and Cindy followed Moira through to her living room, stamping their feet and rubbing their hands to warm them.

Moira went through the ritual of offering tea or coffee while her guests peeled off their jackets and sat side by side on the sofa. They declined. Moira sat askew on the recliner so she faced them. "What can I do for you?"

Cindy and Joe glanced at each other in a way that wasn't reassuring.

"It's the girls," Cindy blurted out.

"Nessa and Meg," clarified Joe unnecessarily.

"They've got themselves into a bit of a scrape."

Joe snorted derisively. "And that's a bit of an understatement."

Cindy eyed Moira apologetically and said more truthfully, "They've got themselves into an unholy mess."

The story came out in fits and spurts. The narrative was disjointed with Cindy and Joe having to backtrack every so often as they remembered additional details, and there were areas where they weren't certain about specific points, possibly because Meg and Nessa hadn't been clear themselves.

Moira got the gist, though, even if a lot of the niceties around Meg's relationship with social media were lost on her. Suffice to say, Meg had reached out on Yapper or SayMate or something, and a journalist had reached back. Not any journalist, either, but Julia Walker, whose flawed exposé refused to stay dead and buried.

Julia Walker had helped Meg, and now Julia Walker wanted payment in blood. If she didn't get the scoop on Moira and Nikki, she would go after everyone Meg held near and dear, and she would smear until their reputations were tattered beyond repair.

Perhaps hers were idle threats. Perhaps they were not. Meg suspected her parents might have been inventive with some of their tax returns.

"We considered the Press Complaints Commission, but it has been replaced by—"

"IPSO," said Moira.

Joe nodded. "But I doubt it can help. It looks as though Walker needs to be attached to some publication or other, and I don't know that she is. It seems as though we can only complain once she's published something—"

"By which time, it'll be too late. Plus, there's the time it would take to process any complaints," said Cindy, "which makes things worse."

"We need something that can stop her before she does anything. A prophylactic if you will. We can't wait until we have something to cure."

When they finished, Cindy and Joe stared expectantly at Moira. To push the point home, Joe said, "The girls didn't know what to do, so they got in touch with us. The thing is we don't know what to do either. The only person we know who has any experience with the media is you, so here we are. Plus, this involves you as much as anyone else."

"You apologised to us," said Cindy. "Now it's our turn to apologise to you."

As much to buy time as anything else, Moira repeated her offer of refreshments. Cindy and Joe accepted, and Moira headed into the kitchen.

She filled the kettle, and as she waited for it to boil, she leaned over the sink, gripping its rim with her fingers so tightly the skin on her knuckles bleached white.

"Julia Walker. Dammit."

*

"I've got an idea. I need to think about it some more, build in some contingencies, but it might work."

They were in Moira's living room again, mugs in hand, and plates balanced on knees.

"What is it?" asked Joe.

Moira had assumed she'd have to think things through on her own. That was what she was used to. But she didn't need to. Joe and Cindy were there, and they were willing to listen. Maybe talking things through, having a sounding board, would be helpful.

"Julia Walker has been obsessed with the Diptych for years. Do you remember what I told you about that party?"

Joe and Cindy nodded.

"For months afterwards, she threw accusations around, suggesting Nikki and I had been involved in the dealing and trafficking and the record label dropped us. We were too much of a liability. Walker wanted to prove there had been some almighty cover-up, we'd paid off the police, or we'd cut a deal, or something. We hadn't, of course. I sued her for libel and won."

"So she has an axe to grind?"

"You could say that. The court case should have put an end to the matter, but it didn't."

Cindy's eyes widened, and she bolted upright as she was hit by an epiphany. "In the summer, you told me your phone had been hacked. But the hacking must have happened years after the Diptych split! Was that her?"

"I've always suspected it was. I don't know for sure. She believes she has something to prove because ours was the scoop that got away. She lost her job soon after I won the case, and she still bears a humongous grudge."

Cindy sank back in her seat. "Ugh. Horrible!"

"I've spent years avoiding her, and anyone like her, and I'm not going to give into her now. But maybe it's time I stop running. And I've got an idea for a story we can use to diffuse her."

"Hopefully once and for all," said Joe.

"Realistically, long enough to get her off Meg's back," said Moira.

Joe looked disheartened, while Cindy said, "What's the plan?"

"First, I need to tell you something. About me. Something you don't know."

"More secrets?" Cindy said without rancour. "Aren't you full of surprises?"

"I'm sorry. I don't mean to be, but I guess I'm not good at sharing things, partly because of bad experiences in the past, but mostly through lack of practice." Moira smiled humourlessly. "After all this time, I suppose secrecy is pretty much a habit. But, anyway, I'm asexual." She frowned. "You know what that is, right?" They were medical professionals, so she hoped they knew, but it wasn't a given.

"Broadly speaking," said Cindy.

"And aromantic?"

Joe nodded but with less conviction. "We came across mentions of them when we were researching LGBT stuff. You know, because of Nessa."

Moira didn't bother telling them that was pretty much how she'd found out too. Her smile slipped as she took in how he'd expressed himself; LGBT was less of a mouthful than stringing together the full alphabet soup of possible orientations, but the omission was exclusionary. She hoped it was simply a careless use of language on his part, but it hurt; however, that was a conversation for another time.

"When I grew up, we didn't have words for any of it. Or maybe we did, but they were the wrong words: frigid, prude, broken, cold. People like me were isolated. We were embarrassed to talk about being virgins or feeling pressured to have sex because that's what we were expected to do, even when we didn't feel any attraction. Do you know how many times people, including Nikki, told me to get over myself and do it? The number of times people reassured me the first time was never good, but you had to do it, get past it, and everything would be fantastic forever after?"

Moira got to her feet and wandered over to the window. She peered into the garden where the frost on the grass had melted in the sun and Mr Gillespie prowled around the flower beds. She'd read enough stories online to know her experiences weren't unique, or even special. Knowing that didn't make it easy to talk about now, but it at least made it easier than it would have been before she'd embarked upon her journey towards self-acceptance.

"You know the song, 'Will You (Ask Me Out)?'"

"Of course," said Joe. "My wife and I played it at our wedding."

"Ah. In that case, you mightn't like what I'm going to tell you."

"Go on."

"The song, my original version of it, anyway, wasn't supposed to be a romance. It was about a lack of romance. About questioning where romance was and whether it was even real. I wrote it decades before I learned about aromanticism. Even if I didn't have the words, I had the feelings, and those feelings have affected my entire life. That's what the story I want to tell would be about."

"About?"

"Asexuality. Aromanticism. About platonic love and what it's like to lose that when your best friend drops you for a lover. The story would be about why words are important, how life is harder when they don't exist, about different kinds of love, and about why, in the end, the Diptych didn't work. It wasn't because of drugs. They might have been the final straw, but they didn't cause the split. The split would have happened anyway. If we tell that story, we raise awareness of something I'm passionate about, and we don't need to say anything more about the drugs than is already on public record."

"Do you think it'll work?"

"I think so because we're not going to let Walker write the story. We're going to tell it ourselves. Let's get Meg and Nessa to make their podcast. That way, we control the message. The scoop Meg'll give Walker is that the podcast exists and when it will premiere. No doubt Walker will twist whatever we say, but the real story will be out there for anyone who cares to look. For once, let's use social media to our advantage."

"And you're okay with that? With the chance that whatever you say will get twisted out of all recognition?"

"It's not a perfect solution. But it's one I can live with, and I hope it'll dig us all out of a hole."

*

It was one thing to have a plan, another to make that plan actionable. From the limited amount Moira had learned about content creation, she'd gathered anyone could make and upload a podcast or a video, but that didn't guarantee people would find it.

For the plan to work, they needed as many people as possible to find Moira's story. The more listeners and publicity they got, the less scope there would be for Julia Walker, or anyone else, to corrupt the narrative. The more people who heard the true version, the less credible any twists Walker might add to it would be.

She would also make sure she knew how to complain if Julia Walker's behaviour got out of hand, and she'd make sure Joe, Cindy, and Meg's parents had information at the ready too.

Just in case.

Moira needed help to execute the plan. They all did.

Once Moira might have had the names of a few people she could call upon to assist, but it was a long time since she'd needed any public relations work done. She'd turned her back on all that when she'd fled London and the ruins of the band. She had no idea where any of the old names were these days let alone whether any of them were still in the business. She didn't even know whether they were still alive.

Moira knew only one person who might have the contacts and connections required to help them spread the word.

Asking for Gareth's help would be pushing their acquaintanceship to its limit.

She dialled his number and hoped he wouldn't mind being pushed.

*

Gareth didn't automatically say no when she told him what she was after. Instead, he said doubtfully, "You know PR's not my thing."

"But surely you know someone who does PR? Can you at least give me a name?"

"I'll see who I can come up with."

That was how at eight in the evening, on a dark and starry November night, Moira consented to talk to Ryan Walker-Price with Gareth acting as a chaperone on a video call.

Moira was reluctant to discuss anything other than the immediate business in hand, but Ryan did not show the same restraint.

Outraged, Ryan asked, "Did my mother really try to groom an eighteen-year-old girl to do her dirty work for her?" Groom was a loaded word, and that Ryan chose so carefully to use it spoke volumes.

"Yes," said Moira while in his tiled window Gareth nodded. "With a dollop of blackmail mixed in for good measure."

"Damn. I didn't want to believe it." He shook his head. "This time, she's gone too far."

This time? Moira resisted the urge to ask.

"Dad?" A young voice in the background of the call went some way towards explaining the reason for Ryan's dismay. There was nothing like having a child to throw the failings of one's parents into sharp relief. Either that, or becoming a parent gave a person a new-found appreciation of how much their own parents had had to deal with.

"Hang on a mo." Ryan got up, leaving Moira and Gareth with a view of an empty room. The height of the ceiling, cornices, and the style of the door, which he'd left ajar, suggested a newish property. Something comfortable but not grand. There were cream walls, sagging bookshelves, a couple of potted plants, and some framed photographs too far away to decipher. Family, maybe? Pets?

Ryan reappeared, sat in his desk chair, fidgeted until he was comfortable, and said, "Before we get down to business, there's something I want to clear up."

"Oh?"

"In the summer—"

"Oh?" said Moira again, this time much more guardedly.

"I wasn't after a story. I was curious. About you. We were on holiday in the area, and I heard you lived nearby. I was looking for answers. Trying to understand, I suppose."

"Understand what?"

"You won't know this, but you were a major part of my childhood."

Moira considered his image on the screen. "You can't have been much more than a baby when I stopped being front page news. Why was I such a big deal?"

"I grew up hearing about the libel case. About how, ultimately, it cost Mum her job. She was demoted from staffer on one of the big tabloids to a jobbing freelancer. To be honest, she was obsessed."

"You told me 'unhinged' earlier," interjected Gareth.

Ryan ducked his head, a reluctant acknowledgement, not a denial.

"According to Dad, Mum always was a workaholic, but she grew bitter too. In the end, Dad couldn't stand it, and he left."

"I'm sorry," said Moira sympathetically. Ryan's childhood sounded miserable.

"I'm not saying this so you feel sorry for me. But I want you to understand, at least a little. Mum always made you out to be a villain, and there you were, only a few miles away from where we were staying. I couldn't help myself. I needed answers."

"And?"

"And I only heard good things. People like you. Admire you. Respect you. I witnessed that first-hand in the pub that night. You're nothing like the villain my mother painted you out to be. I'd long suspected Mum's obsession with you was irrational. After last summer, I was sure. Now she's done this." He glanced down and glanced up again, resolve in his expression. "I know what everyone thinks, and I know what people say. Mother ignored me. I want to prove myself to her. It was true, once, but things changed a long time ago."

"What things?" Moira asked, unable to stop herself. "Sorry, you don't have to tell me. None of my business."

Ryan told her anyway. Perhaps he wanted to garner goodwill and trust, but his response appeared less calculated than that.

"Lots of things. I grew up. I went to therapy. I got tired of trying to get the approval of someone who was never going to give it, not because I don't deserve it, but because she wasn't interested in anyone other than herself. I met my wife, and I saw what her family life was like. They helped me learn what healthy relationships should be. We had children, and I resolved to be a better parent to them than Mum was to me." He recited the list calmly and without any trace of bitterness, but Moira's gut twisted in sympathy anyway.

Ryan stared into the screen. "I'd do anything for my daughters, to protect them. Olivia, the oldest, is fourteen, not much younger than this Meg of yours. The idea of my mother using anyone's child like that is abhorrent!"

Somewhere behind him, a dog barked. A woman chastised it. There was laughter. Ryan turned his head slightly, listening to the noises of family life, reassured himself he wasn't needed, and refocused on the conversation. "Tell me what you need, and I'll get it done."

Moira outlined her plan with Gareth chipping in from time to time, helping to set the ground rules. Ryan nodded a lot, posed a few pertinent questions, made some suggestions, and three-quarters of an hour later, the three of them had managed to piece together a workable proposal ready for Moira to take to Meg, Nessa, and their parents.

Moira came away from the call liking Ryan far more than she'd expected but doubtful about his effectiveness as a journalist. Maybe that was why he had never found himself on staff anywhere. Or, maybe, being a freelancer gave him the option to be more selective about the jobs he took.

Ethics and journalism. Moira doubted she'd ever understand what the links were and where the boundaries of acceptable behaviour lay. Maybe it was best she didn't try. All that mattered was he was willing to help now.

That, plus he held an ace up his sleeve.

Ryan Walker-Price had a bigger hold over Julia Walker than anything Julia had on Meg.

*

Meg cried when Moira explained the full details of their plan. Behind her, her parents seemed relieved and grateful, and Liane pulled Meg into a comforting hug. In other windows, Nessa looked as though half the weight of the world had been lifted from her shoulders, and Cindy and Joe nodded with approval.

Interlude

Coming to terms with this hasn't been easy, and I'm not all the way there. But being on the journey has been a relief. I've had to wrestle with a lot of new ideas, and I'm still learning. I'm still unlearning things too.

Why did it take me so long to figure things out? Why didn't I look for answers earlier?

I was afraid of what I might find. But also, the thing about being aromantic and asexual is you aren't driven to find answers. At least, that's how it was for me. There isn't an imperative to figure out your sexuality when there's nothing there for you to act on.

Another thing I've struggled with is whether I should come out.

But I'm talking to you, so I guess this is it.

This is my big reveal.

Chapter Twenty-Eight

After much debate, they decided instead of making a podcast Meg would livestream on ViewHoo, where the recording would reside forever more. Between them, Gareth and Ryan would call in as many favours as possible to assemble an audience of cultural and lifestyle journalists, and Ryan, who took it upon himself to mediate between his mother and Meg, would make sure Julia Walker tuned in too.

*

While Meg was frantically sorting out the technical preparations for the livestream, putting her learning from media studies along with her experiments the previous summer to good use, the cast and crew of *Little Shop of Horrors* were dealing with multiple challenges of their own.

Ms Markides decided the plant used in the show's finale didn't have enough tentacles, which resulted in a mad panic as everyone involved in the production—and some who weren't—were ordered to track down enough bubble wrap to make more.

Nobody had told wardrobe Becca had been recast as Ronette, and they had made the costume according to the measurements they had taken for Poppy. Becca's costume was now undergoing urgent and major alterations.

Although the tech crew thought they'd fixed the Audrey Two puppet, they were discovering in the worst possible way it still wasn't 100 per cent reliable.

Because Tarone had mistaken Nessa's excessive edginess for a severe case of stage fright and had gone out of his way to try to calm her down, Nessa found herself confiding in him.

She told him she was swamped by everything going on. She had to go to rehearsals; they had the LGBTQIA+ group, now renamed slightly more catchily the Tuesday Club, to run; she needed to keep on top of her schoolwork; but the extracurricular livestream she and Meg were putting together was more important than any of those.

Tarone listened, in turns amused, amazed, and horrified, as she whispered her way through her and Meg's misadventures in sleuthing while, on stage, the technical crew resorted to brute force to free Kai from the guts of Audrey Two.

*

They settled on 6:00 pm on the first Sunday in December for the livestream.

Moira's mouth was dry, and there were butterflies in her stomach.

Moira didn't understand the technology involved, but she didn't need to. All she needed to do was make sure she did everything she'd been told, and Meg would do the rest. Thus, diligently following the instructions Meg had provided, complete with helpful diagrams, Moira made her preparations.

She set up her mic, put on her headphones, and managed to create a virtual background for her call. In honour of the occasion, Moira had made more effort than usual with her make-up, applying the right amount to make sure she would not look peelie-wally on screen. She had also tuned her guitar, and she had a glass of cold water close at hand.

Meg's voice came through her headset. "Ready?"

"As I'll ever be." Moira couldn't remember having been this nervous ahead of an interview before, and she'd been interviewed several times on national television. She'd even appeared on *Wogan* once.

Meg cued the chorus of "Will You (Ask Me Out)?" to start the livestream.

"Okay." Meg swallowed. Apparently, Moira wasn't the only one who was nervous. "Three...two...one... Action!"

Moira wasn't sure whether people usually bothered to say that, or whether Meg had needed to, but it seemed appropriate. She squared her shoulders and looked into the camera.

"Hello, everyone, and welcome to *Moira's Story*. My name's Meg—"

"And I'm Nessa—"

"And today we are delighted to be talking to Moira Cavendish, one of the members of the eighties band, the Diptych. Even if you don't recognise her name, you're sure to recognise the music. Over the years, 'Will You (Ask Me Out)?' has become a staple of weddings and anniversaries. Isn't that right, Moira?"

"Yes, that's right. I'm told it has been played at a few funerals too." Although they had agreed on a list of questions and prompts and had planned out the general content of the interview, they had agreed not to use scripts, wanting to make the conversation flow as naturally as possible. Moira's line about funerals had come out of nowhere.

"Cheery," murmured Nessa.

"Before we talk to Moira," said Meg, "let me tell you a bit about how this video came to be. Last summer, I decided I wanted to make a podcast, but I didn't know what it would be about."

"Meanwhile," Nessa chimed in, "I had moved to Scotland with my dad and the rest of our family, which is where I met Moira. I found out she had been in the band and she and her partner had drifted apart over the years. I had an idea, a stupid idea, as it turned out, to reunite them."

Meg took over again. "As soon as Nessa suggested it, I could see the tagline." Meg mimed quotation marks and melodramatically intoned, "'Two old friends drifted apart. Two younger friends worked to reunite them. This is what happened'."

"Like I said, it was a stupid idea, for lots of reasons, so that's not what this video is about. Instead, Moira would like to tell a different story, right?"

Moira leaned in closer to her mic. "Right." Was her throat closing up? She wasn't about to go into anaphylactic shock, was she? Surely, she hadn't inadvertently eaten any shrimp. She took a noisy swig of her water, cleared her throat, and tried again. "Right." That was better.

"And you're not here to talk about your years in the limelight, are you?" said Meg.

"No. I want to talk about something close to my heart, something most people don't know about me, in fact, something many people don't know about at all."

Moira had never been good at talking about her feelings.

She needed to talk about them now.

"And that would be?" prompted Nessa. Okay, so maybe they had rehearsed this part.

"Asexuality and aromanticism, and what it means to be aroace when you don't have words to describe how you feel. About why words are important, and how without words and concepts to work with, navigating a world that attaches so much importance to romance and sexual relationships can be difficult."

"So you are?"

"I'm an aromantic asexual."

"Can you explain what that means to any listeners who don't know?"

Moira obliged, trotting out the definitions she'd come to think of as Aroace 101.

"You hinted earlier that you didn't know about asexuality or aromanticism when you were our age, so when did you find out about them?"

"Embarrassingly recently. You'd think I'd have figured it out earlier, but if you've never been introduced to the concepts, how can you know you're something when you don't even know that something exists?"

"What was it like, growing up without the words?"

"Difficult, although I don't know I would have said so at the time. I mean, isn't puberty and growing up difficult and confusing for everyone? As a result, it took me a long time to figure out I was more confused than most people."

"What was it like, being a teenager in..."

"The seventies and eighties." Moira smiled into the camera. "Yeah. I'm that old."

"Can you tell us a bit about life when you were younger?"

"All right. I started at the girls' grammar school as the last of the wartime generation of schoolmarms were retiring. They were strict and staid, redoubtable women given to wearing tweed suits, cameo brooches, thick tights, and sensible shoes..."

*

Meg wrapped up the livestream. "We didn't reunite them. And, I guess, we shouldn't have tried. But Moira agreed to let us tell her story. She believes it's a story worth telling. Maybe other people can learn from it. We did. Moira says we wanted to give her a happy ever after, and she says she's found one, even if it's not the one we originally went looking for." Meg signalled it was time for Nessa to say her final lines.

"I'm gay, Moira's ace, we're at peace with who we are, we're friends, and you don't get much happier than that. This was Nessa—"

"And Meg. Thank you for listening to *Moira's Story*." Meg twiddled with a few controls, leaned back in her chair, and heaved a huge sigh. "And we're done!"

Nessa and Moira sagged and grinned with relief.

"Fingers crossed for thousands of likes," said Meg.

Gareth had promised his contacts would plaster mentions of the 'stream on Yapper and write articles about it for their media outlets. If all went well, they'd be trending within the hour, and they'd be viral within the day.

Moira was stretching the kinks out of her spine when Cindy knocked and, without waiting for an answer, came in through the back door. "That went well." Cindy and Joe had promised to watch next door. Had Finlay seen it too? "How do you think it went?"

"Okay," said Moira, though truth be told, she didn't know. She couldn't remember exactly what questions she'd been asked, or their order, or what she had said. "Fingers tightly crossed everyone else thinks so too."

"By the way, are you doing anything on Saturday night?"

Moira was taken aback by the abrupt change in subject.

"Would you like to come over and watch Nessa's show with us?"

*

News of the livestream spread around the school faster than either the rumours of Nessa's being outed or Poppy's expulsion had done. By Monday break, if people hadn't already seen it, they'd heard about it, and by Tuesday everybody in the school had viewed it at least once, along with tens of thousands of other people.

Nessa lost count of the number of mentions it got in the national media, both online and print. There had even been a mention of it on Radio Two. That one would have slipped past Nessa had it not been for Gareth, who was keeping a tally of the coverage the video was getting and passing on the information to Moira. Moira, in turn, messaged Nessa with every new mention she heard about.

Amongst the students, Meg and Nessa had achieved legendary status, although the reactions of St Drogo's staff were more mixed. According to Ms Breckenridge, who was cautiously sympathetic to their cause, a few of the older staff members weren't sure what a livestream was, and most were unsure whether the livestream presented the school, which hadn't been mentioned in the original production, but which had been referred to in a couple of newspaper articles since, in a good or bad light.

*

Frankie led the Tuesday Club in giving Nessa and Meg a standing ovation, which was flattering, although Nessa wasn't sure they deserved it. If anyone deserved the applause, it was Moira, but Moira wasn't there.

"I watched the livestream," said Frankie. "We all did. It was—"

Nessa and Meg waited for Frankie to finish the sentence.

"—good."

"Good? That's it?" said Meg. "You gave us a standing ovation and had trouble spitting out your words because it was only good?"

Nessa nudged Meg to let her know she'd gone too far and handled Frankie's praise with far more finesse. "Thank you."

"Moira—all of you—you made me feel seen. Will you tell Moira I said so?"

Nessa promised she would. "Maybe one day you'll tell her yourself."

*

The person angriest about the livestream was Ms Markides, who at the final dress rehearsal glowered at Nessa and let rip. "I have never been so disappointed in my entire career, Nessa Clarkson! *Little Shop of Horrors* should have been on the front page of the local paper, but your stunt has made such a splash that the paper wants to put you front and centre instead. I have never been upstaged by one of my students before, and the rest of the team are going to be devastated they've had to miss out on their moment of glory because of you!"

Frankie, Becca, and Tarone appeared at Nessa's side, determinedly offering moral support.

"I don't think anyone cares," said Kai, who had been standing nearby. "It's not like anyone reads the paper anyway. *Moira's Story* was great, and more people in the school have watched it than will bother with *Little Shop of Horrors*."

Everyone within earshot murmured agreement.

Ms Markides scowled at Kai for a moment before returning her attention to Nessa. She put her chin in the air and sniped, "You might at least have mentioned the show!" before she flounced off.

"Do you think she's ever going to forgive me?" Nessa asked Frankie, Becca, and Tarone quietly.

"No. Do you care?" asked Tarone.

"I don't think I do. It's not as though I'm ever going to do one of these again!"

"You're not? That's a pity," said Frankie, "since you're getting the hang of this performance lark."

*

Cindy, Joe, Finlay, and Moira had decimated the buffet Cindy had prepared, and Audrey Two was eating Mr Mushnik when Mr Gillespie, appearing from nowhere, jumped onto Moira's knee. "What's he doing here?" Moira asked, astonished.

Cindy sighed. "We can't keep him out, so we've pretty much stopped trying. You don't mind, do you?"

Moira tickled the cat behind his left ear and under his chin. He stretched his neck to give her better access and purred. "I don't think it would make any difference if I did. Dizzy's got a mind of his own."

*

Half an hour after the performance had ended, a tablet that had been positioned in a stand on the dining table in readiness, chimed a notification alert. Joe answered the call while everyone else gathered around.

Nessa's beaming face filled the screen. "Hey, Dad." As she took in the array of faces behind him, she amended her greeting. "Hey, everyone."

"You were great!" said Joe with the guileless untruthfulness only a doting parent could bestow.

Nessa laughed and shook her head. "You have to say that. You're my dad. Anyone want to give me a more honest appraisal?"

Nobody did, although, based on what he chose to comment on, Finlay came closest. "That plant thingy was cool. And the blood! It wasn't real, was it?"

"Of course not. Nobody got eaten, and no dentists were harmed in the making of the show."

"Pity," murmured Moira. "I've never been a fan of the dentist."

"Hey, guess what!" exclaimed Finlay.

"What?" asked Nessa.

"Dizzy's here, and Mum doesn't mind anymore, so we're sharing the cat with Moira!" He twisted around to look at Moira to get confirmation.

Moira made a what-can-you-do gesture. "Dizzy knows how to get what he wants."

Finlay beamed. "Isn't that great?" With that, he wriggled his way out of the conversation, calling the cat's name.

The conversation reverted to *Little Shop of Horrors*, and Nessa told them how they'd been lucky not to witness Audrey Two in one of its crankier moments. "And isn't Frankie brilliant? And Kai and Becca. But Frankie's heart is set on getting into Cambridge and joining the Footlights, so how good she is matters."

"It's good to put a few faces to the names we've heard so much about," said Cindy.

Moira, who had been particularly curious about Frankie, agreed.

Egged on by Nessa, they went on to applaud Tarone's scenery, saying he obviously had talent.

"One more show and the wrap party to go, and I'll never have to do this theatre stuff again!"

"But you've had fun, haven't you?" Joe asked.

"Meh. I guess so. It's cured any curiosity I might have had about what being in these shows involves. But honestly? It's not my kind of thing, and the best bits are all the incidental things that happened."

"Like what?"

"All the drama was horrible, but we wouldn't have formed the Tuesday Club without it. Speaking of..." Nessa reignited her wide grin. "The Club gave Meg and me a standing ovation after the livestream. Frankie organised it." Suddenly sombre, Nessa said, "Don't think I'm ungrateful. I'm not. We're not. But I can't help worrying what we did is a temporary fix. How do we know it will hold?"

"Because Ryan's on our side," Moira said. "He told me Julia Walker wants closer contact with her grandchildren. She's desperate to get to know them better, and that means forging better relations with her son. He's going to allow her more access, but only on certain conditions, one of which is she leaves Meg and her family alone."

"I can see how that might work," said Joe. "The desire for a family is a powerful thing. Speaking of which, there's something we wanted to ask you about."

"Oh?"

"It's about Christmas."

"Oh." Moira's curiosity gave way to wariness.

Cindy said, "This is our first Christmas in this house, and our first as a family. We don't have any traditions to inflict on you, but if you join us, maybe we'll create some together."

The offer was tempting. Extremely tempting, in fact. But Moira was used to doing things alone, to being alone, and Christmas was such a big deal. "I don't want to intrude."

"You wouldn't be intruding. You're part of this family too."

"I am?"

"Yeah. We're sharing a cat after all!"

Moira glanced around at Cindy and Joe, and at Nessa on the tablet screen. She could hear Finlay, who was playing with Mr Gillespie, in the hallway. They'd reached out to her.

She reached back.

"I'd love to share Christmas with you."

Interlude

I've only had one true love in my life, and it wasn't a romantic love.

Nikki was my best friend, the one I used to joke about growing old together with. Only it turned out it was more of a joke to her than to me.

She knows where I am.

I've sometimes thought about moving, but I won't. I want her to find me if she ever decides to come looking.

Maybe I'm a fool.

Epilogue

The fairy lights in Murdo's beer garden, where most of the guests were choosing to congregate, at least until the entertainment got underway, were fighting a losing battle against the evening sun. Cindy was wearing the same suit, a pink pastel affair, as she'd worn for the wedding ceremony held barely three weeks before.

It had been Nessa's idea to combine Cindy and Joe's evening celebration with her eighteenth birthday party. From a practical point of view, it made sense; the guest lists overlapped, and this way, the more distant relatives only had to travel once.

Moira perched her guitar case on the closest picnic table, leaned against its neck, and smiled. Across the garden, Frankie was talking to Fearn, whom Emily had brought as her plus one, and Tarone and Meg, who had offered to carry equipment inside, were doing a better job of distracting the Elephant Twins than helping.

A great deal had happened in the last six months, all of it good.

As Moira had hoped, Meg had heard no more from Julia Walker.

Nessa had finished school and was optimistically awaiting her exam results, keeping her fingers crossed she had earned the grades she needed for Oxford. No doubt, Nessa's friends had equally exciting plans of their own, but Moira hadn't had a chance to talk to them to find out.

Billie and Gordon, the Elephant Twins, had got in touch with her as soon as they'd seen the livestream. They had been rhapsodic about the unfamiliar version of "Will You (Ask Me Out)?" which they'd wanted to play with her the next time they were in the area. Moira assumed that was their way of giving her moral support without having to say the words.

It turned out they did support her, but they were also in deadly earnest about the song.

They didn't get a chance to perform together until after the academic year had ended, however, and in the last month, thanks to another ViewHoo recording, word of mouth, and a large quantity of luck, their version of "Will You (Ask Me Out)?" had turned into a minor internet sensation.

Of course, as Nessa pointed out, this was the same internet that had recently gone mad for *Poppy Crystal's Alternative Careers Advice for Out of Touch Parents and Their Teens*, so that wasn't necessarily a recommendation.

When Moira had asked if Billie and Gordon would perform for Nessa's eighteenth, they'd happily agreed on the condition she join them.

The Elephant Twins hadn't been the only ones to reach out to her in the aftermath of the livestream.

Nikki had too, and she and Moira had been keeping in tentative touch ever since. It would never be like the old days again, but Moira hoped it was a new beginning for them both.

Nikki had known she had an alcohol problem for a long time and had been trying to do something about it ever since she'd got kicked off *the Cats' Meow*; however, it had taken seeing Derek set the dogs after two teenaged girls to give her strength to ditch not only the booze but also her manager.

"Are you having fun?" Nessa had appeared as if by magic at her side. She was wearing a slinky black dress that offered glimpses of artificially tanned thighs. She was also holding a champagne flute, more as a badge of honour, flaunting the fact she could now drink legally, than because she liked the taste.

Moira nodded and smiled. "Happy birthday."

Nessa laughed. "You already said that this morning. When you gave me your present. Which is brilliant, by the way. Thank you. Again."

"You're welcome."

The biggest change to have happened over the last few months had been to Moira herself. She was whole in a way she hadn't felt in years, completed by the social circle she'd gathered around her.

She remembered the Awful Days and, although she couldn't guarantee they'd gone for good, she hadn't had an Awful Day in a long time. The bad days had been reduced to bad moments, which she controlled by focusing on everyone who surrounded her, supported her, and knew her. All of her.

Murdo came out to find her. "The Twins are ready for you."

"Thanks."

Moira picked up her guitar, wove her way through the guests, and into the pub.

She plugged her guitar into the amp. Together with Billie and Gordon, she did the final sound checks and tuning while Murdo herded people inside.

They straightened. "Welcome, everybody," said Gordon. "For those of you who don't already know us, I'm Gordon—"

"I'm Billie—"

"And together we're the Elephant Twins. And it is our immense pleasure to be performing for you tonight along with Moira Cavendish!"

Applause. Whoops. Cheering. Someone, possibly Joe, wolf-whistled.

Moira was transported to the old days, when making music had been fun and exciting, and she'd performed for the joy and friendship of it.

"We're going to play some original pieces in a minute. First, though, we'd like to perform a cover," said Moira. "Anyone over fifty will know this one. Everyone else will pick it up soon enough. Join in when you can."

Billie twitched his sticks, setting the tempo before he started to drum. Rhythm set, Gordon joined in on the keyboard and Moira strummed her guitar. She looked out at the sea of faces. Heads nodded in time with the beat as the room readied itself to belt out the lyrics to "We Are Family".

Acknowledgements

My thanks go to all the people at NineStar Press who have helped to make this book a reality. Particular thanks must go to Barb, my editor, who shows endless patience in the face of my misplaced commas.

About Evelyn Fenn

I lived in five different cities, spanning two continents, before leaving crowds and commuting behind and settling somewhere that official statistics describe as "Very Remote Rural".

I have made up stories for as long as I can remember, and I have been writing them down for almost as long. I cut my creative writing teeth on fan fiction in the days of paper fanzines and, later, online. I had fun but eventually grew tired of playing in other people's sandpits. Turns out, it's more fun to create sandpits of my own.

I have worked in the public, private, and voluntary sectors, with roles ranging from number crunching and lecturing to mucking out cowsheds and toilet cleaning. I currently hold down a day job while daydreaming of writing full time.

Evelyn Fenn is a pseudonym.

Email
evelyn_fenn@btinternet.com

Twitter
@EvelynFenn

Other NineStar books by this author

Friends Without Benefits

www.ninestarpress.com

www.facebook.com/ninestarpress

www.facebook.com/groups/NineStarNiche

www.twitter.com/ninestarpress

www.instagram.com/ninestarpress